WINTER
in
EDEN

BANTAM BOOKS BY HARRY HARRISON

West of Eden

Homeworld

Starworld

Wheelworld

The Stainless Steel Rat for President

The Stainless Steel Rat Wants You

WINTER
in
EDEN

Harry Harrison

ILLUSTRATIONS BY
Bill Sanderson

Book Two
in the WEST OF EDEN *Trilogy*

BANTAM BOOKS
TORONTO · NEW YORK · LONDON · SYDNEY · AUCKLAND

WINTER IN EDEN
A Bantam Spectra Book / November 1986

Library of Congress Cataloging-in-Publication Data

Harrison, Harry.
  Winter in Eden.

  (A Bantam spectra book)
  Second vol. in a proposed trilogy, the 1st of which
is West of Eden.
  I. Title.
PS3558.A667W53   1986   813'.54   86-14168
ISBN 0-553-05163-6

Bantam Books are published by Bantam Books, Inc. Its trademark, consisting
of the words "Bantam Books" and the portrayal of a rooster, is Registered in
U.S. Patent and Trademark Office and in other countries. Marca Registrada.
Bantam Books, Inc., 666 Fifth Avenue, New York, New York 10103.

PRINTED IN THE UNITED STATES OF AMERICA

BP   0 9 8 7 6 5 4 3 2 1

CONTENTS

PROLOGUE

xi

WINTER IN EDEN

1

THE WORLD WEST OF EDEN

351

GENDASI *

PAUKARUTS

SASKU

ALPÈASAK ·DEIFOBEN

ALAKAS ·AKSEHENT

MANINLÈ

ÀMBALASOK

TESKHETS

ULARUAQ

IKHALMENETS

ENTOBAN

DYEBÈISK

8   And the LORD God planted a garden
eastward in Eden;
and there he put the man
whom he had formed.

16   And Cain went out from the presence
of the LORD, and dwelt
in the land of Nod,
on the east of Eden.

GENESIS

The great reptiles were the most successful life forms ever to populate this world. For 140 million years they ruled the Earth, filled the sky, swarmed in the seas. At this time the mammals, the ancestors of mankind, were only tiny, shrew-like animals that were preyed upon by the larger, faster, more intelligent saurians.

Then, 65 million years ago, this all changed. A meteor six miles in diameter struck the Earth and caused disastrous atmospheric upheavals. Within a brief span of time over seventy-five percent of all the species then existent were wiped out. The age of the dinosaurs was over; the evolution of the mammals that they had suppressed for 100 million years began.

But what if that meteor had not fallen?

What would our world be like today?

PROLOGUE: KERRICK

Life is no longer easy. Too much has changed, too many are dead, the winters are too long. It was not always this way. I remember clearly the encampment where I grew up, remember the three families there, the long days, friends, good food. During the warm seasons we stayed on the shore of a great lake filled with fish. My first memories are of that lake, looking across its still water at the high mountains beyond, seeing their peaks grow white with the first snows of winter. When the snow whitened our tents and the grass around as well, that would be the time when the hunters went to the mountains. I was in a hurry to grow up, eager to hunt the deer, and the greatdeer, at their side.

That simple world of simple pleasures is gone forever. Everything has changed—and not for the better. At times I wake at night and wish that what happened had never happened. But these are foolish thoughts and the world is as it is, changed now in every way. What I thought was the entirety of existence has proved to be only a tiny corner of reality. My lake and my mountains are only the smallest part of this great continent that borders an immense ocean to the east.

I also know about the others, the creatures we call murgu, and I learned to hate them even before I saw them. As our flesh is warm, theirs is chill. We have hair upon our heads and a hunter will grow a proud beard, while the animals that we hunt have warm flesh and fur or hair. But this is not true of the murgu. They are cold and smooth and scaled, have claws and teeth to rend and tear, are large and terrible, to be feared. And hated. I knew that they lived in the warm waters of the ocean to the south and on the warm lands to the south. They cannot abide the cold so they did not trouble us.

All that has changed so terribly that nothing will be the same ever again. That is because there are murgu called Yilanè who are intelligent just as we Tanu are intelligent. It is my unhappy knowledge that our world is only a tiny part of the Yilanè world. We live in the north of a great continent. And to the south of us, over all the land, there swarm only Yilanè.

And there is even worse. Across the ocean there are even larger continents—and there there are no hunters at all. None. But Yilanè, only Yilanè. The entire world is theirs except for our small part.

Now I will tell you the worst thing about the Yilanè. They hate us as we hate them. This would not matter if they were only great, insensate beasts. We would stay in the cold north and avoid them in this manner.

But there are those among them who may be as intelligent as hunters, as fierce as hunters. And their number cannot be counted but it is enough to say that they fill all of the lands of this great world.

I know these things because I was captured by the Yilanè, grew up among them, learned from them. The first horror I felt when my father and all the others were killed has been dimmed by the years. When I learned to speak as the Yilanè do I became as one of them, forgot that I was a hunter, even learned to call my people ustuzou, creatures of filth. Since all order and rule among the Yilanè come down from the top I thought very well of myself. Since I was close to Vaintè, the eistaa of the city, its ruler, I was looked upon as a ruler myself.

The living city of Alpèasak was newly grown on these shores, settled by Yilanè from across the ocean who had been driven from their own distant city by the winters that grow colder every year. The same cold that drove my father and the other Tanu south in the search for food sent the Yilanè questing across the sea. They grew their city on our shores and when they found the Tanu there before them they killed them. Just as the Tanu killed Yilanè on sight.

For many years I had no knowledge of this. I grew up among the Yilanè and thought as they did. When they made war I looked upon the enemy as filthy ustuzou, not Tanu, my brothers. This changed only when I met the prisoner, Herilak. A sammadar, a leader of the Tanu, who understood me far better than I understood myself. When I spoke to him as enemy, alien, he spoke to me as flesh of his flesh. As the language of my childhood returned so did my memories of that warm earlier life. Memories of my mother, family, friends. There are no families among the Yilanè, no suckling babies among egg-laying lizards, no possible friendships where these cold females rule, where the males are locked from sight of all for a lifetime.

Herilak showed me that I was Tanu, not Yilanè, so I freed him and we fled. At first I regretted it—but there was no going back. For I had attacked and almost killed Vaintè, she who rules. I joined the sammads, the family groups of the Tanu, joined them in flight from the attacks of those who had once been my companions. But I had other companions now, and friendship of a kind I could never know among the Yilanè. I had Armun, she who came to me and showed me what I had never even known, awoke the feelings I could never have known while I was living among that alien race. Armun who bore our son.

But we still lead our lives under the constant threat of death. Vaintè and her warriors followed the sammads without mercy. We fought—and sometimes won, even capturing some of their living weapons, the death-sticks that killed creatures of any size. With these we could penetrate far to the south, eating well of the teeming murgu, killing the vicious ones when they attacked. Only to flee again when Vaintè and her endless supply of fighters from across the sea found us and attacked.

This time the survivors went where we could not be followed, across the frozen mountain ranges to the land beyond. Yilanè cannot live in the snows; we thought we would be safe.

And we were, for a long time we were. Beyond the mountains we found Tanu who did not live by hunting alone, but grew crops in their hidden valley and could make pots, weave cloth and do many other wondrous things. They are the Sasku and they are our friends, for they worship the god of the mastodon. We brought our mastodons to them and we have been as one people ever since. Life was good in the Sasku valley.

Until Vainté found us once again.

When this happened I realized that we could run no more. Like cornered animals we must turn and fight. At first none would listen to me for they did not know the enemy as I did. But they came to understand that the Yilanè had no knowledge of fire. They would learn of it when we brought the torch to their city.

And this is what we did. Burnt their city of Alpèasak and sent the few survivors fleeing back to their own world and their own cities across the sea. This was good for one of those who lived was Enge who had been my teacher and my friend. She did not believe in killing as all the others did, and led her small band called the Daughters of Life, believers in the sanctity of life. Would that they had been the only survivors.

But Vaintè lived as well. This creature of hatred survived the destruction of her city, fled on the uruketo, the great living vessel the Yilanè used, sailed out to sea.

This is what has happened in the past. Now I stand on the shore with the ashes of the city blowing about me and try to think of what will happen now, what must be done in the years to come.

Tharman i ermani lasfa katiskapri
ap naudinz modia—em bleit
hepellin er atta, so faldar elka
ensi hammar.

MARBAK PROVERB

The tharms in the stars may gaze
down on a hunter with pleasure—
but that is a cold appreciation
that cannot light a fire.

CHAPTER ONE

The storm was ending, blowing out to sea. Sheets of rain swept over the distant uruketo hiding it from sight. It appeared again suddenly as the rain moved past it, farther away now, a dark shape against the whitefoamed waves. Low evening sun pierced the broken clouds and washed the uruketo with russet light, picking out the high outline of the fin. Then it was gone, invisible now in the growing darkness. Herilak stood in the surf and shook his spear after it, shouting aloud with bitterness.

"They should have died too, all of them, none should escape."

"The killing has stopped," Kerrick said wearily. "It is over, done, finished. We have won. We have slain the murgu, burned their city." He pointed to the smoking trees behind them. "You have had your vengeance. For every one of your sammad that they killed you have burned a hault of murgu. You have done that. For every hunter, woman, child dead, you have killed murgu to the count of a man. That is enough. Now we must forget dying and think about living."

"You talked with one of them, let it escape. My spear hand trembled—that was not a good thing for you to do."

Kerrick was aware of the other's anger and his own rose to

meet it—but he kept it under control. They were all tired, close to exhaustion after the events of the day. And he must remember that Herilak had obeyed his order not to slay Enge when he talked with her.

"To you all murgu are the same, all to be killed. But that one, she was my teacher—and she is different from the others. She speaks only of peace. If the murgu listen to her, believe her, there could be an end to this war . . ."

"They will return, return for vengeance."

The tall hunter was still possessed by anger, shaking his blood-drenched spear at the vanished, vanquished enemy, his eyes, burnt by the drifting smoke, were as red as his spearpoint. Both hunters were filthy with soot, their blond beards and long hair thick with pieces of ash. Kerrick knew that it was Herilak's hatred speaking, his need to kill murgu and to go on killing, time without end. But Kerrick knew as well, with a sick feeling that gripped his insides, that Herilak was also speaking the truth. The murgu, the Yilanè, the enemy, they would be back. Vaintè would see to that. She still lived, and while she lived there was no safety, no peace. When he realized this the strength went out of him and he swayed, leaning on his spear for support, shaking his head as though to clear away the vision of despair from before his eyes. He must forget Vaintè and forget the murgu, forget all about them. Now was a time for living; the dying was over. A shout cut through the blackness of his thoughts and he turned to see the Sasku hunter, Keridamas, calling to him from the blackened ruins of Alpèasak.

"There are murgu, still alive, trapped."

Herilak wheeled about with a cry and Kerrick laid a restraining hand on his arm.

"Don't," he said quietly. "Put your spear down. Let me see to this. The killing must end somewhere."

"No, never, not with these creatures. But I stay my spear because you are still margalus, our war counsellor who leads us in battle against the murgu, and I still obey your command."

Kerrick turned about wearily and Herilak followed as he plodded his way through the heavy sand toward the burnt city. He was bone-weary and wanted only to rest, but could not. Were there Yilanè still alive? It did not seem possible. Fargi and Yilanè both had died when their city died—it was the same as being cast out, discarded. When this happened the Yilanè then suffered an irreversible change—he had seen it himself—that always ended in death. But, yes, there were exceptions, it was possible that some could still live. They could be the Daughters of Life: they did not die like the others. He would have to see for himself.

"We found them coming from one of the half-burnt groves of trees," Keridamas said. "Killed one but the others scrambled back inside. It was Simmacho who thought you might like to see them, kill them yourself, margalus."

"Yes!" Herilak said, turning about, an expression of intense hatred stripping his lips from his teeth. Kerrick shook his head with a great weariness.

"Let us see who they are before we slaughter them. Or still better let us take them alive. I will talk to them for there are things that I must know."

They picked their way through the blackened killing ground, between the still-smouldering trees and past the piled corpses. Their path took them through the ambesed and Kerrick stopped, horrified at the tumbled mounds of Yilanè bodies. They looked uninjured, unburnt—yet all were dead. And all were stretched out and facing toward the far wall of the ambesed. Kerrick looked in that direction too, to the seat of power where Vaintè had sat, now barren and empty. The fargi and Yilanè must have rushed here, trampling each other, seeking the protection of the Eistaa. But she was gone, the seat of power was empty, the city dying. So they had died as well. Keridamas led the way, stepping over the tumbled bodies, and Kerrick followed, numbed with shock. All these dead. Something would have to be done about them before they began to rot. Too many to bury. He would think of something.

"There, up ahead," Keridamas said, pointing with his spear.

Simmacho was poking at a splintered and scorched doorway, trying to peer inside in the growing darkness. When he saw Kerrick he pointed at the Yilanè corpse before him on the ground and turned it over with his foot. Kerrick glanced at it—then bent over to look more closely in the dying light. No wonder this place looked familiar. It was the hanalè.

"This one is a male," he said. "The others inside must be males as well." Simmacho poked the corpse in amazement. Like most of the Tanu he could not quite believe that the vicious murgu they had been fighting, killing, were all female.

"This one ran," he said.

"The males don't fight—or do anything else. They are all locked away in this place."

Simmacho was still puzzled. "Why did it not die like the others?"

Why indeed? Kerrick thought. "The females died because their city died, it would be the same for them as being rejected. Something happens to them when they are driven from the city. I'm not quite sure what. But it is deadly enough, you can see proof on all sides. It appears as though the males, being kept apart and protected, always rejected by the city in a way, do not die with the others."

"They will die on our spears," Herilak said. "And quickly before they escape in the darkness."

"It is not their way to move about at night, you know that. Nor is there another door leading out of this place. Let us now stop the killing and all the talk of killing and rest here until morning. Eat and drink and sleep."

None argued with this. Kerrick found water-fruit on an unburnt tree and showed them how to drink from them. Their food was gone but fatigue was greater than hunger and they were asleep almost at once.

Not so Kerrick. He was as tired as the others but the whirl of his thoughts kept him awake. Above him the last clouds blew away and the stars came out. Then he slept, unknowing, and when he looked again dawn was clearing the sky.

There was movement behind him and in the growing light he saw Herilak, knife in hand, walking silently toward the entrance to the hanalè.

"Herilak," he called out as he rose stiffly to his feet. The big hunter spun about, his face grim with anger, hesitated—then pushed the knife into its sling, turned and stalked away. There was nothing that Kerrick could say that would ease the pain that tore at him. Instead of diminishing Herilak's anger and hatred the killings seemed only to have intensified his emotions. Perhaps this would pass soon. Perhaps. Kerrick's thoughts were troubled as he slaked his thirst from one of the water-fruit. There was much still to be done. But first he had to find out if there really were any Yilanè still alive in the hanalè. He looked down wearily at his spear. Was it still needed? There might be females alive inside who did not know of the city's destruction. He took up the weapon and held it before him as he pushed through the burned and warped door.

There was blackened ruin here. Fire had swept along the hall and through the transparent panels overhead. The air was heavy with the smell of smoke—and of burnt flesh. Spear ready he walked the length of the hall, the only part of the hanalè he had ever seen, and on to the turning at the end. A scorched doorway led to a large chamber—where the smell of charred flesh was overpowering. More than enough light filtered down through the burnt ceiling above to reveal the dreadful contents of the room.

Almost at his feet, burned and dead with her mouth gaping wide, was Ikemend, the keeper of the hanalè. Behind her were the huddled shapes of her charges. The room was packed with them, now burnt and as dead as their keeper. Kerrick turned away, shuddering, and made his way deeper into the structure.

It was a maze of connecting rooms and passages, for the most part charred and destroyed. Yet further on the wood was greener, this section recently grown, and scarcely touched by the fire. At the last turning he entered a chamber with ornate hangings on the walls, soft cushions on the floor. Huddled against the far wall, their eyes bulging and their jaws dropped in juvenile fear, were two young males. They moaned when they saw him.

"It is death," they said and closed their eyes.

"No!" Kerrick called out loudly. "Correction of statement. Foolishness of males—attention to a superior speaking."

Their eyes flew open with astonishment at this.

"Speak," he ordered. "Are there others?"

"The creature that talks points the sharp tooth that kills," one of them moaned.

Kerrick dropped his spear onto the matting and moved away from it. "The killing is over. Are you two alone?"

"Alone!" they wailed in unison and their hands flashed the colors of juvenile terror and pain. Kerrick fought to keep his temper with the stupid creatures.

"Listen to me and be silent," he ordered. "I am Kerrick strong-and-important who sits at the Eistaa's side. You have heard of me." They signed agreement: perhaps knowledge of his flight had not penetrated their isolation. Or, more simply, they had forgotten. "Now you will answer my questions. How many of you are here?"

"We hid," the younger one said, "it was a game that we were

playing. The others had to find us. I was over there, Elinman hid with me, and Nadaskè behind the door. But the others never came. Something happened. It was very warm and nice, and then bad smells came in clouds that hurt our eyes and throats. We called for Ikemend to help us, but she never came. We were afraid to go out. I was too frightened, they named me Imehei because I am like that, but Elinman is very bold. He led the way and we followed. What we saw I cannot tell you, it was too dreadful. We wanted to leave the hanalè even though that is forbidden and Elinman did and screamed and we ran back inside. What will become of us?"

What would indeed happen to them? Certain death if the hunters came upon them. They would see only murgu with claws and teeth, the enemy. But Kerrick saw them for what they were; sheltered, stupid creatures, barely able to care for themselves. He couldn't allow them to be killed, was weary of killing at last.

"Stay here," he ordered.

"We are afraid and hungry," Imehei wailed. Soft-to-touch, that was what his name was. True enough. And the other, Nadaskè, looks-out-from-the-enclosure. They were like children, worse than children for they would never grow up.

"Silence—I command it. You have water here and are plump enough to go hungry for a bit. You will not leave this room. Meat will be brought to you. Do you understand?"

They were calm now, signalled ready obedience, secure in being commanded and watched over. Males! He took up his spear and left them there. Went back through the immensity of the structure and when he emerged Herilak was waiting for him. Behind him were the rest of the hunters, while Sanone and his Sasku were grouped to one side.

"We are leaving," Herilak said. He had his anger under control now—but it had been replaced with a cold resolve. "What we came to do—has been done. The murgu and their nest have been destroyed. There is nothing more for us here. We return to the sammads."

"You must stay. There is still work to be done . . ."

"Not for Tanu. You were our margalus, Kerrick, and you led us well against the murgu and we honor you for that and we obeyed you. But now that the murgu are dead you no longer command us. We are leaving."

"Have you been selected to speak for all of them, strong

Herilak?" Kerrick said angrily. "I do not remember this selection."
He turned to the hunters. "Does Herilak speak for you—or have
you minds of your own?"

Some turned away from his anger, but the sammadar Sorli
stepped forward. "We have thoughts of our own, and we have
talked. Herilak tells the truth. There is nothing for us here. What is
done is done and we must return to our sammads before the winter.
You must come as well, Kerrick, your sammad is to the north, not
here."

Armun. At the thought of her this city of death was nothing.
She was his sammad, she and the baby, and he almost gave way,
joined them in the march north. But behind Sorli was Sanone and
his Sasku and they had not moved. Kerrick turned toward them,
spoke.

"And what do the Sasku say of this?"

"We have spoken as well and have not yet finished with the
speaking. We have just come to this new place, there is much here
to be seen and spoken of—and we do not share the same need for
the frozen north that the Tanu do now. We understand them. But
we seek different things."

"Just a small time," Kerrick said, wheeling about to face the
hunters. "We must sit and smoke and confer on this. Decisions
must be made—"

"No," Herilak said. "Decisions have been made. What we
have come to do we have done. We start back today."

"I cannot leave with you now." Kerrick heard the strain in his
voice, hoped the others could not hear it as well. "It is also my wish
to return. Armun is there, my sammad, but I cannot go back with
you yet."

"Armun will be under my care," Herilak said. "If you do not
wish to come with us she will be safe in my sammad until you
return."

"I cannot leave yet. The time is not ready, it requires thought."

He was speaking to their backs. The decision had been taken,
the talking was finished. The battle was done and the hunters were
free again. They followed Herilak in silence down the path through
the trees.

And none glanced back, not one Tanu. Kerrick stood and
watched until the last of them were gone from sight, felt that some
important part of him had gone with them. What had turned his

victory into his defeat? He willed himself to follow them, to plead with them again to come back, and if they did not he wanted to join them on the trail, the trail that led to Armun and his life.

But he did not. Something equally strong kept him here. He knew that he belonged with Armun, with the Tanu, for he was Tanu.

Yet he had talked with the foolish male Yilanè, had commanded them as a Yilanè, had felt the strength and power of his position. Could that be it? Was he at home in this ruined city as he had never been among the sammads in the north?

He felt pulled in two directions and could not decide, could only stand and look at the empty trees, torn by emotions he could not understand, taking in breath after shuddering breath.

"Kerrick," the voice said, speaking as though from a great distance and he realized that Sanone was talking to him. "You are still margalus. What are your orders?"

There was understanding in the old man's eyes; the manduktos of the Sasku knew the hidden secrets of others. Perhaps he knew Kerrick's inner feelings better than he did himself. Enough. There was much to be done. He must put all thought of Armun from him now.

"We will need food," he said. "I will show you the fields where the animals are kept for slaughter. Surely they could not all have been burned. And all of the dead here, something must be done with them."

"Into the river before they rot," Sanone said grimly. "It will carry them out to sea."

"Yes, that will take care of them. Order it done. Then choose those who will come with me. I will show them the way to the animals. We will eat—after that there is much that we will have to do."

belesekesse ambeiguru desguru
kak'kusarod. murubelek murubelek.

YILANÈ APOTHEGM

***

*Those who swim to the top of the
highest wave can only sink in the
deepest trough.*

CHAPTER TWO

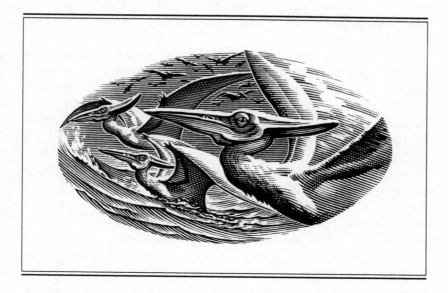

E rafnais ordered everyone below, crewmembers and passengers alike, as the uruketo swam out into the open sea. But she remained there on top of the fin when the storm washed over them, transparent membranes closed over her eyes against the driving rain. Between showers she had a single glimpse of the burnt city, smoke roiling high above it, the beaches empty of life. The vision burned into her memory and she could see it clearly still even when the rain returned; would see it always. She remained there at her station until dark, when the uruketo slowed, swimming easily with the current as it would until daylight returned. Only then did she descend wearily to the base of the fin where she spent the entire night, sleeping at the vacant steering position.

When the transparent viewing disc above her grew light with dawn Erafnais unwrapped her sleeping cloak and climbed wearily to her feet. The old injury to her back hurt as she climbed slowly up the inside of the fin to the observation post above. The morning air was cool and fresh. All the clouds of the previous day's storm had blown away and the sky was clear and bright. The fin swayed as the uruketo stirred and the ponderous creature moved faster in the growing light. Erafnais glanced down, checking that the crew-

member was at her steering station, then looked out at the ocean
again. There was a ripple of foam in front of the great beak as the
pair of accompanying enteesenat surged ahead. All was as it should
be with the voyage.

Yet nothing was as it should be. The dark thoughts that
Erafnais had kept at bay while she slept surged up and overwhelmed her. Her thumbs grasped hard at the uruketo's thick hide;
the sharp claws on her toes sinking deep as well. Inegban* had come
to Alpèasak at last, she had helped in this, and Alpèasak had grown
strong. And had died in a single day. She had watched and not
understood; in her lifetime at sea had never even heard of fire.
Now she knew all about it. It was hot, hotter than the sun, and
cracked and roared and stank and choked those who came close,
grew bright then black. And had killed the city. The handful of
survivors still reeking of the fire's darkness lay below. The rest of
the Yilanè and fargi were as dead as the city, dead in the city that
lay behind them. She shuddered and stared resolutely ahead, afraid
to look behind lest she see that place of sorrow again. If it had been
her city she would be as dead as the others, for those whom the fire
had not consumed had of course died when the city died.

But now she had other problems to face. The scientist Akotolp
was below, still holding to the arm of the male that she had dragged
aboard. But she had not moved since then, had just sat in motionless silence even when addressed. Sat and ignored the pleas and
moans of the male to be released. What could be done with her?
And what of those others below, the deathless ones? What was to
be done? Finally, she must consider—the other. The one whose
name no one spoke.

Erafnais shuddered and drew back as Vaintè climbed up inside
the fin. It was as though in thinking of her Erafnais had summoned
her—the last creature she wished to see this sunbright morning.

Without acknowledging the commander's presence, Vaintè went
to the rear of the fin and stared out at their bubbling wake. Erafnais
was aware of her actions and, despite her fears, turned as well and
also looked out toward the horizon. It was darker there. The
remaining shadow of the night, a storm perhaps, surely it could not
be the land—and the city. That was too far behind them to be
seen. One of Vaintè's eyes rolled back in her direction; Erafnais
spoke.

"You boarded in silence Vaintè and have remained silent since. Are they—dead?"

"All dead. The city dead as well."

Even through the terror of the words, Erafnais was aware of Vaintè's strange manner of speaking. Not as superior to inferior or even equal to equal, but instead in a flat and unfeeling manner that was most unusual. As though she were alone with no one else present, speaking her thoughts to herself.

Erafnais wished to be silent, but spoke despite this, the question coming as though of its own free will. "The fire—where did the fire come from?"

Vaintè's rigid mask vanished in an instant and her entire body shivered in the grip of intense emotion, her jaw gaped so wide in the expression of hatred/death that her meaning was muffled and confused. "Ustuzou who came . . . ustuzou of fire . . . hatred of those . . . hatred of him. Death. Death. Death."

"Death," a voice said harshly, hands moving in the reflexive position of taking-back-upon-self. Erafnais only heard the sound for Enge had climbed up behind her. But Vaintè could see her and understood well enough and there was venom in every motion of her response.

"Daughter of Death, you and yours should be back in that fire-city. The best of the Yilanè who died deserve to be here in your place."

In her anger she had spoken as one of equal to equal, as efenselè to efenselè. When you grew in the sea with others, emerged with them in the same group, your efenburu, it was a fact never considered; like the air one breathed. You were efenselè to the others in your efenburu for life. But Enge would not accept that.

"Your memory is weak, inferior one." She said this in the most insulting manner, the highest of the high to the lowest of the low. Erafnais, standing between them, moaned with terror, her crest flaming first red then orange as she fled below. Vaintè reeled back as though struck a physical blow. Enge was pitiless.

"You have been disowned. Your shame is upon me and I reject you as an efenselè. Your reckless ambition to kill Kerrick-ustuzou, all ustuzou, has destroyed proud Alpèasak instead. You ordered low-creature Stallan to kill my companions. Since the egg of time there has been no one like you. Would you had never emerged from the sea. If our entire efenburu had died there in the wet silence, myself included, it would have been better than *this*."

Vaintè's skin had first flared with rage when Enge spoke, but quickly darkened as her body grew still. Her anger was sealed inside now, to be used when needed—and not to be wasted on this inferior being who was once her equal.

"Leave me," she said, then turned back to the empty sea.

Enge turned away as well, breathing deeply and ashamed of herself for the unbidden anger. This was not what she believed in, what she preached to others. With great effort she stilled the movements of her limbs, the glaring colors of her palms and crest. Only when she was stonelike and as uncommunicative as Vaintè did she permit herself to speak. Below her was the crewmember guiding the uruketo through the sea; close behind her was the commander. Enge leaned down and made the sound of speaking-attention.

"From one-who-follows to one-who-leads, would Erafnais give pleasure by joining here?"

Erafnais climbed reluctantly up, aware of silent Vaintè, back turned and staring out at the sea. "I am here, Enge," she said.

"My thanks and the gratitude of those with me, for saving us from destruction. Where are you bound?"

"Where?" Erafnais echoed the question, then felt shame. She was the commander yet had not thought of their destination at all. She blurted the truth with shallow movements of apology.

"We fled the fire, out to sea, our course as it always is east to Entoban∗. This was done with the panic of flight and not the wisdom of command."

"Dismiss the shame—for you have saved us all and there is only gratitude. Entoban∗ of the Yilanè must be our destination. But which city?"

The question brought the answer instantly.

"Home. Where my efenburu is, where this uruketo first entered the sea. Seagirt Ikhalmenets."

Though still staring out at the surging waves, Vaintè had turned one eye to follow the conversation. She asked for attention to communication but only Erafnais looked her way.

"Ikhalmenets-of-the-islands is not Entoban∗. Respectfully request course to Mesekei."

Erafnais acknowledged the request, yet politely but firmly

reaffirmed their destination. Vaintè could see that her wrong-headedness could not be altered so was silent. There would be other ways to reach her destination—for reach it she must. Mesekei was a great city on a great river, rich and prosperous and far from the cold of the north. More important—they had aided her more than any other city in the war against the ustuzou. The future now was gray and impenetrable when she looked at it, her numbed mind empty of all thought. A time would come when the grayness must lift and she would be able to think once again of the future. At that time it would be good to be in a city among friends. There would be other uruketo in Ikhalmenets; some way would be found.

Companions there—but only enemies here. Through the grayness this ugly fact loomed large. Enge and her Daughters of Death still lived—while all those so deserving of life now lay dead. This should not be—nor would it be. There was nothing that could be done here at sea. She was alone against them all; could expect no aid from Erafnais and her crewmembers. Once ashore this would all change. How could she change it? Her thoughts were stirring to life now and she concealed them by her rigidity of body.

Behind her Enge signed respectful withdrawal to the commander and climbed below. When she had reached the bottom of the fin she looked back at Vaintè's motionless figure, then felt for an instant that she could almost see her mind at work. Evil, dark and deadly. Vaintè's ambitions would never change, never. These thoughts filled Enge so strongly that her limbs stirred despite her attempts at control, even in the dim phosphorescent glow they could be easily understood. She banished them and walked slowly through the semidarkness. Past the immobile Akotolp and her miserable male companion and on to the small group huddled against the wall. Akel stood and turned toward her—then drew back as she approached.

"Enge, follower-to-leader, what unhappiness moves your limbs so that I fear for my very life when you come close?"

Enge halted at this and conveyed apology. "Loyal Akel, what I was feeling was not for you—or for any of you others as well." She looked around at the four remaining Daughters of Life and let her movements show how pleased she was with their companionship. "Once we were many. Now we are few so each of you is more precious than a multitude to me. Since we lived when all others died I feel that this has given us a mission—and a strength to carry out that mission. We will talk of that another time. There are other things that must be done first." With her thumbs against her ribcage she signed listening-ears/watching-eyes. "The sorrow I brought with me is not my own. I will now give thought to the cause of that sorrow."

She sought out a dark angle behind the bladders of preserved meat where she would be hard to see, then lay facing the living wall of the uruketo and forced her body into silent rigidity. Only when this exercise was complete did she let her thoughts return to Vaintè. Inner thoughts that were not echoed in her outer stillness.

Vaintè. She of immense hatreds. Now that Enge was free of any affection for her former efenselè she could see her for what she was. A dark power for evil. And once this fact was realized it became clear that her first act from this darkness would be directed against Enge and her companions. They had lived where all others had died. They would speak out in Ikhalmenets and what they would say would not be to Vaintè's advantage. Therefore in her simple equation of cause and effect they would have to die; nothing could be plainer than that.

Dangers known could be avoided, threats seen counteracted. Plans must be made. The first one was the easiest. Survival. She stirred and rose and went to the others. Akel and Efen greeted her, but Omal and Satsat were asleep, already sinking into the comatose state that would see them through the long, dark voyage.

"Waken, please, we must talk," Enge said, then waited until the others had stirred and were attentive again. "We cannot discuss, so I ask compliance/obedience. Will you do as I ask?"

"You speak for us all, Enge," Omal said simply and the others signed agreement.

"Then this is what we will do. While four sleep one must always be awake—for there are great dangers. That is what must be done. If one is sleepy then another must be awoken. One will always sit awake beside the sleepers." She looked about as they all communicated understanding and agreement. "Then all is well. Now sleep my sisters and I will remain awake at your side."

Enge was sitting in the same position some time later when Vaintè climbed down from the fin, a shiver of hatred running the length of her body when she caught Enge's watching eye. Enge did not respond—nor did she turn away. The placidity of her gaze irritated Vaintè even more so that she was forced to lie at a distance, her back turned, in order to calm herself.

It was a fast and uneventful crossing, for all aboard were so shocked by the death of Alpèasak that they escaped their remembered terrors in sleep, waking only to eat, then sleep again. But one of the appointed five was always awake, always watchful.

Enge was asleep when land was sighted, but she had left her orders.

"It is there, the greentree shore of Entoban∗," Satsat said, touching Enge lightly to awaken her.

Enge signed grateful thanks and waited in silent stolidity until the time came when the commander was alone on top of the fin: she joined her there and they both looked in silent appreciation at the line of white breakers that were drawn against the greens of the jungle beyond.

"Respectful request for knowledge," Enge signed, and Erafnais let acceptance be known. "We are looking at the shore of warm and eternal Entoban∗. But is it known at what position on the coast we see?"

"Somewhere here," Erafnais said, holding out the chart tight-clamped between the thumbs of one hand, the thumbs of the other spanning a distance on the coast. Enge looked closely at it.

"We must proceed north along the shore," Erafnais said, "then on past Yebèisk to the island city of seagirt Ikhalmenets."

"Would impertinence be assumed if I asked the commander to point out warm-beached Yebèisk when we are close?"

"Communication will be made."

Another two days passed before they came to the city. Vaintè was also interested in Yebèisk and stood at the far end of the fin while Erafnais and Enge remained at the other. It was late afternoon when they passed the high trees, the golden curve of the sands on each of the city's flanks, the tiny forms of the fishing boats returning with the day's catch. Surprisingly, after all her earlier curiosity, Enge showed scarcely any interest at all. After one long glance she signed her gratitude for information and went below. Vaintè permitted herself a spasmodic glare of hatred as she passed, then stared back at the shore.

In the morning she listened as a crewmember addressed the commander, and could not control the tremors of anger that shook her body. She should have known—should have known.

"They are gone, Erafnais, all five of them. I saw their sleeping positions vacated when I awoke. They are not here in the uruketo or in the fin."

"Nothing was seen?"

"Nothing. It was my duty to awaken first this day to take the guiding position. It is a mystery. . ."

"No it is not!" Vaintè cried aloud and they drew back from her. "The only mystery is why I did not see what was going to happen. They know that no good will come to them in the bold city of Ikhalmenets. They seek hiding places in Yebèisk. Turn about, Erafnais, and go there at once."

There was command in Vaintè's voice, authority in the stance of her body. Yet Erafnais made no move to obey, instead stood in immobile silence. The watching, listening crewmembers were rigid, each with an eye turned toward one of the speakers. Vaintè signed urgency and obedience and wrath, hovering like a destructive thundercloud over the smaller commander.

Bentback, dragfoot Erafnais—with a will of her own. She had had more than a hint of the motives involved here. Enge had been kind to her and never offended her—while she knew little of the Daughters of Life, cared even less. What she did know was that there had been enough killing. And it was obvious that death lay behind every one of Vaintè's venomous movements.

"We will proceed. We will not turn back. Dismissal of presence from commander to passenger."

Then she turned about and walked away, letting her limp muffle the positions of pleasure and superiority in her body movements.

Vaintè was rigid with anger, paralyzed by impotence. She did not command here—did not command anywhere echoed back darkly from her thoughts—nor could she use violence. The crewmembers would not permit that. She was locked in a silent, internal battle with her anger. Logic must rule; cold thought must vanquish. The inescapable fact was that there was absolutely nothing that could be done at the present time. Enge and her followers had escaped from her for the moment. That was of no importance. In the fullness of time they would meet again and instant justice would follow. Nor could anything be done now about the commander of the uruketo. These things were all too petty to be considered. What she should be thinking about was the riverine city of Mesekei and the important tasks that must be undertaken there. If she were to achieve her ends careful planning would be needed, not mindless anger. For all of her life she had kept her anger carefully in check and she wondered now at the newfound strength of it. It was the ustuzou that had done that, destroyed her calm and turned her into a creature of intemperate justice. Kerrick and his ustuzou had made her like this. It would not be forgotten. In the future her anger would be kept under control at all times, for all things. Except one. Hatred treasured was hatred that grew strong in a hidden place. One day to be released.

With the working of these thoughts the tension eased and her body was hers again. She looked around and found that she was alone. Erafnais was in the fin above with the crewmembers who were on duty; the rest were comatose and asleep. Vaintè looked toward the place where Enge and her followers had slept and it was just an empty area that meant nothing to her. This was as it should be. She was back in control of her body and her emotions again. There was a movement in the darkness beyond and she could clearly hear the sounds of communication-desired. Only then did she remember the presence of the fat scientist and the male. She approached them.

"Aid a helpless male creature, great Vaintè," the captive pleaded, squirming in Akotolp's unyielding grasp.

"I know you from the hanalè," Vaintè said, amused by the thing's mewling. "You are Esetta< who sings—are you not?"

"Vaintè is first-always because she recalls the name of everything, smallest to highest. But now miserable Esetta< has nothing to sing of. The heavy one who now holds me, she pulled me from the hanalè, dragged me through smells and fog that hurt my breathing, half-drowned me on the way to this uruketo, now holds me in her unbreakable grip of great pain. Speak with her I entreat, suggest she release me before death of arm."

"Why aren't you dead completely?" Vaintè asked with brutal candor. Esetta< recoiled and squealed.

"Oh, great Vaintè—why do you wish this one of no importance dead?"

"I do not, but all the others died. Brave Yilanè of Alpèasak. Cast out by their dead city to die with it."

Even as she spoke Vaintè felt the crushing wave of fear. They were dead—not she. Why? She had told loyal-dead Stallan that this was because of their hatred of the ustuzou. Was it? Was that reason enough to stay alive when all others died? She looked at Akotolp as these dark thoughts embraced her and realized for the first time what the scientist was experiencing. Doubt-in-life, avoidance-of-death. Akotolp had labored in many cities, so felt no life-destroying loyalty to any single one. But she was scientist enough to know that the death of rejection could be triggered in an instant. That was what her rigid, silent battle was about. By the force of her will she was keeping herself among the living.

This knowledge was a flow of strength to Vaintè. If this fat one could live by will alone then she, with an eistaa's strength of will could live, survive—and rule once more. Nothing was beyond her!

Before the unseeing eyes of Akotolp, the fear-filled eyes of the male, Vaintè raised clenched thumbs in a forceful gesture of victory, trod strongly with outstretched claws upon the resilient surface. A moan of fear penetrated her consciousness and she looked down with growing pleasure at the cowering Esetta<: desire came instantly.

She bent and her strong thumbs pried loose the scientist's grip on the male's wrist. His repeated sounds of gratitude changed quickly to moans as she pressed him over backward, painfully excited him, mounted him brutally.

Akotolp's tight-locked muscles never relaxed—but her nearest eye moved slowly to gaze at the entwined couple. Even more slowly her stiff features moved with unreadable expressions.

After this Vaintè welcomed deep sleep, slept comatose until the following morning. When she awoke the first thing that she saw was the fat scientist climbing breathlessly up into the fin. Vaintè looked around but did not see the male; hiding from her without doubt. She moved slightly with humor at the thought, then found herself awake, excited by thought of Esetta<. The uruketo rolled as it encountered a large wave and a shaft of bright sunlight from the fin illuminated the interior. The sun looked warm and attractive and Vaintè came fully awake, standing, yawning and stretching. The sunlight drew her on and she went to the fin, climbed slowly up to its top. Akotolp stood there, her eyes in the bright sunshine mere vertical slits in her round face. She glanced at Vaintè and acknowledged grateful presence.

"Come bask in the sun, kind Vaintè, to take pleasure while I thank you."

Vaintè signed acceptance, pleasure—and question of source. Akotolp laced her fat thumbs together in relaxed companionship and spoke.

"I thank you, strong Vaintè, because your example was instrumental in saving my life. The logic of science rules my existence, but I know too well the part the body plays, irrespective of the brain's control. I know that an eistaa's command can trigger the metabolic changes in a Yilanè that will cause her certain death. Then I saw, when all died in tragic Alpèasak, that the death of a city could start this response as well. When I realized what was happening I feared for myself, despite my superior knowledge, feared that I too would be mortally stricken. The male's survival helped. When he remained alive so might I. That is the reason that my hand stayed tight-clamped to him while I fought for survival. Then you came and took him from me and I was aware and vision returned. I saw you magnificently alive, so feminal that I took strength from you and knew that my death was averted. I thank you for my life, strong Vaintè. It is yours to dispose of: I am your fargi and will do as you command."

At this moment another long wave rocked the uruketo and Akotolp's ample form fell sideways. Vaintè reached out and took her arms, stopped her from falling, held her and expressed sincere thanks of equal to equal.

"Now it is I who thank you, great Akotolp. I have much to do and a long way to go. I will need aid. I welcome you as my first follower in that which I must accomplish."

"I take pleasure in that Vaintè, and am yours to command."

They swayed in unison now as the uruketo rose over a greater wave: a shadow blotted out the sun for an instant. They looked up and Akotolp signed joy-of-vision.

It was indeed a rich sight to behold. They were passing the mouth of a great river with limegreen jungle stretching away on both sides. Where river met ocean high waves were formed, rolled and foamed. And here the estekel* fished in numbers too large to count. They bobbed on the waves, great furred wings folded, long beaks plunging deep until just the bony rear extensions of their heads were above water. Others soared in slow circles above, their swift shadows sliding across the sea beneath them. Hoarse cries sounded from the creatures, louder and louder as the uruketo moved into their midst.

"See there, see how they launch themselves into the air," Akotolp cried with pleasure. "I have studied these animals. If you examine them you will see that their wingspan is so great, their legs so short, that it is impossible for them to take flight other than from an estuary like this. Here high waves form and march into the wind rather than away from it. So the estekel*, after eating their fill, launch themselves from the crest of the wave into the wind— and are airborne. Wonderful!"

Vaintè did not share the scientist's enthusiasm for the fish-stinking, fur-matted flying creatures. They dived too close and their shrieking hurt the ears. She left Akotolp there and climbed below and, despite the rocking, fell asleep again. She spent the rest of the voyage this way, comatose and unmoving, was still asleep when Erafnais sent a crewmember to inform her that they had reached their island destination and soon would be coming to Ikhalmenets.

Vaintè climbed the fin to see that the ocean behind them was empty. They had traveled most of the day away from the shores of Entoban* to reach this archipelago, isolated here in the vastness of the sea. They were now passing a large island with a ridge of high mountains in the center of it. The summits were topped by snow, wreathed with clouds and swept by sheets of rain, a grim reminder of the winter that was the enemy of them all. These rocky islands were too far to the north for Vaintè's liking and she felt chill at the thought, looked forward to leaving just as soon as it was possible.

Or should she? They were coming to seagirt Ikhalmenets now, the city backed by green jungles, flanked by yellow sand beaches, a high, snow-topped mountain rising above. This was their destination. She looked at the snow-capped peak of the island, stared at it, unmoving, her body rigid, letting the new idea grow and mature. Perhaps coming to Ikhalmenets had been a good thing after all.

Es et naudiz igo kaloi, thuwot et
freinazmal.

MARBAK ORIGINAL

━━━━━━━━━━━━━━

*If you hunt two rabbits, you miss
both.*

CHAPTER THREE

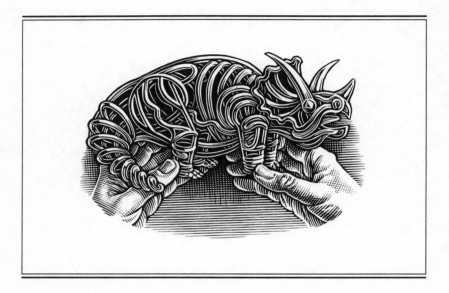

They ate at midday, after the Sasku had killed and butchered one of the deer from the food pens. Kerrick found stones and made a fire-ring in the clear space before the hanalè, then brought dried driftwood from the shore. They could have made their camp anywhere in the ruined city—but he wanted to be close to the surviving Yilanè. While the Sasku hunters did not have the ready tempers and quick spears of the Tanu, they could still not be trusted alone with the two males. Death would come quickly if he were not vigilant.

By the time the hunters returned he had built the fire high so that a hot and glowing bed of coals was ready for the meat. In their hunger they could not wait until it had cooked through completely but hacked away half-raw pieces and chewed on them industriously. Kerrick had the liver, which was his right, but he shared it with Sanone.

"There are many new things to be seen in this place," the old man said, carefully licking his greasy fingers clean before he wiped them on his cloth kirtle. "And many mysteries as well that will require much thought. Are there mastodon here among all the other creatures?"

"No, only murgu in this place, brought here from the other side of the ocean."

"But we are eating this deer, certainly it is not murgu?"

"The deer, greatdeer as well, were all captured and bred here. But in the distant land where those-we-killed came from there are only murgu."

Sanone chewed on this thought—along with another piece of liver. "I do not like to think of a land where only murgu walk. But this place across the ocean that you speak of is certainly part of the world that Kadair made when he stamped his feet and burst the rock asunder. From the rock he brought forth all we see and all we know, brought forth the deer and the mastodon—and the murgu. There is a reason for all this. There is a reason why we came to this place and another reason why this place is here. We must consider all these things until they can be understood."

All of the world beyond the world became of great importance when Sanone spoke as a mandukto. Kerrick had more practical things to consider. The males in the hanalè would have to be fed. And then what would he do with them? Why was he burdening himself with their existence? If he did not intervene they could die quickly enough—there would be no shortage of volunteers for that work. He was sorry for the stupid creatures, but he felt that there must be other reasons than that to keep them alive. He would puzzle over this later. Now they must be fed. Not cooked meat; they would be terrorized by the smell of the smoke. He cut some pieces of flesh from the uncooked forequarters of the deer, then pushed his way through the broken door of the hanalè. The corpses were still there—and beginning to stink. They would have to be removed before dark. As he came to the unburned section he heard singing, though the sounds alone meant nothing by themselves. He stood, unnoticed in the entrance to the chamber and listened while Imehei sang in his hoarse male way. The darkness of the song reminded Kerrick at once of that distant day when Esetta< had sung after the death of Alipol.

> "They walk free,
>   we are shut away.
> They bask in the sun,
>   we look at the dim light.
> They send us to the beaches,
>   Never go themselves . . ."

Imehei broke off when he saw Kerrick—then flashed joy-of-food with juvenile palm colors when he saw the meat that Kerrick was carrying. They both ate greedily, their powerful jaws and sharp, cone-shaped teeth quickly dispatching the meal.

"Did you know Esetta<?" Kerrick asked.

"Brother-in-here," Imehei quickly said, but with more interest he added, "Meat-to-come, interrogative?"

Kerrick signed negative, later time, then asked, "There was another male here, Alipol, did you know him as well? He was my . . . friend."

"Imehei has but recently arrived from Entoban✳" Nadaskè said. "Not I. I was here when Alipol was first in the hanalè, before he went to the beach."

"Alipol worked with his thumbs to make things of great beauty. Do you know of them?"

"We all know of *them*," Imehei broke in. "After all—we are not rough/crude/strong and female. We know of beauty." He turned as soon as he had finished speaking and pulled some of the ornate drapes aside to disclose an opening in the wall. Standing on claw-tip he reached up and took out the wire sculpture, turned and held it out to Kerrick.

A nenitesk—perhaps the very one that Alipol had showed to him on that distant, warm day. The carapace curled high, the three horns sharp and pointed, the eyes gleaming jewels. Imehei held it out proudly and Kerrick took it, turned it so that it caught the light. He felt the same joy that he had felt when Alipol had first revealed his sculpture. There was unhappiness along with the joy—for Alipol was long dead. Sent to certain death on the beach by Stallan. Well, she was dead as well; there was some satisfaction in that.

"I will take this," Kerrick said—then saw their horrified gestures. Imehei was even bold enough to add a suggestion of female-ness to the movements. Kerrick understood. They had accepted him as a male, all the city knew of his maleness and had marveled, but he was now acting brutally female. He tried to make amends.

"Misinterpretation of intent. I *want* to take this thing of beauty but it must remain here in the hanalè where Alipol meant it to be. The esekasak who cared for the hanalè is gone so now the responsibility is yours. Guard it and keep it from harm."

They could not conceal their thoughts, made no attempt to. Hidden away, deprived of responsibility, treated like fargi speechless and fresh from the ocean—how could they be anything but what they were? Now they took in the new thought, recoiled from it, then accepted it, then showed pride. When Kerrick saw this he began to have some understanding why they had to be kept alive. Not only for their own sakes—but for his. For his own selfish reasons. He was Tanu—but was Yilanè as well. With these males he could face that fact, not flee from it nor feel ashamed of it. When he talked with them his thoughts came to life, those parts of his thinking that were Yilanè. Not only thinking, being.

He was what he was: Kerrick of the Tanu; Kerrick of the Yilanè.

"You have water—I will bring more food. Do not leave this chamber."

They signed agreement and acceptance of instructions. With the private expressions of male-to-male. He smiled at their subtle strength. A single suggestion that he had been acting like a female had put him quickly in his place. He was beginning to like them as he understood some of what lay beneath their complaisant exteriors.

The discarded bones were cracking in the cooking fire; the Sasku, bellies full, were dozing in the sun. Sanone looked up when Kerrick reappeared, went over and sat by him.

"There are things I wish to talk about, mandukto of the Sasku," Kerrick said formally.

"I listen."

Kerrick ordered his thoughts before he spoke again. "We have done what we came here to do. The murgu are dead, their threat is no more. Now you will take your hunters and return to your valley and your people. But I must stay here—though the reasons for this are just now becoming clear. I am Tanu—but I am also of the Yilanè, who are the murgu that grew this place. There are things here of great value, of value to the Tanu. I cannot leave without looking at them, thinking about them, considering them. I think of the death-sticks without which the murgu could never have been defeated." He stopped as Sanone raised his hand for silence.

"I hear what you say, Kerrick, and begin to understand a little of the many thoughts that have been troubling me. My way has not been clear, but it is becoming more so. What I can understand now is that when Kadair took the form of the mastodon and shaped the world he stamped hard upon the rock and marked his track deep into the solid rock. What we need is the wisdom to follow that track. That track led you to us and you brought the mastodon to show us where we came from—and where we are destined to go. Karognis sent the murgu to destroy us, but Kadair sent the mastodon to guide us over the ice mountains to this place to wreak his vengeance upon them. And they are destroyed while this place has been burnt but not burnt. You seek wisdom here, which means you are following the mastodon's tracks just as we are. Now I can see that our valley was just a stop along the track while we waited for Kadair to stamp out his path for us. We will remain in this place and the rest of the Sasku will join us here."

While Kerrick had difficulty in following Sanone's reasoning, the depths of the mandukto's knowledge was great and well beyond him, he welcomed the decision enthusiastically.

"Of course—you have said what I was trying to say. There is more here in Alpèasak than one person could understand in a hundred lifetimes. Your people who make cloth from green plants, hard rock from soft mud, you will know about these things. Alpèasak will still live."

"There is a meaning to the sounds and movements you make? Has this place been named?"

"It is called the place of the warm, the shining—I don't exactly know how to say it in Sesek, the sands that lie along the ocean bank."

"Deifoben, the golden beaches. It is well named. Although it is sometimes difficult, even for myself who has been trained in mysteries and in the unraveling of mysteries, to understand that murgu can speak—and that those sounds you make are in reality a language."

"It was not easy to learn."

Kerrick, his thoughts filled with the Yilanè, could not keep all of the pain from his mouth. Sanone nodded with understanding. "That was also a footprint on Kadair's path—and not the easiest part. Now speak to me of the captive murgu. Why do we not kill them?"

"Because we do not war on them—nor do they wish us any harm. They are males, and have rarely left that building, are in reality prisoners of the females. I can talk with them and they give me a . . . companionship that is different from the ways of the hunters. But that is how I feel inside myself. What is more important is that they can aid us in knowing this city for they are more a part of it than I am."

"Kadair's path; all creatures are upon it, even murgu. I will speak to the Sasku. No harm will come to your murgu."

"Sanone is the wisest of the wise and he has the thanks of Kerrick."

Sanone nodded and accepted the praise as was his due. "I will now speak so that the murgu will be safe. Then you will show me more of Deifoben."

They walked until it was too dark to see the path ahead, then returned to the welcoming fire by the hanalè. That day the Sasku who had accompanied them had marveled at the fields of animals— were pleased to discover that only a small portion of them had been destroyed. They ate the fruit until they were sticky with juice, gazed in awe at the nenitesk and the armor-plated onetsensast, swam in the warm waters off the golden sands. While they admired the living model of the city—unharmed, although some of the protecting, transparent ceiling had been burned—Kerrick looked in wonder at how it had grown in the few years that he had been away. His head so filled with memories and visions that, for the first time since they had left the sammads, he did not think once about Armun and the encampment in the snow, so far away in the distant north.

The encampment was the familiar one in the bend in the river. Once again the too-early snows blanketed the ground, covered the ice upon the river as well. There were more tents here than there had ever been before, while all the mastodons of the different sammads made a small herd. They trumpeted in the cold air and dug for the grass that was not there. But they were full-bodied and well fed despite the lack of grazing for they had had their fill of the young branches gathered in the autumn. The Tanu were well fed as well. There was smoked meat and dried squid, even the pre- served murgu meat if it were needed. The children played in the snow and carried bark buckets of it into the tents to be melted for water. All went well, although the women, children too, felt the absence of the hunters. The sammads were not complete. Yes, there were the old men and the handful of younger hunters who had been left behind to guard the sammads. But the others were gone, far to the south where anything could have happened to them. Old Fraken tied knots in his strings and he knew how many days had passed since they had parted company, but this meant nothing. Had they done what they had set out to do?

Or were they all dead?

That thought, which had been just a tiny one soon after they had left, grew day by day until it was like a thunderhead that spread blackness over them all. The women would gather around when Fraken dug into the owl pellets, pushing at the mouse bones until he could see into the future. All was well he reassured them, there had been victory, all was well.

They wanted to hear him say this, so they saw to it that he had the softest pieces of roast meat that his old teeth could chew. But in the night in the darkness of the tents the old fears returned. The hunters—where were the hunters?

Armun had such fear that Kerrick was dead that she would wake up in the night, gasping for air, clutching the baby to her. Awakened and frightened, Arnwheet would wail lustily until solaced by a milky breast. But nothing could bring solace to Armun who would lie awake, tense with fear, until light crept in around the skins. The loneliness of her lifetime was already seeping back. A boy had pointed at her mouth and laughed. Although the laugh had turned to a wail of pain when her quick hand had lashed out, it had still brought back memories long banished. Though she was not aware of it, she once again walked through the camp with a fold of her deerskin over her mouth to hide the split in her lip. The future without Kerrick, cold and empty, did not bear thinking about.

Then it snowed without stopping for many days, for days to the count of two hands, snow that drifted silently into giant drifts that clogged the landscape. When the sun finally returned the river could not be told from the land in this new white world. The mastodons bellowed angrily, their breath forming white clouds against the pale blue sky as they trampled the snow underfoot. Armun wrapped Arnwheet in many layers of deerskin before slinging him on her back. The snow was heaped high over the tent and she had to dig her way up to the outside world. Other women were emerging, calling out to one another. None called to Armun. Anger replaced her old despair and she put the baby in its carrier and walked away from the tents to find peace from the warm cries that were only taunts to her. The snow was waistdeep, but she was strong and it was good to be out of the tent. Arnwheet gurgled on her back, seemingly enjoying the release as much as she did.

Armun walked until trees hid the tents and only then did she stop and catch her breath. Ahead of her the white plain stretched out, not really a plain but the frozen, snow-covered river. Black dots moved upon it in the distance and she was suddenly sorry that she had come this far alone. She had no weapon, not even a knife. Even if she had she would never have been able to stand against the starving predators. They were closer and she turned to run— and stopped.

There were more now, strung out in a single line, more and more of them.

Hunters! Could it be?

Unmoving she watched as they came closer, until it was clear that they were hunters—skinclad, snowshoed hunters. And the one in front, that massive form could be no other, it must be Herilak. Breaking trail, leading the way. She shielded her eyes to see which one was Kerrick, her heart pounding as though it would burst. She laughed aloud and waved. They must have seen her for their ululating cry of victory cut the air. She could not move, only wait as they came closer and closer, until Herilak's frosted beard was clear, until he could hear her cry.

"Kerrick—where are you?"

Herilak did not answer, nor was there any answering shout and she swayed and almost fell.

"He is dead! I am dead!" she screamed when Herilak came close.

"No. Kerrick lives, he is sound. The battle has been won."

"Then why doesn't he answer me? Kerrick!"

She floundered through the snow to get past the big hunter, but he stayed her with one hand.

"He is not here. He did not return with us. He is in the burnt murgu city. He told me to care for you in my sammad and that I will do."

"Kerrick!" she wailed and struggled against his grip.

To no avail.

CHAPTER FOUR

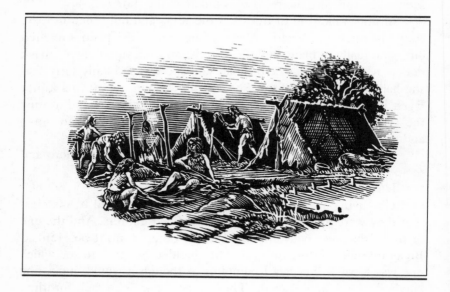

In a single instant Herilak's words had wiped away all of Armun's nameless fears. *He did not return with us. He is in the burnt murgu city. He told me to care for you in my sammad and that I will do.* The world was harsh enough without imagining it worse. In silence she had turned from the hunters and trudged through the snow back to her tent. They had gone swiftly by her, calling out to the encampment as they went, listening for the answering cries from the sammads and hurrying even faster.

Armun heard all this—but was not aware of hearing it for she listened to the far louder inner voice of her thoughts. *Alive.* He was alive. He had not returned with the others, but Kerrick would have a good reason for that. She would ask Herilak, but later, after the first excitement of the homecoming was over. It was enough to know that Kerrick had led them in battle—and that the battle had been won. The murgu destroyed at last. Now the endless fighting would be over. He would come to her and they would live as all the other hunters lived. Unknowing, she hummed aloud with pleasure and Arnwheet chuckled happily on her back.

Later, when the baby slept, she went out and listened to the excited talk of the women. How the hunters had burnt the city of the murgu, killed the murgu, every last one, and had now returned in victory. She moved along the trampled paths in the snow until she came to Herilak's tent. He was standing outside of it but started to go in when he saw her. She called out to him and he turned back with some reluctance.

"I would talk to you, Herilak. I wish to ask about Kerrick."

"He remained behind in the murgu place, I told you that."

"You did not tell me why he did this thing and did not return with the others."

"He did not wish to. Perhaps he likes it there with the murgu. Perhaps he is more murgu than Tanu. There were murgu still alive and he would not kill them—or let us kill them. When this happened we left and came here because we were through at that place."

She sensed the ill feeling, and with it came the quick return of all her fears.

"Did he say when he would return—"

"Leave me, I am through talking," Herilak said, turning and entering the tent and tying it shut behind him. Armun's temper washed away her fear.

"Well I am not through!" she shouted so loudly that people turned to listen. "Come out, Herilak, and tell me everything that happened. There is more that I want to know."

The hunter's silence drove her to fury and she pulled at the skins. But he had sealed them together tightly from the inside. She wanted to shout to him just what she thought of his actions—but desisted. It would only provide amusement for the onlookers. There were other ways of finding out the truth about what had happened. She spun about and the nearest hunters turned away to avoid her anger. After this she stamped away between the tents, toward those of Sorli's sammad, to find Sorli himself where he sat by his fire with some of his hunters, sharing the smoke from a stone pipe. Armun waited until all had smoked and the pipe was laid aside before she stepped forward. Her anger was still there, but well under control now.

"I have heard of how long and hard the path was, Sorli. You and your hunters must surely be tired and in need of rest."

Sorli waved a negligent hand. "The hunter who cannot walk the trail is no hunter."

"It pleases me to hear that. Then the great hunter Sorli is not too tired to talk with Armun."

Sorli narrowed his eyes as he looked at her, feeling that he was somehow being trapped. "I am not tired."

"That is good, because my tent is far distant in the snow and there is something there that I must show you."

Sorli looked around for aid, but there was none. The pipe was being lit again and none of the other hunters were looking his way. "All right, to your tent, but the day is late and there are things to be done."

"You are very kind to a woman alone." She did not speak again until they had reached their destination and had entered the tent. She secured the flaps behind him, then she turned about and pointed to the sleeping infant. "That is what I wanted you to see."

"The baby . . . ?"

"Kerrick's son. Why did he not return with the rest of you to his son, his tent, return to me? Herilak will not speak of it and turns away. Now *you* will speak of it."

Sorli looked about, but there was no escape. He sighed. "Give me water to drink, woman, and I will tell you. There is bad feeling now between Kerrick and Herilak."

"Here, drink this. I know that—but you must tell me why."

Sorli wiped his lips on the back of his sleeve. "The reasons why are hidden from me. I will tell you what happened. We burned the place of the murgu, and the murgu who did not die in the fire died also, I do not know why. They are murgu and therefore incomprehensible. Some escaped on a thing-that-swam. Kerrick talked with a murgu, would not let Herilak kill it. He let it escape. Then other murgu were found alive and these too Kerrick would not allow to be killed. Herilak was great in his anger at this and would not remain in that place and wished to leave at once. The road back was long, we knew that, so the decision was made to leave."

"But Kerrick remained behind. Why? What did he say?"

"He talked with Herilak, I did not listen, it is hard to remember." Sorli shifted uneasily on the furs and gulped down more water. Armun's eyes sparkled in the firelight, her temper barely under control.

"You must do better than that, brave Sorli, bold Sorli. You are strong enough to tell me what happened that day."

"My tongue speaks truth, Armun. Kerrick spoke of things that must be done in that place. I understood little. The Sasku seemed to understand, they remained when we left. We all returned with Herilak. We had done what we had come to do. The trail back was long . . ."

Armun sat with head lowered for a moment, then rose and unlaced the entrances. "My thanks to Sorli for telling me of these things."

He hesitated, but she remained in silence. There was nothing he could add. He hurried out into the growing darkness, glad to be free. Armun sealed the tent again, added wood to the fire and sat beside it.

Her face was grim with anger. How easily these brave hunters had turned their backs on Kerrick. They followed him in battle— then left him. If the Sasku had remained with him he must have asked the hunters to stay as well. And there must be something important in the murgu city, something so important that it had come between the two leaders. She would find out about it in good time. The winter would be over and in the spring Kerrick would return. That is what would happen in the spring.

Armun kept herself occupied so that the winter would go faster, so she would not miss Kerrick too much. Arnwheet was now in his second year and unhappy at the confines of the tent. Armun had cured and scraped the softest deerskins, shaped them, then sewn them into clothing for him with thin lengths of gut. While the other babies his age were still being carried on their mothers' backs he played and rolled in the snow. As was the custom, the other babies were being nursed until they were four, even five years old. Arnwheet was almost weaned by his second year. Armun ignored the dark looks and shouted remarks of the women: she was well used to being an outcast. She knew that they were just jealous of her freedom and nursed only to prevent more pregnancies. So while their babies dangled out of their carriers and gummed their knuckles, Arnwheet grew strong and straight and chewed the tough meat with his growing teeth.

On a sunny, cold day, with no hint of spring in the air, she walked away from the tents with little Arnwheet trotting to keep pace. She carried a spear always now when away from the sammads— and was suddenly glad that she had it with her. There was something up ahead, in among the trees, making a mewling sound. She pointed the spear and stood ready. Arnwheet clung to her leg in wide-eyed silence as she tried to make out what it was. It was then that she saw the footprints leading from the trail, human footprints. She lowered the spear and followed them, then pushed aside the snowy boughs that shielded the boy. He turned about; his snuffling died away as he scrubbed at his face that was streaked with tears and blood.

"I know you," Armun said, reached down with her sleeve to wipe his cheeks. "You are from Herilak's sammad. Your name is Harl?" The boy nodded, eyes brimming. "Did you not come to my fire one night with the story of the owl you had killed?"

When she said this he began wailing again, burying his head in his arms. Armun lifted him with kind hands and brushed the snow from his skins. "Come to my tent. You will have something warm to drink."

The boy pulled back, reluctant to go, until Arnwheet trustingly took his hand. They went back to the tent this way, each holding one of Arnwheet's hands. There Armun stirred sweet bark into warm water and gave it to Harl to drink. Arnwheet wanted some too, but spluttered over the strong flavor and let it dribble down his chin. After Armun had cleaned the blood from the boy's face she sat back and pointed at the bruises. "Tell me about these," she said.

She listened in silence, Arnwheet falling asleep on her lap, and soon understood why the boy had cried when she had mentioned the owl.

"I did not know it was an owl. It was my first bow, my first arrow, my uncle, Nadris, he helped me to make it. The sammadar Kerrick said I did a good thing, for the creature that I killed was not a real owl but a murgu owl and it was right to kill it. That was then, but now the alladjex has said that it was wrong. That killing an owl is wrong. He has told my father that and now my father beats me and won't let me sit by the fire when it is cold."

The boy sobbed again at the thought. Armun reached carefully for the ekkotaz so she would not wake the sleeping infant, then gave Harl a handful of the sweet berry and nut paste. He wolfed it down hungrily.

"What you did was correct," she said. "Old Fraken is wrong about this. The margalus Kerrick knows about murgu, knew that this was a murgu owl, knew that you did the right thing in killing it. Now go back to your tent, tell your father what I have said. What you did was a good thing."

The wind was strengthening so she laced the tent flaps tight after the boy had gone. Old Fraken was wrong more often than right. Since her parents had died, since she had been alone, she had thought less and less of Fraken and his warnings and predictions from owl pellets. Kerrick had laughed at Fraken and his owl vomitings and had helped her lose her fear of the old man. He was stupid and foolish and caused trouble, like this thing with the boy.

Later that same night she awoke, her heart hammering with terror at a scratching on the outside of the tent. She groped for the spear in the darkness until she heard the voice calling her name. Then she blew on the fire until the coals glowed, added fresh wood and unlaced the flap. Harl pushed his bow and arrows in before him then crawled after them.

"He beat me," he said, dry-eyed now. "My father beat me with my own bow when I told him what you had said. He did not want to hear it. He shouted that Kerrick knew all about murgu because he was half murgu himself . . ." His voice died away and he lowered his head. "Just like you, he said. Then he beat me again and I ran away."

Armun burnt with anger; not for herself, she had heard worse insults. "Old Fraken could read the future better from murgu turds. And your father is as bad, listening to stupidities like that. Kerrick who saved the sammads, now he is away they are quick to forget. How old are you?"

"This is my eleventh winter."

"Old enough to beat, too young to be a hunter and fight back. Lie there until morning, Harl, until your father wonders where you are and comes to find you. I'll tell him about murgu!"

Armun went out in the morning and walked among the tents of sammads and listened to what the women were saying. There was concern over the missing boy and hunters were out looking for him. Good, she thought to herself, they only get fat lying around their tents and doing nothing. She waited until the sun was low on the horizon before she went out and stopped the first woman she met.

"Go to the tent of Nivoth, and tell him that the boy Harl has been found and he is in my tent. Hurry."

As she expected the woman was not in that much of a hurry that she did not have time enough to stop along the way to tell others—which was what Armun had expected. She went back to her tent and stayed there until she heard her name being called. Then she went out and closed the flaps behind her.

Nivoth had a scar from an old wound on his cheek that pulled his mouth into a perpetual scowl; his temper matched his face.

"I have come for the boy," he said rudely. Behind him the growing crowd listened with interest: it had been a long and boring winter.

"I am Armun and this is the tent of Kerrick. What is your name?"

"Move aside woman—I want that boy."

"Will you beat him again? And did you say that Kerrick was half murgu?"

"He is all murgu for what I know. I'll beat the boy rightly enough for carrying tales—and beat you too if you don't stand aside."

She did not move and he reached out and pushed her. This was a bad mistake. He should have remembered what happened when she was younger and they called her squirrel-face.

Her closed fist caught him squarely on the nose and he went over backward into the snow. When he struggled up to his knees, blood dripping from his chin, she hit him again in the same place. This was greatly appreciated by the crowd—and by Harl who was peeking through a slitted opening in the tent.

Hunters do not strike women, other than their own women, so Nivoth was not certain what to do. Nor did he have much time to think about it. Armun was as big as he was—and stronger in her wrath. He fled beneath the hail of her blows. The crowd dispersed slowly regretting the end of the fascinating encounter.

It did end with that. Harl stayed on in her tent and no one came for him, nor was the matter discussed in Armun's presence. Harl's mother had died in the last hungry winter and his father seemed to care nothing of the boy. Armun was glad of his companionship and the whole matter rested there.

Spring was late, it was always late now, and when the ice finally cracked on the river and floated away in great floes Armun looked to the east for Kerrick. Each day it was harder and harder to control her impatience, and when the flowers were in full blossom she left Arnwheet playing on the riverbank with Harl and went to find Herilak. He sat in the sun before his tent, restringing his bow with fresh gut for the hunting they had all been awaiting. He only nodded when she spoke to him and did not look up from his work.

"Summer is here and Kerrick has not come."

His only response was a grunt. She looked down at his bowed head and controlled her temper.

"This is now the time to travel. If he does not come to me I will go to him. I will ask some hunters to accompany me who know the track."

There was still silence and she was about to speak again when Herilak lifted his face to her. "No," he said. "There will be no hunters, you will not go. You are in my sammad and I forbid it. Now leave me."

"I want to leave you," she shouted. "Leave you, leave this sammad and go to the place where I belong. You will tell them . . ."

"I will tell you just once more to leave," he said, standing and towering over her. This was not Nivoth. She could not strike Herilak—nor would he listen to her. There was nothing more to be said. She turned on her heel and left him and went to the river, sat and watched the boys playing and rolling in the new grass. She could expect no help from Herilak, the opposite if anything. Then who could she turn to? There was only one she could think of. She went to his tent and found him alone and called the hunter away from the fire.

"You are Ortnar and are the only one still alive from the first sammad of Herilak, you who were of that sammad before it was killed by the murgu."

He nodded agreement, wondering why she was here.

"It was Kerrick who freed your sammadar when the murgu captured him, Kerrick who led us all south when there was no food, who led the attack on the murgu."

"I know these things, Armun. Why do you tell me them now?"

"Then you also know that Kerrick remains in the south and I would be with him. Take me to him. You are his friend."

"I am his friend." Ortnar looked around, then sighed heavily. "But I cannot help you. Herilak has spoken to us of this and has said that you will not go."

Armun looked at him with disbelief. "Are you a little boy who pisses in his skins when Herilak talks? Or are you a hunter who is Tanu and does as he himself sees fit?"

Ortnar ignored the insult, waving it away with a slice of his hand. "I am a hunter. Yet there is still the bond of the dead sammad between Herilak and myself—and that cannot be broken.

Neither will I go against Kerrick who was our margalus when we
needed him."

"Then what will you do?"

"I will help you, if you are strong enough."

"I am strong, Ortnar. So tell me what this help is that will
need my strength."

"You know how to make the death-stick kill murgu, I have
seen you use one when we were attacked. You will have my
death-stick. And I will tell you the way to the murgu city. It is an
easy track to follow after you have reached the ocean. When you
get to the shore, you must decide then what you will do next. You
can wait at that place until Kerrick returns. Or you can go to him."

Armun smiled—then laughed aloud. "You will send me alone
into the land of the murgu! That is a wonderful offer—but still
better than any other I have received. I am strong enough to do
that, brave Ortnar, and I believe that you are also very brave to risk
Herilak's wrath in this manner, because he is sure to find out what
has happened."

"I will tell him myself," Ortnar said with grim determination.

Armun left him then, but returned when it was dark to meet
him and get the death-stick and all the darts that he had made that
winter.

Because her tent was away from the others, and she did not
move among the sammads very much, Armun's tent was laced tight
and silent for two days before it was discovered that she was gone.

After some days the hunters that Herilak had sent out to find
her returned empty-handed. Her woodcraft was too good; there was
no trace of her to be found, no trace at all.

CHAPTER FIVE

"I have something to show you of great interest," Kerrick said. The two Yilanè expressed concerned desire for new information, curiosity and gratitude, all without a sound as they chewed on the raw meat that Kerrick had brought them. "But to see it you are going to have to leave the hanalè."

"Safety and warmth here, cold death there," Imehei said, shuddering delicately at the same time. He looked at the empty leaf and expressed a small desire-for-more-food which Kerrick ignored. Both males liked to overeat and had a tendency to add weight.

"There is nothing to be afraid of outside, I can assure you of that. Follow me and stay close."

They followed him just as closely as they could, almost treading on his heels while they looked about them with frightened eyes. They communicated fear and unhappiness at all of the burnt areas, shuddered away in even greater fear from the hunters they passed, as well as showing loneliness at the sight of the empty city. Only when they were inside the place of the models did they begin to feel more secure.

The model of the city of Alpèasak—Kerrick always thought of

it by that name, though aloud he called it Deifoben like the others—was a physical description only. All of the groves and fields were clearly marked, but no indication was given as to what they contained. Many of them Kerrick knew from his days in the city, almost all of the nearest ones. While the Sasku explored these, and marveled at their wonders, Kerrick wanted to see the parts of the city that had been grown since his departure. He pointed now to a series of canals and swamps.

"We are going here. Not a long way and the exercise will be good for you."

Both males lost their fear as they went, reveling in their unaccustomed freedom, looking at parts of the city they had never known existed. Fields of grazing beasts and swamps and walled stands of jungle with even more animals, both native and imported. In the early afternoon they came to a dike-walled swamp that aroused Kerrick's curiosity. A well-beaten track led along its base, then went up a ramp to the flattened top. From here they could look down into the reed-filled swamp below, on past the reeds to the small lake at the far end. Creatures of some kind stirred the reeds, but they could not make out what they were.

"Emptiness of interest, boredom of watching," Imehei signed.

"Pleasure of companionship, warmth of sun," Nadaskè said, always the more genial of the pair. Kerrick ignored their communication because they seemed to do it most of the time, unike the female Yilanè who talked only when there was something important they wanted to say. Yet Imehei was right; there was little of interest here. He turned about to leave when Nadaskè called for attention and pointed down at the reeds.

"Movement of interest; some creature there."

They watched as one of the reptiles emerged cautiously from the swamp's edge. It was sinuous and snake-like, looking up at them with tiny eyes. Then there was another and still another. They must have been drawn by the forms outlined against the sky. Kerrick looked more closely now and saw the white bones at the swamp's margin. Perhaps the reptiles were fed at this spot. He still could not identify them. With his heel he pried loose a stone and dropped it into the mud at the water's edge. There was a wriggle of motion as the nearest animals slithered over to examine it, then retreated back into the shelter of the reeds. They had sinuous green bodies, snake-like except for their tiny legs, with small blunted heads. He was sure that he had never seen them before—yet they were strangely familiar.

"Do you recognize them?" he asked.

"Slimy, crawlies."

"Not good to eat."

The males were not of much help. Kerrick was about to leave, but turned about for a last look. Then he knew—without a doubt he knew what they were.

"We go back now," he ordered, leading the way down the ramp.

After returning the males to the hanalè, Kerrick sought out the others. Sanone was there, and Kerrick hurried to him, cutting into the mandukto's formal greetings.

"We must get meat at once, we can't have any deaths. And they have gone many days at least without feeding."

"I would aid you, Kerrick, if you would tell me what it is you talk about."

"In my haste I cloud my meaning. I have found a pen, a bit of swamp, that has small murgu in it. We must feed them and look more closely, but I think I know what they are. The shape, the size is right. Immature hèsotsan. Death-sticks."

Sanone shook his head in bewilderment. "Like much of what I see here in Deifoben, what you speak of is beyond my comprehension."

"You can understand this. The murgu do not make things, the way we make bows—or looms for cloth. They grow creatures for their needs. The death-sticks are alive, as you must know since you have fed them yourself. But when they are young, they are as I saw them today, small creatures in a swamp. When they grow older they change into the death-sticks that we use."

Sanone understood now and struck his fists together with pleasure. "Wise-beyond-your-years, Kerrick, you will be our salvation. These creatures you speak of will be fed, will grow and we will have all the weapons we will ever need to live in this murgu-filled world. Now we will bring them food and examine them more closely."

It was obvious when the reptiles slithered out onto the mud to snap up the gobbets of meat that they were immature hèsotsan. Now Kerrick felt that this city that had provided their enemies would now provide them in turn. Sanone agreed with him in this, and with each new discovery they made after that he saw the future inscribed more clearly.

The hunters had found shelter from the rain in one of the unburnt structures. After a hault of days the rains died away, though the nights remained cool. Sanone spent much of his time in deep thought, and went often to examine the city model, as well as the larger one of the landscape stretching west from the ocean. He eventually reached certain conclusions, after which he conferred at great length with the other manduktos. When they were all in agreement they sent for Kerrick.

"A decision has been reached," Sanone said. "We have labored hard to understand Kadair's path and at last all has become clear. We understand now that when Kadair took the form of the mastodon and shaped the world, when he stamped hard upon the ground and marked his track deep into the solid rock, he left a path that we could follow had we but the wisdom. We are his children and we are learning to follow his way. He led you to us and you brought the mastodon to remind us where we came from—and where we are destined to go. Karognis sent the murgu to destroy us, but Kadair then sent the mastodon to guide us over the ice mountains to this place to wreak his vengeance upon them. And they are destroyed while this place has been burnt. But only the evil has been burnt and what remains has been left by his design for our use. I know now that our valley was just a stop along the track while we waited for Kadair to stamp out his path for us. The future lies here. We will meet this evening and drink porro and Kadair will come to us. Then at dawn the first hunters will find the track that leads from here in Deifoben along the ocean to the west, the track that goes to the south of the ice mountains, the track that the murgu followed when they attacked us. Once this way is known our people will come here and this will be our home."

Kerrick drank the fermented porro with the others that night and once again felt himself invaded by strange forces, and knew that the manduktos who did this were strong indeed and what they were doing had to be right. He wanted to tell them this, and in the end he did, standing and swaying, his voice raised in a hoarse shout.

"This city will be born again and you will be here and I will be here and you will be here and I will be Tanu and Yilanè, and this city will be the same."

The manduktos approved of this and the manner in which he

moved and spoke, though of course they did not understand since he spoke in Yilanè. But the alien language made his speaking it that much more impressive.

The next morning Kerrick lay asleep late, his head throbbing when he moved. So he kept his eyes shut—and for the first time since the hunters had gone north without him he thought of Armun. He must bring her here to join him. But the year was late already—if he left now he would have to journey through the worst part of the winter before he reached the encampment. He did not want to be trapped there by the snow; it was better here in the warmth. Nor could Armun travel in the cold. And the baby, he had forgotten about the child, it must stay in the security of the tent until winter's end. So there was nothing that could be done now. When the days began lengthening again he would make plans. Right now he needed some cold water to wash over his head.

Armun had planned her escape in the greatest detail. She knew that Herilak would send swift hunters after her, and knew also that there was no way that she could stay ahead of them or escape them. Therefore she would have to outsmart them, escape in a way that they would never consider. No one paid attention to her comings and goings so she was able to carry what she needed away from the encampment, a little at a time, with Harl's help. When this had been done and all of her plans were completed it was time to leave. She sealed the flaps at dusk, put out the fire and saw to it that they all retired early in the empty tent.

The morning star was just on the horizon when she rose, took up the still-sleeping baby, gave Harl the furs to carry, and led the way out into the night. By the light of the stars they went silently between the black tents of the sleeping sammads, staying on well-trampled paths, past the dark shadows of the mastodons to the rocky hills that lay beyond, to the north. Everything that they needed had been concealed there, in the deep crevasse under a shelf of over-hanging rock.

And there they stayed for three days and three nights. There was dried meat and ekkotaz, sealed bladders of murgu meat, as well as all the water they needed from the stream close by. During the day, well-hidden from sight, she cut the long poles into shape and made a travois which she packed with their supplies. On the fourth day they again were up before dawn. Arnwheet crowed happily when he was secured into the seat on the travois. Harl took up his bow and arrows: Armun lifted up the poles of the travois and the long walk began. They worked their way south through the forest, making a wide circle around the encampment, and by midafternoon had crossed the track the sammads had made when they had come north to their encampment. New grass grew in the ruts but could not conceal the deep-cut tracks of the travois poles and prints of the mastodons. Harl scouted ahead for deer as Armun leaned into the poles and started east. Rocked by the steady motion the baby fell asleep.

They camped at dark, ate cold food because she dared not risk a fire, fell asleep rolled in their furs.

It was not easy, but she had never thought that it would be an easy thing to do. If the track had not taken the flattest route she would never have made it at all. Some days, when the path led uphill, no matter how hard she labored between the poles she still could only manage a small portion of a day's march that the sammad might have achieved. She did not let this bother her, nor did she let her fatigue come between her and what must be done. Each evening Harl gathered wood and they had a fire, warm cooked food. She would play with the baby and tell him stories that Harl listened to with close attention. The children were not afraid of the darkness that began just beyond the light of the fire, that stretched out forever, and she would not permit herself any fear as well. The fire burned all night and she slept with the spear in her hand.

There were many days of sunshine—then heavy summer rain. This went on for a long time until the muddy track became impassable for the travois. In the end she built a shelter of leafy branches and they crawled into it. She needed the rest, but despaired of the wasted time. Summer was too short as it was. Harl went out to hunt each day—and one evening returned with a rabbit. She skinned and cooked it at once and the fresh meat was delicious. The rain eventually stopped and the ground dried enough for them to start on again. But the next night, just before dawn, there was a frost that left the blades of grass tufted with white. Winter was drawing near again. With this realization there came the bitter knowledge that she would never make the long trek south along the shore before winter closed in. When she went to pack the travois she saw that she had been struck another unkindness. The death-stick was dead, the tiny mouth gaping open, killed by the frost. It was a

creature of the south and could not live in the cold. It was a portent
of the future.

That night, long after the two boys were well asleep, she still
lay awake in her furs staring up at the twinkling lights of the stars.
The moon had set and the stars stretched above her in an immense
bowl, the River of the Tharms running across it from horizon to
horizon. Each star was the tharm of a dead hunter, held up there in
a glitter of cold light. Yet none of them could help her now. Had
she been a fool to come on this helpless trek, to risk not only her
own life but the lives of the two children? Perhaps, but it was too
late to begin questioning. It was done. She was here. Now she had
to decide what would come next. Had she any choice? Ortnar had
told her she could wait on the shore for Kerrick, but he had been
speaking stupidity, just to give himself an excuse for not going with
her. She did not have enough supplies to last the winter on the
shore, no tent, nothing to keep the winter at bay. So it was a choice
then of camping and freezing—or starting south and freezing. There
seemed little chance now that she could move south faster than the
winter did. For the first time since she had left the encampment
she felt tears in her eyes and was furious at herself for the weakness, wiped them away, rolled over and slept because she would
need all of her strength for the next day's walking.

The following night the first snow arrived and she shook it
from the furs in the morning, packed them away and pressed on.
That night, as they were eating, she found Harl looking at her
across the fire.

"Eat it," she said. "I like the murgu meat as little as you do,
but it keeps us strong."

"It is not the meat," he said, "but the snow. When do we get
to the place you have told us about, where Kerrick is waiting?"

"I wish I knew . . ." She reached over and brushed his fine
blond hair, noticing the drawn lines about his eyes. He was eleven
years old, a strong boy, but they had been walking steadily for far
too long. "Sleep now, we want to be fresh when we start in the
morning."

There was no snow that night, but the last fall still lay un-
melted on the ground. The day was clear yet there was little
warmth in the sun. The track lay along the river valley now and she
was sure that she recognized this place. The sammads had camped
here before, not far from the ocean. Armun even thought that she

could smell salt in the air—she moved along strongly with the wind in her face.

Yes there it was, white breakers rolling up onto the sand, the shore just beyond the bluff. She had her head down, pulling on the poles with steady endurance, following the track. She stopped only when she heard Harl's warning cry.

There was a turf hut ahead, built into the base of the bluff and sheltered by it, with a fur-clad hunter standing before it. Motionless, apparently just as startled by her arrival as she was. She started to raise her voice and call to him—then the words choked in her throat.

He wasn't Tanu, what he wore was not right. And his face . . .

It was covered with fur. Not just a beard on the lower part of his face—but there was fur, soft brown fur over all of his face.

uposmelikfarigi ikemespèyilanè.
uposmelikyilanè ikemespènèyil.
eleiensi topaa abalesso.

YILANÈ APOTHEGM

———————

*A fargi lies down to sleep and one
morning awakes a Yilanè. Since the
egg of time a Yilanè who sleeps awakes
always a Yilanè.*

CHAPTER SIX

Vaintè looked at the activity in the port with great interest. Up until this moment Ikhalmenets had just been a name to her, sea-girt Ikhalmenets, almost always expressed that way and now she could see why. Ikhalmenets had grown along a curving natural harbor—the reason for the city's existence. All of the other islands in this group were rocky and barren. But not this one. It lay on the shore, at the base of the high mountain that caught the moist winds, cooled them to cloud as they rose up, until heavily burdened they released their moisture as snow and rain. The snow tipped white the mountain top while the rain ran down the slopes until it was funneled into the city.

But Ikhalmenets was more of the sea than of the land. Uruketo lined the shore, mixing with the smaller fishing boats heavy-laden with their catch. Erafnais called down instructions to guide the uruketo through the rush to a berth at the dock. Vaintè stood aside as the crewmembers climbed down from the fin and made the creature secure.

"All to remain on board," Erafnais ordered as she prepared to leave. Vaintè listened, then was careful to express no antipathy when she spoke.

"Is your order addressed to me as well, commander?"

Erafnais was immobile with thought; then she spoke. "I do not wish wild accounts of what occurred in Alpèasak to be spread through the city. I will talk with the Eistaa first and await her commands. But you—I cannot command you Vaintè. I can only ask you to—"

"The need to ask is superfluous/close-to-insult, commander."

"Never my intent!"

"That I realize, so no insult is taken. Vaintè does not gossip in the ambesed."

There was a wheezing behind them as Akotolp pulled her bulk to the top of the fin, laboring even harder as she hauled the protesting Esetta< after her. She signed dutiful-request to Erafnais.

"It is required that I relieve myself of the burden of this male creature. Your discussion was overhead, so take my assurance that in the doing of this labor in the city none shall hear from me of Alpèasak's destruction."

"It will be my duty to aid you," Vaintè said. "The male shall proceed between us to the hanalè. This will cause the least amount of disturbance/attraction among the fargi."

"I am in Vaintè's debt," Akotolp said with pleasure-of-gratitude. "A single male is a sight rarely seen. I do not wish to arouse unseemly emotions."

Erafnais turned her back, closed her mind on the matter. The stories would get out soon enough, though not from Vaintè and the scientist. But her crewmembers would be quick to gossip. Before this happened she had to seek out Lanefenuu, the Eistaa of Ikhalmenets, to report everything that she knew, everything that she had seen. It was a burden for an eistaa not for her and she yearned to be free of it.

While Akotolp climbed slowly down, Vaintè waited on the scarred wood of the dockside, her nostril flaps open wide to the drifting smells of the city, almost forgotten during the days at sea. Pungent odor of fish, warm breath of fargi, hints of decay from the undergrowth, while over it all lay the lush embrace of the growing city itself. Unexpected pleasure to be ashore moved through her body.

"Truly felt, Vaintè, and I share your emotion," Akotolp said as she came wide-mouthed to her side. Esetta<, held firmly by the wrist, looked around at the city with interest—though he shied

away with quick fear when Vaintè took his other arm. Vaintè felt
pleasure at this reaction and squeezed both of her thumbs together
harder than she need. In this way they proceeded toward the main
avenue leading into Ikhalmenets. Fargi turned to look at them with
eye-widened interest and soon joined together and walked in a train
behind. Vaintè examined her followers with one backward-turned
eye, then signalled for attention.

"Whichever of you is with perfection-of-speaking and knowledge-
of-city come forward."

There was a milling about as the gap-mouth youngsters in front
pushed back with fear of confrontation. They were shoved aside by
an older fargi.

"From one below to her highest with male attached. I have
some knowledge and wish to be of aid."

"You know where the hanalè is?"

"The location is known to me."

"Lead us."

The fargi, swollen with importance, waddled quickly to the
fore and the procession wound its way along the avenue. Large
boughs overhung it, providing protection from the sun, but the cool
north wind made the sun desirable. They proceeded along the
sunlit strip to one side, to a great structure with a sealed door. Two
fargi, holding dried and preserved hèsotsan as symbols of their
status, stood before it.

"Summon the esekasak who is in charge of all affairs here,"
Vaintè ordered. The guards writhed with inferior confusion until
Vaintè snapped a clarification to the command.

"That one will go; that one will remain on guard."

The esekasak radiated lack-of-knowledge of arrival and willing-
ness-to obey when she appeared and saw them waiting. Vaintè,
every movement of her body demanding obedience and respect,
addressed her.

"Here is a new male for your loyal protection. We will bring
him into the entrance for you."

Once inside, with the heavy door closed behind them, they
could not be overheard.

"This is what must be done," Vaintè said. "This is Esetta<
and he has just crossed the ocean from a far city. He is tired and
needs rest. He also needs privacy-without-end until your eistaa
commands different. You will bring his meat and he will speak only

to you. If you are asked who issued these orders, you will say that Vaintè has done this. Do you understand?"

"Great Vaintè crossed the ocean to be eistaa in a distant city," Akotolp said, humbly and proudly, deliberately speaking of things past in such a manner a listener might consider them things present as well. Vaintè appreciated the adroit assistance.

"As Vaintè has ordered—so shall it be," the esekasak said instantly, signalled request for permission to leave, then took Esetta< away as soon as she received it. Esetta< knew better than to express the hatred and fear of the recent events that he felt, instead he looked about at the warm security of the hanalè and let his motions show pleasure-at-arrival—which was certainly true enough.

There was still a small crowd of fargi waiting outside; nothing new had caught their attention and they waited dimly at the site of their last interesting observation. The older one who had led them here stood to one side, signing respective obedience when Vaintè looked her way. Vaintè waved her over.

"Your name?"

"Melikelè. Is low one permitted to know identity of high one who is speaking?"

"This is Vaintè," Akotolp said, making sure that all the highest marks of respect were associated with the name.

"Do you wish to follow me, Melikelè?" Vaintè asked.

"Wherever the path goes; I am your fargi."

"To the place of eating first. Then I wish to know more of this city."

Akotolp had seen Vaintè's radiant leadership before, yet respected it anew. In this city on a rock in the sea, where she had never set foot before—she still commanded instant obedience. And she spoke of food, excellent idea. Akotolp snapped her jaws together loudly at the thought.

Melikelè led the way back down the hillside to the shore, and along it to an enclosure beside the beach. Since it was not the usual time for eating, the open area under the translucent cover was empty. Tanks lined the wall and the attendant fargi were pulling large fish from them, slicing them with string-knives, gutting and cleaning them and putting the resultant slabs of meat into enzyme solutions.

"A waste," Akotolp pronounced. "For hundred-year-old nenitesk steaks this treatment might be needed—not for fish. Let me see what they have in the tanks. Small crustacea, delightful when fresh—behold!"

She seized a large one between her thumbs, snapped off its head and limbs and shelled it in one practiced movement, popped it into her mouth and chewed with pleasure. Vaintè cared little for the food she ate and took a slab of fish on a leaf instead. Melikelè did the same as soon as Vaintè had turned away.

Akotolp muttered to herself with happiness while a mound of discarded husks grew at her feet. Radiating pleasure-with-eating she took no notice of the fargi working around her, or of the Yilanè who emerged from an adjoining structure. Who looked at her, then looked again more closely, who then approached.

"Passing of time—ending of separation," the newcomer said excitedly. "You are Akotolp, you must be Akotolp, there is but one Akotolp."

Akotolp looked up in amazement, a fragment of white flesh caught on her mouth, the nictitating membranes of her eyes fluttering with surprise.

"A voice familiar, a face familiar—can that be you, thinner-then-ever Ukhereb?"

"Fatter-as-always, years-since-parting."

Vaintè watched with interest as Akotolp and the newcomer laced thumbs in the affectionate embrace of efenselè, though the gesture contained a modifier that slightly altered that relationship.

"Vaintè, this is Ukhereb. Though we are not of the same efenburu we are as close as efenselè. We grew together, studied and learned with ancient Ambalasi, she who was old as the egg of time, who knew everything."

"My greetings to you, Vaintè, and welcome to sea-girt Ikhalmenets. Friend-of-friend is doubly welcome. Now away from this public place to my private one of great comfort for pleasure-of-eating there."

They passed through the adjoining laboratory, Akotolp making a great fuss over all of the equipment, and on to the comfortable chamber beyond. Soft places to lie or sit, decorative hangings around them to relax the eye. Vaintè did just that, leaning back and listening to the two scientists as they talked. She was patient and waited until the conversation left the area of old associates and new discoveries, until Ukhereb asked a more pointed question.

"I have heard that you were in Alpèasak, when all of Inegban* went there. I have read of some of the research carried out, the abundance of new species discovered—what a wealth of joy-in-discovery it must have been! But now you are here in Ikhalmenets. Why travel here to our islands when you had a continent of discovery at your feet?"

Akotolp did not answer, but instead turned to Vaintè for aid. Vaintè silenced her with a gesture of understanding and desire-to-aid before Akotolp could request her assistance.

"Unspeakable things have happened, Ukhereb, and Akotolp hesitates to tell you of them. It is my desire to answer your question if it is permitted, since I was a part of everything that happened. This is what occurred."

Vaintè spoke in the simplest manner, without elaboration or asides; told the scientist, to her growing horror, of the destruction of distant Alpèasak. When she was done Ukhereb emitted a cry of pain and briefly shielded her eyes with her forearm in the childish gesture of unwillingness-to-behold.

"I cannot bear to think of the things that you have told me—and you have lived through them with strength incredible. What is to be done, to be done?" She swayed from side to side slowly, again a juvenile gesture of being moved without thought by strong currents of water.

"Your eistaa is now being informed of events tragic-beyond-understanding. When this has been done I shall confer with her. But you, Ukhereb, you should not be disturbed by events since-finished. We will talk of other things, objects of beauty, consideration of which will ease your pain. Such as the mountain on this island, black rock pinnacled with white snow. Most attractive. Is there always snow upon the summit?"

Ukhereb signed fear-of-novelty. "In the past it was unknown; now the snow on the mountain does not melt at all. Our winters are cold and windy, summer very short. That is why I expressed double-pain at destruction in distant Gendasi∗ There was hope of our salvation there as well. Cities have died—and Ikhalmenets grows cold. Now there is fear where before there was hope."

"Hope cannot be destroyed—and the future will be bright!" Vaintè spoke with such enthusiasm and such assurance of happiness that both Akotolp and Ukhereb were warmed by the strength of her spirit.

Of course she was happy. Vague ideas were turning into positive plans. The details would become clear soon, and then she would be certain of just what must be done.

Not so Enge. For a Daughter of Life, death seemed too close to her, too often.

They had left the uruketo at dawn, had not been seen as they climbed the fin and slipped easily into the water from the creature's back. But the seas had been heavy, waves broke over their heads and forced them under. It had been a long and exhausting swim to shore. The uruketo had vanished behind them in the dawn mists and they had been alone. At first they called out to each other, but only at first. After that they needed all of their strength to reach the beckoning sands. Enge, fearful for her companions, had pulled herself through the breakers first, had found the strength to go back into the waves and drag out one wet form after another. Until they were stretched on the sand in the warmth of the sun.

All except one. Now Enge splashed helplessly through the surf, first in one direction then the other, but the one she sought had never come ashore. Kind Akel, strong Akel, eaten by the ocean.

Then the others pulled her back, touched her with understanding and made her rest while they looked. To no avail. The sea was empty, Akel vanished forever.

Enge finally found the strength to sit up, then to stand, to brush the sand from her skin with tired movements. Before her the water stirred and foamed; small heads of an immature efenburu looked out at her, vanished with fright when she moved. Even this delightful sight did not penetrate the blackness of her despair. Yet it did distract her, bring her to herself, make her realize that the others depended upon her and that her duty was to the living, not the dead. She looked along the sand to the distant outline of Yebèisk at the ocean's edge.

"You must go to the city," she said. "You must mix with the fargi and lose yourselves among them. You must move with caution and remember always the terrible lessons that we learned in deadly Gendasi∗. Many of our sisters died there, but their deaths may still have some meaning if we have learned our lessons well. Learned how Ugunenapsa saw the truth clearly, spoke it clearly, gave it to us. Some were weak and did not understand. But now we know that Ugunenapsa spoke the complete truth. We have the knowledge—but what shall we do with it?"

"Share it with others!" Efen said with joy-of-tomorrow expressed with great feeling. "That is our mission—and it will not fail."

"We must never forget that. But I must consider carefully how to go about doing that. I will find a place to rest—and to think. I will wait there for your return."

With silent movements of agreement and perseverance they touched thumbs lightly. Then turned and with Enge leading went toward the city.

Hoatil ham tina grunnan, sassi
peria malom skermom mallivo.

MARBAK ORIGINAL

*Anyone can bear misery, few are
the better for good times.*

CHAPTER SEVEN

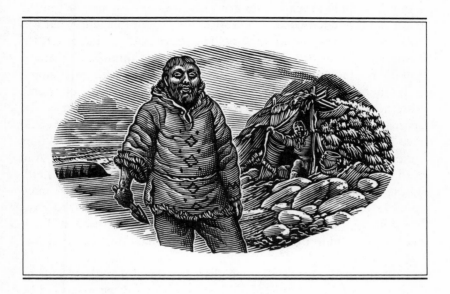

There was much to be done in the city of Deifoben. To Kerrick seemingly far more than there ever needed to be done when the city was called Alpèasak and Vaintè was eistaa. Kerrick remembered those lazy, heat-filled days with regret that he had not observed more, learned more how the immense city was governed. Although he now sat in the eistaa's place, against the wall of the ambesed where the sun first struck in the morning, he could never rule from here as she had done. Where she had had assistants, aides, scientists, fargi beyond counting—he had a few willing but inept Sasku. If a task was simple, and could be repeated, they could be taught and it would be done. But none of them ever understood the skein of intermeshed life that made the city a single complex unit. He knew little enough about it himself, but at least he knew it was there. Each part dependent upon the others in ways unknown. And now the city was wounded. It was self-healing for the most part—but not always. A great stretch of growth along the shore, untouched by the fire, had simply turned brown and died. Trees, vines, undergrowth, walls and windows, warehouses and living quarters. Dead. And there was absolutely nothing that Kerrick could do about it.

What could be done was to care for the animals, or a good number of them at least. The giant nenitesk and onetsensast in the outer fields needed no attention since they could forage in what was still natural swamp and jungle. The deer and greatdeer grazed easily enough, as did some of the murgu meat animals. But others had to be fed with fruit, and this was easy enough to arrange. Still others were simply beyond his understanding. And died. Some were not missed. The riding tarakast were vicious and could not be approached. Yilanè had ridden them, could control them, but he could not. They did not graze, so might be carnivores. Yet when they were given meat they screamed and stamped it into the dirt. And died. As did the surviving uruktop in a swampy outlying field. These eight-legged creatures had been bred to carry fargi, seemed suitable for nothing else. They looked at him with glazed eyes when he approached, did not run or attack. They refused all food, even water, and in their dumb, helpless way fell down and perished one by one.

In the end Kerrick decided that this was a Tanu city and no longer a Yilanè one. They would keep what suited them and not be too troubled about the rest. This decision made the work a little easier, but it was still dawn to dusk every day, with conferences many times late into the night.

Therefore he had good reason to forget the season in the frozen north, to lose track of the passing days in this hot and almost changeless climate. Winter ended without his being aware, and late spring had come before he gave serious thought to the sammads. And Armun. It was the arrival of the first Sasku women that gave him pause to remember, to feel a certain guilt about his forgetfulness. It was easy to forget the seasons in this hot climate. Kerrick knew that the manduktos understood many things and he sought out Sanone for help.

"The leaves here never fall," Kerrick said, "and the fruit ripens year round. It is difficult to keep track of the time of year."

Sanone was sitting cross-legged in the sun, soaking in the warmth. "That is true," he said. "But there are other ways of marking the seasons of the year. This is done by watching the moon as it waxes and wanes and keeping track of when this happens. You have heard of this?"

"The alladjex talks of it, that is all I know."

Sanone sniffed his disapproval of primitive shamanism and

smoothed out the sand before him. He was versed in all the secrets of the earth and sky. With his index finger he carefully scratched a moon-calendar into the sand.

"Here and here are the two moons of change. Death of Summer, Death of Winter. Here the days get longer, here the nights begin to grow blacker. I looked at the moon when it rose last night and it was new—which means we are here in its travels." He pushed the twig into the ground and sat back on his heels, well satisfied with the diagram. Kerrick voiced his ignorance.

"To you, mandukto of the Sasku, this means many things. Unhappily, wise Sanone, I see only sand and a twig. Read it for me, I implore you. Tell me if now, far to the north, has the ice broken and have the flowers opened?"

"They did that here," Sanone said, moving the twig back in the circle. "Since then the moon has been full and full again."

Kerrick's remorse grew at this revelation. But when he thought about it some more he realized that summer had just begun, there would still be time. And there were so many things here that had to be done first. Then one night he dreamt of Armun and touched her split lip with his tongue and awoke shaking and determined to start at once to reach her, bring her here. The baby too, of course.

Good as his intentions were the tasks that had to be finished to make Deifoben inhabitable never seemed to end. One day ran into another, stretched on through the long days of summer, until, suddenly, it was autumn again. Kerrick was torn two ways then. Angry at himself for not making the time to leave and go north for Armun. Yet feeling a relief that it would be impossible to go now since he would never get there and back before the winter snows. He would plan better now, finish his work by early spring, have Sanone remind him of the passing days. Then go north and bring her here. At least she was safe, she and the baby; that gave him a feeling of security whenever he missed her the most.

Kalaleq was not frightened by the sudden appearance of the Tanu. He had met them before—and was also well aware that he was now in their hunting grounds. But he could see that the woman was afraid of him.

"Be without fear, snow-hair," he called out, then laughed aloud to show how friendly he was. This had little good effect for the woman stepped back, still fearful, and raised her spear. As did the child with her. The baby on the travois began to cry lustily. Kalaleq lowered his eyes, unhappy that he had caused distress, then saw his hands and knife dripping with blood from the slaughter of the fur-creature that lay before him. He quickly dropped the knife and put his hands beind his back, smiling what he hoped was a friendly smile.

"What did you say?" Angajorqaq called out, pushing aside the skins that hung in the open doorway as she emerged from the hut— stopping rigid when she saw the newcomers there.

"Look how their hair shines! Their skins, so white. Are they Tanu?" she asked.

"They are."

"Where are the hunters?"

"I have no knowledge—I see but these."

"A woman, a child, a baby. Their hunter must be dead if they are alone and they will grieve. Speak to them, make them at ease."

Kalaleq sighed heavily. "I have no skill in their tongue. I can say only meat and water and goodbye."

"Do not say goodbye yet. Offer water, that is always nice."

Armun's first fear was eased when the furry-faced one dropped his knife and stepped back. He was a Paramutan, if he were here on the shore, one of the hunters who lived always in the north by the sea. She had heard of them but had never seen one before. Slowly she lowered the point of her spear, yet still gripped it tightly when another one of them emerged from the hut. But it was a woman, not another hunter, and she was greatly relieved. The two of them talked in incomprehensible, high-pitched voices. Then the hunter smiled broadly and spoke a single word.

"Waw-terr." The smile faded when she did not respond and he repeated it. "Waw-terr, waw-terr!"

"Is he saying water?" Harl asked.

"Perhaps he is. Water, yes—water." She nodded and smiled as well and the dark woman slipped back into the tent. When she emerged again she was carrying a black leather cup; she held it out. Harl stepped forward and took it, looked inside—then drank.

"Water," he said. "Tastes terrible."

His words disarmed Armun. Her fear was gone but was replaced by a great tiredness, so much so that she swayed and had to jam the butt of the spear into the ground and lean on it for support. The sight of the friendly, fur-covered faces, the knowledge that she was no longer alone let in the fatigue she had so long kept at bay. The other woman saw this and waddled quickly over to her, took the spear from her loose grasp and eased her down to the ground. Armun submitted without thinking, there seemed no danger here— and if there were it was too late to turn back. The baby was crying so lustily now that she had to stand and take him up, balance him on one hip while she found a piece of smoked meat for him to suck upon. The Paramutan woman made appreciative clucking noises as she reached down and touched Arnwheet's pale hair.

Armun was not even startled when there was a call from the distance, a highpitched shout. A small boy, his face-fur a lighter brown than the adults', trotted along the shore holding a rabbit high by the snare that had caught it. He stopped and gaped when he saw the newcomers. Harl, with the curiosity of all boys, went over to look at the rabbit. The Paramutan boy appeared to be older than Harl, though he was half a head shorter. They accepted each other's presence easily. Through her great fatigue Armun felt a sudden welling of hope. They might still be alive in the spring!

Kalaleq was a good hunter and well able to provide food for many. Also, as was the Paramutan way, he would have shared everything he had with a stranger, even if it meant going hungry himself. The only battle they had in the frozen north was against the weather. A stranger was always welcome and everything placed at his disposal. And a woman like this one—he could see the fullness of her breasts inside her clothing and he yearned to touch them. And a baby as well—even more welcome. Particularly a child such as this with hair like sunshine on ice. They would be taken care of. And she would know where the hunters were that they had come to trade with. The Erqigdlit hunters always came to this campsite on the shore, always. But this summer he had waited and seen no sign of them. The snow-haired one would know.

Although Armun could understand nothing of what the Paramutan woman said, she felt the warmth and ready acceptance of their presence. She was coaxed into the hut by gentle patting hands, given soft furs to sit upon. She looked about her with curiosity; so much was different here. Her attention went back to the woman who was hitting her breastbone loudly with her fist and repeating Angajorqaq over and over again. It could be her name.

"Angajorqaq? You are called Angajorqaq. I am Armun." She tapped herself as the other had done and they laughed aloud,

Angajorqaq shrieking with laughter, as they called each other by name.

Kalaleq hummed happily to himself as he skinned the still-warm rabbit, both boys watching with great interest. Then Kalaleq cut off the right hind foot, a trophy considered good luck, and threw it into the air. The white-haired boy caught it with a mighty jump, then ran off with Kukujuk screaming after him. They dodged along the shore, then began to play catch with the bloody bit of fur. Kalaleq looked on with great pleasure. Kukujuk had no others to play with here and had been lonely for his friends. This was a very good day and he would long remember it and think about it during the long night of winter. He returned to his quick butchery of the rabbit, then called out when he had extracted the liver. Kukujuk came when he was called and Kalaleq handed it to him, the choice piece, since he had caught the animal.

"I will share it with my friend," he said.

Kalaleq beamed with happiness as he quickly slashed the liver in half with his flint knife. Kukujuk was a boy who was thinking like a man, knowing it was always right to share, better to give than to take.

Harl took the bloody gobbet, unsure what to do with it. Kukujuk showed him, chewing on his own piece industriously, rubbing his stomach at the same time. Harl hesitated—then watched with amazement as Kalaleq made a little hole in the back of the rabbit's skull and sucked the brain out. After seeing this chewing the raw liver was nothing. It even tasted good.

CHAPTER EIGHT

Armun was not as ready to eat her meat raw as the boy had been. Freshly caught prey was one thing, she had eaten that before, but not the kind of meat Angajorqaq took from a niche in the dirt wall. It was ancient, decayed and stinking. Angajorqaq took little notice of this, as she cut off a piece for herself, then one for Armun. Armun could not refuse—but neither could she put it into her mouth. She held it reluctantly in her fingertips, it was slimy to the touch, and wondered what to do. If she refused to eat it would be an insult to hospitality. She looked desperately for a way out. She put Arnwheet down onto the furs where he chewed happily on the leathery smoked meat, then turned away, raising her hand to her mouth as though eating the piece she had been given. She kept this pretense up as she pushed aside the door hangings and went to the travois. Out of sight now she hid the meat among her skins and found the open bladder of murgu meat. The jellified, almost-raw flesh that the Tanu ate so reluctantly might appeal to the Paramutan.

It did, tremendously. Angajorqaq found the flavor wonderful and called out to Kalaleq to join them, to try this new thing. He ate it with bloodied hands, crying aloud how fine it was between chewing on large mouthfuls. They also gave some to Kukujuk and Harl took a portion as well. While they ate Angajorqaq had heated water over a small fire in a stone bowl, poured it over dried leaves in the leather cups to make an infused tea. Kalaleq sipped his noisily, then ate the leaves from the bowl. Armun tried hers and liked it. This day was ending far better than it had begun. The dugout was warm and free of drafts. She could eat and rest—and not fall asleep, as she had every other night—with the fear of the next day's walk heavy upon her.

In the morning Kalaleq rooted deep in the back of the hut and dragged rolled bundles out for her inspection. Some were cured skins, black lengths so large she could not imagine the creature they had been taken from. There were also sewn hides filled with thick white fat. Kalaleq scooped out some to taste, offered it to her. The flavor was rich and filling. Arnwheet wanted to try it too. "Eat, eat!" he said and she let him lick her fingers.

Now Kalaleq went through a great amount of play-acting. Rolling and unrolling the hides, pointing to Armun, then pointing back down the trail, holding out his flint knife in one hand, shaking a hide out with the other, then changing hands and calling out, "goodbye". It was all quite mysterious.

Not to Harl, who seemed to understand these people better than she did.

"I think he wants to know where other Tanu are. He wants to give them some of the fat."

Armun pointed to herself and the two boys, then back down the trail and said goodbye over and over. When Kalaleq finally understood her meaning he sighed deeply and rerolled the hides, then carried them down to the shore. Kukujuk hurried to help him and Harl joined in as well. After one trip to the water's edge he ran back to Armun shouting with excitement and pointing.

"See, see that big black rock there! It's not a rock, not at all. Come see. It's a boat, that's what it is."

Arnwheet stumbled after them, through the dunes and over the dried clumps of grass to the sandy shore. Harl was right, the black lump had the lines of a boat, upside down with its bottom in the air. Kalaleq was going over this carefully, poking it to be sure that there were no openings. It was a strange boat, not hollowed out from a tree like Tanu boats, but made instead from a single large black hide. When Kalaleq was satisfied with his inspection he bent and seized one edge and heaved the boat over. Harl hung from the gunwhale to look inside and Arnwheet shouted until he had been picked up and could see in too.

It was of amazing construction. Thin lengths of wood had been tied together to shape it and give it strength. The hide had been stretched over this to make the outer fabric of the boat. Armun could see now how the hide had been cut to fit the shape of the boat, then sewn back together again. The seams were covered with the same black substance that made the leather cups waterproof. It was a wonder to behold.

Now that Kalaleq had decided to leave, no time was wasted at all. Their belongings were carried down from the dugout, even the hide door cover, and piled on the sand. Everyone joined in, even Arnwheet staggered under the burden of one of the furs. When everything had been tumbled onto the shore, Kalaleq pushed the boat out into the water. It rode there, rocking in the small waves, and Kalaleq climbed inside. There seemed to be a special place for stowing everything that only he knew about, so there was much shouted instruction as the stores were handed to him a piece at a time. When Angajorqaq passed him the supplies from Armun's travois she knew it was time for a decision to be made—or perhaps it had already been made for her. She looked back at the dunes, with the hills beyond, and knew that only frozen death awaited her there. There was really no choice, none whatsoever. Wherever the Paramutan were bound she must go with them.

Harl clambered in after Kukujuk and Armun handed up Arnwheet who laughed and thought it was great fun. Angajorqaq urged her ahead with soft pats and she climbed into the boat herself. Angajorqaq sat on the sand and unwrapped her leg coverings and threw them into the boat. Like her face and hands, soft brown fur covered her legs as well. Then she hiked up her leather skirts and stepped into the water to push out the boat, shrieking at its icy embrace. Kalaleq had an oar and when the boat was free of the sand Angajorqaq hurled herself headfirst into it, her squeals of laughter muffled by her clothing that had fallen over her face. Armun helped her to pull it free and down over the wet fur of her legs, smiling to herself and amazed at the way the Paramutan laughed so much of the time.

Kalaleq paddled strongly for the rest of the day, right through the discomfort of a rain squall, driving rain with sleet mixed into it,

and on into the afternoon. He called out when he was hungry and
Angajorqaq fed him deliciously rotten bits of meat, once laughing
so hard he almost could not paddle when he bit her finger instead
of the meat. Armun huddled under an open hide, holding the boys
to her for warmth, and marveled at everything. Only at dusk did
Kalaleq paddle back closer to shore, looking for a spot to land for
the night. He ran the boat up on a smooth sand beach and they all
labored to drag it above the tide line.

For days without number it went on like this. Kalaleq rowed
steadily all day, every day, apparently immune to fatigue. Angajorqaq
hummed when she baled out the boat with a leather cup, as much
at home here as she had been on land. Armun grew sick with the
constant motion, lay under the furs and shivered most of the day,
holding to Arnwheet who shared her queasiness. After the first few
days Harl became used to the movement and joined Kukujuk in the
bow where they hung out fishing lines and talked to each other—
each in his own language.

The days passed like this and there was no way to keep track
of time. The weather worsened as they went north, the waves
growing higher so that they bobbed like a bit of driftwood over the
mountainous seas. The storms finally died away, but the air remained cold and dry. Armun was lying under the furs, clutching
Arnwheet, more than half-asleep when she became aware that Harl
was shouting her name.

"We're coming to something, look ahead. Ice, black things on
it, can't tell what they are."

The ice was a solid sheet that filled the large bay. There was
more ice floating in the sea and they had to thread their way
between the floating lumps. To the north even larger icebergs were
visible in the hazy distance. Kalaleq was pointing the boat toward
dark lumps that littered the icy surface ahead. When they came
closer it could be seen that they were boats lying bottom up. Only
when they had reached the ice sheet did Armun see that most of
the boats were many times larger than the one that they were in. It
was an incredible sight.

Kukujuk stood on the gunwhale—then jumped up onto the ice
when they brushed against it. He used the braided leather line to
secure them to one of the broken irregularities of ice—then ran
away toward the shore.

Armun had not realized how weak she had become from the

voyage. It took Kalaleq and Angajorqaq together to help her up
onto the ice. Arnwheet was passed up to her and she sat, shivering
and holding him squirming to her, while the unloading started. It
had barely begun when Kukujuk came running back with a number of
Paramutan hurrying after him. Hunters and women, they marveled
at the strangers' skin and hair, running their hands over Harl's head
until he darted away from them. There were shrieks of laughter at
this: then the unloading began in earnest. Soon the bundles were
being carried toward the shore and the boat dragged from the sea to
join the others on the ice. Armun staggered after them, Arnwheet
stumbling in her wake, until one of the hunters seized him and
carried him, shouting happily, on his shoulders.

They passed a group that had been erecting a black-skin tent
on the ice; they stopped work and gaped at the newcomers. Behind
them were other tents, some of them protected against the wind by
an outer covering of snow blocks. They were scattered over the ice,
as many of them as there were tents in two, maybe three sammads
Armun thought, stumbling with fatigue. Smoke rose up from most
of them and she knew that there would be fires and warmth.
And safety. The wind caught up snow from the drifts and blew it
stinging against her face. Winter had already arrived here in the
north, snow and ice.

But they passed the security of the tents and walked on toward
the shore. Here the snow-covered sea ice was piled high and
broken where it reached the land, difficult to climb over. Beyond it
the shore was smooth, rising up to a steep hill. Huddled at the base
of this hill, half dug into the soil of its slopes, were a few more of
the black-skin tents.

Angajorqaq pulled at her hand, hurried her toward one of the
black-domed tents. It was sealed shut and Kalaleq was unlacing the
entrance. All of the bundles from the boat had been dumped beside
it in the snow. Kalaleq pushed his way in and must have lit a fire
that was already laid, for smoke quickly burst from the opening at
the top. With the feel of solid ground beneath her feet Armun's
sickness from the voyage soon disappeared and she joined the
others in dragging in the bundles and furs. It was all right. Everything was going to be all right. She was safe, Arnwheet and Harl
were safe. They would all live to see the spring. With this thought
she seized up the child, held him tightly to her as she sat down
heavily on the heaped furs.

"Build the fire quickly," Angajorqaq called out. "Hair-of-sunlight is tired, I can tell by looking at her. Hungry and cold. I will get food."

"We must move this paukarut onto the ice," Kalaleq said between puffs of breath to encourage the fire. "The bay is frozen, winter is really here."

"Tomorrow. All will rest first."

"We will do it tomorrow. The ice is warmer than the land now, the sea water below it will keep the cold away. And I will cut snow to keep out the wind. It will be warm and we will eat and have good fun."

Thinking of this made him smile with pleasure and anticipation and he reached for Angajorqaq to have some fun now, but she slapped his hand away.

"No time," she said. "Later. Eat first."

"Yes—eat first! Hunger makes me weak." He groaned in mock agony, but could not stop himself from smiling at the same time. It was going to be a good winter, a very, very good winter.

esseka>asak, elinaabele nefalaktus*
tus'ilebtsan tus'toptsan. alaktus'tsan
nindedei yilanènè.

YILANÈ APOTHEGM

---

*When the wave breaks on the shore, small
swimming things in it die, are eaten by
the birds that fly. they are eaten by
animals that run. Yilanè eat them all.*

CHAPTER NINE

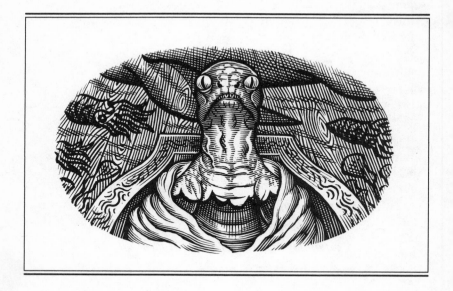

Lanefenuu had been Eistaa of Ikhalmenets for so many years that only the oldest of her associates could remember the previous eistaa; even fewer of these could recall her name. Lanefenuu was large in spirit as well as body—a head taller than most Yilanè—and as eistaa had wrought great physical changes to the city. The ambesed, where she now sat in the place of honor, had been constructed by her: the old ambesed continued its existence as a field of fruit trees. Here, in a natural bowl on the hillside above the city and the harbor, she had shaped an ambesed for her own pleasure. The morning sun fell full upon her raised seat of inlaid wood to the rear of the bowl, even while the rest was in shadow. Behind her, conforming to the natural curve of the land, were beautifully worked wooden panels, carved and painted so realistically that during the daylight hours there were always fargi pressed close and gazing in gape-jawed admiration. It was a seascape of dark blue waves and pale blue sky, enteesenat leaping high while the dark form of an uruketo stretched from one end to the other, almost life-size. At the top of the high fin a figure had been carved, the replica of the uruketo's commander, which bore more than a chance resemblance to the Eistaa seated below it.

Lanefenuu had commanded an uruketo before rising to the emi-
nence of her present position, still commanded one in spirit. Her
arms and the upper portion of her body were painted with patterns
of breaking waves. Every morning Elililep, accompanied by another
male to carry his brushes and pigments, was brought from the
hanalè in a shrouded palanquin to trace the designs. It was obvious
to Lanefenuu that males were more sensitive and artistic: it was
also good to take a male every morning. Elililep's brush-carrier was
made to satisfy her, for Elililep himself was too valuable to end up
on the beaches. It was Lanefenuu's firm belief—though she never
mentioned it to Ukhereb knowing that the scientist would sneer—
that this daily sexual satisfaction was the reason for her continued
longevity.

This day she was feeling her years. The wintry sunlight did
not warm her and only the body heat of the living cloak wrapped
around her kept her from sinking into a comatose sleep. And now
she had added to all her other worries the burden of despair that the
newly arrived commander had placed upon her. Alpèasak the jewel
to the west, the hope of her own city, gone. Destroyed by crazed
ustuzou—if Erafnais could be believed. Yet she must be believed
for this was no second or thirdhand report passed on by yiliebe
fargi. Erafnais, who commanded an uruketo, the supreme responsibility, had been there, had seen with her own eyes. And the other
survivor, Vaintè, she who had grown the city and had witnessed its
destruction. She would know more about what had happened than
the commander, who had been in her uruketo the entire time.
Lanefenuu shifted on her seat and signed for attention. Muruspe,
the aide who never left her side, moved quickly forward, ready for
instruction.

"Muruspe, I wish to see the newcomer called Vaintè who
arrived on the uruketo this day. Bring her to me."

Muruspe signed instant obedience and hurried to the attendant
fargi and repeated Lanefenuu's message precisely. When she asked
them to speak it back to her some of them fumbled, bad memory or
weakness in speech, it did not matter. She sent these away, shame-
of-failure hurrying them from sight, then made the rest repeat the
Eistaa's command until they all had it right.

Out of the ambesed they went in all directions, hurrying with
pride as they bore their Eistaa's message. Each one they asked
spread the word even further through the city until, within a very

short length of time, one of Ukhereb's assistants hurried into her presence signing information-of-great-importance.

"The Eistaa has sent word through the city. The presence of your guest Vaintè is required."

"I go," Vaintè said, standing. "Lead me there."

Ukhereb waved her assistant away. "I will take you Vaintè. It is more appropriate. The Eistaa and I labor together for the cause of Ikhalmenets—and I fear I know what she wishes to discuss with you. My place is there at her side."

The ambesed was as empty as though it were night, not clouded day. The milling fargi had been driven away and now minor officials and their assistants stood at all the entrances to prevent their return. Facing outward to assure the Eistaa's privacy. Lanefenuu's rule was firm, this was her city, and if she preferred the privacy of the entire ambesed rather than that of a small chamber, why then that was what she had. Vaintè admired the erect strength of the tall, stern figure sitting against the painted carvings, felt at once that she was with an equal.

Vaintè's feelings were in the firmness of her pace as she came forward, not following but walking beside Ukhereb, and Lanefenuu found great interest in this, for none had approached her as an equal since the egg of time.

"You are Vaintè from Alpèasak just arrrived. Tell me of your city."

"It has been destroyed." Movements of pain and death. "By ustuzou." Qualifiers that multiplied the earlier statements manifold.

"Tell me everything you know, in greatest detail, starting from the beginning, and leave nothing out for I want to know why and how this came about."

Vaintè stood legs widespread and straight and was long in the telling. Lanefenuu did not stir or react all of that time, although Ukhereb was moved to pained motions and small cries more than once. If Vaintè was less than frank about some of her relationships with the ustuzou captive, particularly in the matter of the new thing called lies, this was only an error of omission and the story was a long one. She also left out all references to the Daughters of Death as not being relevant, to be discussed at some future time. Now she told simply and straightforwardly how she had built the city, how the ustuzou had killed the males on the birth-beaches, how she had defended the city against the enemy from without and had been forced into peaceful aggression in that defense. If she stressed the creatures' implacable hatred of Yilanè that was merely a fact. When she reached the end she controlled all of her feelings as she described the final destructions and death, the flight of the few survivors. Then she was finished, but the position of her arms suggested that there was more to be spoken of.

"What more can be added to these terrors?" Lanefenuu asked, speaking for the first time.

"Two things. It is important that I tell you in private of others who left the city, are even now on the shores of Entoban∗. This is a most serious yet completely separate matter."

"And the second item of importance?"

"Relevant!" She spoke this loudly with modifiers of great urgency, strength and utmost certainty. "Relevant to all that I have told you. Now I know how to defend a city against the fire. Now I know how to destroy ustuzou in great numbers. Now I know what was done wrong by those who died that we could have that knowledge. Now I know that Yilanè are destined for Gendasi∗, the empty lands across the sea. This is a thing that must happen. Not since the egg of time have such cold winds blown as those that are blowing now, destroying Yilanè cities to the north of us. No one knows where this will stop. There is Eregtpe, with dead leaves the only thing stirring in the streets. There is Soromset with Yilanè bones white in the white dust. There is my city of Inegban∗ that would have died in Entoban∗ but went instead to Gendasi∗ to live. And now I feel the cold winds blowing through sea-girt Ikhalmenets and I fear for all here. Will the cold come here? That I do not know. But I do know this, strong Lanefenuu. If it does and Ikhalmenets is to live, it must live in Gendasi∗ for there is no other place to go."

Lanefenuu looked for some sign of weakness or doubt in Vaintè's words or stance—but there were none.

"Can this be done, Vaintè?" Lanefenuu asked.

"It can be done."

"When the cold winds come to Ikhalmenets, can Ikhalmenets go to Gendasi∗?"

"The warm world there awaits them. You will take Ikhalmenets there, Lanefenuu, for I see that you have the strength. I ask only to aid you. When we are there I ask only to be permitted to kill the ustuzou that are killing us. Let me serve you."

Vaintè and Ukhereb turned away as politeness dictated when Lanefenuu dropped into the immobility of deep thought. But each kept one eye to the rear awaiting any movements she might make. It took a very long time for there was much for Lanefenuu to consider. The clouds opened and the sun moved across the sky, yet all three remained as immobile as though carved of stone, as only Yilanè can.

When Lanefenuu finally stirred they faced her and waited attentively.

"There is a decision here that must be made. But it is too important a decision to be made at once. Ukhereb must first tell me more of what the scientists in the north tell her. Vaintè must tell me of this other matter that cannot be spoken of in public. Does it relate to warm Gendasi*?"

"Indirectly it could have the greatest bearing upon it."

"Attend me then and we will talk."

Lanefenuu walked slowly, the gravity of the decisions that must be made weighing her down. Her sleeping chamber was small and dark and had been designed to be more like the interior of an uruketo than a room in a city. The light came from phosphorescent patches and there was a round, transparent port in one wall that looked out onto a cunningly lit design of a seascape. Lanefenuu seized up a water-fruit and half drained it, then settled back onto her resting board. There were two other boards for visitors, one against the rear wall, one near the entrance. Lanefenuu signed Vaintè to use the one at the entrance.

"Speak," Lanefenuu ordered.

"I shall. I shall speak of the Daughters of Death. Do you know of them?"

Lanefenuu's great sigh was not one of despair but of unhappy awareness. "I know of them. And from what Erafnais told me, I was sure they were her other passengers. And they are now free to spread the poison of their thoughts in warm Yebèisk. What are your feelings about these creatures?"

This simple question opened the well of hatred that Vaintè kept sealed within her, let loose the flood. She could not stop it or control it. Her body and her limbs writhed with all the shapes of disgust and loathing, while only inarticulate sounds emerged from her throat as her teeth ground together with enfoamed rage. It took long moments to get her body back under control and only when it was still and motionless again did she dare to speak.

"I find it hard to express my hatred of these creatures in any rational manner. I feel shame at my display of uncontrolled rage. But they are the reason I am here. I have come to tell you of their perversions, to warn you of their danger if you did not know already, to ask you if they and their mind-venom have reached sea-girt Ikhalmenets yet."

"They have—and then they haven't." Although Lanefenuu sat solid and firm, there was more than a suggestion of dissolution and death in the way she spoke. "I learned of these creatures long ago. I determined then that their sickness would not spread here. Ikhalmenets is called sea-girt with a reason, for our young are born here and stay here and no fargi come from other cities. Our uruketo are our only contact with the world. And what they bring here I know of at once. Some of these Daughters of Death have come and have been returned without touching a foot on land. This can be done with those of no rank."

"Yet a Yilanè goes where a Yilanè goes," Vaintè said, wondering, for free passage was like the air one breathed, the water one swam in, and she could consider no other possibility.

"That is true," Lanefenuu said, speaking with immense difficulty for some strong emotion had locked her muscles. "When I first saw you, Vaintè, I sensed one who felt as I did, who trod the same path. What you have told me has only deepened that feeling. I see a future shared, so I now tell you what no others know. Yes, Yilanè have come to sea-girt Ikhalmenets, and among them were those who spoke well of the Daughters of Death. All those whom I suspected might be capable of subversion I have had brought to me here in this chamber and they have talked to me and I have listened."

Lanefenuu paused for a long time, her eyes peering inward, backward in time, seeing events long past that only she knew of.

"Those who were determined to speak their subversion, despite my requests for them to leave Ikhalmenets, these and only these, I have dealt with here. After we talked I instructed them to be seated, just as I instructed you. But on that other board. If you examine it in the light you will see a shining area in the middle. A living creature that contains one of the glands from the hèsotsan. Do you understand what I am saying? They never left this chamber,

Vaintè. Do you know what that means? They are all in there," she gestured toward a small door in the wall. "They nurture the roots of this city with their bodies, not their ideas, and that is as it should be."

When the import of what Lanefenuu had said penetrated Vaintè's numbed senses she dropped forward in the position of lowest to highest, then spoke with this same relationship.

"Let me serve you, Lanefenuu, for all my days. For you have the strength that has been denied me, the strength to act as you know best, irrespective of what others may think, the strength to pit yourself against the custom of ages in the defense of your city. I will be your fargi and obey your commands and will serve you always."

Lanefenuu reached down and touched her thumbs lightly to Vaintè's crest, in the gesture that means shared happiness. When she spoke there were overtones of burdens cast down in what she said.

"Serve me, strong Vaintè, as I will serve you. We have the same journey to make—it is just that we have taken different paths. But I see that our paths have now been joined. We will journey on together now. Neither ustuzou nor Daughters of Death will prevail before us. All will be swept away. Tomorrow's tomorrow will be as yesterday's yesterday—with no memory of these unspeakable creatures in between."

Uveigil as nep, as rath at
stakkiz—markiz fallar ey to marni.

MARBAK ORIGINAL

═══════════════

*No matter how long and hot the
summer—winter always awaits at its end.*

CHAPTER TEN

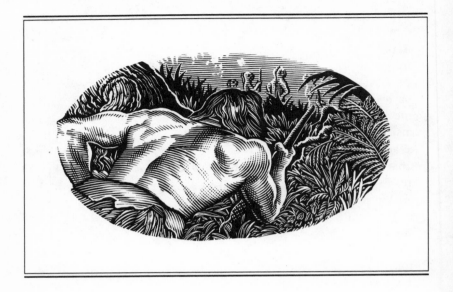

Winter had come again to Deifoben. The rains were heavy this year and a north wind that whistled through the branches of the trees sent dead leaves tumbling before it. This morning Kerrick had been woken in the darkness by the drumming of the rain on the translucent coverings above. He had not fallen asleep again. At the first grayness of dawn he had taken his hèsotsan and fed it, pushing into its tiny mouth the fragments of meat that he had saved from his evening meal the night before. The weapon was at his side most of the time now. He had issued firm orders that anyone going out of the confines of the city must be armed. There were no exceptions—himself included. When it had fed he went out, walking as he did almost every day now, along the paths that led between the fields to the north of the city, to the last grove where the nenitesk tore at the leaves, loudly crunching great mouthfuls. The clinging vines that the Yilanè had planted to block the path still stretched from side to side and he stepped over them carefully. But the poison thorn bushes had been cleared away since they were there to trap humans, not animals. He kept his weapon ready, wary of the many predators that prowled the city's fringes. Looking and listening carefully. But he was alone, the path to the north was open.

And empty. Kerrick stood there, unaware of the rain that soaked his long hair and beard, dripped from the large and the small metal knives that hung from the collar about his neck, ran in runnels down his skins. Empty. He came here most mornings: this was the worst time. Later when the day's work involved him he would forget for awhile. Not now, not when he first awoke. Perhaps Herilak would return and bring Armun back, or there would be a hunter with some word of her. Yet he knew, even before he came here that this hope was an empty one. He should have gone himself in the spring, gone north to bring her back. Now it was too late and spring was far away. What made this city so important that he had stayed when all of the others had returned? He was still not sure. But it had been done and could not be undone. He would go after her in the spring and nothing would prevent him this time.

When he turned away the path was just as empty as it had been when he first came.

The rain was easing up and patches of blue sky were breaking through above. There were problems awaiting him in the city, decisions to be made. He did not want to face them, to talk to anyone, not yet. The ocean was not far, he could hear the muted thunder of the surf even here: there would be no one on the shore. He would go along the beach and back to the city that way.

Sun broke through as he emerged from under the trees, shining on the clean sand and the white-capped surf. Alpèasak, the beautiful beaches, the words sprang unbidden to his mind, his right arm and chin moved at the same time, unknown to him, with the correct modifiers. Head down he scuffed through the sand, the beauty of the beach meaning nothing. The world was a very empty place.

The docks had been overgrown by scrub, unused for over a year, one of the many changes in the city now that the Yilanè were gone and the Tanu had taken their place. He climbed over a litter of windblown branches and up onto the dock. The guard should be close by. The one thing that he and Sanone agreed upon was that watch should be kept from before dawn until after dark at the sea approaches to the city. The enemy had been driven away; that did not mean that they would never return. There was the guard, sitting with his back against a tree. Kerrick did not want to talk to him so he started toward the track to the city. The Sasku did not move, sat slumped, took no notice of him.

In sudden fear Kerrick stopped, fell to the ground, looked around him hèsotsan ready. Nothing moved. A bird called out: there were no other sounds. On elbows and knees he crept forward under cover of the brush until he could see the hunter clearly. Slumped down, eyes closed, his fingers resting lightly on his spear. Asleep.

Kerrick stood up, smiled at his own irrational unease, walked forward and started to call out.

Then saw the dart in the side of the hunter's neck and knew that all of his worse fears had been realized.

The Yilanè had returned!

He dropped back under cover, looking around wildly. Where were they, where had they gone? Before panic took over he forced himself to think, not react. The Yilanè were here, that was certain. This was no accident—or possible murder by another hunter. They all made their own darts now, took patient care with their construction so they would be more accurate in flight. Yet the one before him that had killed the guard, this one had been grown on a bush. Picked by a fargi—and fired by a Yilanè. They had come from the sea. But how many? He had to give the warning. Where were the nearest Sasku working? As warily as he could he hurried toward the center of the city, making a swing away from the most direct route.

There were voices ahead—speaking Sasku! He ran toward them, ready to call out when he saw the two warriors among the orange trees. There was a sharp cracking sound and one of them stumbled and fell. The other turned about, startled, kept turning and fell on top of the first hunter.

The words caught in Kerrick's throat and he hurled himself to the ground, dropping behind the trunk of a tree, seeing the two Sasku dead before him.

Dried leaves crackled in the small grove while he lay motionless, not breathing, staring at the dark form that slowly emerged into the sunlight.

A Yilanè!

She stopped, motionless, just her eyes moving, looking about but not seeing him. Her arms were half-lowered in the gesture of fear, the hèsotsan pointed at the ground. She was young, just a fargi he realized. But there would be others with her. He was right, for a moment later he heard an irritated voice say *Forward*. The fargi writhed with fear and indecision and finally moved. Two others emerged from cover behind her, showing the same overriding fear as the first. Then a fourth figure became visible in the shadows, erect and commanding, familiar. Stepping forward into the light.

Vaintè.

Kerrick shook with the wave of fierce sensations that swept over him. Hatred and loathing—and something else, he couldn't tell what it was, did not want to know. Vaintè had returned, there were invading forces, he had to give the warning.

He had to kill her, that was all that he knew. Once before he had plunged a spear into her and she had lived. Now, a single bite from his dart, an invisible drop of poison on its tip—and instant death. Yes!

Raise the weapon slowly, sight along it, a touch of moving air on his cheek, allow for it, she was turning toward him, how well he knew that face . . .

Squeeze.

The weapon cracked loudly in his hand just as one of the fargi stepped forward. To receive the dart in her flesh, stumble and fall.

"You!" Vaintè said, staring at his face, hatred coloring the word, rippling her flesh with its strength.

Without conscious thought Kerrick fired again—but she was gone. The two remaining fargi turned to follow her. His weapon snapped again and one of them dropped. Loud footsteps crashed away through the trees.

They were running, fleeing. It was not the invasion then, perhaps only a scouting party.

"They are here!" he shouted as loudly as he could, then howled the Tanu war cry. Then shouted in Yilanè "Kill, kill, kill—Vaintè, Vaintè, Vaintè!" in the hope that she would get the meaning.

There were shouts in the distance and he called out the warning again. Then ran, suddenly heedless of all danger, following the receding footsteps. Crashed after them, panting, wanting to kill some more. Came out of the trees and saw the two figures on the dockside ahead hurling themselves from it into the water.

Kerrick stood on the scarred wood and fired at the two heads moving away from him in the sea, over and over until the depleted hèsotsan writhed feebly in his grip. His darts had missed; the two swimmers were well out of range. Moving toward the black object far out in the harbor.

The fin of an uruketo, waiting there for them.

Only then did Kerrick realize how he was shaking. He lowered the weapon and watched the heads grow smaller until they were lost in the waves. Vaintè here, and he could have killed her. There was the sound of hurrying feet behind him and two hunters ran up.

"We saw them, two murgu, dead, they killed Keridamas and Simmacho; what is happening?"

Kerrick pointed, still trembling. "There, the murgu, they are still alive. They have one of their boat-beasts out there. They came to see the city; they know that we are here now."

"Will they be back?"

"Of course they will be back!" Kerrick screamed, his lips drawn back from his teeth. "She is with them, the leader, the one who keeps alive the battle against us, who wants to kill us all. As long as she is out there—they'll be back."

The hunters stepped away from Kerrick and eyed him uneasily. "This is a thing that Sanone must be told about," Meskawino said. "We must run and tell him."

They started away and Kerrick had to call after them. "One can carry the news. You, Meskawino, stay here."

Meskawino hesitated, then obeyed since Kerrick ordered things in the city. Sanone was their mandukto whom the Sasku still looked to for leadership, but he had instructed them to obey Kerrick at all times. Meskawino gripped his mattock and looked around apprehensively. Kerrick saw this and struggled to get himself under control. The time for blind anger was past. He must think coldly now, like a Yilanè, think for all of them. He reached out and touched the hunter's trembling arm.

"They are gone, so your fear must go as well. I saw the one who leads; she and another swam to safety. They are gone, all gone. Now you must remain here and keep watch in case they return."

This was a positive command, something to do. Meskawino raised his mattock like a weapon. "I will watch," he said, turning and looking out to sea. When he did this he saw the slumped body of the guard for the first time and began to wail.

"He too—my brother!" The mattock slipped to the ground as he stumbled over to the body and dropped to his knees beside it.

More killing and more death, Kerrick thought, looking out at the now empty harbor. Vaintè, the creature of death. Yet it could not be her alone. She would receive no aid from the cities were it not for the cold winters that brought fear to the Yilanè of Entoban* where one city stretched out to brush against another city. When winter came to the northern cities they could stay and die. Or cross the ocean—and make war. That was what Vaintè told them; he had heard her, knew that she would go on doing that until she was killed.

Someday. Not now; she was beyond his reach. What he must do now was to get inside her head and discover what she was planning. He knew her as well as anyone did, far better than the other Yilanè. So what would she do next?

One thing was certain, she was not alone. An entire fleet of uruketo could be lying just over the horizon, filled with armed fargi, ready to invade. It was a frightening thought. A wail of agony cut through his thoughts and he turned to see that the Sasku had arrived. Sanone came first, the women following behind tearing at their hair when they saw the dead hunter. Sanone looked from the corpse to Kerrick, then out to sea.

"They have returned as you said they would. Now we must defend ourselves. What must we do?"

"Post guards night and day. The beaches and all of the ways into the city must be watched. They will come back."

"By sea?"

Kerrick hesitated. "I don't know. They have always attacked from the ocean before, when they could, that is their way. But that was when they had this city and small boats. And they did attack us by land. No, it won't be from the water next time, I am sure of that. We must keep watch here—and on all sides."

"Is that all that we do? Just stand and watch and wait like animals to be slaughtered?" Kerrick caught the bitterness in his voice.

"We will do more than that, Sanone. We know about them now. You will have your best trackers go north and south along the coast to find their base. When we have found them—then we will kill them. And for that we will need help. The sammadar who lives for the death of the murgu. We need those Tanu hunters, their knowledge of the forests and their strength. You must find your two strongest runners, who can go day after day and still keep on. Send them north to find the Tanu, to get the message to

Herilak that he must join us with all the hunters he can bring. If he is told there are murgu for the killing—then he'll come."

"Winter is here and the snows are deep in the north. They would never reach the sammads. Even if they did the hunters might not leave in the depths of winter. You ask too much, Kerrick, ask Sasku to die without reason."

"Death may be here already. We need their aid. We must get it."

Sanone shook his head unhappily. "If we are to die then we will die. Where Kadair leads we can only follow. He brought us here for his reasons. Here we must stay for we came in the mastodon's footsteps. But I cannot ask Sasku to die in winter snow just for an idea. In the spring it will be different. We will decide then what must be done. All we can do now is try to divine Kadair's will."

Kerrick started to speak in anger—then controlled himself. He was not quite sure just what Kadair did will, except he always seemed to will it when the old man needed his arguments reinforced. Yet there was truth in what he said. Sasku might not get through where Tanu could, they were not used to the winter. And even if they did—there was no way to be sure that Herilak would answer his call for help. They would have to wait until spring.

If they had that much time.

CHAPTER ELEVEN

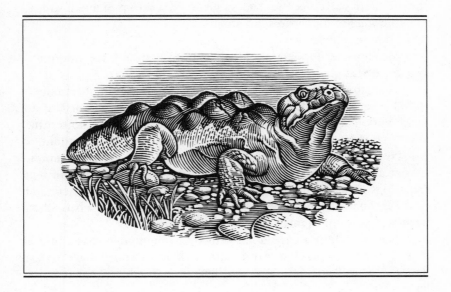

South of the city, south of the river, the swamps began. Here the tangled jungle and marsh came down almost to the ocean's edge, made walking impossible except along the beach. Just above the surf line, long-legged sea birds were tearing at a dead hardalt that had been washed ashore. They suddenly took alarm and hurled themselves into the air, flying and screeching in circles as the two Sasku came warily along the beach. Their white headbands were each daubed with a spot of ochre to show that they were on a very serious mission. They did not seem happy about it. They looked at the jungle wall with obvious fear, pointing their deathsticks at invisible threats. As they passed the corpse of the hardalt Meskawino looked at it with disgust.

"It was better in the valley," he said. "We should have stayed there."

"The murgu came to the valley to destroy us—have you forgotten that already?" Nenne said. "It was Kadair's will that we come to this place to destroy them, and that we have done."

"They return."

"We will kill these too. You whimper like a baby, Meskawino."

Meskawino was too filled with fear to even notice the insult.

Life here by the ocean was not at all to his liking, too different from the ordered existence he had enjoyed in their protected valley. How he longed for those solid stone walls.

"There, ahead, what is it?" Nenne said.

Meskawino stopped, took a backward step. "I see nothing." His voice was hoarse with fear.

"Out to sea, floating in the water—and there is another one."

There were indeed things there, objects, but too distant to make out what they were. Meskawino tried to pull back, to return.

"We must tell Kerrick what we have seen, this is important."

Nenne stuck his tongue far out, a gesture of great contempt. "What are you, Meskawino? Woman or Sasku? Do you run in fear from logs floating in the ocean? What do you tell Kerrick and Sanone? That we have seen something. They will ask us what—then what will you tell them?"

"You should not have done with your tongue like that at me."

"My tongue stays in my mouth as long as you behave like a Sasku. We will go south and see if we can discover what it is we have seen."

"We go south," Meskawino said with resignation, sure that he was going to his certain death.

They kept away from the surf, as close to the trees as they could get, walking in careful fear. But the beach was empty. When they came to a surf-eroded headland they climbed up through the scrub and palmettos, still going warily although they knew they could not be seen from the ocean. At the crest they parted the boughs with care and looked through.

"Murgu!" Meskawino moaned, falling forward with his face in his hands.

Nenne was not that easily frightened. The murgu were not close but were farther down the shore and in the sea. There were ship-beasts, the same as the one that had taken the survivors away when they had burned the city. He had seen it with his own eyes so knew what it looked like. But there were more of them in the ocean here, the count of two hands. And smaller ones as well plying back and forth to the shore bearing the killer murgu. They were being landed on the shore, were doing something there, he could not tell what because a wall of brush hid them from sight. Out to sea he could see more of the ship-beasts approaching, coming from the direction of the island there. It was all very strange.

"We must get closer, see what they are doing," Nenne said. Meskawino just moaned, his face still buried in his hands. Nenne looked down at him and felt sorrow. Meskawino's father and his only brother had been killed by the murgu. Anger and revenge had brought Meskawino here and he had fought well. That time was past. All of the deaths had done something to him and he was like a broken thing. Nenne had tried to shame him into being a Sasku once again, but it was no good. He reached down and touched him lightly on the shoulder. "Go back, Meskawino. Tell them what we have found. I am going to get closer, to see if I can find out what work of Karognis they are up to. Go back."

The fear was still there when Meskawino lifted his face, but relief as well. "I cannot help it, Nenne, it is not of my doing. I would go with you if I could. But my feet will not go forward, only back. I will tell them."

Nenne watched as he sped back along the beach, his feet indeed working very well in that direction, then turned away. Now he would find out what was happening on the shore. With all the woodcraft he possessed he moved into the forest and went forward in silence.

It took a very long time and the sun was slanting down the sky before he was close enough to see the barrier clearly. It rose high, shielding the beach and the land behind it, stretching out into the sea. It was made of bushes of some kind, with large green leaves, though other kinds of darker growths were mixed in with it. He started forward along the forest's edge when he saw the first body. Then another and another. He stood as paralyzed as Meskawino for a long time, horrified, before he could make himself take step after careful step back away from the place.

Although he trotted back along the sand at a steady ground-eating pace, he never caught up with Meskawino who must have run far faster, driven by his fears. For the first time Nenne could understand how the other felt.

Kerrick had heard of the Yilanè presence from Meskawino so had to labor hard to control his impatience as Nenne gasped water from a drinking-fruit, squeezed the remainder over his head and sweat-drenched body. When he could speak at last, Nenne's eyes grew wide with the memory of what he had seen and his dark skin seemed paler as he talked.

"At first it was just one, a deer that had come to graze the shrubs. Dead, the vine with thorns wrapped about its leg. Then I saw the others, some just bones, creatures of all kinds, even murgu beasts, that had died on the growing wall. Birds as well, sea birds and others who had landed—and never left. Whatever grows there is living death that kills whatever comes near it."

"But why? What can it mean?" Sanone asked, and the other listeners nodded in puzzled agreement.

"What does it mean?" Kerrick's voice was grim when he spoke. "Nothing good for us. Think of it. The murgu are here in force with many of their beast-ships. They have a base on that island offshore where we cannot reach them. We could build boats—but I think we would die if we tried to land there. As long as they are on their island and we are here, why then there is no problem. But they have grown this death-place on the shore."

"It is far from us," Meskawino said in a faint but hopeful voice.

"It is now," Kerrick said with no hope at all in his. "It will come closer or another one will grow closer, we can be sure of that. They are changing their tactics and I grow afraid. When they attacked us before this they sent armed fargi against us and they were destroyed. Now I have the great fear that the one who leads them is planning something much more intricate and deadly."

How deadly was it—and how vulnerable? With this thought came a sickening fear. When he spoke again they could all hear it in his voice.

"I must go see this barrier on the shore. Will you show me, Nenne? Help me carry some things that I will need?"

"I will go with you. Now?"

"No, you must rest, and it is late. We will go in the morning."

They left at dawn, going forward carefully and steadily, following the footsteps made the day before where they were still visible above the high-tide mark. By midday they had the barrier in sight, a green arc cut in from the sea. But there was one difference.

"They are gone," Nenne said. "It was not this way before. The beast-ships were there and others were moving between them and the shore, large ones coming from the island. Now they are gone."

Kerrick suspected some trap. The sea was empty, the afternoon haze making the island gray in the distance. There were other, smaller islands beyond it; Kerrick remembered them when he had passed in the uruketo, an entire chain of them. Alakas-aksehent, the succession of golden, tumbled stones. A perfect place to come ashore from the sea, to be safe from anyone on the mainland. But the arc of death planted on the shore—what did it mean?

"I will climb that tree, the tall one," Nenne said. "From the upper limbs I can see over the barrier, see what lies behind it."

He was a good climber, had climbed the valley wall many times, and this was much easier. Small twigs and leaves rained down as he swarmed up the wide branches. He stayed just a moment, then returned as quickly as he had gone.

"Nothing," he said, his voice puzzled. "There is simply sand inside. Empty, the creatures who were there yesterday are gone. Unless they are buried in the sand—they are gone."

"We will go to the place you watched from before, close to the killing area," Kerrick said, taking up his bow while Nenne swung the leather bag to his shoulder.

The corpse of the deer was there, now buzzing with flies, beyond it the green wall studded with the dead creatures. Kerrick flexed his bow and selected an arrow while Nenne opened the bag.

Kerrick carefully tied the strip of cloth around his arrow, then dripped the charadis oil onto it from the skin container. Nenne was hunched over to keep off the breeze while he scratched fire from the stones. He added dry twigs until small flames were crackling in the pit in the sand. Kerrick stood, half-drew his bow with the arrow he had prepared, bent and touched the oil-soaked rag to the flames. It caught fire, the flames invisible in the sunlight but the dark smoke clearly seen. Then he stood, drew the arrow far back, aimed high in the air—and released it.

It rose in a great arc and dropped into the green barrier. They could see it there, where it had impaled a leaf, smoking slightly. When the smoking died away Kerrick sent another burning arrow after the first, then another and another. The results each time were the same.

"They have learned," he said, his voice grim as death. "They know about fire now. We won't be able to burn them out a second time."

Nenne tapped his forehead with puzzlement. "None of this do I understand."

"I do. They have a base on land, one we cannot attack or burn."

"We can use arrows and spears; they will not be safe behind this barrier."

"This one, this size, I agree that they would not be safe. But if they grow a larger one they could retreat behind it at night—out of range."

"These murgu do strange things," Nenne said, spitting with distaste in the direction of the green wall.

"They do—because they do not think as we do. But I know them, I should be able to understand what they are doing. I must think hard about it. This has not been done without meaning—and I should be able to understand the reason for it being here. Let us get closer."

"That is certain death."

"For animals, yes. Just go carefully."

Kerrick found his legs trembling as he put one foot carefully in front of the other on the hard-packed sand. As they came close to the deer Nenne seized him by the arm, stopping him.

"The vine with thorns that has the deer by the leg, see how it arises from the sand. Just where the deer is standing, near the grass it was eating. Why did the deer not see it and avoid it?"

"I think I know." Kerrick bent and dug a half-buried clamshell from the sand, then threw it carefully underhand so that it dropped beside the corpse.

Sand flew aside as a green, thorn-tipped length lashed out of the sand and struck the shell.

"Lying just under the surface," Kerrick said. "They are released when there is pressure above."

"They could be growing anywhere here," Nenne said, stepping carefully backward, walking in the tracks they had just made. "This is a place of death where nothing can live."

"Not quite, look there, right at the base of the wall."

They stood, unmoving and scarcely breathing as the leaves rustled and parted. A mottled, orange and purple head appeared, bright eyes looked about, withdrew. It was back a moment later, further out this time, a lizard of some kind. With quick movements it darted across the sand—then stopped, frozen. Only its eyes moved as it looked about. An ugly creature with a flat, thick tail, with swollen bulges on its back, shining in the sun as though it were wet. Then it moved on again leaving a trail of slime in its path, stopping at a clump of grass. It began to chew this with sideways motions of its jaw. Kerrick reached slowly into his quiver when it looked away, nocked an arrow, drew it back.

Released it.

"Good," Nenne said, nodding approval as he looked at the impaled creature that kicked out sporadically then lay still. They retreated in a long circle and approached it from the ocean side, walking in the edge of the surf, bent over and looked at it.

"Ugly," Nenne said. "See it drips with slime like a slug."

"Perhaps that is protection from the poisons in the wall, probably the thorns as well. This creature was grown to live where everything else dies. There has to be a reason for that; the Yilanè who grow things do everything with a reason."

"It is sick though—those boils on its back, one is opened."

"Those aren't boils or sores; see how regularly spaced they are." With the tip of his bow Kerrick reached down and prodded the open bulge, disturbing it so that brown particles fell free. Nenne bent close over and looked at them.

"They are dry, I do not understand. They look like seeds."

Kerrick stood slowly and turned to look at the deadly green barrier, felt a chill at the same time despite the warm sun upon him. "I understand," he said. "I understand only too well. We are looking at defeat, Nenne. Certain defeat. I see no way that we can win this battle, no way for us to survive."

CHAPTER TWELVE

O ne of the younger manduktos stirred the fire and added fresh wood. The light of the flames flickered over the small group about Sanone who were sitting across the fire from Kerrick. He had wanted to talk to all the hunters, but this was not the Sasku way. The manduktos made the decisions and they were obeyed. They were conferring now in low murmurs as Kerrick looked deep into the fire, trying to look into the future as well, seeing only despair in that warm light.

"We cannot agree," Sanone said, turning back to Kerrick. "You are just guessing, you have no proof, we must wait and see."

"Must you wait until we have the first deaths here? Can you not see clearly what has been done? Look south, to the beach there, to what appears to be an empty encampment. It does not matter that none of the murgu are there now—it is meant to be empty. Those plants are poisonous and deadly, but they must be grown somewhere so they can be harvested. Why not on the shore here? This is the environment they will have to grow in. They were planted there to grow and flourish—and when they are ripe, their seed will be harvested. And that explains as well the small murgu we killed."

"This is just guessing . . ."

"Perhaps. But it has the real smell of truth to it. Think of that creature, designed to live among the vines and plants where everything else dies. Why bother breeding such a creature in the first place if the plants are just for protection? No, they have a more terrible significance. They are meant to be spread. Spread here. The little murgu will run and hide, and wherever it goes it will leave those seeds behind. It will run here in Deifoben until our city is filled with death and we will have to leave or die ourselves."

"If the little murgu try to come here we will kill them," one of the manduktos called out and the others murmured agreement. Kerrick fought to keep his anger under control.

"Will you? You are such a wonderful killer with the bow and the death-stick that you can hunt by night and day, over all this vast place, under every shrub and tree, kill each murgu as it appears? If you think that you are a fool. You are all being foolish. I feel as you do; I don't want to believe this thing. But I must. We will have to leave here—and as soon as possible."

"No, this will not happen." Sanone was on his feet. "Kadair led us here, he will not desert us now."

"Maybe Karognis brought you here instead," Kerrick said, hearing the horrified gasps around him, hoping that they might be shocked into understanding. "We cannot kill all of the creatures when they begin coming here, we cannot stop the seeds from growing. We must leave before the first deaths happen."

"It cannot be," Sanone said. "They would not do such a thing because it would leave this city useless. What kills us would kill the murgu just as quickly."

Kerrick ignored the cries of agreement and shouted louder than they did. "You reason like children. Do you think the murgu would design and grow these plants without knowing how to destroy them just as well? When this city is theirs again all the growing bushes of destruction will be cleared away."

"If they can do it—so can we."

"No we can't. We have not the knowledge that they have."

Sanone raised his hand and the others were silent. "We get angry and wisdom vanishes. We say things we will regret later. Perhaps everything that Kerrick has said will come to pass. But even if it does—do we have a choice? If they can kill this place, can they not follow and kill our valley, or wherever else we choose to camp? Perhaps Kadair led us here to die, perhaps that is part of his plan. We cannot know. It appears that we have little choice. It will be easier to stay."

For the first time Kerrick was silent for he could not answer Sanone's words. Was that the only choice? Stay here and die, or run away, across the great land. And find death waiting for your arrival. Without another word he wrapped his deerskin cloak around him, stood and went to his sleeping chamber. It had been a long and hard day and he was tired, yet he could not sleep. Lying in the darkness he sought a way out, a path to follow that they had not noticed yet. They would send for Herilak in the spring and he would come with the Tanu. They would launch an attack on the island where the Yilanè were, drive them off. Capture a scientist, make her reveal how the deadly plants could be killed. Kill the lizards when they appeared, dig up the plants when they started to grow. A lot could be done—had to be done . . .

The morning was clear, the sun warm, the fears of the night diminished by daylight. Kerrick was peeling an orange when he saw Sanone emerge from the leafy mouth of one of the connecting passageways. His face was twisted with lines of pain, and he shuffled as he walked. Kerrick stood, the fruit, forgotten, dropping to the ground.

"The first," Sanone said. "As you said, so it begins. A child, a small girl, playing at the riverbank when a thorn rose out of the sand and drove into her foot and she died. We dug the plant out of the ground with spears, it was as small as my hand, burnt it in the fire. But how could it come there—in the center of the city?"

"Many ways. They could put seeds in the river upstream. They could be fed to birds to fall with their excrement. They are very wise, the Yilanè who make new things grow. When they do a thing they do it well. Everyone must be warned, precautions taken. Or do we leave?"

Sanone seemed older than his years at this moment, the lines in his face deeper. "I do not know. We will talk again tonight. Meanwhile there are certain things I must do to understand Kadair's meaning in all this. It is very hard to know exactly what is the correct thing that must be done."

Kerrick went with Sanone to see the remains of the plant, poked at it with a stick. "Very small—but the thorns are just as big as those on the full-size plants. Were there any more?"

"We searched. Just this one."

"Everyone must wear leather around their feet. Strange plants must not be touched. The bigger children must look after the smaller ones. The children must stay in certain areas which will be gone over very carefully every morning."

After this Kerrick was hungry and went to the fire where Nenne's woman, Matili, always made room for him. She baked delicious meat in the ashes, coated it with clay that hardened so the meat was both tender and juicy. With this she had a paste in little dishes, made of fruit that had been mashed with salt and hot chilies, that the meat could be dipped into. It was very good and he was hungry.

Yet when he came to the fire Matili looked up at him coldly and made a gesture he had never seen before; with her hand held vertically in front of her nose, between her eyes. When he spoke to her she did not answer, but instead turned away and ran into the room where she and Nenne slept. It was mystifying and Kerrick was about to leave when Nenne appeared.

"I hope you are not hungry, Kerrick, for there is no meat." He kept his face averted when he said this, which was not his way.

"What is wrong with Matili?" Kerrick asked. "And why did she hold her hand like this?"

He repeated the gesture with his hand. But like a Yilanè he saw the hand gesture as part of a whole that involved the entire body, all of the limbs. So without realizing it he dropped his shoulder, held his hand before his chest in a protective, feminine gesture, even for one instant stood with his legs just as Matili had stood. Nenne saw this writhing movement and did not understand it, like many things he did not understand about Kerrick. He did not like them either, but he kept his feelings to himself. The moment had come to tell Kerrick; it was time that he understood. "Come over here, I will try to explain."

They walked under the trees until they could not be overhead. "It was the words you spoke last night. You talked with the manduktos, you shouted and many heard. Matili has been told what you said. What she did with her hand when she saw you, that is what foolish women do to turn Karognis away from them."

Kerrick was puzzled. "My words last night—and Karognis? I do not understand."

"Karognis is the evil one, as evil as the murgu, his eyes must not rest upon one or harm will befall."

"What have I to do with Karognis?"

"Some say you speak with the tongue of Karognis. You spoke—words about Kadair that were overhead. That was not a good thing to do."

Kerrick looked at the grim expression on Nenne's face and knew that although he might deny it, he really felt the same as Matili did. The Sasku listened to the manduktos and understood them when they talked about the living world, how Kadair had made all of the world, and how all things in the world knew that. In this they were like the Tanu who saw life around them in everything, the animals and the birds, even the rivers and trees. Knowing where this life came from they would never speak of Ermanpadar with other than deepest respect. Kerrick always forgot this, had not grown up with these strong beliefs as the Tanu and the Sasku had done. He tried to make amends.

"I spoke in anger and fear. Tell Matili that it was not myself talking, what I said I did not mean."

"I must return." Nenne turned and walked away without answering. It was obvious now that he really believed as the women did. Kerrick did not display his instant anger and call out after him the words that would only have added to the ill feeling. But he hated their stupidities.

They are only ustuzou.

They were, yes, but that was a Yilanè thought that he should not have—would not have. He was ustuzou just as they were, he was not Yilanè at all.

Yet even while he was thinking this he was walking toward the hanalè, wondering how the two males were faring. He was Tanu—but at this moment he felt like being with the Yilanè.

"Very boring," Nadaskè said, and added a movement that signified asleep-forever. "We are here all the time, none come to see us. One time in the remote past you would take us around the city in the sunshine and that was pleasure. But you do it no more and we have only each other to talk to and very little to say after all these days. Once we had you to talk to, but of course you have other preoccupations and are rarely here."

"You are still alive," Kerrick said with some anger and bitterness. "That should be some satisfaction."

Nadaskè turned away, signing female and interrogative as he did. Kerrick smiled at that, the suggestion that he had been acting harsh and insulting. Just like a female. Yet a short while ago it had been a female who had sent him hungry away from her fire. And he still had not eaten. He looked about. The males had fussy appetites and there was still some of the preserved meat left from the previous day. Kerrick peeled off a piece and ate it. Imehei wailed.

"We will die here, locked away—and we will starve too."

"Don't be stupid." Signing equality of males and foolishness, a confusing thing to do since it was a gesture used only by females. Yet these two assigned him the dominant-female role when he was with them. Quick anger grew; was he accepted nowhere?

"Vaintè has returned," he said. "She and many others are close by."

He had their attention then and they were apologizing for their bad temper, assuring him of his strength and generosity, begging for information. He stayed some time, happy in their companionship, realizing that he had much in common with them. He could speak of what interested him in the deep and complex manner of Yilanè communication. He cared not for Kadair, Karognis—or Ermanpadar either for that matter. For the moment his many troubles were forgotten. It was midday when he left and he saw to it that he returned before dark, bringing meat with him. They ate together in joined pleasure.

Yet behind the pleasure lay the dark shadow of the future. Vaintè was close by and death was between her thumbs. The poisonous plants would grow well in the sun and the little lizards would run and spread their deadly seeds. The future was inescapable—and inescapably grim.

CHAPTER THIRTEEN

When the weather warmed in the spring and the winter storms died away, there was greater activity at sea south of the city. More of the poison plants had been found to the south, though none in the city itself for some undetermined reason. It was as though the Yilanè had made all of their preparations, tested the efficacy of their attack—and were now waiting for some signal to begin. Yet days passed and there was still no sign of it; even Kerrick was beginning to doubt his earlier fears. Not really doubt, just cover up and hide them. He knew that sooner or later the final battle would begin. Vaintè was out there. She would never stop until they were all destroyed. So, despite the complaints, Kerrick saw to it that all of the approaches to the city were watched and guarded, night and day, while armed parties made longer patrols north and south along the shore to look out for any Yilanè activity. Kerrick himself led the sweeps south, he had the certainty that the attack would come from this direction, but other than the ever-growing wall of death there was still no sign of activity on shore. It was a hot afternoon when he returned from one of these scouting expeditions and saw Nenne waiting for him on the trail.

"There is a hunter from the north, a Tanu who has come and

says only that he will talk with you. Sanone has gone to him but he
will not speak with the mandukto, other than to repeat that his
words are only for you."

"Do you know his name?"

"He is the sammadar, Herilak."

When he spoke the name a chill of apprehension washed over
Kerrick. Armun—something had happened to Armun. There was
no reason for this fear, but it was there, filling him so full that his
hands were shaking.

"He is alone?" Kerrick asked, not moving.

"None are with him—though it can be seen that there are
other hunters who wait outside the city, among the trees."

Alone, others in the forest, what could the reasons be? And
Armun, what of her? Nenne stood waiting, half turned away as
Kerrick's body moved with his thoughts, in the Yilanè way with
physical echoes. With an effort Kerrick broke the paralysis of inac-
tion and fear. "Take me to him—at once."

They trotted through the city, gasping in the hot air, their
bodies running with sweat, to the open space of the ambesed where
Herilak stood waiting. He was leaning on his spear but straightened
up when Kerrick came close, speaking before Kerrick could.

"I have come with a request. It is our death-sticks that are . . ."

"We will talk of them after you tell me of Armun."

"She is not with me," he said, unsmiling and grim.

"I see that, Herilak. She is well, the baby?"

"I have no knowledge of that."

All Kerrick's fears had been true. Something had happened to
her. He shook his hèsotsan angrily.

"Speak clearly, sammadar. You took her to your sammad,
to protect her, you told me that. Now why do you say you have
no knowledge?"

"Because she is gone. She did that alone, although I ordered
her not to, ordered that none should help her. What she has done,
she has only herself to blame. Though the hunter, Ortnar, dis-
obeyed me and helped her to leave. It was last year at this time. He
is no longer in my sammad. I sent hunters after her but they could
not find her. Now we will talk of other matters . . ."

"We will talk of Armun. She asked you for aid and you did not
give it. Now you tell me that she is gone. Where has she gone?"

"She went south to join you. She must be here."

"She is not—she never arrived."

Herilak's words were as cold as winter. "Then she is dead on the trail. We will talk of other things."

In a red haze of anger and hatred Kerrick raised his hèsotsan with shaking hands, aimed it at Herilak who stood unmoving and unafraid, his spear butt on the ground. Herilak shook his head and spoke.

"Killing me will not bring her back to life. And Tanu does not kill Tanu. There are other women."

Other women. These words disarmed Kerrick and he lowered his weapon. There were no other women for him, just Armun. And she was dead. And Herilak was not to blame. It was his fault, his alone. If he had returned to the sammads she would be alive now. It was over. There was nothing else to say about it.

"You want to talk about the death-sticks," Kerrick said, all feeling gone from his voice. "What of them?"

"They are dead, all of them. It was the cold of winter. Even though we tried to keep them warm many died the first winter, the rest were dead before this spring. Now we must go and hunt in the land of the murgu for there is no game to the north. We need more of the death-sticks. The sammads need them to live. You have more here. Will you share them?"

"I have many here, young ones growing here. Where are the sammads?"

"North, on the beach with the mastodons, waiting. Half of the hunters stay to guard them, the other half are here waiting in the forest. I came alone. It was my feeling you would kill me and I did not want them to see this happen."

"You were right in that. But I give you no death-sticks for hunting on the plains."

"You what?" Herilak shook his spear in anger. "You will refuse me, refuse the sammads? You could have had my life if you wished it. I gave you that—for the sammads—and now you refuse me?"

Without realizing it he half-raised the spear and Kerrick pointed to it, smiling coldly.

"Tanu does not kill Tanu—yet you raise your spear." He waited until Herilak had conquered his anger, lowered his spear, before he spoke again. "I said there would be no death-sticks for hunting in the plains. There is danger in this city and hunters are needed to defend it. The Sasku are here. As they once aided the

Tanu I now ask you to aid them in turn. Stay and help them here. There are death-sticks for all."

"That is not for me to decide. There are other sammadars, and all in the sammads as well."

"Bring them here. A decision must be made."

Herilak scowled darkly with anger, yet had no choice. In the end he turned on his heel and stamped away, brushing past Sanone without even a sideward glance.

"There is trouble?" Sanone asked.

Trouble? Armun dead. Kerrick still could not accept this reality. It took an effort to speak to Sanone.

"The sammadars of the Tanu are coming here. I have told them if they want death-sticks they must stay in the city. They must bring the sammads here. We will band together to defend each other—there is no other way."

Nor was there. The sammadars talked, long and angrily, sucked smoke from the pipe and passed it on. They would decide to stay; they had no other choice. Kerrick did not take part in the discussion, ignored the angry looks from them when Herilak told of his ultimatum. How they felt was of no importance to him. Tanu and Sasku would stay here, would leave only if they were driven out. Through the haze of his troubled and angry thoughts he became aware that a hunter stood before him. It took him a moment to realize that it was Ortnar. When he saw this he waved the hunter forward.

"Here, sit in the shade beside me and tell me about Armun."

"You have spoken of this to Herilak already?"

"He told me that he ordered her to stay in the encampment, ordered that she not be helped. Yet you went to her aid. What happened?"

Ortnar was not happy. He spoke in a low whisper, his head lowered, his long hair hanging over his face. "This has pulled me in two directions at the same time, Kerrick, still pulls me. Herilak was my sammadar, we two are the only two still alive from the sammad killed by the murgu. That is a bond that is hard to break. When Herilak ordered none to help Armun I obeyed for it was a good decision. The path was long and dangerous. Yet when she asked me to help her I felt that she was right too. This pulled me apart and in my stupidity I gave her only half the help she needed. I should have given her all, gone with her, I know that now. I told her the path and gave her my death-stick. Half help."

"The others gave her none, Ortnar. You were her only friend."

"I told Herilak what I had done. He struck me down and I lay as one dead for two days, this I have been told. Here is where he struck in his anger." Ortnar's fingers crept to the crown of his head, fingered the scar there on his scalp. "I am no longer of his sammad; he has not spoken to me since."

He raised his face and interrupted before Kerrick could speak. "I had to tell you this first, so you would know what happened. Since then I have looked for traces of her, scouting as we came east. I could find nothing—no bones or skeletons of any of them. There were three of them who left together, Armun and your son, and a boy who she took with them. There should have been some trace. I asked all the hunters we met but none had seen them. But there was one, a hunter who traded stone knives for furs, who traded with the Paramutan to the north. He understands some of their talk. He was told that a woman with hair like ours was with them in their place, a woman with children."

Kerrick seized him by the arms, pulled him to his feet and shook him wildly.

"What are you saying—do you know what you are saying?"

Ortnar smiled and nodded his head. "I know. I came south to tell you this. Now I go north while it is still summer to find the Paramutan, to find Armun if I can. I will bring her to you . . ."

"No, no need for that."

In an instant everything had changed for Kerrick. He straightened up as though an invisible weight had slipped from his shoulders. The future was suddenly as clear as a path, stretching sharply marked out ahead of him, like Kadair's footsteps stamped into stone that Sanone always talked about. He looked past Ortnar, to the city street that led to the north.

"There is no need for you to go—I will do that myself. The sammads will stay here; the city will be defended. Herilak knows how to kill the murgu—he won't need any instructions from me for that. I will go north and find her."

"Not alone, Kerrick. I have no sammad except yours now. Lead and I will follow. We will do this together for two spears are stronger than one."

"You are right—I will not stop you." Kerrick smiled. "And you are the better hunter by far. We would go hungry if we depended upon the skill of my bow."

"We will go fast with little time for hunting. If there is the gray murgu meat we will take that to eat."

"Yes, there is still a good supply. Fresh meat is much preferred by the Sasku."

Kerrick had found a large stock of bladders of preserved meat, had been bringing it to the hanalè for the males. And what would become of them? Certain death if he left them, that was clear. They deserved better than that. He must think about that as well. Much had to be decided.

"We will leave in the morning," he said. "We will meet here when it is light. By that time the sammadars will have come to an agreement since they have little choice."

Kerrick went to the hanalè, closed the heavy door behind him and called out his name. Nadaskè hurried down the corridor toward him, claws clattering on the wood, making motions of greeting and happiness.

"Days without number have passed, loneliness and starvation batter at us."

"I will not ask which comes first, hunger or companionship. Now where is Imehei? There is important talking to be done before I leave the city."

"Leave!" Nadaskè wailed with agony and signed death-by-despair. Imehei heard the sounds and came hurrying up.

"I'll not leave you to die," Kerrick said, "so stop your bad imitation of a mindless fargi and listen closely. We are going for a walk around the city now. The Sasku will take no notice, they have seen us walking before and have been ordered not to harm you. They obey their mandukto far better than you obey me. We will walk to the edge of the city and beyond. Then you will go south by yourselves until you see the island I have told you about, and the place of death. You will find Yilanè and uruketo there and you will be safe away from ustuzou forever."

Nadaskè and Imehei looked at each other, signed agreement and firmness of purpose. It was Nadaskè who spoke, indicating that what he said was spoken for both of them.

"We have talked. In the many hours alone we have talked. We have seen the city and the ustuzou here and walked about it and have talked. I will tell you what we have talked about. How strange it has been to be away from females and to walk with Kerrick-ustuzou-male-female. Very strange. We have marveled at what we have seen, eyes as wide as fargi fresh from the sea, for we have seen ustuzou living as Yilanè in this city. Strangest of all we have seen the ustuzou males with hèsotsan and the females with the young. We have talked and talked about this . . ."

"And you talk too much," Imehei interrupted. "Not only did we talk, we decided. Decided that we did not want to go to the beaches ever again. Decided that we never wanted to see a female-grasping-painly-deadly Yilanè ever again. We will not walk south."

They signalled firmness-of-decision together and Kerrick marveled. "You have a braveness I have never seen—for males."

"How can it be seen when our lives are in the hanalè," Nadaskè said. "We are as much Yilanè as the females."

"But what will you do?"

"We will stay with you. We will not go south."

"But I am leaving here in the morning. Going north."

"Then we go north as well. It will be better than the hanalè, better than the beaches."

"There is cold, certain death to the north."

"There is warm, certain death on the beaches. And this way we will at least have seen something more than the hanalè before we die."

CHAPTER FOURTEEN

Kerrick slept little that night; there was too much to think about. The sammads would come south, that had been decided; the hunters with their new hèsotsan were leaving in the morning to bring them back. With the hunters here the city was safe—or as safe as it might possibly ever be. Kerrick must turn his back on it now and think of his own sammad. He had left Armun behind with the sammads, and she had tried to join him. He would not even think of the possibility that she was dead; she was alive in the north, she had to be. He would find her, with Ortnar's aid they would seek out the Paramutan. They would find her, and the baby too—which left only a single thing to be concerned about. The two male Yilanè.

But why should he bother about them? They were nothing to him. But that was wrong. They were important. They had been imprisoned as he had been imprisoned. He had been tied by the neck—his fingers touched the iron ring about his neck at the thought—and they had been locked in the hanalè. It was the same thing. And they had a courage that he did not have, wanting to go bravely forth into a world they knew nothing about. Ready to follow him—because they had faith in him. They wanted to be part of his

sammad. At this thought he laughed into the darkness. A strange
sammad it would be! A sammadar who could rarely shoot an arrow
straight, a hunter with a hole in his skull put there by his former
sammadar, a woman, a baby—and two frightened murgu! A sammad
indeed to strike fear into the hearts of others—if not into that of the
sammadar himself.

What else could he do with the poor, helpless creatures? To
leave them here would mean certain death; better to kill them
himself than abandon them to that. And they would not return to
the female Yilanè, which was very understandable. Yet if they went
north with him they would surely die in the snow. Then what could
he do? Take them out of here—then what?

An idea began to form and the more he thought about it the
more possible it became. It was clear by morning and he slept on it.

Ortnar was waiting for him in the ambesed, with all of his
weapons, his pack upon his back.

"We go later today," Kerrick said. "Leave your things here
and come with me for I want to study our track north." They went
to the still-intact model that the Yilanè had built, of the land on all
sides of the city, and Kerrick looked at it closely.

"There is no need," Ortnar said. "I know the track well, have
been over it many times."

"We will go a different way, at least at the beginning. Tell me,
Ortnar, will you obey my orders, even if they do not suit you, or
will you go to another sammad?"

"It may be that one day I will, since a hunter only obeys a
sammadar who is right in what he says. But not now, not until we
have gone north to find Armun and your son. For I feel I did wrong
in not helping her when she first asked for aid. Because of that I
will follow wherever you lead until we have done that thing."

"Those are hard words to say and I believe every one of them.
Then you will go north with me—even though the two murgu
males come with us?"

"They mean nothing to me. They will die in the snow in any
case."

"Good. We will go after midday, when the hunters have gone,
since I feel that the Tanu who leave now would enjoy using their
new death-sticks on the males."

"I would enjoy doing that myself—were you not my sammadar."

"I can believe that. Now let us get a large supply of murgu

meat from the store. If anyone asks you why we are taking the murgu north with us, it is because they will carry much meat for us so we can go faster and not stop to hunt. Tell them that we will kill the males when the meat is used up and we no longer need them."

"Now I understand, sammadar. It is a good plan and I will let you kill them yourself when the time comes."

They went to the hanalè then, and when they entered the two Yilanè eyed the newcomer with great fright.

"Act like males," Kerrick ordered. "We all travel together and you must get used to one another. This is Ortnar who follows me."

"He smells of death-smoke, horrible," Imehei said, shuddering delicately.

"And he thinks that your breath is foul from eating raw meat. Now be still while I fit these on you."

Ortnar had made leather packs to hold the meat and the two Yilanè were already wailing over the weight of their loads.

"Silence!" Kerrick ordered, "or I will give you more to carry. You are like still-wet fargi and have never worked in your lives. Outside the hanalè there is much work to be done and you will have to share it. Or do you wish to go south—to the birth-beaches?"

They were silent after that, though Imehei made a movement of extreme hatred when he thought Kerrick had looked away. Good. A little anger would be of big help to them. Nadaskè turned and reached up to the niche in the wall and took down the metal sculpture of a nenitesk that long-dead Alipol had made.

"Where we go this goes," Nadaskè said firmly. Kerrick signed agreement.

"Wrap it well and put it in the pack. Then remain here with the ustuzou until I return," he said, then turned to Ortnar and spoke in Marbak. "I am going for my pack and weapons. Remain with these murgu until I return."

"With these?" Ortnar said, worried, grasping his spear. "They have teeth and claws—and are two to one."

"They are more afraid of you than you are of them. You will all have to be together without me at some time. Now is that time."

"We die, death is upon us," Nadaskè moaned. "When you go through the door the ustuzou will spear us. I sing my death song . . ."

"Silence!" Kerrick ordered, speaking as mightiest on high to lowest below. "I tell you this now, and will tell him the same words. We will stay together. You will all obey me. You will be my fargi.

He will be my fargi. You will be efenselè to each other. This is our efenburu."

When he had told Ortnar the same thing he turned on his heel and left. Sanone was waiting for him when he came out of the hanalè.

"You leave us," Sanone said.

"I will come back—with Armun."

"We all follow the footsteps of Kadair. Do you go alone?"

"Ortnar goes with me. He is a good hunter and knows the path. And we take the murgu to carry food."

"That is well, for I could not promise their safety once you were gone. We will be here when you return."

There was little enough to take for Kerrick had few possessions. The unbreakable ring was always around his neck, the little knife and the big one hung from it. He would need all the furs he had for the north and he rolled these carefully and tied them to his pack and pulled it on.

Back in the hanalè he was relieved to discover that his small sammad was still intact—although Ortnar stood against one wall, the two Yilanè against the other. They all moved with relief when he entered.

The word had spread, and it seemed that every Sasku was there to watch the strange procession when they emerged. Kerrick went first, looking neither to right nor left, while the two males stumbled after him, bent under the weight of their packs, fear in every movement of their bodies. Ortnar came last looking as though he wished he were somewhere else. He carried two of the hèsotsan, as did Kerrick—the extra weapons in case the first died, Kerrick had explained. Through the city they went, to the northernmost exit among the fields, where the nenitesk turned placid eyes upon them as they passed. Only when they had marched for some time, were well clear of the city, did Kerrick order a stop. Ortnar merely stood and waited but the males fell to the ground, writhing with expressions of fatigue and despair.

"Death is better—the birth-beaches are better!"

"The hanalè is our home, we belong there."

"Useless males be still," Kerrick ordered. "Rest while you can, then we go on."

"Why do they moan and shake like that?" Ortnar asked.

"They are like children. They have never been out of the city before—nor have they ever done any work like carrying those packs."

"That is not work," he said scornfully. "They are big and ugly and strong. We'll make them work before we kill them."

"They are my friends—and we will not kill them."

"Then the winter will. It is the same to me."

"That will not happen either. When we looked at the plan of the land—did you notice the large lake north of here?"

"We call it Round Lake. I have been there."

"Good. We go there first—if you will lead the way."

Because of the complaints of Nadaskè and Imehei, and their slow gait, it was not until the third day that they reached the lake. There was swamp to the south of it, but Ortnar knew the path that took them around it to the lakeshore.

"Good fishing here," Ortnar said. "Hunting as well."

"All for the best," Kerrick said. "Because we are leaving the murgu here with a supply of meat. We go on alone. We will go faster that way."

"We do not kill them? I cannot understand this."

"I won't kill them—because they are my friends. And they are of my sammad. They do not ask me to kill you."

Ortnar found this difficult to understand. "But you are Tanu—and they are just filthy murgu. I will kill them for you, do not worry."

"Part of me is filthy murgu too, Ortnar, you must never forget that. I grew up with them—and do not see them as you do. Put aside thoughts of hatred for a short while. Help me make this place safe for them, then we will go on."

Ortnar looked at the murgu: one of them yawned and he stepped back at the sight of the rows of conical teeth. "If this is what you want, sammadar, then I will help you. But I cannot lie and say that I like it—or even understand your reasons for doing this thing."

"Thank you for your help—that is all I ask. Now let me tell them what has been decided."

Kerrick waited until the screams of agony had turned to wails of despair before he silenced them.

"Wet-from-ocean—or fearless-males? Which are you? Here is your opportunity to live, to be free of the females and the hanalè. To be strong and independent. We will build a shelter against the rain. Before we go you will be shown how to use the hèsotsan, to hunt and to fish. And when I return from the north I will come for you. Meanwhile all you have to do is stay alive." They trembled with fear. "A female could do it," he added maliciously.

Ortnar cut branches with his knife to make a shelter, then cut poles to place them upon. The two Yilanè watched him with great interest.

"I could do that as well, even better," Nadaskè said. "Ustuzou hands are clumsy, not enough thumbs."

"Try it then," Kerrick said, passing over his flint knife. Ortnar saw the motion and jumped away from them, his own knife ready before him. Kerrick sighed.

"Ortnar—it is only fit that they build their own shelter. I think your skills would be better used if you took your death-stick and hunted some fresh meat for us."

"That I will do," Ortnar said, happy to be away from them. Nadaskè and Imehei were equally pleased when he left.

"Waxy-uncommunicative," Imehei said. "And I fear the stone tooth on the stick."

"He is hunting for us—so let us finish this work. Take my stone tooth and cut more branches. We will use them to finish the shelter. But first I will show you the secrets of the hèsotsan so you will be able to defend yourselves and kill fresh meat. There are fish and shellfish in the lake and they will be easy to catch—if you know how."

Kerrick finished the instruction on the hèsotsan well before the hunter returned, knowing that Ortnar would have reacted strongly if he had seen the Yilanè holding weapons. They were hidden out of sight in the completed shelter before Kerrick issued his final instructions.

"Only use the preserved meat when there is no fresh meat or fish, since there is not a big enough supply to last very long."

"Pain-in-hands, fatigue-of-body," Nadaskè signed. Imehei flashed palm colors in agreement. Kerrick controlled his temper.

"Forceful-demand for all of your attention. You must do as I have said—or you will die of starvation. A slow death as the flesh wastes away, the skin hangs in loose folds, the teeth decay and drop out . . ."

Nadaskè's wail of agony and movements of submission meant he had their attention.

"That won't happen if you are wise, for there is plenty of game about. Your biggest danger may be the female Yilanè who will find you unless you take precautions." He had their wide-eyed and silent attention now. "You know of the birds that fly and return with pictures. So keep under cover as much as you can—and look out for the large birds. When the boughs on the shelter die replace them with fresh ones. Do these things, and you will not be found and returned to the hanalè—and the beaches."

Kerrick and Ortnar left at dawn, the two Yilanè watching their departure with widened, fright-filled eyes. Yet they were here by choice. Kerrick had done what he could for them, supplied them with food and weapons. He hoped that they would learn how to hunt before the preserved meat ran out. If it did, they at least had a choice the Tanu did not. They could return to their own. Enough. He had done what he could for them. Now he would think of himself and the long trek ahead of them. Think of Armun somewhere in the north, somewhere there. Alive.

The lake and the shelter vanished behind them, hidden by a curve in the trail.

efenabbu kakhalabbu hanefensat
sathanapté.

═══════════

*Life is the balance of death, just as
sea is the balance of sky. If one
kills life—then one kills oneself.*

CHAPTER FIFTEEN

Enge had woven a shelter for herself from the broad leaves of the palms, then had secured it between the tree trunks to protect her from the nightly storms. The rainy season had begun here on the coast of Entoban✳ and the ground under the trees never dried out. To keep off the damp she had also made a platform of branches and was sitting on this now, facing out into the sun-filled clearing. Large and colorful dragonflies, each as long as her arm, drifted through the air before her—yet she did not see them. She was looking instead inside herself, at her memories of Ugunenapsa's words, at the multilayered truths behind their apparent simplicities. She had water in a gourd from the nearby stream, as well as food that her followers had brought from the city. She needed nothing else—not when she had the words to examine. She was grateful for this opportunity for uninterrupted meditation, day after warm day, and could have asked for nothing else.

So great was her attention to this inner voice that she was not aware when Efen and Satsat came from the forest and crossed the clearing before her. Only when they stood close and their bodies came between Enge and the bright sky did awareness penetrate.

"You are here," she said, signing welcome with her thumbs.

"We bring you fresh meat, Enge," Satsat said. "That beside you has gone rotten from the heat."

Enge moved one eye downward. "So it has. I did not notice."

"You did not notice, nor did you eat any part of it. Your flesh is going—and from your arms down to your legs I can see each bone of your ribcage clearly. To eat is to live."

"I have been eating the words of Ugunenapsa so living a life of endless splendor. But you are right, the flesh needs life as well. Tell me of the city." She listened attentively as she ate the cool, limp flesh.

"As you have told us we mingled with the fargi and have gone through the city and have seen the life of Yebèisk. There is a stream that flows through the ambesed, crossed by many golden bridges, and fargi crowd into the ambesed in large numbers. The fields are rich, the animals are beyond counting, the harbor busy with uruketo, the sun warm, a city of delights."

"What of the Daughters of Life? Are there any in the city?"

Efen sat back on her tail with motions of unease and unhappiness, as did Satsat. "I spoke of the day things first in order to bring light to events of the night. The Daughters are here, we have seen them but cannot talk to them. They work in the orchards, are imprisoned there as well, behind a tall wall of poison thorns. Each day they bring fruit for the beasts to the exit, but may not leave. The fruit is taken away and meat put in its place. There are many guards there. We asked and were told only that inside were the Daughters of Death, no further questions permitted, prompt orders to leave. When Omal heard this she touched our thumbs and told us to bring this message to you. Those within must not be kept from the truth of Ugunenapsa and the truths of her teaching that we have received. She said that you would understand. She went forward then and spoke with the guards who struck her to the ground and then locked her in with the others."

Enge recoiled at the thought of the violence done in the name of Life, but made motions of appreciation at the same time. "Omal is the strongest of us and she has done what I would have done myself had I her strength."

"Yours is the strength that carries us all, Enge. She knows your will, knew you would go. So she went in your place so you would not be the one who was trapped. You must be free to teach the words of Ugunenapsa."

"And I shall—and Omal will be freed. Tell me of the eistaa."

"She is much liked and respected," Satsat said. "All may approach her in the ambesed if there is need."

"There is need," Enge said, rising and brushing bits of meat from around her mouth. "In the days of peace here I have thought of Ugunenapsa's words and how their clarity can be applied to our lives. I have considered how best to bring her teachings to all and the answer when it came was simplicity itself. I ask the question—why are we hated and feared? I answer the question—because our beliefs are seen by the misinformed as a threat to the rule of the eistaa and the succession of power that descends from her to the city. She commands the power of life and death, and when the power of death is taken from her she feels that power is diminished. So here is what I must do. I must talk to the eistaa and reveal the truth of Ugunenapsa's words. When she understands she will be a Daughter of Life and will find that her rule is not diminished but enhanced. This is what I have to do."

"Don't!" Efen's voice was a wail of pain; Satsat echoed her movements as her own limbs twitched in expressions of despair. "We are too few and they are too many. You will be taken to the orchards and all will end there."

Enge made calming motions of trust. "This is imminent-pain-of-departure speaking, not strong Efen. Each of us is unimportant; speaking of Ugunenapsa's words is all. I do what must be done. Follow me to the ambesed but do not reveal yourselves. Wait and watch and learn. If I fail here you may succeed here or in the next city. Now—let us go."

They went along the shore because this was the easiest way to enter the city. And here they could look with pleasure at the young playing in the sea, even a juvenile efenburu standing waist deep in the water, staring at them with wide, worried eyes. Mature, yet afraid to face the unknown land. Enge made colored motions of warmth and welcome with her palms but they took fright and vanished back into the sea. Farther along were the guarded beaches and they paused on the hill that overlooked them, stopping at a much-visited viewing place. Below them the torpid males basked in the sun on the sand, or were rocked by the shallow water. It was beautiful and relaxing and gave them strength to go on.

The ambesed was as Efen had described it. The fresh stream of water ran through it and many bent over to drink from it. Light bridges of golden metal spanned the water at various places and the most decorative bridge of all rose high, then dropped down before the eistaa where she sat in her place of honor. Graceful designs were painted on her body, and about each wrist were decorations of golden wire worked in patterns that echoed the design of the metal bridges.

Enge waved the others away from her, then bent over when she reached the stream and let the cool water wash over her hand. With the wetness she cleaned the dust from her face and forearms, let them dry for a moment in the sun. Then, head high, she walked steadily forward across the golden bridge to stand before Saagakel, Eistaa of Yebèisk, stood in the posture of expectancy, lower to higher.

"You are new to my city, welcome," Saagakel said, appreciating the strength of line of the new arrival, noting at the same time the positive recognition of her authority from one with authority of her own. She liked that. It was seldom seen any more and even the best of her assistants used the formal lowest-of-low to highest-on-high.

"I am Enge and I have come from far Gendasi* and bring you word of what has happened there." The circle of advisers around Saagakel gasped at the signs of death and destruction behind her words. "Do I have permission to speak now?"

"Speak, for these my closest are all of my efenburu and will know what I know. The water behind you is not there by chance. All are free to cross, none are free to stay unless I will it. Speak freely, though I bend like a tree before a storm at the sense of despair your thoughts tell us."

"All will be told. How Inegban* came to Alpèasak, how Yilanè came to battle with ustuzou—and how that great city was destroyed."

Though Enge could not lie she could tell the record of events in any manner she cared to. Therefore she waited until the very end to reveal the part that she had taken.

"Thus the city died. The fire consumed it and all there died within the burning city."

"Yet you are here, Enge, are you not? And there was no indication of ending to your last words which signifies that there is more to come. But before you speak let me drink from a water-fruit for I feel that fire in my throat. Once when I was very young I saw fire and touched it. See."

Saagakel held up her right hand, and there was a murmur from

the watchers when they saw the white scars that replaced one of her
thumbs. Then, while she drank, those about her spoke pained
questions.

"All dead?"

"The city gone?"

"Ustuzou that use fire and talk and kill?"

Instant silence fell when Saagakel willed it. She put the fruit
aside and signed Enge to continue. They all watched in horrified
silence as she spoke.

"I have told you that Vaintè was my efenselè and I know of
these events because I was the one who taught the ustuzou to
speak. I did not teach it to hate, yet it hates Vaintè just as she hates
it. The ustuzou lives, Vaintè lives, one of the very few who came
away on the uruketo. For when the city died all who had not been
eaten by the flames died as well—for how can a Yilanè live without
her city?" There was a murmur of horrified agreement from the
advisers but not from Saagakel who sat unmoving and still. "The
commander lived, for the uruketo is her city. Vaintè lived, perhaps
because she had been eistaa and the eistaa is the city. I lived as
well."

Saagakel understood, even if her advisers did not. "Tell me
why you lived, Enge—or should I tell you."

"Whichever pleases you, Eistaa. You are the city."

"I am indeed. You did not die because you are a Daughter of
Death."

"Daughter of Life, Eistaa, for I am alive."

Both spoke with the minimum of revealing motion. The advisers looked on in shocked silence.

"Have you heard of our fruit groves?" Enge signed response in
the positive. "Good. Is there any reason why I should not send you
there at once?"

"Every reason, Eistaa. I know things about Gendasi∗ known to
no others alive. I know of the ustuzou there and can speak with
them through the one I taught—who spared my life when the other
ustuzou would have killed me."

"Yes, these are matters of interest. But not sufficiently interesting enough to keep you from the groves, would you not agree?"

"I agree. There is only one reason to keep me from the groves.
I know of life and death and have lived where all others have died.
That is knowledge you should have, Eistaa—and I can teach it to

you. You now have the power of death of every Yilanè in this ambesed, even your efenselè. You have only to command—and they die. But that is only half of what you should have. Life is the balance of death, as sea is the balance of sky. I can teach you of the power of life."

With that Enge fell into static silence, looking and waiting. Ignoring the uproar from Saagakel's advisers, just as the Eistaa did. She looked back at Enge in the same silence, the process of her thoughts invisible.

"All here will be silent," Saagakel ordered. "I have decided. As interesting as your arguments are—they are equally dangerous. You said it yourself—the existence of the Daughters of Death threatens an eistaa's rule. Therefore an eistaa has but a single choice." She made a gesture calling the nearest two of her advisers forward. "Seize this bold creature, bind her and lead her to the groves. There will be no sedition spread in my city."

CHAPTER SIXTEEN

Strong thumbs bit deep into Enge's flesh as she was seized and pushed down to her knees, held there as one of the retinue hurried away for bindings. Saagakel sat back with dignity as an excited babble of conversation sounded behind her. Above all this one voice rang out clearly, ordering them aside; there was one yipe of pain as a foot was trod upon. Through the assemblange a Yilanè pushed, made her way forward to stand before Enge, to look down at her closely.

"I am Ambalasi," she said hoarsely. Now that she was close Enge could see the lines of age on her face, the ragged edge to her pale crest. Then she turned about to face the eistaa and raked the claws of one foot along the ground in a sign of great disapproval. "I don't think that this is wise, Saagakel. There is much of importance in what Enge says, much to be learned from her."

"Too much of importance in what she says, wise Ambalasi, to let her remain free to spread her poison. I respect your great knowledge of the working of science—but this is a matter of politics and I listen only to my own advice."

"Do not close your mind, Eistaa. The teachings of the Daughters relate directly to our biological selves which in turn relate directly to our very existence."

"What do you know of their teachings?" Saagakel broke in, astonished.

"A good deal—since I have talked with the Daughters at length. In a crude way they have stumbled across a mind-body link that is of immense importance to the biology of longevity and aging. Therefore it is my polite request that the prisoner, Enge, be released in my custody for study in the place of science. Will you permit that?"

Although the expressions were polite, they were spoken loosely with only surface formality, close to insult since there were hints of negative qualifiers in the mode of address-to-Eistaa, and superiority-to-all in relation to science.

Saagakel roared with anger as she sprang to her feet. "Insult of insults—and in my own ambesed! I have respected your great knowledge and great age, Ambalasi, respect them still. Therefore I do not order your instant death but instead order you from my presence and from my ambesed, to return here again only if I will it. Or better still—leave my city. You have been talking of leaving, have made your plans to go far too many times to remember. Now is the time to do as you have threatened . . ."

"I do not threaten. I will leave as planned. And I will relieve you of the burden and take Enge with me."

Saagakel was quivering with rage, her thumbs snapping with anger. "Go from my presence at once and do not ever return. Go from this city as well for your presence strains my leniency."

"You are about as lenient as an epetruk at the kill. Since you see your absolute rule as absolutely vital to your existence why not put it to the test? Expel me from this city, order me to die. It will be a most interesting experiment. . ."

Ambalasi's voice was drowned out by Saagakel's roar of rage as she lept forward, towered above her tormentor, jaws agape and thumbs spread wide for the kill. The old scientist stood, unfrightened, making just the brief expression of respect-for-age, respect-for-learning with a questioning modifier.

Saagakel howled with inarticulate anger again, spraying Ambalasi with saliva, trembling for control. In the end, she wheeled about and dropped back into her chair. There was shocked silence all about her and the only sound was the running footsteps of the fleeing fargi who poured out of the ambesed shaking with fear. Three of them lay unconscious on the sand, perhaps dead so great had been the Eistaa's wrath.

When Saagakel finally spoke it was to signal removal-of-both who stood before her. "It is my wish never to see either of these again. Both, to the orchards, instantly."

Willing thumbs seized Enge and Ambalasi and hurried them from the ambesed. Once out of the Eistaa's sight they all went slower, for it was a hot afternoon, but none released their tight grip on the prisoners' arms. Enge had much to think about and did not speak until they had reached the sealed entrance to the orchard compound, had been roughly pushed inside. When the heavy entrance gate was sealed shut behind them she turned to Ambalasi and signed gratitude.

"You risked all, strong Ambalasi, and I thank you." ·

"I risked nothing. Saagakel's words could not kill me, nor would she have physically attacked me."

"Yes, I can see that now. I also see that you deliberately angered her so you would be imprisoned here."

Ambalasi made a motion of joined pleasure and humor, her mouth parted to reveal her ancient yellowed teeth. "I like you, Enge, and appreciate your presence here. And you are correct. I have been planning to visit this orchard—your being sent here has just accelerated my actions by a few days. This is a city of great boredom and paralyzed ideas and I wonder why I ever came here. Only because of the research facilities I assure you. I would have moved on long before this—but then they began arresting your Daughters of Despair . . ."

"Daughters of Life, I beg."

"Life, death, despair—all are the same to me. It is not the name or the philosophy that I care about, only the physiological results. I say they are Daughters of Despair because it was I who despaired of ever carrying my research any further. A long time ago, when the walls for this imprisoning orchard were first grown I came here to supervise the work. At that time I talked to some of the Daughters, but I despaired of their intelligence. They reminded me of onetsensast cropping the leaves of a single tree. Having once made a leap into the dark of this philosophy they are happy to remain unmoving ever again. I think you will move for me, Enge, in fact know that you will."

"If you will tell me what your moving involves I will attempt to help. Thus do I welcome you as a Daughter of Life . . ."

"Don't do that—I am not one of you."

It was Enge's turn to be baffled. "Yet—you said that you would not risk death if the eistaa ordered your death. Then you must believe . . ."

"No, I do not believe. I understand—and that is a different matter altogether. I am a creature of science, not of faith. Can you understand the difference? Or would you find that too disconcerting to your beliefs?"

"I do not find it disconcerting in the slightest," Enge said, registering joy-of-thought. "Quite the opposite. I see it as a testing of my courage and of Ugunenapsa's words and would talk long with you about this."

"I as well. Welcome to the fruit groves of Yebèisk, welcome. Now I ask you a question. If you and your Daughters were free of this place, all of you, would you come with me to a city where you would be welcome? Where you could be free, not oppressed, able to go your own way?"

"We ask nothing else, wise Ambalasi. That is our only desire and we would be your fargi if you could do that."

"It is possible. But before I aid you, I have another request, and you must think carefully before you answer. When you are free I want to make you captive again to my studies. I wish to understand how this new phenomenon operates and the string-knife of my research may cut deep." When Enge registered fear-of-pain Ambalasi signed negative in return. "You misunderstand. It is the string-knife of thought that I wish to use, to cut deep into your philosophy and see what makes it operate."

"That indeed I would welcome. It is what I do myself. If you can aid me in that, then I welcome your help."

"More than aid, Enge. I may dig so deep that I destroy the roots of your tree of knowledge and pull it out."

"If you do then it was a dead tree, a false tree, and I would welcome that as well. I open to you. Embrace my thoughts—do as you will."

Ambalasi seized Enge's arm in the quick gesture of greatest-pleasure. "Then it is agreed. I must now give my attention to our exodus. Since I have long been determined to leave this city I have already made all the necessary arrangements with my assistants and within a day—two at the most—there will be firm results."

Enge signed apologies and lack of understanding.

"You will understand when the time comes. Now there are other things to do. There is one here among the daughters whom I would speak to. Her name is Shakasas<."

"Confusion-naming," Enge said. "Shakasas<, speed-in-changing-movement is a name that one of us would not use, a name that belongs to the existence before the understanding. As a sign of our acceptance of Ugunenapsa's wisdom we take new names."

"I was aware of the ritual. But I am sure that your convert will remember her earlier existence before conversion. Send for her under that name and I will address her in any manner she wishes."

Enge signed respectful understanding and turned away to issue the order. Only then did she realize for the first time that they had been talking in the middle of a circle of silent listeners. Omal stepped forward and welcomed her.

"The one whose presence has been requested has been sent for. But I have pleasure-to-see you, unhappiness-your-imprisonment."

"We must discard unhappiness. This Yilanè of great wisdom whom I have been speaking with may be our salvation. Now let me see and meet with our sisters here, for I wish to know them all."

Ambalasi stepped aside as they greeted each other and waited with stolid patience until she was aware of a Yilanè who appeared before her and signed respectful attention.

"Are you Shakasas<?" Ambalasi asked.

"I was, before the time of my understanding. Because of my joy at accepting Ugunenapsa's words I am now called Elem. What do you wish of me, Ambalasi?"

The answer to a single question. I have heard that you once served on the crew of an uruketo. Is this true?"

"When I was first Yilanè it was my pleasure. This led me to my interest in air and sea currents. The mysteries of navigation became my study, and through them my interest in the work of Ugunenapsa."

"Explanation satisfactory. Now tell me who leads you?"

"Ugunenapsa, for it is her example—"

"Enough! I refer to your physical presence in this despicable orchard. Who among you is in charge?"

"None, for we are all equal. . . ."

Ambalasi silenced her with a rude gesture normally used only when commanding fargi, raking her toenails along the ground with great agitation. "Silence! Your Ugunenapsa has a lot to answer for. There must be someone who stands above you in this hierarchy of mindlessness. Enge, do you see her there?, good. Can she command you?"

"Certainly. I have heard much of her and her wisdom and would willingly do as she commanded."

"At last, communication. The three of us will speak together at once. After that has been done you will stay by my side at all times and will do as I order. Will you do this if she tells you to?"

Elem signed pleased agreement and Ambalasi dismissed her quickly before she could begin again on Ugunenapsa.

The island just off the coast of Gendasi∗, south of Alpèasak, was small and crowded with quickly grown structures, most of them little more than covers to keep the rain off. Only the joined rooms where Ukhereb labored had any look of permanence, solidity. The eistaa, Lanefenuu, had been taken there when she emerged from the uruketo that had brought her across the ocean, but she listened to the explanations with bored disinterest, caring only about the results of the scientists' labors, not the details. Only the masinduu drew more than casual attention.

"This is very amusing," Lanefenuu said. "You must grow me one to take back to Ikhalmenets. I have never seen anything like it before."

"The reason for that, Eistaa," Akotolp said with some pride, "is that it has never existed before. Ukhereb and I needed to work with the new plants we developed, to work together on their modification. But they are most difficult to handle since they are so poisonous. For this we needed the magnifying abilities of the sanduu. You know the creature I refer to?"

"I do not," Lanefenuu said, proud of her ignorance. "I am much too busy to devote my time to a study of your squalid beasts."

"Perfectly correct, Eistaa," Akotolp said. "It is a messy occupation. Explanation-offered. The sanduu magnifies, that is it makes things look bigger, up to two hundred times bigger and is an essential scientific tool. However, only one Yilanè at a time can use it—Ukhereb and I needed to work together. Therefore we developed this masinduu, which might be called an image-projecting sanduu. We use it in microsurgery, but now we are using it to show you pictures of what we have done, without the necessity of exposing your honored body to the dangers involved."

"This honored body is much pleased by your efforts. And what may this thing be that we are looking at?"

Akotolp turned one eye toward the brightly lit image on the wall. Sunlight fell on the eye of the masinduu in the outer wall, was amplified to project the multifaceted and brilliant image. "Those are diatoms, Eistaa, tiny creatures that live in the sea. We use them to adjust the masinduu. The colors that you see are generated by a polarized filter . . ." Akotolp broke off when Lanefenuu signed boredom-of-scientific-detail.

The room brightened as Ukhereb entered, followed by a fargi carrying a tray of pictures.

"All is ready, Eistaa," she said, motioning the fargi to put down the tray and leave. "Here are the latest prints and they will show you the unqualified success of our efforts on your behalf."

"Begin at once," Lanefenuu commanded.

The imaged diatoms vanished and a seascape took its place. Beyond the sea was a green coastline above white beaches. As Ukhereb talked she manipulated the masinduu so that one image faded into another so it appeared that the coast grew closer.

"This is the shore of Gendasi*, south of the city of Alpèasak. We selected this site since we could establish ourselves there unobserved. The temperature and soil are the same as the city so our plants could develop in the correct environment."

"Why not go to the city itself?" Lanefenuu asked.

"The ustuzou have occupied it," Vaintè said as she entered. "I went there to see. Not all of the city was burned—but it is filled with these vermin."

"Whose destiny is death, Vaintè," Lanefenuu said. "I ordered your presence because these accomplished scientists have arranged a demonstration of what has been accomplished here in my name. You will watch with me since you have created all this."

Vaintè signed pleasure-in-gratitude and settled down on her tail next to the eistaa—who ordered continuation-of-seeing.

Green shrubbery grew larger until dead animals could be seen around it, impaled on the thorns. "The mutated vines and shrubs," Akotolp explained. "All of them growing and mingled with those broad-leaved plants which are rich with water and therefore fire resistant, protecting the others. All of this was not hard to do, simple variations of the walls that protect most cities. While these were being developed and grown in enough numbers to raise for seed, we were also developing this creature."

The image of a multi-colored, shining lizard filled the screen. Akotolp walked over to point to the rows of nodules on the creature's back. "These cysts develop when the lizard matures, burst, then regrow. You will notice the thick skin and slime coating that protects the animal from the deadly environment that it sows. A perfect development."

"Need-for-clarity," Lanefenuu communicated sharply.

"Apologies without count, Eistaa. I proceed out of sequence. The deadly plants we have just seen were designed to be sown in the city that the ustuzou occupy. Various self-perpetuating techniques were considered and this system was devised. When the cysts burst the seeds of poisonous plants are released. They grow and the lizards live beneath their protection—where no other animal could survive. So without any further effort on our part, without the loss of a single Yilanè life, the city itself drives out the invaders. It will not happen at once, but it will happen with the inexorable and unopposable persistance of the incoming tide. The plants will fill the city, the ustuzou will be forced out—and tomorrow's tomorrow will be as yesterday's yesterday."

"Admirable." Lanefenuu expressed pleasure and happiness. "But how will Yilanè live in this city of death?"

"With great ease. Parasites and viruses have already been developed to destroy the growths and wipe out the lizards—affecting nothing else."

"It is indeed an excellent plan. Then why has it not been put into effect?"

"A single detail," Akotolp said, "since resolved. It required the development of a parasitical worm that carries the encysted seeds in its body. This worm infects the lizards, causing the cysts that spread the seeds. The worm's eggs, also with the encysted seeds, emerge in the lizard's droppings . . ."

She broke off at the Eistaa's gesture of termination. "Good Akotolp, I know these details fascinate you Yilanè of science, but I find them both repulsive and boring. Terminate your talk with details of progress."

"All is ready, Eistaa," Vaintè said, opening the door and pointing out into the sunshine. "As soon as Ukhereb and Akotolp reported success I sent for you. While you traveled here generations of lizards have been bred, are in an enclosure which I will now show you. All is in readiness—simply awaiting your command."

"This is admirable. I now speak. Let it be done. Alpèasak will be cleansed of vermin and rebuilt. So when the cold winds come to Ikhalmenets, Ikhalmenets will come to Alpèasak. Do this thing now."

"It begins, Eistaa," Vaintè said.

It begins—but does not end there, she added, but in unmoving silence so that none could hear her thoughts. *The city will be cleansed and will be Yilanè again. When that is done I will ask a boon and it will be granted. I will ask the eistaa only that I be permitted to use the seed-lizards to make the rest of this land uninhabitable for ustuzou. Then will I seek them out and destroy them. Thus will I kill the Kerrick-ustuzou at last.*

CHAPTER SEVENTEEN

Saagakel was swollen with anger, her pendulous cheeks trembling with rage. The ambesed was empty and so silent that the bubbling of the water beneath the golden bridges could be clearly heard—since all had fled at the first signs of her great displeasure. Only the single, helpless fargi remained, the one who had brought the displeasing message. In silence Saagakel fought to control her emotions: this simple creature was not responsible and must not be made to die because of the information that she had brought. Saagakel believed in ruling justly, and there would be no justice in killing the young thing. But she could kill her, indeed she could, with a single word. Knowing this she took pleasure in her power and leaned back on the sunwarmed wood, took pleasure from its warmth as well and from her city that surrounded the ambesed. When she spoke again it was with clear strength.

"Rise, young one, and face your Eistaa and know that your life will be a long one in her service and that of her city."

At this the fargi stopped trembling and stood, her eyes moist with adoration of her Eistaa, her body shaped to receive any command. Saagakel accepted her due and her voice was still gentle when she spoke.

"Repeat again what you were instructed to come and tell me. No harm will befall you—that is an Eistaa's promise."

The fargi's body grew rigid with concentration as she fought to remember the exact phrasing. "From one who serves lowly in the service of Saagakel, Eistaa of Yebèisk and highest. Motions and colors of greatest sadness. In two days a sickness has descended upon the groves where the okhalakx graze and many are unmoving. Even more dead. Aid is sought to save the living."

It could be no accident. Saagakel's eyes blazed with anger— but her body was unmoving, under control. The fargi waited in rapt silence. No accident. Some years ago this same sickness had spread among the okhalakx, but Ambalasi had cured it. Now, just a few days after Ambalasi's imprisonment, the disease had returned.

"Speak my desire-of-presence to those who council me. Go. Through that gateway—you will find them there."

They came, shaking with fright when they saw her deadly stance. The thought cheered Saagakel: it was good to remind even the highest in the city that her rule was absolute. When the first of them shuffled fearfully into her presence her good humor had returned.

"I have been told that the okhalakx are dying in great numbers— and you, and everyone else, know that they are my favorite meat. I see the shadow of Ambalasi darkening those bodies. Go to the orchard, you Ostuku, go quickly for you are getting fat and the walking will do you good, go and bring Ambalasi to me at once. That is my order."

Just thinking about the terrible fact that the okhalakx might be destroyed gave Saagakel a sudden pang of hunger; she sent at once for a haunch of meat. It arrived with great promptness and she tore off a large mouthful, was still grinding the last slivers of flesh from the bone with her back teeth when the small procession entered the ambesed. Ostuku led, while strong guards walked on both sides. Ambalasi was between them, moving slowly and leaning on the broad shoulders of her companion.

"I ordered the presence of Ambalasi alone," Saagakel said. "Remove the other."

"Then remove me too," Ambalasi said, signing indignant irritation. "You condemn me to that wet orchard, to sleep on the ground at my age. Chilled and damp at night so now I lean on this one when I walk. This strong one remains—I will not walk without her."

Saagakel made a gesture that showed this part of the discussion was beneath her attention, then stressed the importance of what she said next.

"The okhalakx die in the groves. What do you know of that?"

"Do they stiffen and lie helpless? If they do it is the lung disease brought by the wild ones from the forest."

"But you cured that disease a long time ago. How can it return now?"

"In the forest of ecology there are countless paths."

"Did you infect them?"

"You can believe that if you wish." A dubious answer that could be taken two ways. Before Saagakel could order a clarification Ambalasi spoke again. "But no matter how disease reaches the beasts in the field it is a fact that only I can cure it. Do you wish this done?"

"It will be done and I order you to do it."

"I will accept your desire—but not your order. In return I ask my release from that damp orchard, the release as well of she-I-rest-my-weight-upon. When I decide that my legs are as they should be you can send her back to the orchard."

And you as well, ancient fool, Saagakel thought in unmoving silence. "Do your work at once," she ordered aloud, then turned her attention away with movements of distaste and dismissal.

Ambalasi waved the guards back with irritated movements and hobbled from the ambesed, leaning heavily on Elem's broad shoulders. She did not speak while they went through the city, remained silent until the outside doors of her own buildings had closed behind them. Only then did she straighten up and walk easily to her private laboratory. There was a gulawatsan on the wall here, claws holding tight, mouth clamped to a sapvine. Ambalasi pushed hard on the ganglion in the center of its back and it turned sightless eyes to her, liquid dripping from its lips—then screamed piercingly through its wide-gaped mouth. Elem stepped back, numbed by the volume of the sound. Ambalasi nodded approvingly at the clatter of rapid footsteps as her assistants hurried in.

"You," she ordered the first arrival. "Get the okhalakx serum from the cold cabinet and administer it to the sick animals. While you, Setèssei, will accompany this Yilanè to her place of studies to obtain charts."

"I have been forbidden entrance," Elem said.

"Only the Eistaa stands above me in this city," Ambalasi said warmly. "Therefore in this city I will be obeyed. Setèssei will speak in my name and will take you there. You will return with all of your navigation charts. Is the order understood?"

As Elem started her gesture of acceptance, Ambalasi turned away and issued rapid instructions to her other assistants. There was much to be done and very little time to do it in. Only the fact that she had been preparing for this move for over a year enabled its completion now. Enge's arrival was fortuitous and, on impulse, Ambalasi had angered the Eistaa and brought her léaving time forward. It was a minor matter. She had long been dissatisfied with this boring city and had been prepared to move on. Life was certainly going to be more interesting in the near future.

Her only fear was that the Eistaa had cancelled an earlier order putting an uruketo at her disposal. But the order had been issued a long time ago, when there had been need to go upriver for wild specimens, and would hopefully be forgotten until it was too late. As it proved to be.

"The crewmembers obeyed my orders," Setèssei said when she returned. "They loaded all of the equipment aboard. Have you reached a decision yet about those who aid you?"

"I have. All stay here."

"Must I stay as well? I who was your fargi and am now your first assistant. Am I to stay behind?"

"Do you wish to?"

"No. I wish only to continue serving Ambalasi of great genius. This city is of no importance to me."

"Well spoken, faithful Setèssei. Would you then slip away with me—even though your destination is completely unknown?"

"I am your fargi." Setèssei added qualifiers of loyalty and strength.

"Well said. You join me. Now see to the loading of the rest of my goods."

When Elem returned with her charts she had them sent to the uruketo with the remaining bundles. Then she signed the navigator to follow her.

"Get two large cloaks for I have had enough of sleeping on the damp ground. All of the others are remaining here—but you are coming with me." As their course took them through a garden that was open to the sky, she let one eye roll in the direction of the setting sun. "Walk faster, we have very little time."

Elem's mouth gaped wide as they hurried through the city, for in addition to the cloaks she was burdened with a heavy cylinder that Ambalasi had pressed upon her. She was dizzy with heat, when they finally stopped, gasping hoarsely to cool herself.

"Move into the shade of those trees—and stay motionless for you are too warm," Ambalasi ordered, taking the cylinder from her. "I will do what is needed for it must be finished before dark."

Elem looked on with total incomprehension as Ambalasi twisted the end of the cylinder so that a fine spray of liquid emerged. Holding it at arm's length she used it to moisten the barrier of vines and plants that stretched between the row of trees. They were in a region of the city that she had never visited before so she did not realize that the trees were part of the living wall of the orchard where they had been imprisoned. When Ambalasi discarded the empty cylinder and made her way slowly back through the growing dusk, Elem was already cool enough to drape the cloak loosely about herself. Ambalasi took the other cloak and placed it on the ground, signing great annoyance as she stretched out upon it.

"This is the last time that I ever intend to sleep upon the ground. We must awaken at first light, before the city stirs." She said this with motions of utmost importance and great urgency. Elem signed acceptance of commands then closed her eyes and slept.

Bird calls awakened her and she knew that dawn was close. She pulled the warm cloak closer about her and looked up through the branches above. When the sky grew light between them she rose and called out respectfully to the old scientist.

"Light . . . orders . . . goes . . ."

Her meaning was unclear because of the darkness but the sound of her voice had the desired affect. Ambalasi rose and discarded the cloak, walked stiffly over to the wall of plants. There was enough light now to see that there was a marked difference in the vegetation where she had sprayed: the leaves were wilted and yellow. She signed pleasure of accomplishment as she reached out and tugged at a thick vine. It broke in her hand, crumbling into dust.

"Forward," she ordered Elem. "With nostrils closed, membranes over eyes, force your way through this."

A cloud of dust and fragments boiled out as Elem flailed with her arms. In a moment she had broken through the thick barrier and found herself staring down at two of the Daughters of Life—as startled at her presence as she was at theirs.

"Don't gape like fargi," Ambalasi ordered, with accompanying gestures of silence and speed of movement. "Wake everyone, command them to join me here. They must come quickly and in absolute silence."

The first of the Daughters appeared in the growing light and Ambalasi ordered them forward. "You," she said to the first arrival, "stand by this opening and sign all that come to follow those before her. When all are through follow them yourself. You others follow me."

She turned and led the way through the wakening city, all of the Daughters following her in silent progression. The few Yilanè they passed ignored them; lacking all curiosity. Only the fargi took interest and many of them joined the procession, eager to see and learn new things. The sun was well above the horizon when Ambalasi halted the march at the waterfront, behind the rounded warehouses, and passed on the order to send Enge to her.

"Come with me and do not speak," she responded to Enge's interrogative, then led the way out of the shadows toward the high fin of the nearest uruketo. A crewmember had just appeared above, eyes slitted in the morning sun, and Ambalasi called out to her.

"Commander's presence before me ordered immediately."

The crewmember vanished from sight and a few moments later the commander climbed down and jumped from the back of the gently rocking uruketo to the rough wood of the dock.

"Orders to be obeyed at once," Ambalasi said, with modifiers of urgency. "Go to the Eistaa."

The commander signalled assent as she hurried away. When she was out of sight Ambalasi spoke to the curious crewmembers on top of the fin above. "Onto the dock, everyone aboard. There are others coming and I do not want you in the way." She turned to Enge as the first of them began climbing down. "Now—bring them all at once. But stop the fargi—there is no room for them. When the eistaa questions the commander she will know at once that something is wrong. We must be gone by then."

Ambalasi, never known for her patience, prowled the dock as the Daughters hurried by. She signed the curious crewmembers to move back, then signalled presence-needed, first to Enge, then to Elem.

"We leave as soon as the last one is aboard. And we leave without the crew. You will be commander, Elem, since you informed me that you served on an uruketo." She cut off the other's protest with a sharp command. "I have watched the commander work. It is not a skilled occupation. You will teach others what they must know."

"There is risk in this," Enge said.

"There is no alternative. Where we are going we must not be found. We want no witnesses who might return and inform the Eistaa where we are."

"Where do we go?"

Ambalasi answered only with silence—and the gesture that meant end of communication.

The shocked crewmembers cried out fearful questions and milled about in confusion when the dock-bindings were cast loose and the uruketo moved out into the river behind the sporting enteesenat. They wailed unhappily when the first waves broke over its back as it grew smaller in the distance.

They were still standing there, staring out toward the flocks of estekel* fishing at the river's mouth, when the first gape-mouthed messengers of the Eistaa stumbled up. They answered the mumbled enquiries with forceful negatives.

The sea was empty, the uruketo gone.

CHAPTER

Mer sensta.

TANU DEATH-CRY

═══════

We die.

CHAPTER EIGHTEEN

As they moved steadily northward Kerrick was filled with an elation that made him want to shout loudly—even though he knew that a hunter was always silent on the trail. With each forward step he left a little more responsibility behind, walked that much more easily.

He had done what he could to save the city; it was now up to the others to carry on where he had left off. It was no longer his burden to carry. Ortnar's broad back, running with sweat, moved steadily along before him. Mosquitoes hummed around the hunter's head and he brushed them away with his free hand. Kerrick felt a sudden affection for him, for they had come a long way together, ever since Ortnar had killed his leashed Yilanè, Inlènu<, and Kerrick had tried hard to kill him in return. There was a bond between them now that could never be broken. That was the reality, that and the forest around him. The city and all of its problems grew distant as they moved steadily north. By nightfall he was very tired and more than ready to stop, but did not want to be the first to order a halt. It was Ortnar who stopped when they came to the grassy hollow by the stream. He pointed at the gray remains of an ancient campfire.

"A good place for the night."

The words were in Marbak and the thought was a Tanu one. There was no need now for Kerrick to speak Yilanè—or Sesek for that matter—and follow the complicated arguments of the manduktos. Sky and forest, these were reality. While at the end of their march Armun would be waiting. He felt the relief at laying down a burden—one he had not even known that he was carrying. He was twenty-four years of age and had traveled a great distance, through many different worlds, in the sixteen years since his capture by the Yilanè. That night he slept more soundly and more deeply than he had in a very long time.

There was a thin mist above the stream when he awoke in the morning. Ortnar touched his shoulder and motioned him to silence as he slowly lifted and aimed his hèsotsan. The small buck, knee-deep in the water, raised its head at some sudden warning—but fell forward when the dart imbedded itself in his side.

The rich flesh was a change from the preserved murgu meat and they ate their fill, drying and preserving the rest in the ashes.

"Tell me of the Paramutan," Kerrick said, muffled through a mouthful of meat. "I know only the name, that they live in the north."

"I saw one once, our sammad traded with him. He had fur all over his face, not a real beard like ours, but all covered with hair like a longtooth. And he was short, only a little taller than I was and I was still young. I have heard that they live on the shore far to the north where the sea ice never melts. They fish in the sea. They have boats."

"How will we find them? Do they have different sammads?"

Ortnar patted his cheeks in the gesture meaning he did not know. "If they do, I was never told. But I listened when they spoke and they are too stupid to talk Marbak. A hunter in our sammad had a few of their words and they talked. I think that all we can do is go north, stay on the shore, look for their tracks."

"It will be winter before we get there."

"It is always winter there. We have furs, we will bring dried meat. If we stay on this path we will meet the sammads on their way south. We will get ekkotaz from them. That is what we must do."

"Dried hardalt as well—they will surely have some."

Many days later they smelt smoke under the trees, carried to them by the rain-filled wind. They followed it to the meadow where the dark tents of the sammad of Sorli were staked out, half-seen in the downpour. The mastodon trumpeted as they passed and they were grateful for the welcome and the chance to eat until they could eat no more, then sleep dry and out of the rain. They went their separate ways in the morning: these were the last Tanu that they met.

They walked north, out of summer and into the colors of autumn. Drifted leaves lay heavy across the trail and the rabbit that Kerrick shot—with his bow, his aim was improving steadily—was already showing white in its fur.

"Very early winter," Ortnar said, his face grim.

"The winters are all early now, we know that. All we can do is keep on, keep moving north as fast as we can."

The sky was gray and they could smell snow in the air when they reached the camping place by the river. Kerrick recognized it at once as he stood on the rise above the beach, standing among the few bits of ancient leather and crumbled bones that was all that was left of his father's sammad. Herilak had found Amahast's knife of sky metal here, among his father's bones. He touched it where it hung about his neck. The Yilanè had come out of the ocean there, had destroyed the sammad here. It had been very long ago and he had only memories of memories now. His sammad was now to the north with Armun—and that is where they must go. He turned away at Ortnar's call and they moved west along the riverbank.

It wasn't until late the next day that they found a dead tree caught on the riverbank, one large enough to support them both, yet still not so big they could not cut it free from the tangled undergrowth. They worked it clear that night, finishing well after dark.

The water was as freezing as fresh-melted snow when they waded out into it in the morning—calling out loudly in protest. With their packs and weapons tied securely to the projecting roots they pushed the tree free of the shore, hung onto it and kicked out, slowly working the clumsy bulk of the thing across the fast-flowing river. By the time they had reached the far bank they were numb, blue with cold, their teeth chattering uncontrollably. While Kerrick dragged their possessions ashore Ortnar built a roaring blaze. They stayed only as long as it took to dry themselves and warm their clothing through, pullled the still-wet skins on and went north again. They would not get chilled again if they kept walking fast; there was little or no time to spare—for the first flakes of snow were already drifting down under the trees.

The days were growing shorter now and they were up before dawn every morning, walking in the dark under the pale illumination of the stars until the pallid sun rose. They were strong and fit. And beginning to be afraid.

"There is not much meat left," Ortnar said. "What do we do when it is gone?"

"We will find the Paramutan before then."

"And if we do not?"

They looked at each other in silence for they both knew the answer to that question. Though neither wished to speak it aloud. They built the fire higher and stayed close to it, soaking in its warmth.

The endless forest of giant firs came right down to the coast, to the sandy beaches at the shore. At times as they walked they had to cut inland when the beach gave way to high cliffs with the waves breaking against them. The forest was silent and trackless, the snowdrifts beneath the trees were very deep and made the passage slow and tiring. Each time they worked their way back to the shore they looked eagerly in both directions, for some sign of habitation. Nothing. Just the barren coast and empty sea.

The food was almost gone when the blizzard struck. They had no choice, they could only go on, leaning against the north wind, looking for shelter of some kind. They were numb, half frozen when they found the shallow cave at the foot of the cliffs, just above the beach.

"There," Kerrick called out, shouting to be heard above the roaring of the wind, pointing out the dark opening barely visible through the driving snow. "We must get inside, out of the wind."

"We'll need wood—a great deal of it. Leave what we carry inside, then get wood."

They kicked through the drift that half-blocked the entrance, stumbling and falling. Away from the wind it seemed almost warm, although they knew the air was far below freezing.

"We cannot lie here," Ortnar said, stumbling to his feet. He seized Kerrick's hand and helped him to rise, pushed him out ahead of him back into the storm.

They hacked and chopped clumsily at the low branches, breaking off what they could with hands that were unable to close properly. Ortnar dropped his knife from his numb fingers and they wasted precious time digging through the drifts until they found it. With the last of their strength they dragged the wood back; it would have to do, they could not go back for more now. Kerrick fumbled out the firebox, but could not feel the stones inside until he had put his hand inside his furs to warm them against his body.

The fire was finally lit and they built it high, huddled next to it gasping in the smoke yet feeling the life return to their numb bodies. It was dark outside now, the wind howling incessantly, while the snow drifted across the entrance so that they had to keep digging it free to allow the smoke to escape.

"We are not the first ones to shelter here," Kerrick said, pointing to the low ceiling of rock where the outline of a greatdeer had been traced with a charred stick. Ortnar grunted and kicked at the ground next to the fire.

"At least they did not leave their bones here."

"And we might?" Kerrick said.

In silent answer Ortnar pulled over his pack and shook out the remaining food. "This is all we have left, about the same in your pack. Not enough to get back with."

"Then we must go forward. We will find the Paramutan. They *must* be here. Somewhere."

"We go forward only when the storm lets us."

They took turns, one tending the fire, one getting wood. Darkness came quickly and Ortnar had difficulty in finding the cave with the last load of wood. The temperature had dropped sharply and there were white spots on his cheek that he rubbed with snow. They were both silent now because the time for talking was past. There was nothing more to be said.

The storm continued for days to the count of a hunter's hand. One day for every finger—including the thumb. They went out only for wood, melted snow for water. And felt the first knife of hunger in their guts as they rationed out the remaining scraps of food.

It was on the next day that there was the first break in the storm. The wind died down and the snow seemed to be thinning.

"It is over," Kerrick said, hopefully.

"We cannot be sure yet."

They emerged into grim daylight. Snowflakes still drifted down from the dark gray sky. For a short while the falling snow thinned a little and they could see the waves breaking on the beach, running high up on the pebbled shore. The seas were heavy, foam-topped, dark.

"There!" Kerrick shouted. "I saw something out there—it's a boat of some kind. Wave to them, wave!"

They stumbled down to the shore, into the edge of the foaming sea and stood there, leaping and shouting hoarsely. Once the boat rode high onto a wave and they thought that they could even make out some figures aboard it. Then the waves rose up again and hid it from sight. The next time they saw the boat it was further out, going north.

It disappeared once again among the mountainous waves and never reappeared.

Wet and exhausted they stumbled back to the cave, barely visible now through the driving snow as the storm struck again with redoubled fury.

The next day they ate the last of their food. Kerrick was licking the crumbled bits of sour meat from his fingers when he looked up and caught Ortnar's eye. He wanted to speak but could not.

What could he say?

Ortnar pulled the furs about him and turned away.

Outside the storm winds blew, screaming along the cliffs. The ground beneath them trembled as the high waves thundered down onto the beach.

Darkness came and with it a great and all-possessing despair.

CHAPTER NINETEEN

Outside the paukarut the blizzard blew with unceasing fury, the wind hurling the snow before it across the arctic ice. Nothing could live before its blast, nothing moved in this totally barren landscape—other than the attacking blizzard. It heaped high around the snow-banked paukaruts until each had a downwind drift like a white beard. In the frozen desert of endless night there was only darkness and certain death.

Inside the paukarut the yellow light of the oil lamp shone on the black ularuaq skin, the white-arched ribs that supported it, the furs and skins and laughing faces of the Paramutan as they dipped bits of rotten meat into the open skin of blubber, fed mouthfuls to the children, roared with laughter when they rubbed it into their faces instead.

Armun enjoyed their presence and was not too disturbed at Kalaleq's constant attentions, his hands always reaching out to touch her when she came close. They were different, that was all. They even shared their women and no one seemed to mind. Laughed about that too. Her temperament was not theirs so she could not join in the wild laughter.

But she smiled at their antics and was not bothered when

Harl joined in with the others. They moved aside to make room for him—some reaching out to touch his light hair. They never tired of the novelty of this and always talked of the Tanu as Erqigdlit, meaning fantasy-people in their own language, for they were Angurpiaq, real people as they called themselves. Armun could understand their talk, this was the second winter that they had spent in the paukaruts on the ice, and that was long enough. When they had first arrived among the Paramutan she had been grateful just to be alive. She had been weak, had lost weight, was worried about Arnwheet in this strange place. It was so different in every way—the food, the language, the way they lived. Time passed very quickly while she was finding out how to adjust to this new life, so that the second winter was upon them even before she realized it.

There would be no third one for her here—she was steadfast in her conviction about that. In the spring she would make them understand that it was time for her to leave. She had her strength back: she and the two boys were well fed. An even more important reason to leave was the disturbing knowledge that by this time Kerrick would have discovered that they had left the sammads; he would be sure that they were dead. The smile slipped from her face at the darkness of this thought. Kerrick! She must go to him, go south to that strange murgu place that they had burnt, go wherever he was . . .

"Alutoragdlaq, alutoragdlaqoq!" Arnwheet said, shaking her by the knee. A strong little boy who had already seen his third summer, talking excitedly through his uneven new teeth. She smiled again as she wiped some of the grease from his face.

"What is it you want?" she asked, speaking Marbak. She could understand him well enough, but did not want him to only talk in Paramutan. If the two boys were left alone, he and Harl only spoke to one another in what had now become their daily manner of communication.

"I want my deer! My deer!" He beat on her knee with hard little fists, laughing. Armun dug into the jumbled furs until she found the toy. She had made it from a strip of deerskin, adding bits of carved bones for antlers. He seized it to him and tumbled away, laughing.

"You should eat more," Angajorqaq said, sitting down at her

side and holding out a handful of the white blubber. She had thrown most of her skin clothes aside in the heat of the paukarut and her fur-covered breasts swung free when she extended her arm. Armun dipped out a small bit of the greasy substance and licked at it. Angajorqaq made unhappy clicking noises with her tongue.

"There was a woman once who did not eat the fish when it was caught." She had a story about everything, saw hidden meanings in any event no matter how commonplace. "It was a silver fish and very big and fat and it looked at her and did not understand. Tell me, the fish said, why you do not eat me? Deep in the ocean I heard the right spells that the fisherman said, saw the hook with the bright bait. I ate it as I should and now I am here and you do not eat me. Why?

"When the woman heard this she was very angry and told the fish it was only a fish and she could eat him or not, whichever pleased her. But of course when the fish-spirit heard this he was even angrier and swam up from the dark bottom of the sea where he lives, swam faster and faster until he hit the ice and broke up through that and opened his mouth and ate the paukarut and all the furs and the baby and the oil lamp and then ate the woman too. So you see what happens when you do not eat. Eat!"

Armun licked some more of the fat from her finger. "When the storm stops and the sun comes back and it is warm—then I am leaving with the boys. . ."

Angajorqaq screeched aloud and dropped the blubber, grasped her ears and rocked from side to side. Kalaleq looked up when he heard this, eyes wide with astonishment, then climbed to his feet and walked over to see what had caused the commotion. In the warmth of the paukarut he had thrown all of his clothing aside: his smooth brown fur shone in the lamplight. Even after all this time Armun found it hard to realize that all the Paramutan were like this, covered with fur from head to foot. Kalaleq's tail came forward decently up between his legs, the furry end spread out to cover his maleness.

"Angajorqaq made a sound of great unhappiness," he said, then held out the bone he was carving to distract her. "This will be a whistle, and see—there will be a ularuaq on it and the whistle will come from its mouth when it is blown."

She pushed his hand aside, was not going to be deprived of her misery this easily.

"It is winter and dark—but the hair of the Erqigdlit is like the sun inside the paukarut and we laugh and eat and are warm. But now . . ." she wailed again, still rocking from side to side" . . . now Armun will go and the light of the boys will go and all will be black."

Kalaleq gaped at this outburst. "But they cannot go," he said. "When the blizzard blows, death sits outside the paukarut with open mouth. When you walk from the paukarut you walk into his teeth. So they cannot go and you do not have to cry out."

"In the spring," Armun said. "We must go then."

"See," Kalaleq said, stroking Angajorqaq's fur to quiet her. "See, they are not going. Eat something. They stay."

The Paramutan lived one day at a time and each new day came as a wonderful surprise. Armun was silent now, but her mind was still made up. They were going to leave as soon as the weather was warm enough to travel. She licked the rest of the blubber from her finger. They would eat well now so they would be strong. And go south as soon as they were able.

The storm blew itself out during the night and when Kalaleq loosened the laces on the smokehole in the morning a tiny shaft of sunlight lanced in. Everyone shouted with excitement at that and searched among the tumbled furs for their discarded clothing, shrieking with laughter when they found someone else's skins. They had been trapped by the storm for days without number and the children screamed with eagerness. Armun held tight to the wriggling Arnwheet with one hand while she pulled on the soft undergarments that had the fur facing inward for greater warmth. Over them went the thicker outer furs, with the hood, then boots, gloves, everything that made existence possible in ther polar north.

Kalaleq was lying stretched out flat, grunting with exertion as he pushed aside the snow that was blocking the end of the entrance tunnel. Light filtered in, then darkened as he wriggled into the opening. They blinked in the glare when he pulled himself free. There was more laughter and they pushed at one another seeing who would be the next one out.

Armun let the boys go first, then followed them. Shielding her eyes against the brightness when she stood up. After the close, damp air of the paukarut, smelling of rotten meat, urine and babies, the cold crispness of the fresh air was wonderful. She breathed it in gratefully, though it stung her nose and throat.

The scattered paukaruts were white lumps in a white landscape. From them other Paramutan were crawling out into the sunshine; there were shouted greetings and much laughter. The bowl of the sky was pale blue with a few high clouds, arching down to the darker blue of the ocean at the edge of the ice sheet. The boats secured there were just white mounds, completely concealed by the snow.

Someone trilled a warning, then pointed and shouted.

"In the sea—a ularuaq!"

"It cannot be!"

"Not a ularuaq—it is one of our boats."

"Then it is Niumak's boat, his is the only one not here. But he must be dead, we sang his death song and the death songs of those with him."

"We sang them too early," Kalaleq laughed. "They fooled us good this time. They will never let us forget this."

Harl ran with all the others toward the approaching boat. Arnwheet ran behind him, but tripped and fell and howled loudly. Armun picked him up and dried his tears: he was more shocked than hurt.

With everyone helping the boat was soon out of the water and secured alongside the others. Arnwheet stood in the snow, dry-eyed now, holding Armun's hand and watching the joyous return. Niumak led the way back to the tents, others running beside him to touch him, pat his arms. To share some of the good luck he and the three others with him must possess. To have lived through this storm was something very special. All four dropped down wearily onto the snow, drinking eagerly from the bowls that were brought to them, snapping up the preferred bits of meat. Only when they were patting their stomachs were the first eager questions asked. Niumak raised his hands for silence and even the smallest children grew still.

"Here is what happened," he said, and there was a shuffle of feet as they grew close to listen. "We could see the ice here when the storm began. Could see through the walls of the paukaruts and see the warmth and the food and the babies playing, could smell their fur and lick them with our tongues. But the storm blew us away."

He paused dramatically, hand raised, and his listeners wailed in agony since they knew what was proper—stopping the instant his hand fell.

"We could not reach the ice and the paukaruts; we could only sail before the storm. There is the headland known as the Broken Leg and we sheltered there for a long time, but could not go ashore because there is no landing there as you know. Then the wind changed and we were blown out to sea again and that is when we sang our death songs."

This brought another wail from his listeners and the tale continued in this manner for a long time. But no one protested because it was a good and exciting story to hear. But Niumak was getting tired and cold so the end came quickly then.

"On the last day the storm was breaking up and we came close into shore, but the seas were still too heavy so we could not land. Now here is a strange thing. There is the cave on the shore that is known as the Deer Cave because of the drawings there and we passed this place and saw two of our brothers come out of the cave and run and wave their arms. We could only sail on for the wind was behind us. And they had a warm cave and we wished to join them but could not. But who were they? All are here, all of our boats are here. Are there other Paramutan close by? But there would not be in the winter. And then we sailed back and you saw us and we are here and now I rest."

He crawled into his paukarut followed by shouted questions. Who had they seen? What did they look like? Was there another boat nearby?

Armun stood as though carved of ice, as cold as ice, staring but unseeing. She knew who was in that cave on the shore, knew as surely as if the name had been whispered in her ear. *Kerrick.* It had to be him, one of those two hunters had to be him. There was no doubt in her mind, none at all. It was as though the knowledge had been there all the time, waiting for Niumak's words to release it. He had come after her. He had found out that she had gone north and had come to find her. She must go to him.

The paralysis left her and she wheeled about. "Kalaleq," she cried. "We must go to that cave. I know who is there. My hunter is there. Kerrick is there."

Kalaleq gaped with amazement. The Erqigdlit did so many

things that were surprising. Yet he did not doubt her for an instant. He pulled himself up and remembered Niumak's words.

"It is good that your hunter is there, and he is safe and warm as Niumak said."

"He is not," she said angrily. "He is not a Paramutan so he is not safe. He is a Tanu who has walked to that place, has carried his food, who was caught by the blizzard. I must go to him—at once."

When the import of this soaked in, Kalaleq shouted aloud. "A boat, my boat, we must launch my boat. There is a thing that must be done."

Armun turned and saw Angajorqaq staring at her with widened eyes. "You must help me," Armun said. "Take care of Arnwheet until we get back. Will you do that?"

"You should not go," Angajorqaq said without much conviction.

"I am going."

The boat was already in the water by the time she reached it and stores were being handed in. Four other Paramutan were there with Kalaleq, putting the oars into the water even as the last of the bundles came aboard. Then they were away, helped on their way by the light wind from the north.

At nightfall they were still rowing south. The coast here was a continuous cliff so there was no thought of going ashore for the night. They hove to and threw out a length of leather with a heavy skin on the end so they would not drift too far during the night. They ate fragments of rotten meat and dug out and sucked on pieces of snow from the supply that had been shoveled aboard. Many of them came over to touch Armun and pat her and make soothing noises. She did not answer, only looked at the shore and waited. Towards dawn, exhausted, she slept and when she awoke they were rowing south again.

To Armun the snow-covered shore looked featureless and blank. Not so to the Paramutan who pointed out invisible landmarks with shouted enthusiasm. There were cries of agreement and they rowed with growing enthusiasm towards a pebbled beach. As they surged up on a wave and grated to a halt two of them were over the side and waist-deep in the icy sea, pulling the boat higher up. Armun jumped from the bow, landed heavily but climbed to her feet and ran swiftly towards the wooded hills. Her long legs outdistanced the others—but she had to stop, to look about desperately at the unmarked snow.

"We go there," Kalaleq cried out as he passed her, pointed, stumbling and falling in the drifts. There was no laughter now, for the snow reached up to the tree line, unbroken, concealing anything there.

They dug, throwing the snow in all directions with desperate urgency. Blackness appeared, the hole was enlarged. Armun was digging as desperately as the others, fell into the opening as they burrowed through. There was a mound of furs covering—what?

She crept forward and reached them first, pulling back the stiff, frozen furs that covered Kerrick's face. Gray and frost covered. She tore off her glove and reached out, not breathing in the fear that overwhelmed her.

Touched his skin, so cold. So cold.

He was dead.

Yet even as she cried aloud with the thought his eyes trembled and opened.

She was not too late.

CHAPTER TWENTY

The wastes of the frozen north were home to the Paramutan. They knew how to live here and survive, knew everything that there was to know about frostbite and freezing. Now they called out in excitement to each other as they pushed Armun aside and jammed their way into the cave. While Kalaleq opened Kerrick's furs and tore them off him, two of the others were undressing as well, laying their still-warm clothing out on the frozen ground. Kerrick's chilled body was placed carefully on the furs and the naked hunters lay beside him, holding him tight to them, using their body heat to warm him. The others piled all of the rest of the furs over them.

"Such cold—I will freeze myself for sure, sing my death song!" Kalaleq cried out.

The others laughed, their good spirits returned now that they had found the hunters alive.

"Get wood, make a fire, melt snow. They must be warmed and will need to drink."

Ortnar was treated in the same manner. Armun realized that she could help best by getting the wood. And he was alive! The sun was warm on her face, warmth penetrating her body at the realization that both she and Kerrick were safe now, alive and together again. At that moment, as she leaned her weight on a branch and cracked it free, she made a promise to herself that nothing would ever separate them again. They had been apart too long. The invisible cord that bound them one to the other had been stretched too far, had been near to breaking. She would not let that happen another time. Where he was—there she would be as well. No thing and no person would ever come between them. Another frozen branch broke free with a loud crack as she hauled on it with all her strength, a mixture of anger and happiness filling her. Never again!

The fire roared, the cave was warm. Kalaleq had gone over Kerrick's unconscious body, pushing at his extremities and nodding happily.

"Good, very good, he is strong—how white his body is! Only here on his face is there freezing, those dark spots. The skin will come off, that is all right. But the other, look how bad."

He pulled the furs back from Ortnar's feet. All of the toes on his left foot were frozen, black.

"Must cut them off. Do it now and he won't feel anything, you'll see."

Ortnar groaned aloud, even though still unconscioous, and she ignored the grisly chopping sounds behind her as she bent over Kerrick. His forehead was warm now, becoming moist. She stroked it with her fingertips and his eyelids moved, opened, closed again. She took him around the shoulders and lifted his body, held the leather cup of water to his lips. "Drink it, please drink it." He stirred and swallowed, then slumped back again.

"They must stay warm, have food, get some strength before they can be moved," Kalaleq said. "We'll leave meat here from the boat, then maybe go catch some fish. Back at dark."

The Paramutan left her a great mound of wood as well. She kept the fire banked high, stirred it, and uncovered the glowing coals. When she turned away from it later in the afternoon she found Kerrick's eyes open, his mouth moving as he tried unsuccessfully to talk. She touched his lips with hers, then stroked them as she would silence a baby.

"I'll talk. You are alive—and so is Ortnar. I found you in time. You will be all right. There is food here—and water—you must drink that first."

She supported him again as he drank the water, coughing a bit

at the dryness of his throat. When she laid him back down she held
tight to him, whispering, her lips close to his ear.

"I made an oath to myself. I swore that I would never allow
you to leave me alone again. Where you go, I go. That is the way it
must be."

"The way . . . it must be," he said hoarsely. His eyes closed
and he slept again: he had been at the brink of death and it is
most difficult to return once you have come that close. Ortnar
stirred and made a sound and Armun brought water to him as
well.

It was almost dark when the Paramutan returned, shouting and
calling out to her. "Look at this tiny thing I bring," Kalaleq called
out as he pushed into the cave—holding up a great, ugly fish
covered with plates, its mouth bristling with teeth. "This will give
them the strength they need. Now they eat."

"They are still unconscious—"

"Too long, not good. Need meat now. I show you."

Two of them lifted Ortnar until he was sitting up, then Kalaleq,
moved the hunter's head gently, pinched his cheeks, whispered in
his ear—then clapped his hands loudly. Everyone shouted encouragement when Ortnar's eyes opened slightly and he groaned. One
held his mouth open while Kalaleq hacked off chunks of fish,
then squeezed the juice from this into the hunter's mouth. He
spluttered, coughed, and swallowed and there was more excited
cheering. When he came blurrily awake they pushed bits of raw fish
in between his lips and encouraged him to chew and swallow.

"Tell him in your Erqigdlit tongue, he must eat. Chew, chew,
that is it."

She fed Kerrick herself, would let no other near him, tried to
give him her strength as she held him tightly against her breasts.

It was two days before Ortnar was fit to travel. He bit his lip
until there was blood upon it when they cut more black flesh from
his feet.

"But we are alive," Kerrick told him when the ordeal was
finished.

"Part of me isn't," Ortnar gasped, the beads of moisture standing out on his face. "But we have found them—or they have found
us—and that is what is important."

Kerrick had to lean most of his weight on Armun when they
went down to the boat: Ortnar was carried on a litter of branches.

He was in too much pain to take much notice of his surroundings, but Kerrick was wide-eyed and appreciative when he looked about him at the boat as he climbed in.

"Made of skins, light and strong. And all the oars! These Paramutan can build as well as the Sasku."

"Some of what they make is even better," Armun said, pleased at his interest. "Look at this—do you know what it is?"

She handed him the length of carved bone and he turned it over and over in his hands.

"It is from some large beast, I don't know what kind. And it has been hollowed out—but what is this?" He shook the dangling leather tube, put his eye to the hole on top of the bone, pulled the knob next to it and discovered that a length of round wood, the thickness of an arrow, was attached to it. "It is wonderfully made, that is all I know."

Armun smiled, her split lip revealing the evenness of her teeth, as she poked the end of the tube down into the water that was sloshing at their feet. When she pulled up on the knob there was a sucking sound, and when she pulled a second time a thin gush of water shot from the top opening and over the side of the boat. He gaped—then they both laughed at his astonishment. Kerrick took it from her hands again.

"It is like something that the Yilanè have grown—but this was made, not grown. I like this kind of thing." He turned it over and over with admiration, tracing the carvings on its length that pictured a fish spitting out a great stream of water.

The return to the paukaruts was a great triumph with the women pushing each other, screaming with laughter, for the privilege of carrying the litter with the blond giant on it. Ortnar looked at them with amazement as they fought to touch his hair, barking at each other all the time in their strange language.

Arnwheet stared at his father in wonder; he had very little memory of any Tanu hunters. Kerrick knelt in the snow to look at him more closely, a solid, wide-eyed boy with little resemblance to the baby he had left. "You are Arnwheet," he said and the boy nodded gravely—but shied back when Kerrick put his hand out to touch him.

"He is your father," Armun said, "and you must not be afraid of him." But the child clung to her leg at the strangeness of it all.

Kerrick stood up, the word bringing up long buried memories.

Father. He dug into his furs and found the two knives that hung about his neck, his fingers touched the smaller one and pulled it free. This time when he knelt down the child did not pull back. Kerrick held out the shining metal blade, glinting in the sunlight.

"As my father gave this to me—so do I give it to you."

Arnwheet reached out hesitantly and touched it, looked up at Kerrick and smiled. "Father," he said.

Before winter ended Ortnar was on the mend. He had lost flesh, was still in pain, but his great strength had pulled him through. There had been more black flesh on his feet, pus and an awful smell, but the Paramutan knew how to treat this as well. As the days grew longer the flesh healed and scars formed. With fur padding in his boots he hobbled out of the paukarut each day and learned to walk again. The foot without the toes made this difficult, but he learned nevertheless. He was walking far out along the edge of the ice one day when he saw the boat approaching from the distance. It was one of the larger ones with a large skin tied to a pole and did not look familiar. Nor was it. When he stumbled back to the paukaruts he found that everyone had turned out, were shouting and waving as the boat came close.

"What is it?" he asked Armun, for he had learned only a word or two of the strange tongue.

"Newcomers, they are not from our paukaruts. It is very exciting."

"What's happening now—all the loud talking and arm waving? They seem very worked up about something."

"I can't tell, they are all shouting at once. You have been walking too long. Go to the paukarut and I will find out what is happening and meet you there and tell you."

Ortnar was alone in the paukarut for the Paramutan—Kerrick, Arnwheet, and Harl as well—were all at the boats. He sat down heavily and groaned aloud, since there was none there to hear, at the pain in his feet. He chewed on a piece of meat, grateful for the rest, as he waited for Armun to come.

"Something very good seems to have happened," she said when she returned. "It is about the ularuaq. They talked about how bad it was all winter, how there were less and less. Now they seem to have found them again. It is very important."

"What are ularuaq?" Ortnar asked.

"They hunt them, in the sea. I have never seen one but they must be very large, larger even than a mastodon." She pointed at the arched ribs above. "Those are from the ularuaq. And the skin cover as well—all in one piece. Most of the meat we eat, the blubber too, comes from the ularuaq. The Paramutan will eat any kind of meat, anything at all." She indicated the seabird hanging by its legs from the ribs above, rotting nicely. "But almost all of their food, the boats, everything comes from the ularuaq. They say that it is the weather, the long winters, that have been driving them away. The ice comes further south every year and something in the water, I don't understand all of it, has changed. So the ularuaq have been harder and harder to kill and this is the worst thing that could happen to the Paramutan. We'll have to wait to find out what has happened now."

It was some time before anyone else returned to the paukarut. Kalaleq was first, crawling in through the entrance and pushing a lattice of thin bones before him, while the others followed. He waved it happily, an intricate array, tied by gut and secured in angles and curves. Armun made him talk slowly as he pointed out the importance of it, translating into Marbak as he spoke.

It was Kerrick who finally understood what Kalaleq was talking about.

"The bones are a chart of some kind—they use them to find their way about the ocean just as the Yilanè do with their charts. Ask him to point out where we are now."

After much reference to the skein of bones, questions and confused answers, what had happened finally became clear. Kerrick, who had crossed the ocean understood the significance.

"It is the winters. They have changed the ocean just as they have the land, changed the things that live in it. The ice sheet we are on stretches across the northern ocean to the land on the other side. I have been on the land there, though not in the north. For some reason the ularuaq are no longer on this side of the ocean but seem to be all over there now. The ikkergak that just arrived has actually crossed to the other side of the ocean and has seen them. What are the Paramutan going to do?"

Kalaleq was graphic in his demonstration when he understood the question. He pulled on invisible lines, rode over imaginary waves as he talked. They could almost follow without Armun's translation.

"They are getting the ikkergaks into the water and preparing them for a long voyage. They went to cross over as soon as the ice begins to break and hunt the ularuaq—and return before winter sets in again."

"Then it is time for us to leave as well," Kerrick said. "We take their food and give nothing in return." But as he said this he looked out of the corner of his eyes at Ortnar who smiled grimly.

"Yes, time to go south," he said. "But it is a walk I do not look forward to."

"You won't have to walk," Armun said impulsively, reaching out to touch his arm. "I know the Paramutan. They will help us. They brought me and the boys here without hesitating at all. They like us, they think we are so different. They will want us to stay but when we insist they will take us south in the spring. I know they will."

"But won't they need all the ikkergaks for the hunting trip?" Kerrick asked.

"I have no idea. I will just have to ask and find out."

"We must leave as soon as we can," Ortnar said. "We must go back to the sammads."

Kerrick's face hardened at these words and his mouth set grimly for the thought of their return brought memories flooding back. Bringing with them fears long forgotten, pushed aside.

And his first thought was of Vaintè, she of eternal hatred. She was out there, planning the destruction of Tanu and Sasku, of all the ustuzou in the world. He had turned his back on the city and the Yilanè that threatened it because he had to find Armun. Well he had done that. They were together again, all safe. Or would they ever be safe? Not while Vaintè was alive, not while she lived on hatred. They would have to return to the city. Back to Yilanè and hèsotsan, the world of ustuzou and murgu, of a battle that had no ending. Or no ending that did not allow the destruction of the sammads.

Armun looked at him and his thoughts were clear to her, for while he thought the murgu words his body writhed their echo, his face worked and grew grim.

They would be going back.

But to what?

ambesetepsa ugunenapsossi, nefatep
lemefenatep. epsatsast efentopeneh.
deesetefen eedeninef.

YILANÈ APOTHEGM

=========

*Ugunenapsa taught that since we know
death we know the limits of life,
and that is the strength of the
Daughters of Life who live when others
die.*

CHAPTER TWENTY-ONE

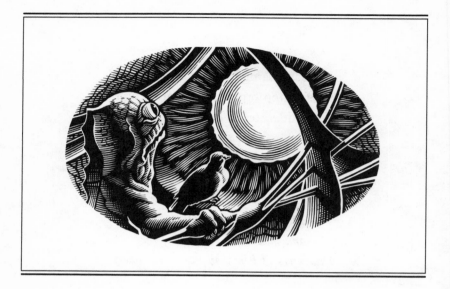

When the uruketo left the harbor of Yebèisk, Ambalasi ordered that it swim west, directly into the open sea. This was the quickest way for them to get out of sight of land— and would give no clue to the watchers on shore as to their possible future course. Elem clambered up to the top of the fin and found the scientist already there, staring out at the dark forms of the enteesenat swimming beside them. Elem made a courteous sound of speaking-attention desired.

"I have never commanded an uruketo, but have only served aboard. There are problems . . ."

"Solve them," Ambalasi said firmly with modifiers end-of-participation, query-next. "Who is on steering duty?"

"Omal, a Yilanè of calm intelligence who learned quickly."

"I said you could command. Now we will examine the charts."

As they left the bottom of the fin they passed Omal who stood with her hands close to the nodules of the nerve endings that guided the uruketo, peering out through the transparent disc at the sea. On the ledge before her perched a gray and pink bird which was looking in the same direction. Ambalasi stopped and ran her thumbs along the creature's feathers; it cooed in response.

"A new compass," Elem explained, "far more useful than the old ones."

"Of course—my design. Accurate, reliable—and provides companionship on long voyages. Once it has been aligned in the right direction it will point that way until it dies."

"I have never understood . . ."

"I have. Magnetized particles in the forebrain. Where are the charts?"

"In here."

Although the alcove was barely illuminated, when the first chart was unrolled it glowed brightly under the dim purple patch on the wall of flesh above it.

"This is designed to the largest scale," Elem said. "As well as being the latest. Here is Entoban* and across the wide ocean is Gendasi*."

"And these swirls of color?"

"These, of the cooler colors, are the winds of the sky that sweep like great rivers through the atmosphere. They rise here in the tropics where the sun heats the air, then move north and south affected by the rotation of this planet. These are of utmost importance to me in my studies, but for practical navigation these warm oranges and reds that mark the ocean currents, these are what guide us."

"Explanation-in-detail."

"Pleasure-in-expatiation. We are here now, in the ocean west of Yebèisk. At your instructions we continue to swim west until dark in case others follow. We will then be about here, in this red stream, a south-flowing current. We will drift with it during the night; then at dawn, after a position check, we will begin the voyage to our destination. Accuracy-of-swimming, desire-for-knowledge of our destination?"

"Uncertainty-now. Show me what you would do if our destination were Gendasi*."

"Eagerness-in-enumerating. For Gendasi* we must follow this current as it sweeps south and west to midocean. This is a most interesting area, quite abundant with life. When we reach it we will choose the correct current for our destination. This is the one we seek, which sweeps here past Alakas-aksehent to the green land beyond."

Ambalasi studied the chart closely, staring at Yebèisk, then allowing her left eye to move across the ocean to Gendasi*.

"A question. We swim in a great arc southwest to midocean, then another arc northwest to our destination. Think how much faster it would be if we simply cut straight across the ocean like this." She ran the edge of her thumb across the chart in a swift motion. Elem stepped back and gasped, her crest flaring red.

"Impossible!" Modifiers of despair and fear. "What you suggest is . . . unnatural. For short periods, yes, as we do now, or crossing from one island to another, then it is in order. But nothing moves in a straight line. The sea creatures follow the currents of the sea, the birds the invisible currents of the air. Such a course that you suggest, why—it goes against nature. The uruketo would have to be forced away from the currents, though at night it would drift with them, then in the morning recalculation . . . plainly impossible!"

"A simple query of scientific interest, Elem, compose yourself. Since you are a worker-with-knowledge, for the greater good of your labors, I will tell you of the two different states of matter. Or do you already know Atepenepsa's law?"

"Humble-ignorance, desire-for-input."

"Stated in its most basic form, invisible matter moves in straight lines, visible matter does not. Remove the glaze from your eyes and close your mouth—you are a picture of fargi stupidity! Do you know of invisible matter?"

"No . . ."

"Lump of ignorance! Gravity is invisible—if I drop this chartweight it goes straight down. That-which-carries light is itself invisible and it moves the light in a straight line from object to eye. Inertia is invisible, yet it keeps a moving object . . . enough. I see that this is all beyond you. Do not feel shame for your imbecility. There are very few Yilanè like myself who have no intellectual limitations. Now, to our course. What lies here?"

Ambalasi placed her splayed fingers and thumbs upon the empty area of the chart beyond Maninlè, south of Gendasi∗. Elem gaped. "Nothing, nothing at all."

"Empty-of-mind, unconscious-of-being-alive! Must I teach you your own speciality? What are these on the chart, here and here?"

"Currents, ocean currents of course."

"Wonderful. Now, amplification-of-detail, what causes currents?"

"Temperature differentials of sea water, wind, planetary rotation, impact on coastlines, gradient of ocean floor . . ."

"Good. Now these currents, here and here, examine them

closely. They do not appear out of outer darkness so suddenly. Trace them backward."

"I see, I see! Great Ambalasi you have drawn me from ignorance as a fargi is drawn from the sea. There *must* be a large mass of land here, where you have indicated. Though no one has ever seen it or recorded it—you have deduced its existence from these charts . . ."

As the significance of this was driven home, Elem lowered her head and signed from lowest-of-low to highest-on-high, as she suddenly realized that Ambalasi knew as much as she did of navigation. Perhaps more. Ambalasi nodded, accepting the awareness.

"You are skilled in your own science, Elem," she said. "But it is I who am skilled in all sciences—as I have just proven. This is not the work of a moment, I have been looking at navigation charts for some years now, making these deductions. This voyage will prove that my contentions are correct. We are going here, to this blank spot on the map. It will never be blank again after we have reached it. Now go, bring Enge here to attend me."

Enge went with Elem as soon as she was summoned. Ambalasi was standing in an arrogant pose when they joined her, as erect as her aged spine would permit, a chart grasped firmly in her hand. Elem approached the scientist as humble as a fargi. Enge, shaping her limbs with utmost respect, did not quite go that far. Ambalasi held out the chart at arm's length, utmost gravity-importance in the gesture.

"Now I will show you, Enge. Now I will reveal our destination and the city that is awaiting you there."

"We have true gratitude for what you have done for us." Her arms shaped the curved gesture that indicated she spoke for everyone in her group.

"Excellent. Here, here on this chart, at this place, is our destination. While here—is our city."

She opened her other hand as she spoke, extended it. Resting on her palm was a large and convoluted seed. Enge looked from chart to seed, then back again, before bending her head in appreciative acceptance.

"We are grateful. Since there is only an emptiness here on the chart I can only assume that with your superior knowledge you know of a new land that is there. A land without cities, without

Yilanè, so therefore the seed is a city seed that will be grown to shape a city of our own."

"Precisely," Ambalasi said sharply, putting seed and chart down with unnecessary violence, ripples of color running along her crest. "You have a first-class brain, Enge, and I look forward to besting it."

She did not add that she had not succeeded this time, nor did Enge make a point of mentioning it, but signed gratitude and agreement instead. The aged scientist was set in her ways and irascible—but could be allowed any eccentricities after all that she had done for them.

"Is it permitted to ask for more information on our destination in order to enjoy the working of a brain of such infinite magnitude?"

"It is permitted." The colors died from Ambalasi's crest as she accepted what was only her due. "Look closely and learn. The strength, the width, the temperature of these currents, these rivers in the sea, are noted on the charts for those with the capacity to understand them. Whose number of course includes me. I will not go into details, you would not understand them, but will give you my conclusions instead. Here is no small island or string of islands, but a great land mass whose size we will discover when we reach it. It lies to the south of Alpèasak which means that it will be gloriously warmer. Do you know the name of this new land, Enge?"

"I do," she answered firmly.

"Then tell us all," Ambalasi said with uncontrollable movements of pleasure.

"It is named Ambalasokei so that in tomorrow's tomorrow, as long as Yilanè speak one to another, they will speak the name of she who brought life to this distant and unknown place."

"Well composed," Ambalasi acknowledged and Elem signalled agreement with modifiers of enlargement. "Now I will rest and conserve my energy. You will of course need my guidance so do not hesitate to waken me then even though it troubles you to do so."

Word of what was happening spread quickly and there was great excitement. The Daughters of Life pressed Enge to reveal the significance of Ambalasi's disclosures and she did, standing in the shaft of light that fell from the open fin so all could hear.

"Ugunenapsa, our teacher, told us that the weakest is the strongest, the strongest the weakest. By this parable she meant to instruct us in the oneness of life, to make the point that the life of a still-ocean-wet fargi was as important to that fargi as the life of an eistaa would be to the eistaa. Ugunenapsa spoke this long ago, but the eternal truth of it has been driven home to us again today. Ambalasi, even though she is not yet a Daughter of Life, has profited from Ugunenapsa's teaching so much so that she has led us from captivity and is leading us now to a new world where we will grow a city—that will be our city. Be humble before the wonder of that thought. A city without persecution for beliefs. A city without death. A city where we can grow together and learn together—and welcome fargi to grow and learn with us. I have said, with gratitude and without a moment's hesitation, that this new land where we will grow this city will be called Ambalasokei."

A wave of emotion swept her listeners, a wave of agreement that rippled their bodies in unison as a field of grass is moved by the wind. They were of a single mind.

"Now we will rest, for there will be much to be done upon arrival. Elem will need aid with this uruketo, so all with skills or the desire to assist should go to her and sign readiness and cooperation. The rest of us will compose our thoughts and prepare for that which is to come."

Ambalasi, as befitted her age, lay dormant for the greater part of the voyage, though she was the only one. For the Daughters of Life the situation was too novel, too exciting, since for the first time they were in a majority and not being persecuted or derided. They could speak openly of their beliefs, discuss them and seek guidance from those, like Enge, whose clarity of thought they appreciated. While the passing of each day brought them closer to the shining reality of their new existence.

As she had instructed, Ambalasi was not disturbed until they entered the current that carried them away from the route that would have taken them past Maninlè and Alakas-aksehent to the mainland of Gendasi*. After drinking cool water and eating some meat, she rose and climbed slowly up to the summit of the uruketo's fin. Elem and Enge were waiting for her there and signed respected greetings.

"Warm," Ambalasi said, her eyes closing to vertical slits in the bright sunlight, signing modifers of pleasure and comfort.

"We are here," Elem said, indicating their position on the

chart with one thumb. "The waters are rich with life and contain unknown fish of giant size."

"Unknown to you perhaps, and others of limited knowledge, but the ocean keeps no secrets from me. Have you captured any of these unknown fish?"

"They are delicious." Elem signed pleasure of eating. Ambalasi instantly signed displeasure-of-gluttony and primacy of knowledge.

"You think of your stomach first and your brains last," Ambalasi said testily. "Before you consume all the scientific resources of this ocean have a specimen brought before me."

It was indeed impressive, a transparent, smooth length fringed with green fins—that when stretched out proved to be as long as a Yilanè is tall. Ambalasi took one look and expressed dislike-of-ignorance and superiority-of-knowledge.

"A fish indeed! Am I the only one with eyes to see, a brain to use? This is no more a fish than I am. It is an elver. And I see by the glaze in your eyes that the technical term is meaningless to you. Elvers are the larvae of eels—and I presume you know what eels are?"

"Very edible," Enge said, knowing this would encourage the scientist to greater flights of insult which she obviously took great pleasure in.

"Edible! Again the processes of digestion not of cerebration! I find it hard to believe that we are of the same species. Once again I fill your empty brains with new information. Do you not realize that the largest elver known is no longer than the smallest nail on my foot? And you must know that mature eels grow to respectable— and I hurry to say it before you do—edible sizes."

Enge looked down at the slowly writhing elver and conveyed appreciation of information—and growing amazement as she spoke. "That will mean that the adult forms will be gigantic!"

"It does indeed. Which is further proof that an unknown land is out there—for eels of that size have been completly unknown— up until this moment."

A few days later Ambalasi ordered that a sample of the seawater be brought to her. A Yilanè climbed down from the fin to the uruketo's broad back and dipped the transparent container into the waves that broke about her legs. Ambalasi raised it before her eyes, looked at it quizzically—then put it to her lips. Elem signed danger, knowing that the drinking of seawater could lead to dehydration and death.

"I am pleased at your concern," Ambalasi said, "but it is misplaced. Taste for yourself."

Elem hesitantly sipped from the container—then registered shock and surprise. Ambalasi agreed knowingly.

"Only a great river, greater than any we have ever known, could carry fresh water this far out to sea. I feel that we are on the edge of a mighty discovery."

The next day they noted that sea birds were circling them in large numbers, sure evidence that they were close to land. Soon they saw floating vegetation in the water which was no longer as transparent and clear as it had been in midocean. Ambalasi took samples for examination before she made another of her positive statements.

"Suspended soil, bacterial life, egg cases, plankton, seeds. We are approaching an immense river that drains a vast area of an even larger continent. I predict, with some accuracy, that we are close to our destination, close to Ambalasokei."

It rained for most of the next day, but stopped before evening. As the clouds cleared from the horizon ahead they witnessed a sunset of great majesty and color. As the uruketo surged over the long waves they glimpsed a dark line on the horizon below the flaming sky.

They slept that night, as Yilanè always sleep, unmoving and deeply, but all were awake at the first light of dawn. Elem ordered many of them below for the crush on top of the fin was unbearable. Ambalasi took the front position, as was her due, as the land on the horizon grew, came closer. It eventually opened out to reveal a wealth of small islands.

"No river," Elem said with movements of disappointment.

Incapable-of-comprehension Ambalasi signed with some vehemence. "Small rivers have large mouths. A river that drains a continent carries silt and forms a delta of many islands. Find one of the channels through those islands and you will find our river rightly enough. And on the banks of its rich waters we shall plant the seed of the city."

"There is no slight doubt within me that Ambalasi is right, for she is never wrong," Enge said. "Out there, coming close, is our destiny, the beginning of a new life for us all. The new land of Ambalasokei where our city will grow."

Angurpiamik nagsoqipadluinarpoq
mungataq ingekaqaq.

PARAMUTAN SAYING

===

To a Paramutan a fresh fish is as good
as a quick screw any day.

CHAPTER TWENTY-TWO

In the end the decision was made. It took a long time for that is the Paramutan way. Endless conversation, interrupted only by quick mouthfuls of blubber and rotten meat, was the only manner in which to settle important matters. When the meat in one paukarut began to run out the conference was moved to another one. People came and went, some even fell asleep, and when they returned or woke up, they had to be told what had happened in the interim so even more discussion was needed.

Yet the decision had been made. Most of the ikkergaks would cross the ocean to catch ularuaq. But this was a long voyage and they would not be back until the end of autumn, might even have to wait until next spring, and food would be needed in the paukaruts before then. There were fish that could be found in the coastal waters here—so it was decided that one ikkergak would venture south to see what could be caught there, while at the same time it would carry the Erqigdlit visitors back to their own land. This was something new and exciting and all of the Paramutan wanted to go, but they also accepted the fact that Kalaleq would command the ikkergak since he was the one who had the foresight to bring the Erqigdlit here in the first place.

Once the decision had been made no time was wasted. The ice was beginning to break up as the sun warmed and the days grew longer. The summer would be short—then winter would be upon them once again. With almost unseemly haste, after the protracted deliberations, supplies were struggled out to the ikkergaks. They were stowed aboard and one by one, with much shouting and laughter—long faces and tears would guarantee bad luck on the voyage—the vessels got under way. Angajorqaq hid when their ikkergak was ready to leave, but Armun stopped them from sailing and went back to find her hiding under the furs in the rear of the paukarut.

"You are being foolish," Armun said, using her knuckle to wipe the tears from the brown fur of the other woman's face.

"That is why I hid from you."

"Among the Erqigdlit it is a sign of good fortune to be unhappy when someone leaves."

"You are strange people and I do not want you to go."

"We must. But we will return soon."

Angajorqaq's eyes widened and she whistled softly, a sign of great respect. "You must be able to see through the ice and through snow and into tomorrow if you say that. I did not know."

Armun had not known herself—the words had just come as naturally as talking about something sure and certain. Her mother had been able to do that, lift the darkness of night a little and see tomorrow before anyone else could. Perhaps she could do that herself. She patted Angajorqaq's face, stood and left her. The ikkergak was waiting, and they all shouted for her to run—and she did. Arnwheet jumping up and down happily and Harl shouting. Even Ortnar looked pleased. Only Kerrick still had the black expression that had captured his features ever since the decision to leave had been made. He tried to control it, to smile and to talk lightly, but he never succeeded for long. The look was always close by, ready to return. At night Armun could make him forget the future for awhile when he held her—but in the morning it always came back.

Until the voyage south began. The novelty of being at sea in the ikkergak kept his mind and his body occupied, for it was like nothing he had ever seen or experienced in his life before. Crossing the ocean in an uruketo had been completely different, trapped in a living, leathery compartment with smells and stinks and constant semidarkness, nothing to see, nothing to do. The ikkergak could not have been more different. Now they moved over the sea, not under it, seabirds crying out, winging close, with the creaking of the ikkergak's structure all about as the big sail was spread and they rode before the fresh wind. Here he was not a stupefied passenger but played an active role in the ikkergak's passage. There was always water to be pumped out and he never tired of working the handle and watching the gush of clear water over the side. He puzzled over it, but never quite understood the mystery. It had something to do with the air, like the popping toy, but just exactly what he was never sure. It did not matter—it was enough to know that with a pull of his arm he could lift water from below his feet and send it back into the ocean.

Setting sail was less of a mystery. He could feel the wind on his face, saw it fill the leather sail, could see the strain on the woven lines that passed the strength of the wind on to the fabric of the ikkergak itself. Following instructions carefully he learned to pull on the correct lines and mastered the knots that held them into position. He even took his turn at the tiller. He was needed because they sailed all night as well as all day, sailing from winter into spring. Steering the craft at night was beyond him, he had not the skill to guide it by the feel of the air on his face and the pressure on the tiller. But during the day, with a good following wind, he could hold the ikkergak on its course as well as any of the Paramutan.

The ikkergak was an intricate and marvelous construction. Big as it was, the outer skin was made from the hide of a single ularuaq, and he wondered what the immense creatures could possibly be like. The skin had been stretched over a framework made of thin strips of strong wood, countless lengths that crossed each other and were tied together with leather thongs. In some ways it was like sailing in an uruketo for the flexible sides moved as the ikkergak rode over the waves, moving in and out as though it were breathing.

Traveling south in the ikkergak was far better for Armun than the trip north had been in the little boat. The motion was easier and she was no longer sick. While the days grew warmer instead of colder: she had had enough of ice and snow. But she worried about the boys falling into the water and watched them closely when they were playing. Despite this, in a moment of daring, Harl did lose his balance and topple over the side. Her scream alerted the helmsman who brought the ikkergak all aback, sail flapping, while Kalaleq scrambled over and threw a line to the frightened boy. It had happened in moments, the air in his clothes had kept him afloat, and all the Paramutan rolled about with laughter when his dripping form was hauled aboard. He was much more careful after this experience and even Arnwheet was more cautious after having seen his friend vanish over the side.

The Paramutan were good fishermen and kept lines out most of the time. The hooks were carved from two small bones, one sharpened at the end and the other drilled for the line, tied together with ligament where they joined. Three or four of them would be tied to the line and baited with bits of leather that had been stained yellow and red. A large rock with a hole drilled through it was used for a weight and this was secured at the end of an immense length of line. The weight would be thrown over the side and the line paid out. Many times when it was hauled up again it would be heavy with fish. Of course the catch was eaten raw, as was all the meat that formed the Paramutan diet, but the Tanu had long grown accustomed to this.

Water was carried in skins and refreshed often from streams along the shore. The coast was green with new grass now and the first leaves were opening. Sooner than they had imagined they reached the great river where it emptied into the sea, where the sammads had camped on their trek south. The weather was warmer too, the days longer. The Tanu relished the heat but the Paramutan became more and more uncomfortable. They had long since shed all of their clothing and stayed out of the sun whenever they were able, but their soft brown fur was still sheened with perspiration. There was no laughter now. It was after a warm and sunny day that Kalaleq drew Armun aside in the dusk. He was crouched down, exhausted, fanning himself with his outstretched tail.

"You must learn to sail the ikkergak, make sure all the other Erqigdlit know how as well, for now is the time for the Paramutan to part. We leave you, we die . . ."

"Don't say that!" she cried, horrified, for it was known that death always waited close by, eager to come if he were called. "It is the warm air, we will land, you must go back north."

For many days now the Paramutan had been suffering from the heat, but they still insisted on going on, nor would they permit the Tanu to go ashore so the ikkergak could turn back. Something had to be done, she did not know what—when the decision was made for them. The sails flapped suddenly and the ikkergak turned and wallowed in the water. Kerrick was steering and had thrown the tiller hard over, he was pointing at the shore and shouting.

They were just outside the breaking waves, passing a long beach that stretched away to the horizon in both directions. It was low tide and most of the sand was exposed, smooth and unbroken. Except for the dark object that Kerrick was pointing to. Gray rock. Armun could not understand why he was bothered. Then her breath caught in her throat as she recognized it.

A mastodon. Dead.

They ran the ikkergak up onto the beach close to the body. Kerrick was first over the side, pushing through the surf toward the great, still form. Its trunk lay in the water, washing back and forth in the waves. Seabirds had already torn the creature's eyes out. Kerrick was hidden by the mastodon's bulk for a moment, then reappeared, walking slowly now. His face was as grim as death itself when he held up the Yilanè dart that he had plucked from the wrinkled hide.

"You must go back," Armun said, shouting in Paramutan, her voice shaking with fear. "Go north, this night, keep going. We are going inland, away from the ocean." She reached up for Arnwheet as Harl landed with a splash in the water beside her. Ortnar climbed painfully down from the bow. She explained what had happened to the horrified Paramutan, her words coming out in a rush. "Those creatures I told you about, the murgu, they have been here. They strike from the sea, from the south. You are safe if you go north."

"The mastodon came down from there," Kerrick said, pointing to the trees beyond the dunes. "You can still make out the tracks. They are two or three days old. Tell them to pass down our packs. Tell them to leave."

The dead bulk of the mastodon made argument impossible. "We will go," Kalaleq said, unable to keep the fear out of his voice. "We will go north and fish and bring the catch back to the paukaruts. Come with us or the murgu will kill you as well."

"We must stay."

"Then we will return. To this place. Before the winter comes again. We must catch more fish. You will come back with us."

"Understand me, please, we cannot do that. This is where we must remain. Now—go, quickly, you must leave."

She stood on the shore, their few possessions tumbled about

them, her arms around the boys, as the ikkergak caught the wind and moved quickly away from the shore. The Paramutan had remembered to do the correct thing when they departed so were laughing and making loud jokes as they went, growing more distant until their sharp voices were drowned in the rustle of the waves upon the shore.

Ortnar went slowly ahead, leaning heavily on his spear, while they lifted the packs onto their shoulders. They followed his footsteps and caught up with him at the edge of the trees. At the place where this sammad had been slaughtered.

It was hideously familiar to all of them except for the four-year-old Arnwheet who fiercely clutched his mother's hand in numbed silence.

The collapsed tents, the sprawled bodies, the dead mastodon.

"It is sammad Sorli. They were going north," Ortnar said grimly. "Yet we met them last autumn, going south. What reason . . . ?"

"You know the reason," Kerrick said, his voice as deadly grim as the death that surrounded them. "Something has happened in the city. I must go there, find out—"

He stopped when he heard the sound from the forest, dim and distant. A sound familiar to them all. The bellow of a mastodon. Kerrick ran toward it, through the slaughtered sammad and beyond, toward the opening in the trees where a path had been torn, clearly marked by broken branches and shrubs. The mastodons had panicked during the attack, had broken away. He came to one dead body, then another. He stopped to listen and heard the trumpeting call again, much closer this time.

Moving quietly he slipped through the darkening forest until he saw the beast: he called out softly. It turned toward him and lifted its trunk, made a burbling cry in response.

When it moved, in the shadows behind it, he saw the small girl standing forlornly against a tree. Tear-stained and frightened, no more than eight years old, speechless. He made soothing noises as he approached, both child and animal were still afraid, bent and picked her up.

"Let me," Armun said as she came through the trees. He gave her the child.

It was getting too dark to move on. They stayed there, in the protection of the trees, waiting for the others. The boys were close behind Armun, but Ortnar did not come hobbling up that quickly.

"No fire," Kerrick said. "We don't know where they have gone. They could have come by land, might still be close."

The child finally talked to Armun, but could add nothing to what they already knew had happened. Her name was Darras. She had been alone in the woods, squatting down in the shelter of the bushes, when everyone screamed. She had been frightened, had not known what to do, so had remained hidden. Later she found the mastodon and stayed with it. She was hungry. When she was asked why the sammad had trekked north she had no idea. She ate the cold meat ravenously and fell asleep soon afterward.

There was little to be said until Kerrick broke the silence.

"In the morning I will see if there is any trace of the Yilanè, though they must be gone by now. If they are, we will start south, to the lake where I left the two male murgu. If those two are still alive we can get their death-sticks. There will be food there too; it will be a safe place to stay. I must find out what has happened in Deifoben. But I will have to do that alone while you remain at the lake."

"That is what you must do," Ortnar said, grimly. "The sammads are there—or were there. We must find out what has happened."

CHAPTER TWENTY-THREE

Ortnar hobbled off at dawn, leaning heavily on his spear, to find the track of the Yilanè. Kerrick wanted to go in his place, but he knew that the big hunter was a far better tracker and woodsman. While Armun fed the children he cut long, stout poles to make a travois, using the straps from their packs to bind it together. He was fixing it to the mastodon when Ortnar returned.

"They came from the sea," he said, dropping wearily to the ground, his face running with sweat and taut with pain. "I found where they came ashore, where they laid an ambush that the sammad walked into. They're gone, back to sea."

Kerrick looked up at the sky. "We are safe enough until we get further south. They won't have any birds looking at this area, not after the killing. We'll leave now, go as far south as we can before we have to travel by night."

"The owl . . ." Armun said. Kerrick nodded.

"We are still better moving at night. The raptors fly high, can watch a bigger area. That is all we can do."

Once they had passed the dead sammad they came to the well-marked track it had made, then followed this south. Arnwheet ran behind the plodding mastodon, thinking it was all exciting and fun, stopping to admire the giant heaps of fresh dung. Darras walked in silence, numbed by what had happened, staying close to Armun. Arnwheet quickly tired of walking and swung onto the travois where the little girl soon joined him. Harl at thirteen was far too old for this babyish comfort and walked on with the others.

Ortnar refused to ride on the travois—though his toeless foot kept him in constant agony. He was a hunter, not a child. Kerrick mentioned it just once, did not speak of it again after the hunter's snarled refusal. In midmorning a spring rain began to fall in a fine drizzle, becoming heavier as the day progressed. Slowed by the glutinous mud, Ortnar fell farther and farther behind until he was out of sight.

"We should wait for him," Armun said. Kerrick shook his head.

"No. He is a hunter and has his pride. He must do what he must do."

"Hunters are stupid. If my foot hurt I would be riding."

"So would I. That must make me only half a hunter because a Yilanè would not walk unnecessarily."

"You are no murgu!" she protested.

"No—but at times I think like one." His smile faded and he strode on unhappily through the rain. "They are out there somewhere—and something terrible is happening. I must find out what it is, go to the city."

Kerrick was reluctant to stop at midday—but Armun insisted because they had not seen Ortnar since the storm had begun. While she took out the food, he cut some pine branches to shelter them from the cold rain. Harl brought water from a nearby stream and they gulped mouthfuls of it to wash down the repellent meat. Kerrick finally spat his out. They must hunt, get fresh meat, cook it. He had not noticed any game, but it must be there. Something moved in the forest and he grabbed up his bow, fitted an arrow to it—but it was Ortnar. Stumbling forward, slowly and steadily. He had a brace of woods pigeons slung over his shoulder.

"Thought we could use . . . the fresh meat," he gasped as he slumped to the ground.

"Let us eat them now," Kerrick said, worried by the drawn lines in Ortnar's face. "We can light a fire, the smoke won't be seen in the rain. Harl, you know how to find dry wood. Get some."

Armun plucked the birds, with Darras's enthusiastic if not too skilled help, while Kerrick built the fire. Even Ortnar sat up and smiled at the smell of birds roasting on green-wood spits. The birds were half raw, barely warmed through when they ate them, but they could not wait. They had had enough of frozen fish and stinking meat.

All they left were the well-gnawed bones. Then, warmed and with their stomachs filled, they resumed the walk with more energy than they had started the day with. Even Ortnar kept up with them at first, though as time passed he fell farther behind until he was out of sight again. The rain stopped and the sun was visible behind the thin clouds. Kerrick looked up at it and decided that they would make an early halt. He must allow enough daylight for the injured hunter to reach them before dark. When they came to a glade of large oak trees, with a stream nearby, he decided that they had gone far enough.

Cutting branches from a stand of pine and building them into a shelter for the night kept him busy for some time. But not long enough. Ortnar still had not appeared.

"I'm going back along the track," he said. "I'll look out for game."

"You will need me to help," Harl said, reaching for his small spear.

"No, you have a more important task. You must stay here and be on your guard. There could be murgu."

The hunting was only an excuse: he was worried about Ortnar. Walking back along the track he did not even think of hunting. Something had to be done—but Ortnar could not be forced to ride in the travois. Yet he should. When they had been eating the birds he had noticed that there was blood dripping from the wrappings of Ortnar's bad foot. Kerrick must talk to him, say that he was slowing them up, endangering them all. No, this would be no good, for the hunter would then leave them and strike out on his own. He began to worry. He had come a long way and the hunter was still not in sight. There was something ahead—dark on the track. He raised his spear and went forward warily.

It was long after dark and Armun was torn by worry and fear. The sun had set and they had not returned. Should she send Harl to see what was happening? No, best to stay together. Was that a shout? She listened and heard it more clearly this time.

"Harl, watch the children," she said, seizing up her own spear and hurrying back along the rutted path.

There Kerrick was, coming along slowly, a dark bulk over his shoulders. Ortnar, hanging limply.

"Is he dead?"

"No, but something is very wrong," he gasped out the words for he had carried the motionless body a long way. "Help me."

There was little they could do other than cover the unconscious hunter with furs, make him comfortable under the shelter. There was foam on his lips and Armun wiped it gently away. "Do you know what happened?" she asked.

"This is the way I found him, just collapsed in the mud. Can you tell what is wrong with him?"

"There are no wounds, no bones seem to be broken. I have never seen anything like it."

The clouds blew away and the night was clear: they dare not light a fire. They took turns sitting by the unconscious figure, making sure he stayed covered. Near dawn Harl awoke and offered to help, but Kerrick told him to go to sleep again. When the first light filtered through the leaves, Ortnar stirred and moaned. Kerrick bent over him when he opened his right eye.

"What happened?" Kerrick asked.

Ortnar struggled to speak and the words came out slowly, mumbled, for his lips were twisted. Kerrick saw that not only was his left eye closed but the entire left side of his face was slack and ummoving.

"Hurt . . . fell down . . ." was all he could say.

"Drink some water, you must be thirsty."

He supported the big hunter's dead weight as he drank. Most of the water dribbled down his chin because of his slack lip. After this Ortnar slept, a more natural sleep, and his breathing was easier.

"I knew one like this in our sammad, when I was small," Armun said. "She was like this with the eye closed, the arm and the leg on the same side unmoving. It is called the falling curse and the alladjex said it was because she had a spirit of evil inside her." Kerrick shook his head.

"It is the wounds in his feet. He pushed himself too hard. He should have rode."

"He will now," Armun said, calmly practical. "We will spread some of the branches on the travois, then tie him on. We will be able to go faster."

Ortnar was too ill to make any protests about being carried. For some days he lay as one dead, waking only to drink and eat a bit. As the days grew warmer the game became more plentiful—and more dangerous. There were murgu here. They killed and ate the small ones—but knew that the giant flesh eaters were out there as well. Kerrick walked always with his bow ready and an arrow notched—and wished often that their hèsotsan had survived the winter.

Ortnar could sit up now and hold his meat with his right hand. He could even hobble a few steps leaning on a crutch Kerrick had cut for him, dragging his useless left leg.

"I can hold a spear in my right hand still—that is the only reason I stay with you. If there were other hunters here I would sit under a tree when you left."

"You will get better," Kerrick said.

"Perhaps. But I am a hunter, not a drag-leg. It is Herilak who has killed me. Before I fell my head was on fire, here, where he struck me. It burned there and through my body, then I fell. Now I am half-dead and useless."

"We need you, Ortnar. You are the one who knows the forest. You must guide us to the lake."

"I can do that. I wonder if your pet murgu are still alive?"

"I wonder, too." Kerrick was glad to talk of something else. "Those two are like—I don't know what. Children who have never grown up."

"They look grown up enough to me—and ugly."

"Their bodies, yes. But you saw where they were kept. Locked away, fed, watched over, never allowed out. This must be the first time that they have been alone and on their own since they came out of the sea. The murgu take the males and lock them away even before they learn to talk. If those two are still alive after the winter it will be something to see."

"It will be something better to see them dead," Ortnar said bitterly. "All of the murgu dead."

They traveled only at night as they moved steadily south, concealing themselves and the mastodon under the trees during the day. Hunting was good: raw fish and stinking meat only a bad memory. They were lucky in that none of the bigger murgu ranged the thick forest and the smaller ones, even the flesh eaters, fled before them. Ortnar was watching the trail carefully and found where they had to turn off toward the round lake. This path was narrow and overgrown and had not been used for a long time. It was impossible to follow it at night so they were forced to travel by day, hurrying across the infrequent open places, looking worriedly up at the sky.

Kerrick led the way, spear ready, for Ortnar had said that they were getting close to the lake. Going cautiously and as silently as he could he looked about carefully under the trees and into the shadows. Behind him he could hear the distant cracking of branches as the mastodon pushed through the forest. Ahead of him there was the snap of a breaking twig; he froze.

Something was moving in the shadows. A dark figure, a familiar form, too familiar . . .

A Yilanè—armed!

Should he try to reach his bow? No, the movement would be seen. She was coming closer, stepping into the sunlight.

Kerrick stood and cried out.

"Greetings, mighty hunter!"

The Yilanè spun about, staggered back, mouth gaping with fear, struggling to point the hèsotsan.

"Since when do males kill males, Nadaskè?" Kerrick asked.

Nadaskè stumbled back and sat down heavily on his tail, signing fright and death-approaching.

"Oh ustuzou who talks, you have brought me to the edge of death!"

"But not over the brink as I can see. You are alive and I am happy to see that. What of Imehei?"

"He is like me—strong and alert, and of course a mighty hunter . . ."

"And a fat one too?"

Nadaskè made motions of rejection and anger. "If I look fat to you now it is just because of our prowess in the forest. When all the good meat was gone we grew lean before mastering the craft of the hunt and of the fishing. Now we excel—there is something horrible coming!"

He raised his hèsotsan, then turned to flee. Kerrick called out to stop him.

"Dispose-of-fear, entertain-joy. My comrades come with a great beast of burden. Do not flee—but do go to Imehei now and tell him what is happening so he does not shoot us for our meat."

Nadaskè signed agreement as he waddled quickly off down the track. There was more cracking as tree limbs broke and the mastodon pushed up beside him.

"We are very close," he called out to Armun. "I have just talked to one of the murgu I told you about. Come ahead, all of you, and do not be afraid. They will not hurt you. They are—my friends."

It sounded strange when he said it like that, in Marbak, but it was the closest word that he could think of for the concept of efenselè. Family, that would be a better word, but he did not think that Armun would take to that very kindly. Or even saying that the murgu were part of this sammad. He hurried ahead, anxious to see and speak with the two males again.

Ortnar rolled free of the travois and dragged himself to his feet, stumbled after it. They came to the lakefront in this way, pausing under the trees beside the immense stretch of sunlit water. Imehei and Nadaskè were waiting in motionless silence under a canopy of green vines, hèsotsan clutched in their hands. The mastodon was pulled to a halt and Kerrick was aware of the Tanu behind him, stopping, standing as unmoving as the Yilanè males. In the silence a flock of brightly colored birds flew low over the water, calling loudly as they went.

"These are my efenselè," he called out to the males, stepping out into the sunlight so he could be understood. "The large-gray-beast-unintelligent carries for us. There is no need for weapons."

When he turned back he saw that the little girl had her face buried in Armun's clothes: she and Arnwheet were the only Tanu not holding spears. "Ortnar," he said, softly, "you marched with these males, they never harmed you. Armun, you don't need that spear—you either, Harl. These murgu are no threat to you."

Ortnar leaned his weight on his spear and the others lowered theirs. Kerrick turned away from them and crossed to the still rigid males.

"You have worked hard here," he said, "have done much while I was away."

"Are those small-ugly ustuzou young?" Imehei asked, weapon still at the ready.

"They are, and they are Yilanè even when small unlike your young. Do you stand all day like gaping fargi or do you bid me welcome, offer me cool water, fresh meat? A female would. Are males inferior to females?"

Imehei's crest reddened and he put the hèsotsan aside. "It has been so peaceful here I have forgotten the sharpness of your female-male speech. There is food and drink. We make your ugly efenselè welcome."

Nadaskè with some reluctance put his weapon aside as well. Kerrick let out a deep breath.

"Pleasure-companionship," Kerrick said. "Welcome-at-last."

He fervently hoped that it would stay that way.

CHAPTER TWENTY-FOUR

For the moment the sammadar was happy to see the two halves of sammad Kerrick staying well apart from each other. They were too distant, too alien, separated by more than language. He had freed the mastodon from the travois and hobbled it under the trees where it grazed the young leaves happily. The creature was going to be a problem—since it was so large it was sure to be seen from the air. The answer was obvious; kill it and smoke the meat. They would have to do that, but not right now. There had been so much killing.

Armun had lit a small and smokeless fire under a spreading, wide-branched tree; the children played close by. Ortnar was sleeping, while Harl had gone off to hunt—carefully slipping into the forest far away from the other half of the encampment. There was peace for the moment, time to think. Time for him to talk to the males. Keeping to the shadows he walked over to their encampment close to the lake shore. He admired the thick, leafy covering overhead.

"You did this?" he asked. "Grew this cover so you could not be seen from the air?"

"Brute force is a female trait, intelligence male," Nadaskè said smugly, leaning back on his tail.

"Endless labor cutting fresh boughs," Imehei added. "They dried and changed colors most quickly. So we cut poles and trained the ivy along them."

"Work of intelligence, admiration-unbounded."

Kerrick reinforced it with strong modifiers. The two males had worked in this unknown environment, facing difficulties they had never imagined in the security of the hanalè. They had secure cover now, and certainly had been eating well. "The hunting is good?"

"We are expert," Imehei said. "In the art of fishing also." He waddled over to a pit in the ground filled with wet leaves, rooted through the leaves until he found what he wanted, returned with two large freshwater crustacea. "We catch these. Desire-to-eat?"

"Later. Hunger-dispersed-presently."

"Better than meat," Imehei said, putting one in his mouth and passing the second over to Nadaskè. He chewed happily, his sharp, conical teeth making quick work of the creature, bits of shell pushing out between his lips as he ground away.

Nadaskè finished his quickly as well, spitting the bits of shell into the bushes. "Without these the food would not be as good. We do not know the secret of meat preparation—do you?"

Kerrick signed negative. "I have seen them do it in the city. The fresh-killed meat is put into tubs with a liquid, that is what changes it. I have no idea of what the liquid is."

"Joyful-jellied-flesh," Imehei said; Nadaskè added qualifiers of agreement. "But perhaps that is all we miss of the city. Freedom of spirit and body makes all work worthwhile."

"Have you seen other Yilanè—do you know anything of the city?" Kerrick asked.

"Nothing!" Imehei said with some vehemence. "That is the way we wish it. Free, strong—and forgetful of the birth-beaches." His words were muffled as he used clamped thumbs to remove a large fragment of shell from his teeth. "We take pride in what we have done—but we have also talked of it often. Death and hatred to ustuzou for killing the city. Gratitude to Kerrick-ustuzou for saving of lives, freeing of bodies."

"Reinforcement many times over," Nadaskè said.

Both Yilanè were silent then, their bodies still formed into the shapes of gratitude. After the winter among the Paramutan the males looked squat and ugly, with their clawed feet and great teeth, eyes that very often looked in two directions at once. That was as a Tanu would see them. He saw them as steadfast friends, intelligent and grateful.

"Efenselè," Kerrick said, unthinking, with overtones of gratitude and acceptance. Their agreement was automatic in return. When he returned to the Tanu encampment he walked slowly, bearing with him a strong feeling of accomplishment.

The feeling did not last. Once they were settled in he found that his thoughts returned always to the city and his concern over its fate. He had to see for himself what was happening there. He controlled his impatience, knowing that he dare not leave the two different groups alone until they had lost their fear of each other. Darras would not come near the two males, burst into tears when she saw them, for she knew that others of their kind had slaughtered her sammad. Harl was like Ortnar, wary and troubled when near the males. Only Arnwheet had no fear of the Yilanè, nor they of him, calling him small-harmless and fresh-from-sea. They knew that his connection with Kerrick was something close and of great importance, but could not understand how a parent could be related to a child. Yilanè were born from the fertile eggs carried by the males and entered the sea soon after they were hatched. The only relationships they knew were those of their efenburu, those they had grown up with in the ocean. Even the males' memories of this were dim since they had been separated from the females as soon as possible. Arnwheet went with Kerrick whenever he spoke to the males, sat wide-eyed in appreciation of their twitching forms and grating voices. It was all great fun.

Days passed without the two groups growing any closer, and Kerrick despaired of any real progress. When the others were asleep he tried to talk to Armun about it.

"How can I like the murgu?" she said, and he felt her body grow rigid beneath his hand. "After the things they have done, all they have killed."

"These males did not do that—they were in the city, imprisoned . . ."

"Good. Put them back in prison. Or kill them. I will do that if you do not want to. Why must you talk to them, be with them? Make those awful noises and shake your body? You don't have to."

"I do. They are my friends."

He despaired of any explanation; he had said it all too many times before. He stroked her hair in the darkness, then touched her lovely forked lip with his tongue and made her giggle. That was better, this was better. But good as it was, he wished that the rest of his life could be as satisfying, that the two halves to his nature could be one.

"I must go to Deifoben," he told Armun the next day. "I must find out what has happened."

"I will go with you."

"No, your place is here. I will be away just for a few days, just time enough to walk there and back."

"It is dangerous. You could wait . . ."

"Nothing will change. I won't be long, I promise that. I will go there—carefully—and come back as soon as I can. You will be all right here; there is plenty of meat." He caught her gaze moving across the camp. "And those two won't hurt you, that I promise. The males are not like that. They are more afraid of you than you are of them."

He went to tell the two Yilanè that he was leaving—and it had the expected reaction. "Instant death—end of life!" Imehei wailed. "Without your presence ustuzou will kill, they always kill."

"They will die with us, this I promise," Nadaskè signed with grim confidence. "We are not strong-feminile, but although only mere males we have learned to defend themselves."

"Enough!" Kerrick ordered with exasperation, using the form of female-above to male-below forms, the only imperative he could think of in this strange situation. "There will be no killing. I have ordered it."

"How can you order it—mere male—to a female ustuzou?" Imehei said, with slight overtones of revenge. Kerrick's anger faded and he began to laugh. The males would never understand that Armun, being female, was not in command of everything, that he was not just her spokesman.

"Respectful-imploring," he signed. "Simply stay away from them—and I promise they will stay away from you. Will you at least do that for me?"

They both reluctantly weight-shifted in agreement.

"Good. Now I go to tell the ustuzou the same thing. But in leaving I ask you a favor. Let me take one of your hèsotsan. The other two we took with us died in the cold."

"Death-from-darts!"

"Starvation—lack of meat!"

"You forget who gave you the weapons, trained you to use them, gave you your freedom, saved your worthless lives. Disgusting display of typical male lack of gratitude."

There was more wailing and complaints of female brutality on his part, but in the end they reluctantly handed over one of their weapons.

"It looks well fed?" he asked, stroking the creature's lips to see its teeth.

"Care has been lavished, they eat before we do," Nadaskè said with slight exaggeration.

"Gratitude. It will be returned when I return. A few days, no more."

He left at dawn the next day, taking a small supply of smoked meat. This, and the hèsotsan, were his only burdens so he traveled fast and easily. The track was clear; he made good time. Only when he came to the outermost fields of the city did he slow and proceed with utmost caution. These had been the limits of Alpèasak, the creatures penned here long dead, the barriers long gone. Ahead he could see the fresh green of one of the outer thorn barriers.

Greener than he had remembered it—and when he came closer he could see why. It was covered now with great, flat wet leaves. And long thorns with the corpses of birds and small animals rotting on them.

Yilanè.

But had the barrier been grown here to keep the enemy in—or out? Who was occupying the city now? Was it still Deifoben—or had Alpèasak been reborn?

There was no point in going inland; the new barrier would surely encircle the city. He might take days to work his way slowly all the way around it—and he would still be no wiser. The sea, it had to be the sea. He forgot all attempt at keeping cover and began to run. Only when he was panting, dripping with sweat, did he slow and stop in the shade of a tree. This would not do. It was just suicide to go on like this. He must proceed slowly and carefully, watching all about him. And it was almost dark. He would find water and rest for the night. At first light he would go on to the shore.

He chewed some of the meat and thought he would not be able to sleep. But it had been a long and trying day and the next thing he knew the sky was gray and a chill fog had left him beaded with dew. It was not far from this place to the shore. But the fog was thicker now, obscuring everything. Close by he could hear waves running up on an invisible beach. Carefully, he pushed through the last undergrowth until he reached the familiar dunes. He would stay here until the fog lifted.

It would be another warm day and the sun quickly burned through. As the fog thinned he could see a dark form in the water, moving offshore. Concealed by the undergrowth he watched as it emerged from the haze. Black hide, tall fin. An uruketo.

It swam slowly south toward the harbor. It could mean anything; it could be a patrol, watching for activity on the shore. Or it could be based there.

Any faint hopes that he might still have had vanished when the two small boats appeared, the rising sun glinting off the shells of their bows. Fargi in each, going out to fish for the day.

Deifoben had become Alpèasak once again. There had been a battle, an invasion, destruction. It had all happened while he had been away.

But where were the Tanu and the Sasku who had been living there when he left? What had happened to them? The barrier of deadly thorns stretched off into the distance. He could see nothing on the other side of it, but the activity at sea was positive proof that this city was Yilanè once again. The evidence overwhelmed him, drove him to the ground with the black fist of despair. Were they all dead? His cheek lay on the sand; a spider ran quickly by. He reached out to crush it, then stayed his hand and watched it hurry out of sight. Were they dead, all of them, dead?

He would never discover what had happened just lying there. He knew that, but his feeling of loss was so great that he felt disarmed and helpless. Only when distant shouts penetrated his daylight darkness did he stir and raise his head. More fishing boats were going by and a Yilanè was standing in one, calling out to the others. It was too distant to make out her meaning.

But were they just fishing boats? Or were they part of another raiding party going north? He had to know; there might be Tanu out there. He dropped behind the dunes and hurried north as well.

He ran until he was tired, then crawled up the dunes again to look at the ocean, to check the progress of the boats.

The wind was freshening from the east, sending thick rain clouds hurtling before it. Soon the first drops splattered down, grew heavier and heavier. He no longer ran, but head lowered against the storm, trudged slowly through the sand. The boats were still there, just outside the surf, he checked often. It was midday when he stopped to rest and eat some of the meat. The feelings of despair seeped back when he stopped moving. What was the point of it—what was he accomplishing? The boats were there, in the sea, and nothing he might do could effect them in any way. Was there any point to this futile pursuit?

This time when he raised his head carefully over the crest of the dune he saw that the boats had stopped, were being joined by others who had been fishing on the far side of the narrow channel that separated the beach from the sandy islets beyond. He could see the nets being hauled in, the catch being shared out to the new arrivals. So it was not an attacking force—they were just fishing boats after all. The sea was far rougher now as the wind gathered force; a tropical storm was building. The Yilanè in the boats must have been aware of this as well because on some unheard command they all turned and moved back toward the harbor and the city.

Kerrick climbed to his feet and watched them leave, slowly vanishing from sight in the driving sheets of rain. He was soaked through himself, his hair and beard plastered across his face, but it was a warm rain and he scarcely noticed it. The hèsotsan he was holding stirred feebly as it felt the water, opening its tiny mouth to suck at a rivulet. Kerrick turned his face to the rain too, drinking it in. Enough. He would leave now. Was there anything else he could do? He could think of nothing.

There were dark forms in the water where the boats had been, leaping high and splashing back into the sea. The waves were much higher now, breaking across the islets on the other side of the channel. These were really just large sand bars, the waves now washing right over them and surging far up on the beach. These were enteesenat; he recognized them, he had watched them playing about the uruketo often enough. They never ventured out alone— there must be an uruketo near by—yes there it was. Moving solidly along in their wake, waves breaking across its back, surging about its fin. It was going slowly, having trouble in fighting the growing seas. There was no room for the creature to turn, the waves were hitting it broadside, and there was no escape to the open ocean.

The boats were now out of sight, Kerrick and the enteesenat the only witnesses of the disaster. The uruketo was thrashing its mighty tail—but it was not moving. It was aground. The waves were still higher, breaking over the creature, rolling it up onto the sand. Their force sent it over on its side, dipping the high dorsal fin into the water. There were Yilanè there, holding on, being washed away: a flood of dark water entered the opening on the top. Then the backsurge of the waves straightened it up again and he saw the round, empty eye of the creature well above the water.

It was beached, injured, half out of the water. The enteesenat were hurrying back and forth just outside the breaking waves, still leaping high in their consternation. They were strong swimmers, they were safe; it was their charge the uruketo that was lost.

The next time a large wave hit the great dumb beast it was rolled still further over on its side, its fin flat in the water. Nor could it recover. One great flipper stuck straight up, beating feebly, sporadically. Kerrick could see the water surging in and out of the open dorsal fin. When the water drained back down the beach the crew began to emerge. They were battered, dragging themselves out desperately before the next wave washed over them. One of them was just emerging, dragging one of her companions, when the wave hit. They both disappeared in the breaking wall of water. When it rushed on, far up the beach, they had vanished.

Though the uruketo was doomed, the flailing fin now motionless, the crewmembers were still struggling. The waves were not breaking with the same terrible strength, the tide was on the way out and the wind was dying. Kerrick could see one of them, probably the commander, standing waistdeep in the streaming water, directing the survivors. They emerged from the gaping fin with bundles, dragged them up onto the beach, then went back for more. They did not salvage very much for the opening in the top of the fin was collapsing; they had to drag the last crewmember free.

There were only five survivors who dropped down wearily next to the little that had been salvaged. Four of them had collapsed onto the sand, but the other one stood stiffly, staring as they all were at the dying creature in the waves.

Hèsotsan held ready Kerrick walked slowly toward them. Why not? None of them were armed, they were battered by the sea,

192 • HARRY HARRISON

would offer no resistance. But they were still able to talk. They would have to speak to him, tell him what had happened in the city. He could hear the blood pounding loudly in his ears as he approached them. Now he would know.

He could see them clearly as he came close, noted the way the one who was standing was bent forward. A familiar stance. Of course!

"Erafnais," he called out, and when the commander turned to stare at him in undisguised astonishment he smiled wryly. "You must remember me, commander. How many other ustuzou have you ever talked to?"

CHAPTER TWENTY-FIVE

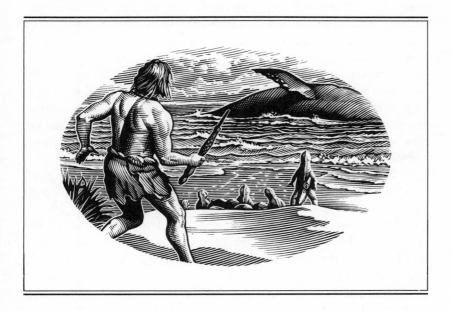

E rafnais looked at the tall form standing before her, befuddled, shocked. Her head was tired, heavy. She swept the transparent membranes over her eyes to clear away the last of the salt water. "Kerrick?" she said numbly.

"The same."

The crew turned at the sound of voices, registering confusion and concern. "Give them orders," Kerrick said, using the forms of she-who-is-highest to those-who-are-lowest. "Tell them to do nothing, to obey you. If they do this they will not be hurt. Do you understand?"

Erafnais seemed numbed and incapable of comprehending what was being said to her. They all were like that, Kerrick realized. Erafnais pointed at the dead, or dying, beast and spoke slowly with fargi-like simplicity.

"My first command. I was there soon after it was born, fed it fresh caught fish with my own hand. That is what a commander must do. They have some intelligence, not much, but it is there. It knew me. I helped with the training, doing what the instructors taught me. I know the creature is old, fifty-five, almost fifty-six, they don't live much longer than that, but it was still strong. We should have been at sea, this never would have happened, not in this restricted channel with a storm on its way. But those were the orders." She turned a hopeless look of despair upon Kerrick. "You sailed in her, I remember. We had a good crossing, rode out a storm, never a problem."

The crewmembers were on their feet now, listening as he was, for they had lived aboard the uruketo, too. It was their home, their world. One of the crewmembers dropped to the sand again; the movement drew Kerrick's attention. No, she wasn't sitting, she was taking something from among the bladders and containers on the beach.

"Get away from there," Kerrick ordered, modifiers of urgency and immense danger. She did not listen, was reaching down, sitting up now—with a hèsotsan.

Kerrick shouted and fired, saw the dart strike one of the containers. The opening of the other weapon swung toward him and he dived to the sand, scrambling into a dip, hearing the other fire. Raising his own weapon to fire again.

More successfully this time. The dart struck her in the chest and she fell face down in the sand. Kerrick ran forward, before the other crewmembers could react, grabbing up the other hèsotsan with his free hand, spinning about and pointing his own at the crew.

It had taken only instants—yet everything had changed. Another of the Yilanè was huddled on her side, dead. The dart that had missed him had found her instead. Kerrick pointed at Erafnais and the other two survivors.

"I warned you, ordered you to stop them. This need not have happened. Now all of you, move back away from these things. Two are dead. That is enough."

"Eight others dead in the uruketo," Erafnais said, speaking so softly he could barely hear the sounds, her limbs scarcely moving with the qualifiers.

"Tell me of the city," Kerrick said, loudly, urgency-of-speech in his sharp movements. "What has happened there? Tell me of Alplèasak."

"You were not there?" Erafnais asked as the meaning of his words finally penetrated.

Kerrick signed a quick negative, glancing quickly at the

crewmembers, then back at the commander. "I was very distant. I have just returned. What happened?"

"Vaintè said there would be no battle, but she was wrong. The eistaa listened, helped her, for the winter winds are blowing toward Ikhalmenets and she wanted to believe. Vaintè told her of this city, sought her aid, came here, promised no battle. The seeds were spread, the ustuzou were to die, then Alpèasak would be Yilanè once again. But they attacked our island base from the sea, the ustuzou, and were beaten off. I carried Vaintè in this uruketo, so I know, at first she was gorgeous in her victory, then when she discovered that it was a ruse her anger was so great fargi died about her."

"Ruse, what ruse?" Kerrick pleaded, movements of explanation, greater clarity requested.

"Only a small force attacked the island. It is believed that all of them died. But while this was happening, all of the others in the city escaped, fled, could be traced, not caught. And it does not end." Erafnais turned to face Kerrick, drawing herself up as straight as she could with her twisted back, spoke with feeling.

"Why does she do it, Kerrick ustuzou? You know her. What hatred drives her? The city is Yilanè again, that is why we came here, why so many died. Yet she talks to the eistaa, has convinced her that the ustuzou will return, talked to her on the fin of my uruketo, so I know. And the eistaa agreed with her and they plan to follow and attack. And more Yilanè will die."

"Ustuzou will die as well, Erafnais," Kerrick said, lowering the hèsotsan. "It is not my wish either that this go on."

Erafnais seemed to have forgotten his presence. She was looking out to sea, past the dead bulk of the uruketo. "The enteesenat are upset—see how they jump high. But they are intelligent creatures and will not stay here. They will return to the harbor, they can be trained to follow and feed another uruketo. We must go too. We must report what has happened . . ."

"No," Kerrick said, pointing the weapon again. "You cannot do that. You cannot tell Vaintè of my existence. And you will have to tell her, won't you?"

Erafnais signed agreement and lack of understanding. "When we report what happened your presence will be noted."

"I know. Even if you could lie you would not."

"The expression 'lie', I do not know it. Clarification requested."

"It is a term that Vaintè invented to describe a certain ustuzou concept unknown to Yilanè. It is not relevant. What is relevant is that I cannot permit your return. She would be after me, the birds would fly, we would be found. I suppose the males would live—but not for long. I know how they would pay for their attempt at freedom. The beaches, as many times as was needed. I am sorry, you cannot return."

"We will take my charts," Erafnais said, picking them up. "They should not be left here. The rest can remain; others will come and retrieve anything of value . . ."

"Stop!" Kerrick ordered. "What are you doing?"

"Taking my charts," Erafnais said, her arms full so that her meaning was muffled. "They are very singular and precious."

"Where do you think you are taking them?"

"To Alpèasak."

"You cannot." The hèsotsan was leveled. "You have been a friend, have never injured me. But the lives of others come first. If you attempt to leave you will be shot. Is that clear?"

"But my uruketo is dead. There is just the city now."

"No."

Kerrick spun about at the sharp cry. One of the crewmembers was running down the beach. He aimed and fired and she fell. He turned quickly toward the other in case she should try to flee as well. But he was too late for she had already escaped—fled from him and from life itself. She lay on her side on the sand, her mouth gaping open, her eyes already glazing.

"You understand," Erafnais said. "The uruketo is dead. She would have been all right if she could have returned to the city. But you have stopped her—so she dies as though she had been rejected by the eistaa." She turned her troubled eyes to Kerrick. "Nor shall I command ever again."

"No!" Kerrick cried out, "Don't."

Erafnais turned away from him and sat down heavily. He ran to her side, he did not want her to die, as well, but she toppled over onto the wet sand before he reached her. He looked down at her, turned and saw the other dead and dying Yilanè, felt their loss. He had not wanted them to die—yet there was no way he could have prevented it. It was just waste, terrible waste.

Out to sea the enteesenat were moving off, swimming swiftly

toward the city. They knew the uruketo was dead, knew that there was nothing for them here.

Kerrick watched the enteesenat leave—and realized that there was danger. When they returned alone there would be alarm, for it was unknown for them to ever abandon their uruketo. A search would be made, boats would be sent out, possibly another uruketo would come this way. He looked up at the sky. There was still daylight, they might even be here before dark. Panic started to rise and he forced it down. He must plan, there was no urgency, he had the rest of the day, all the time he needed. First and most obvious—he must leave no traces of his presence here, none at all.

With this thought he turned and looked back up the beach, at the clear line of his footprints stretching down from the dunes. The rain was lighter now, it might wash them away, but he could not be sure. He laid the hèsotsan aside and walked carefully back in his own tracks to the place where they emerged from the coarse grass. Far enough. Then he bent over, moving backward, and smoothed the tracks with his hands as he went. The rain would obscure these signs quickly enough.

Now the dead. He plucked the darts from the two bodies and buried the deadly missiles in the sand. Then, one by one, he dragged the heavy Yilanè corpses down to the water's edge and out into the surging waves. Erafnais was the last and her grip, even in death, was strong; he had to pry her clasped thumbs open before he could free the charts, drop them onto the sand.

He poked through the salvaged bundles but there was nothing that he could use. Food and water, better to leave it. He would take the other hèsotsan, of course. He laid it beside his, then dragged the supplies into the ocean to join the bodies there. They might be washed ashore now, it didn't matter. He would smooth out all the marks on the sand, then walk north in the water's edge. As long as his presence was not suspected it would appear to be only a natural tragedy. The uruketo beached in a storm, its crew drowned trying to salvage what they could. All signs of his presence had to be destroyed.

What about the charts? He was about to throw them into the ocean as well—then changed his mind. Could the charts tell him anything about the new eistaa? All the Yilanè were from Ikhalmenets, that is what Erafnais had said. He remembered the name but did not know where the city was. Not that it made any difference: it just seemed wrong to discard them without an examination—and there was no time now. He would take them, along with the weapons. He stood up to his knees in the surf taking a long last look at the sand. It would do. He moved deeper into the bubbling waves and walked north. Walked with a lighter step as memory came flooding back. He had been so busy on the beach that he had forgotten for the moment.

They were alive! Some had escaped before the city fell, that is what Erafnais had said, perhaps most of them. They would have gone back to the valley of the Sasku, all of the survivors, and the Tanu would have gone with them. Vaintè had sworn to follow, had not done it yet. They were still alive.

It rained again during the night but stopped soon after dawn. Kerrick wanted to go faster but it was too hot and damp here under the trees. The sun was out, bright fingers of light piercing the green canopy above, but water still dripped from the leaves. The moss and grass underfoot made it easy to walk quietly as long as he took care. His hèsotsan was ready in his hands, the other one slung across his back with the maps, for there were predators here. Game as well, though he did not want to take the time to hunt. He wanted to return to the camping place by the lake as soon as possible.

"I heard you coming," Harl said from behind the tree. "Thought you were a murgu."

Kerrick turned, startled, then smiled at the boy. Harl was a Tanu raised in the forest; Kerrick knew that he would never be as good a tracker or hunter. "Tell me of the camp," he said.

"I killed a deer yesterday, a buck; it had seven points on its horns."

"We will all eat well. Other than that, has there been . . . any trouble?"

"The murgu you mean? They stay far away from us; we never see them." The boy's eyes never rested as they moved through the forest, searching on all sides. Though he apparently did not look where he was walking he never made a sound; a twig hidden by the grass cracked when Kerrick stepped on it. "I'll go ahead, tell them that you are coming," Harl said.

"Do that." To carry the good news—or to get away from his

mastodon tread? Kerrick smiled as the boy swiftly moved out of sight.

They were all waiting for him when he came to the camp, Arnwheet running out shrieking with happiness, to be swung high into the air. Armun smiling, Ortnar leaning heavily on his crutch, looking grim as always. Kerrick told them at once what he had discovered.

"The sammads are no longer in Deifoben—but they are alive. And I have another death-stick and these maps. There is more— but water first, I've come a long way."

He sluiced it over his head, gasping, drank great mouthfuls. Then sat and told them what he had seen, what had happened.

"But you cannot know where the sammads are," Ortnar said when he had done.

"There is only one place to go—back to the valley. The Sasku know the trail very well. They have many death-sticks. The murgu will find them hard to kill."

"Yet the murgu you spoke with said they would be followed, attacked," Armun said, worriedly. "Should we not go to them, warn them."

"They know well enough." His words were grim as were his thoughts. What could he do? What could anyone do? Was there never to be an end to the killing? It was Vaintè who did this. Without her there might be an end to the fighting. But she was far from his spear or arrow, could not be killed.

There was nothing that could be done, that was the answer. Nothing. The sammads would flee—and the Yilanè would follow. That was the repellent yet inescapable truth.

CHAPTER TWENTY-SIX

That afternoon Kerrick crossed the invisible boundary between the two camps to return the hèsotsan to the males. They would need it for their hunting, having no proficiency with spear or bow. Arnwheet saw him leave, called out then ran after him. The boy had one of Erafnais's charts tucked under his arm; he was fascinated by the colors and was the only one besides his father who seemed at all interested in the Yilanè artefacts. Kerrick took him by the free hand and they walked slowly together under the trees. Kerrick was cheered by the small hand in his, the boy's presence and affection, but could not escape from the ever-present feeling of despair.

"One who has gone returns," Kerrick called out when he saw Imehei. "Information to impart of great importance."

Nadaskè heard the sound of his voice and pushed his head out of their sleeping shelter to see what he was saying. "Pleasure to see-again," he said, and there was a movement of undisguised relief as he spoke.

"Agreement," Imehei said. "Death from vicious ustuzou threatened us each instant you were departed."

Kerrick ignored the obvious exaggeration and returned the

hèsotsan with a signed gratitude-for-use. In response to the querying movements from the two he told them what had happened in Alpèasak.

"Ustuzou fled, Yilanè once again."

"Females and death, too close, too close," Imehei wailed.

"Well you weren't very happy when the city was ustuzou," Kerrick reminded him. "You had better decide which you prefer."

"Equally bad," Nadaskè said. "Death from stone tooth, death on the beaches."

"Then stay away from the city."

"Look, see," Arnwheet said, coming between them and holding out the chart.

Imehei took it from him with appreciative movements at the rich colors. Kerrick started to speak—then stopped, shocked.

Arnwheet had spoken in Yilanè. Crudely and simply—but Yilanè it was!

Imehei and Nadaskè admired the detailed lines and colors of the map while the boy looked on proudly. He watched and listened when they spoke and seemed to understand some part of what they said. Kerrick was overwhelmed by affection for the boy, bent and seized him, hurled him laughing into the air, sat him proudly on his shoulders. Why shouldn't he understand? He was young, he learned like all children by listening to others—Kerrick as a boy had been far older and he had learned Yilanè. He was proud of his son's accomplishment, more than proud. It was an important thing to have happen, a greater bond between them. Up until this moment he had been alone, the only living creature in the world who could speak with both Yilanè and Tanu. This was no longer true.

"Objects of great delight," Imehei said, holding the chart up to the sun the better to admire the colors. "Great artistry, see how the lines penetrate from one side to the other."

"They have a function and a purpose," Kerrick said. "They are aids to navigation, directions for crossing the ocean."

"Little purpose, no importance," Imehei said.

"They were needed by the uruketo that brought you here," Kerrick said with overtones of malice. "Without them, you could have ended up in the frozen sea."

"Since I shall never venture aboard an uruketo again, smelling-boring, they are useless. Except for wall hangings, color to place of living; could be placed beside the sculpture of the nenitesk, polite request."

"No," Kerrick said. "I want to study them. They are from Ikhalmenets—do you know where that is?"

"Distant—fish-filled."

"Island of little importance."

As always the males took no interest in anything other than their own comforts, their own survival. They could be no different, Kerrick thought. In the hanalè they had no responsibilities. But they had made the break, were self-sufficient now; he must give them credit for that.

He carried Arnwheet and the map back in a strangely thoughtful mood. The fact that the boy was beginning to speak Yilanè was of great importance. He felt that—but logically knew no reason why. When the others were asleep that night he lay awake in the darkness speaking softly to Armun.

"Arnwheet can speak with the murgu a bit—he will get better at it."

"He should not go near them, disgusting. I will see that Darras plays with him more. When do we go back to the sammads?"

"I don't know. I don't know what to do." To her in the darkness he admitted his worries and fears, held tight to her, as she to him. "The valley is distant and the murgu will be watching all of the trails. How can we escape them? Ortnar cannot walk. And I do not think he would go with us if he had to ride like an infant in the travois. I think that he would walk into the forest alone if he had to go that way. What would that leave us? Children—and one half-grown boy who is probably the best hunter here, better than I am I know."

"I have a strong arm and a good spear."

"I know." He held her, smelling the freshness of her hair. "Your strength is my strength. But you know as little of hunting as I do. We will need food. The hunting is good here, Harl gets what we need, and we have the fish in the lake. But it would be a long and hard trail if we left. I think we have been on enough trails like that. Far too many."

"Then you want us to stay here?"

"I don't know what I want, not yet. When I try to think about it I feel a knot of pain and my thoughts twist away. But now we are safe here. We must take time to decide what to do. And the sammads, I think about them too, and wonder if there is anything we can do to help them. The murgu will be after them."

"Their hunters are strong. They can take care of themselves. It is not yours to worry about," she said.

It was a true and practical answer. She understood his feelings—but did not share his sense of responsibility for all the others. What she had received in her life she had fought for. He, their son, this tiny sammad, this was her world and the only thing of any importance to her. To live in peace with them, to survive, that was her only desire. The sammads were not her concern.

Nothing was that simple and straightforward for Kerrick. He rolled and turned and finally fell asleep.

He awoke at dawn, went to sit at the lake's edge and looked across the still water. The surface rippled as unseen fish arrowed under it. A flight of great coral-colored birds flew by in line, calling to each other. The world, here, at this moment at least, was at peace. Arnwheet had left the Yilanè charts blowing about the camp so Kerrick had picked them up as he walked, gathered them together. Now he spread out the top one and tried to make sense of it. It was useless. Perhaps some colors meant land, some meant ocean, yet they turned and twisted over each other in a manner quite impossible to understand. In this they resembled the Paramutan frames of joined bone. But those were just possible to comprehend. Kalaleq had pointed out the ice cap, the distant land, and Kerrick had understood that much. But other things about them were beyond him. Perhaps the Paramutan might understand these masses of color, he certainly could not. Maybe he should give them to the males to hang up for decorations. He tossed them to the ground and looked unseeing and uncomprehending at their swirls.

What could he do? When he looked at the future he saw only blackness. To remain here by the lake provided only temporary salvation; it had no future. Here they were like animals burying themselves in the ground, hiding from the enemy outside. The spy-birds flew, the Yilanè watched, and one day they would be seen. It would end then. But what other choice had they? To trek west to the valley? A dangerous trip—yet at the other end there would be friends, all of the sammads. Under a threat of disaster because Vaintè was on her way there as well. So what should he do? What could he do? In all directions he saw nothing, nothing but certain despair, despair ending in certain death. There was nothing he could do, nothing at all, no way out. He sat in the shadows beside the water until the sun was high in the sky and the flies busy around his nose and eyes. He brushed his hand across his face but was really not aware of them at all, so deep and intense were his fears.

Later they ate most of the leg of the deer Harl had killed, admiring it and his skill greatly so that the boy was red with pleasure and turned away. Only Ortnar disagreed.

"You should be ashamed. You needed three arrows."

"The undergrowth was thick and there were leaves in the way," Harl protested.

"The brush is always heavy. Come over here and bring your bow. We will say that tree is a deer. Now you will kill it for me."

Ortnar moved only with a great effort. He could no longer use his bow—but was still deadly with his spear. And he knew how to hunt: there were many things that he could teach Harl. Arnwheet too Kerrick thought, as the smaller boy ran over to join the fun, to watch and learn.

"It is not yet time for Ortnar to go alone into the forest," Kerrick said to Armun. She followed his eye and nodded agreement.

"The boys must learn. Ortnar is a hunter who knows all the important things."

"And I am one who doesn't."

She was angry in his defense. "You know things stupid hunters will never know! You can speak with the murgu and have crossed the ocean. You are the one who led the sammads in battle to victory. Any hunter can shoot a bow or throw a spear—but did they know how to use the death-sticks until you showed them? You are more than all of them." Her anger faded as fast as it had come and she smiled at him. "All of those things are true."

"If you say so. But you must know that nothing now is clear to me. I look at the sunshine and I see only darkness. If we stay here we will certainly be found by the murgu one day. If we go to the other sammads we join them in death when Vaintè attacks them. What shall we do?" He thought of what she had said, searching her words for some help. There was a glimmering there. "What you said just now about crossing the ocean. I did that in the belly of a murgu beast. But there are others who cross on top of the water."

Armun nodded. "The Paramutan. They sail the ocean to spear the uluruaq, that is what they told us."

"Yes, they must be able to do that. The Paramutan who brought us south, they said that they would return here to fish. If only we could go with them. But we don't know what is on the other side of the ocean. Death could wait there as well as it waits here. We should not cross until we know what is there. By then it could be too late. What should we do? Perhaps I should join them. Cross with them to the other side of the ocean. They said that there was a cold land there. But south of the cold land it will be warm; I know because I have been there. It is the land of the murgu and they only live where it is hot. But perhaps I can find a land between the heat and the ice where we could live and hunt. Perhaps."

He seized her hands, trembling with excitement. "I could go with the Paramutan now and search for a place of safety over there, find somewhere to the south of the ice and north of the murgu. It might be all right, there might be hunting. Then I would come back for you. We would be able to leave here and find a place that is safe. While I am away you will be all right as long as you stay under cover and watch out for the birds. You will have food and you will be safe until I return. Don't you think this is something that I could do, that might save us all?"

Kerrick was so absorbed with his new plans, at the thought that there might be a way out of this trap, that he was not aware of the coldness that replaced the warmth in her face, the stillness of her features, was unaware of how she felt until she spoke.

"No. You cannot do that. You will not leave me."

He looked at her, shocked at the rebuff, his temper rising.

"You cannot order me. I do this for all of us and it is I who will risk crossing the cold sea . . ."

He grew silent as she reached over and placed her fingers gently over his mouth.

"You take the wrong meaning from my words and that is my fault. I spoke quickly out of fear. My true meaning is that I will not leave you, ever again. Where you go, there will I go also. Once we were apart and each came to the very edge of death seeking the other. That was too terrible and must never happen again. You are my sammadar—and I am your sammad. If you wish to cross the sea, we will cross the sea. But you will not go alone. I will go with you wherever you want to go. I will aid you with my strength and ask only a single thing. Never leave me again. We will both go together."

He understood for he felt the same way. Had been alone all of his life—as she had been—until he had found her. He had no words to speak his feelings and held to her tightly, as she did him.

But there were still dangers that must be considered.

"I must go," he said. "If you will go with me that will be better. But we cannot bring all the others until we are sure there is a safe place for them to go to."

For Armun this was a bad thought, a tearing thought. Must she leave her son here and cross the sea? Was there no alternative? She could think of none. It would have to be done this way. It was not a good answer—but it was the only answer. She would have to be the strong one and the practical one now. She considered carefully before she spoke.

"You yourself have said how safe it is here. Harl will hunt, he is no longer a child. Ortnar is needed to watch over everything until we return. Arnwheet and the girl will be no trouble—she is already learning to find plants in the forest, to cook and to do woman's work."

"You would leave the boy?" he asked, stunned. This is not what he would have expected.

"I would. He is everything to me and I do not wish to be parted from him—but I will leave him. I can go away from him, leave him in another's care until I return, I can do that. It is you whom I will never leave."

"I must think about this," Kerrick said, shocked by the granite-like hardness of her feelings, her resolve.

"There is nothing to think about," she said with steadfast determination. "It has been decided. Now you will make the detailed plans and we will do as you say."

The strength of her support forced him to believe that it could be done. What were the alternatives? Follow the sammads to the valley? And if they did not die during the march they would die there when Vaintè brought her poison thorns and darts, her numberless fargi. Stay here? It was a life with no future. There would only be a lifetime hiding here with the Yilanè city close by, and they would surely be discovered one day. It was all right for the two males, they had no choice, had nowhere else to go. Yet he would have to think about them as well; he must talk to them about his plan.

Imehei moaned aloud when he went to speak to them. "Do not leave again, too terrible to consider."

"Satisfactory here, desire you stay," Nadaskè said firmly.

Kerrick shaped his limbs into orders from her-on-high to lowest-creatures-below. "You will not be eaten or killed. Now all I ask you to do is simply to cross over with me to the other camp now and talk about this thing. I want you all there when I speak of the future. You do not fear fresh-from-sea, Arnwheet, and have marched with Ortnar. Nothing will happen to you. Now come."

It took a long time for him to convince them—but he was firm. His plans were made; he must cross the ocean and find a safe haven for his sammad. He was not going to let these two stand in his way. He forced them to go with him then, but they sat as far from the others as they could, leaning against each other, filled with fear.

Kerrick stood between the two groups. He looked at the two Yilanè males to one side, rigid with terror—or at least pretending to be. On the other side Ortnar sat slumped against a tree and glowered. The rest of the Tanu beside him seemed accustomed to the murgu now, particularly when Arnwheet crossed over and showed Imehei his latest treasure, a bone whistle that Ortnar had made. And there were no weapons present, he had seen to that.

It was going to be all right. It had to be all right. Perhaps this was only a plan born of desperation. That did not matter. He must see it through.

"What I am going to tell you now is important—to all of us," he said in Tanu, then turned to the Yilanè.

"A speaking-of-importance. Attention and obedience."

Then he told them all that Armun and he were going away for a time, but they would be back.

umnuniheikel tsanapsoruud marikekso.

YILANÈ APOTHEGM

========

*Good meat cannot be prepared without
the death of a beast.*

CHAPTER TWENTY-SEVEN

"And what are these," Vaintè asked, laying the pictures out on the work area before her.

"Just received—just formed," Anatempè said, sorting the prints in order in a line, then pointing at the nearby model of the Gendasi∗ landscape with her thumb. "A high-flying bird which went along this part of the coastline here, almost due west of us. The fleeing ustuzou could be along the shore here."

"But nothing is visible!" Vaintè made sharp snapping motions of disgust and annoyance. "There are only clouds in the picture."

"Unhappily that is true. But another bird has been dispatched—"

"And by the time it gets there the ustuzou will be long gone. I want *them*—not pictures of clouds!" Her hands shook with the violence of her emotions and she dashed all of the pictures to the ground with a sweep of her thumbs.

"I control the birds, but cannot control the clouds," Anatempè said, as meekly as she could, yet some of her true feelings penetrated her movements. She no longer enjoyed being the butt of Vaintè's foul moods. Vaintè saw this and her anger became cold and dangerous.

"You take issue with my orders? You find them offensive?"

"I obey your orders implicitly for I have been ordered to do so by Ukhereb who obeys the Eistaa. I seek only to do my duty." This last spoken with modifiers of eternal-service, obedience.

Vaintè started to remonstrate, then grew rigid and silent, signing only a curt dismissal to the scientist, letting her displeasure show only when the other had turned away. When she had been eistaa that sort of insult would have carried certain death as its reward. But there was too much truth in what the creature conveyed. Lanefenuu was Eistaa who ordered others and who ordered her. It was a situation she must live with. Turning about with disgust she saw the fargi standing just inside the entrance of the landscape model building. She had stood patiently for some time, waiting to catch Vaintè's attention.

"Message for Vaintè highest," she said, her meaning muffled by her weakness of language. Vaintè controlled her temper: the creature would forget the message or die of despair if she let it know just how she felt.

"I am Vaintè. Speak, carefully-slowly, I attend you."

"Yilanè Naalpè uruketo presence harbor communication requested."

It was almost to much to bear, but Vaintè still controlled her temper and wondered at her own patience. "Need for clarification. Are you informing me that Naalpè is now in the harbor aboard her uruketo and wishes to talk with me?"

"Agreement!" The fargi writhed with pleasure of communication and turned away at Vaintè's sign of dismissal, therefore she did not see Vaintè's glare of displeasure at the abominable quality of her speech. As she left her place was taken by a second fargi also signing desire-to-communicate.

"Do." Vaintè said curtly. "And strongly-desired superiority of speech over last messenger."

Far better indeed, because this one was from the Eistaa and she only used fargi whose speech was yilanè most of the time.

"Request from highest through lowest to Vaintè of rank. Warm salutations and upon completion of present labors presence desired in the ambesed."

"Return pleasure-of-acceptance to Eistaa, soonest arrival." No matter how politely it was expressed an order from the Eistaa was an order instantly obeyed. As much as she wanted to talk to Naalpè the meeting would have to wait.

But Vaintè was not going to hurry and arrive breathless and speechless. She moved along shadowed walks in the direction of the ambesed, knowing the messenger would be there first to report her compliance with the order.

Walking these familiar ways had a bitter-sweet taste for Vaintè. Sweet, in that the city was again Yilanè: bitter in that much of it was still in ruins—and the ustuzou had escaped. That they must never do. They would flee, but they would be found.

The large ambesed was quite empty, for only the advance forces had arrived from across the sea. The city must be repaired and regrown and further preparations made before Ikhalmenets came to Alpèasak. Its defenses strengthened, that was the first priority. No ustuzou must set foot in this city ever again. Lanefenuu was sprawled back in the warm sunlight in the place of honor against the far wall. There nobly dead Malsas< had sat, there Vaintè herself had sat and ruled once long ago when the city had been young. It was strange to see another there—and Vaintè instantly wiped away the feeling of jealousy that came to the fore. Never! She was no longer an eistaa nor did she want to rule ever again. Lanefenuu was an eistaa of power, one to respect and obey. In her generosity to Vaintè she had permitted her to prepare armed forces and enlist the genius of science to recapture this city. To kill ustuzou. Lanefenuu was an eistaa of two cities, a leader among leaders.

Lanefenuu saw these expressions clearly when Vaintè approached and accepted them as was her due. Her advisers drew back to make room for Vaintè in the attendant circle.

"An uruketo has arrived with reports and questions," Lanefenuu said. "The thought of it stirs me and I feel the need to once more breathe the air of sea-girt Ikhalmenets. I have been too long here and my nose-flaps close at the stench of ustuzou and smoke that drenches this city."

"It will be cleansed, Eistaa, just as you cleansed the city of the ustuzou who befouled it."

"Gracefully said and appreciated. Ukhereb will remain here and will oversee that process. It is a scientific one and not a political one so it will be her responsibility. Yours will be to watch and guard and preserve the city for the Yilanè. Is there clarity of meaning here?"

"With certainty, Eistaa. We shall not rule together but work together, one to build, one to guard. There is only one ruler here."

"Agreed. Now tell me of the ustuzou."

"Those that fled north are all dead. Though we are on constant guard, keeping watch in all directions always in case some are in hiding, for they are as deadly as serpents when concealed by the forest."

Lanefenuu signed agreement and understanding, with more than a trace of unhappiness.

"How well I am aware of that. Far too many Yilanè are dead who should have lived to see this city theirs again."

"Good meat cannot be prepared without the death of a beast." Vaintè offered this, with overtones of understanding, in at attempt at solace. But Lanefenuu's temper was short this day.

"There were just a few too many deaths, far more than you led me to believe. But that is in the past—though I still grieve for Erafnais who was close to me. There is a gap in my existence that she and that great uruketo filled."

The way the Eistaa shaded her meaning it seemed almost as if the loss of the uruketo, not the commander, was the more important. The listening circle stood motionless and obedient. As she reminded them, quite often, Lanefenuu had commanded an uruketo herself, before her elevation to Eistaa, so her feelings could be appreciated. When Lanefenuu silently touched thumb to arm in cognition of sadness-loss they echoed the motion sympathetically. But the Eistaa was too much a Yilanè of action to brood long. She looked at Vaintè with a query.

"Your ustuzou then, they are all gone?"

"Fleeing in fear and despair. We watch them at all times."

"None are close?"

"None. To the north, death. To the west—death follows and retribution waits."

"And you are sure of their destination?"

"I know where they go for I have been there before, seen it for myself. Their city will be their trap, their death. They shall not escape."

"They did last time," Lanefenuu said with brutal frankness.

Vaintè moved with remorse and acknowledgment of truth, hoping that her signs were strong enough to conceal her more than slight feelings of anger at this reminder. "I know this and accept the Eistaa's rebuke. If there is any value in past defeat it is preparation for future victory. This time the attack will be more subtle and more prolonged. The vines of death will grow about their city, throttle and kill it. There will be only corpses."

"That is acceptable—as long as they are ustuzou corpses. You were profligate with fargi on your last visit there. It will take an efenburu of males at the birth-beaches to replenish them."

Vaintè, like the others, stated only motionless acceptance. The Eistaa could be as vulgar as a low crew member when she wanted to be—but she was still Eistaa and could do just as she wished.

"After I leave you will command Yilanè and fargi of my city—and I hold each one of them dear."

"Their existence respected," Vaintè said, "guarded with my own life. My gratitude is great that you will permit me to pursue and kill these creatures before they can return and attack again. I will do this as I have been bid, filled with awareness of the preciousness of all Ikhalmenets lives to you."

There was no more to be said on the subject and when Vaintè asked for respectful withdrawal a motion of the Eistaa's thumb released her. She left the ambesed without unseemly haste, but once out of sight she moved faster in the gathering dusk. It was almost nightfall and she was most anxious to hear what Naalpè had to report.

The uruketo had been secured to the wharf where its cargo was still being unloaded. Its commander stood to one side, but when she saw Vaintè approach she signed one of her officers to take command and went to meet her.

"Greetings, Vaintè," signs of greatest respect. "Information to be conveyed, privacy important."

They moved out of sight of any watchers before Naalpè spoke again.

"As requested I stopped at Yebèisk upon our return voyage from Ikhalmenets. I spoke with many there and it was easy to learn of the one whose name you gave me because none talk of any other matter."

"Clarification of meaning requested." Vaintè was polite and concealed her growing impatience.

"This Enge, the Daughter of Death of whom you spoke, she went boldly to the eistaa and told of her beliefs, and for this she was imprisoned with others of her kind . . ."

"Excellent, most excellent and warming information, kind Naalpè—" She broke off as she saw the commander's signs of agitation and alarm.

"Not like that, not at all. How it happened does not seem to be clear, the details confused by time-elapsed and many opinions. What did happen I can vouch for with sincerity, because I myself talked to the commander of the uruketo. She spoke to me as she would to no other since ours is the same labor, told me what happened."

"But—what did happen?"

"The Enge you inquired after, she and all of the others, the others being all of the Daughters of Death in the city of Yebèisk, they boarded the uruketo and left. They could not be followed. No one knows where they have gone."

Vaintè froze, incapable of speech, her thoughts racing in circles of unknowingness. What could it mean? How had they done it? Who had aided her? How many were they? Gone where?

She spoke this last aloud but there was none to answer her.

"Gone . . . but *where*!?"

CHAPTER TWENTY-EIGHT

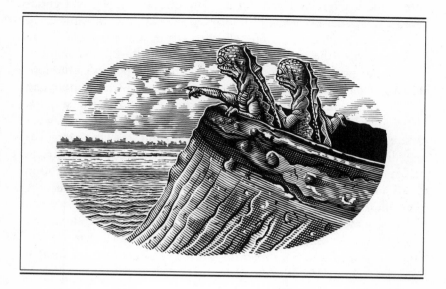

This land in the river delta was low-lying and half swamp. But a cypress tree had taken root on the southern tip, grown high and wide, its leafy branches creating a welcome pool of shade and relief from the blistering sun. Most of the Daughters were assembled here now, luxuriating in close study of Ugunenapsa's words. The circle of intent students sitting rigid with the effort of concentration, following Enge's every gesture and sound. When she had finished her explanation there was only silence as each looked inside herself, seeing if Ugunenapsa's words were hers as well.

"Questions?" Enge said.

Long moments passed before one of the students, a young, slim Yilanè, a recent convert, tentatively made a motion of attention. Enge signed authority-for-speaking. The student sought for clarity of expression, then spoke.

"Before Ugunenapsa recorded her thoughts, made this momentous discovery, were there others who, perhaps, contribution-of-effort . . ." She stumbled over her question and Enge came to her rescue.

"Are you asking if Ugunenapsa, our teacher was first in

everything—or did she learn from earlier teachers and thinkers?"
The student expressed grateful agreement. "If you study Ugunenapsa's works closely you will find her discussing just this question.
She *did* seek guidance from all the Yilanè thinkers who were
concerned with the questions of life and death, but found none to
aid her, no prior reference to the problem of its possible solution.
When she sought for an explanation of this, for she was humble and
would not think that she alone had been graced with singular
knowledge, she reached a certain conclusion. What lives and what
dies? she asked herself. A Yilanè may die, but a Yilanè city lives
forever. Yet at just this time a Yilanè city had died, the first one
ever recorded for she searched and searched and found no mention
of any other. Yet a city had died of the cold. Then she turned the
question over and asked it from the other side. If a city can live and
not die—why cannot a Yilanè live and not die? A city had died, just
as a Yilanè dies. She was humble and did not believe that the city
had died just to lead her to her discoveries. But grateful also in that
from death she had discovered life . . ."

"Attention, information of importance."

There was a murmur and movement of horror as Ambalasi
blocked their view of Enge, interrupting her while she was speaking. Only Enge remained undisturbed by the discourteous act.

"How may we be of aid to Ambalasi, she who salved us."
Reminding them all that the scientist deserved respect above all
others.

"I wait patiently for your talking to finish, but finally observe
it is endless. Therefore interruption. There is work that needs
doing before dark. I need strong thumbs to help me."

"Request for assistance, eager to help." Enge looked around at
her audience. "Which of you shall be first in the hurry to assist
Ambalasi?"

If Enge was eager to help, her cooperative mood was not
shared by the Sisters. They had obviously not relished the interruption and had no desire to substitute heavy labor for heady philosophizing. None moved, though one briefly communicated importance-
of-teaching. Enge was embarrassed, not angered, by their reluctance.

"I have failed you as a teacher," she said. "Ugunenapsa has
taught us that all life is equal, so all Yilanè are equal, and a request
for aid is to be honored as if it were a request for life." She turned

to Ambalasi and signed humility-of-submission. "I shall be the first to hurry to assist you."

At this the students forgot their pique and pushed forward to show their understanding and compassion.

"Without Enge's guidance you are stupid as fargi," said Ambalasi unappreciatively. "I need five of you to carry and assist in planting." She looked them up and down critically for many were thin and cerebral; selected the ones who looked the strongest and sent them off with her assistant for the supplies.

"You must excuse them," Enge said. "In their excitement of seeking knowledge they forget the labors of the day."

"Time-wasters, the lot. Walk with me, there are things we must discuss."

"Pleasure in obedience to desires."

"That is true, you sincerely feel that way. But you alone, Enge, you alone. I have never tried to work with creatures as resistant to orders as your Daughters of Lassitude."

Enge signed understanding and apologies. "There is a reason for this—as there is for everything. Pleasures of association and mutual discovery, without persecution for beliefs, is a strong mixture. It is hard to descend from the heights of cerebration to the depths of manual labor."

"Perhaps. But it must be done. To eat we must work; I wish you would tell them that with strength-of-argument. Did not Ugunenapsa once say that?"

"Never!"

"Better for all of us if she had. Now come to the shore here and look outward. Can you see the peninsula over there?"

"Not too clearly," Enge said, peering across the muddy rush of the river. This island was low and flat, as were all the islands of the estuary. Ambalasi made gestures of distaste then indicated the uruketo nearby.

"We can see better from the top of the fin."

Since there was no dock on this ready shore, the uruketo had been encouraged, by tempting it with fresh fish, to push a channel into the mud with its toothed beak. Now that it was well fed it kept its head wedged into the opening it had made. They stepped carefully onto its slippery, muddy hide and clambered toward the dorsal fin above. The uruketo's round, bone-refinforced eye moved slightly when they passed, but this was the creature's only re-

sponse. They hooked thumbs and toe-claws into the rough skin and
climbed. Enge going very slow to match the efforts of the elderly
scientist.

"At times . . . I am that sorry I ever decided to leave
Yebèisk . . ." Ambalasi said, gasping with the effort. "But no
sacrifice is too great to advance knowledge. You and I know that,
but this intelligence is lost upon your followers."

Enge made no response, other than signing agreement, re-
specting Ambalasi's age and intelligence—and knowing from experience that if anything were to be accomplished, other than
interminable arguments, it was better to agree with her most of the
time. Ambalasi gaped in air, looked about and registered displeasure, finally recovered enough breath to enable her to talk clearly.

"Look there, you can make it out from up here, on the
peninsula, the green patch."

From this height the long narrow neck of land in the bend of
the river, that was to be their city, could be clearly seen. All of the
vegetation was yellow and dead—except for a green line in the
distance.

"The wall of thorns," Ambalasi said with satisfaction, the first
sign of pleasure she had displayed this day. "The fungus infection
has killed off the rest of the plant life—it goes without my saying
that the thorns are immune—and the animals have fled or died for
lack of nourishment. It is almost time for our ecology to replace the
native one."

"You will plant the seed of the city and it will grow high and
strong." Enge signed great pleasure—which vanished before the
angry burst of Ambalasi's anger.

"End-of-intelligence, closure-of-mind. I make some attempt to
study your absurd philosophy—is it asking too much for you to pay
attention and understand the most basic facts of the biological
sciences? Why are we living in discomfort on this swampy island?
We are doing that because it is surrounded by water—as are all
islands. The swift-moving stream protects us from being consumed
by the carnivores of the mainland. It also means we sleep under
rough covering and eat only the few tasteless fish that your sisters
so reluctantly catch. We do this while we wait for the wall of thorns
to grow that will protect our city. And while we do this we admire
and feed the young hèsotsan so they will mature quickly and supply
us with weapons to defend ourselves. We do this while we wait for

the boats in the pond to mature so we can use them instead of the uruketo which is not suited for inshore work. What we do *not* do is plant the highly-precious city seed!"

"Interrogative expressed with humble desire for knowledge. Why not?"

"Why not? Why not?" Ambalasi's ragged crest flared red, as did the palms of her outstretched hands. "Because if we planted it at this time it would be eaten by worms, consumed by beetles, destroyed by fungus, crushed under foot by one of your clumsy Daughters!"

"Now I understand," Enge said calmly. "Apologies extended for ignorance."

Ambalasi turned to look across the river, muttering to herself with sharp growls and twitches of her limbs. When she had composed herself she picked up the lecture again.

"I think that the thorn wall is high enough for protection now. I want a large force, at least half your number, to cross with me in the morning. If our flank is secured we will begin the much-needed labors of clearing the land, spreading the carefully nurtured larvae to purify the soil. Then we will add the nitrogen-fixing bacteria, followed by the shrubs of rapid-growth, rapid-decay for fertilizer. *Then*, if all goes well, and I say that the time is ripe, then we plant the city seed. Is it remotely possible that now my meaning is clear?"

"Admirably so," Enge said, majestically immune to sarcasm. "And I thank you for the detailed explanation. I now await your orders."

"I wish that the others did. That is the next problem. We need some leadership here, someone to tell these worthless creatures what to do."

"Indeed that is our problem," Enge agreed enthusiastically, "for that is what brings us here. My Sisters, who are willing to die for their beliefs, do so by first understanding the inability of an eistaa to destroy them, then relish the joy of that newfound freedom. They will work together, they will not be ordered to."

"If they won't be led—how may they be induced to follow?"

"A very serious question—and one I have pondered over deeply."

"You had better ponder a little more deeply and a little more quickly," Ambalasi said testily. "Or we may all be dead before you have found a solution. All social creatures have a leader, a decision-maker—look there." She indicated a school of bright, tiny fish in the water alongside. Something disturbed them and they turned instantly, heading off in a new direction.

"One of them is always first," Ambalasi said. "When bees swarm they follow the new queen. Ants have a queen from whose fruitful loins all the others spring. As ants, so Sisters. They must be led."

"I understand the problem . . ."

"You do not. If you did you would give it the highest priority, the first attention. Your play-groups and discussions would stop and you would address yourself to this problem, the only problem, until a solution was reached. There must be leadership, delegation of authority, cooperation."

"You have just described an eistaa and her joined descent of command," Enge said calmly. "That is what we have rejected."

"Then find something to put in its place before we all die of starvation or are eaten by the creatures of the night." She was aware of a motion for attention and turned to Elem who had joined them on the fin. "Speak."

"Apologies for interruption: matter of great importance. The uruketo has been too long on the shore. We must go to sea, beyond the river mouth."

"Impossible!" Ambalasi qualified this with dismissal-from-presence which Elem steadfastly ignored.

"I beg permission to amplify reasons. They were explained to me by the commander of the uruketo, a long time ago, when I served as a crewmember. Memory returns as I observe the uruketo now. And the enteesenat who plunge in the water and utter shrill cries. It is time to go to sea, away from these muddy waters, for this creature must feed."

"Tomorrow. After we have crossed to the city site."

"No. Too late. We swim now with the tide. We must be one or two days at sea. That is most important."

Enge tensed her muscles and waited for Ambalasi to turn and maim this upstart who went against her will. But she had forgotten that Ambalasi was a scientist first and always.

"You are right, of course. Make sure that it is well fed before your return for it is needed. And in the future give me advance warning before any of these feeding trips."

"As you order, so shall I obey."

"Our expedition will wait. Perhaps this delay is fortuitous. You have two days to solve your problem. Let us go ashore."

"I despair of an answer in that time. This is not an easy problem because it strikes close to the very heart of our beliefs."

Ambalasi stopped when they reached the ground and settled back onto her tail, suddenly very tired. There was far too much physical work to do and she was not used to it. Enge waited patiently as the scientist, deep in thought watched the river, only half-aware, as the uruketo moved out. There was much splashing and thrashing before it worked itself clear of the bank, then turned and followed the excited enteesenat downriver toward the sea. Ambalasi closed her eyes for a long time, then opened them and turned one toward Enge's silently expectant form.

"Desire to make suggestion."

"Respectful of great wisdom, keenly attentive."

"Reverse the decision-making, look at the question from the other side, if I may quote your Ugunenapsa. Let decisions come from the bottom, not the top. You are Daughters of Life, so the basic needs of life must be your basic tenets. We will begin with one of them. Food. Do you follow this line of reasoning so far?"

Enge signed respect and comprehension. "I admire as well the clarity of your thought processes and exposition."

"As well you might—since the burden of all responsibility here seems to fall upon my strong shoulders. Repetition of argument. Food. Once you get them to admit that they need food to live, ask them if they wish to obtain it collectively or individually."

"Wonderful!" Enge radiated agreement and enthusiasm. "Permit me to continue your thought. As we did in the sea, collectively catching schools of fish, so shall we do in the efenburu of sisterhood. We will all catch fish . . ."

"No! You are missing the point. You are no longer yilieb young in the ocean, but Yilanè with the need to work together for your mutual good. *Some* of you must be selected to fish for all the others, and one of the group of fishers must order the others in the manner of fishing."

"I understand and appreciate your point. But this decision will be difficult, difficult."

Ambalasi was in complete agreement. "That is the story of survival: nothing is easy. We have had our cities so long we forget that once we competed on equal terms with all of the other life forms. Now we bend them to our will. And now we had better find a way to bend your Sisters before they become prematurely extinct."

It took most of the entire day of discussion before the Daughters reached an agreement. Ambalasi busied herself with her seedlings and growing animals, registering extremes-of-disgust only when her glance passed over the talking multitude. When Enge approached her in the late afternoon she looked up with an expression of expectancy and impatience

"Can it be that we will have fish after all?"

"A decision has been reached that conforms to all of Ugunenapsa's teachings. Equality in all things, equality of effort. Ten of us will fish at a time, for ten is a complete number that represents the total of the fingers of two hands that will be doing the work. The first of the ten will lead the ten and issue the orders for the first day. On the second day the second of the ten will be in command, and so on, until the tenth of the ten commands and on the following day the next ten will take their place and so on until all have served—then the tens of tens of tens will begin over again. Is that not a circular, complete and satisfying solution?"

Ambalasi signed disgust and horror. "Absolute rubbish! The most confusing bit of nonsense I have ever heard. What was wrong with appointing a fisher-in-charge who will choose all the others— all right. I see your frenzied motions—it would not be Ugunenapsa's way. So do it as you have decided. When does the fishing begin?"

"Now. And I am first of the ten. We go with pleasure to supply the food for all."

Ambalasi watched Enge's receding back, erect and proud. It was unbelievable. But understandable. And analyzable. Once you trapped yourself in a belief you had to follow through to the very end of all its permutations—or abandon the belief. She was beginning to regret her journey into the realms of darkest philosophy. Delicately, she cleaned the dirt from the roots of the seedling she was transplanting. How true, clear and satisfying biology was by comparison! But she dare not shy away. Their repellent philosophy produced biological results. She was determined to probe and discover the reasons for this. It was hard to be the first in science, the first in intelligence, the first in reason. Ambalasi sighed happily: it was a burden she would just have to bear.

CHAPTER TWENTY-NINE

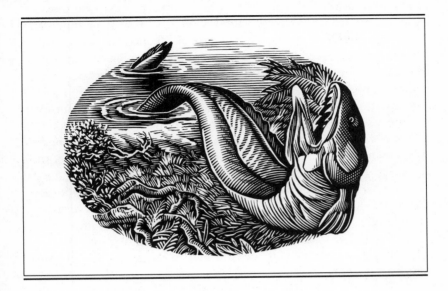

"Attention and urgency, attention and urgency!"

The Yilanè was repeating herself incoherently like a fargi. Ambalasi looked up from her work prepared to indulge her biting temper. But she saw that the mud-covered creature was shaking with worry and fear so she signed for explanation-amplification instead.

"One is injured while fishing. A bite, much blood."

"Wait—then take me to her."

Ambalasi kept a bundle of medical needs ready for just such emergencies. She found it and handed it over. "Carry this—and proceed."

They pushed through the circle of excited Daughters to find Enge kneeling in the mud, supporting the head of a blood-drenched Yilanè.

"Quickly," she implored. "It is Efen, she who is closest to me. I have covered the wound to staunch the flow of blood."

Ambalasi looked down at the blood-sodden wad of leaves that Enge held to the other's side. "An intelligent action, Enge," she said. "Hold it there still while I bring some comfort."

The little snake lay coiled and sluggish in its basket. Ambalasi took it behind the head and squeezed it so that its mouth opened and exposed the single long fang. With her free hand she took out a nefmakel and exposed its moist underside, used it to wipe clean the skin in Efen's groin. This not only cleaned off the mud—it destroyed any bacteria with its antiseptic action. She discarded the creature and pressed Efen's damp skin to reveal the artery pulsing there; with delicate touch pushed the sharp fang into it. The modified venom flowed into Efen's blood; she was unconscious within moments. Only then did Ambalasi uncover the wound.

"A clean bite. It took out a lot of muscle but did not penetrate the omentum. I'll just have to clean it up a bit." The string knife removed the ragged flesh. As the wound began to bleed again she unrolled a larger nefmakel and placed it over the damaged area. The creature stuck there, stopping the bleeding and sealing it completely. "Take her some place to rest. She will be all right."

"Gratitude to Ambalasi as always," Enge said, rising slowly.

"Wash yourself—you are filthy with mud and blood. What creature bit her?"

"That." Enge indicated the riverbank. "It was tangled in our net."

Ambalasi turned to look—and for the first time in living memory was struck speechless.

It was still alive, writhing on the ground, crushing bushes and small trees. A great, undulating gray length, as thick through as a fargi's body, stretched out on the ground the length of two, three Yilanè—with more of its serpentine form still in the water. Its jaw of great bony plates gaped wide, its tiny and deadly eyes staring sightlessly.

"We have found it," Ambalasi said finally, with some satisfaction. "You saw the elvers in midocean. This is the adult."

"An eel?" Enge signed awe and understanding. "This new world of Ambalasokei is indeed a world of many surprises."

"By its very nature it must be," Ambalasi said, sinking back into her normal didactic personality now that the first shock of recognition had passed. "I doubt if you are capable of understanding the theory of tectonic plates and continental drift so I will not trouble your mind with it. But you will be able to appreciate the results. This land, and distant Entoban* were once one. All of the creatures were the same. This was soon after the cracking of the egg of time. Since then slow differentiation and the process of natural selection have caused major changes—*must* have caused major changes in the species. I imagine we will find others, though none perhaps as dramatic as this."

Within a few days Ambalasi was to remember saying this with some chagrin. It was perhaps the most erroneous assumption that she had ever made.

Efen's wound healed easily. On the positive side of the accident was the acquisition of the large eel. It was gigantic—and very tasty, and fed them all with much left over. Stronger nets were constructed, more precautions taken, and their source of food guaranteed. Softened by enzymes, it was the best food they had known since their imprisonment.

When the well-fed uruketo returned they used it to cross the river to the site of their new city. The Daughters were eager to see this place of great importance and there was no shortage of volunteers for this expedition.

"Would that this eagerness for work was more evenly apportioned," Ambalasi grumbled, selected only the strongest then drove the rest away. As soon as they were aboard, and despite their protests, she ordered them all into the interior, sharing the fin-top only with Enge and Elem.

"Make note," Ambalasi ordered, "that your Sisters while avoiding all real work are always ready to volunteer for an outing. Perhaps you ought to consider some system of awards for labor since you cannot order them to do it."

"There is much truth in what you say, as always, and I will think about it," Enge said. "Although I understand them and know their feelings, yet I also know that we must devise some way of sharing the work. I will study the thoughts of Ugunenapsa more closely because she may have considered this problem as well."

"Study quickly or we starve. I assume you have noted the breakdown already in your voluntary fishing organization? With earlier tens feeling cheated now that later tens are not working as hard as they did before the eels were caught. They are already asking for a reorganization of the system."

"I know—and I grieve. It has my fullest attention."

The uruketo shuddered beneath them as the ponderous creature swam aside to avoid a floating tree that was sweeping down the river in their direction. A forest giant that had been undercut by the flood until it had toppled in. Birds flew up from its still-green foliage as it drifted majestically by them. Under Elem's guidance the uruketo turned again and drew up to the neck of land that was to be their city.

Ambalasi climbed down first and splashed ashore. The ground was covered with yellowed, dead shrubbery, with the bare branches of the dead trees stark above. Ambalasi made a sharp sign of satisfaction.

"The beetles will soon take care of the trunks and stumps. Put your Daughters to work pulling down branches and small trees. Throw everything into the river. Then we will inspect the barrier of thorns."

Ambalasi led the way, walking slowly in the heat. Before they reached the green wall they had to stop in the meager shadow of a skeletal tree to cool before they could go on.

"Hot," Enge said with some difficulty, her jaw thrown wide.

"Of necessity, since we are precisely on the equator, a geographical term you would not be acquainted with."

"The place on the surface of a sphere equidistant from the poles that mark the axis of rotation." Enge was looking at the barrier so missed Ambalasi's gesture of irritation. "In my attempts to understand Ugunenapsa's works I discovered that her philosophy was based in part upon her study of certain natural sciences. So I emulated her fine example . . ."

"Emulate my fine example and let us keep walking. We must be absolutely sure there are no breaks in the barrier. Come."

As they walked along beside the wall of flat leaves and sharp thorns, Ambalasi reached in among the branches to remove ripe seed pods, which she gave to Enge to carry. When they reached the riverbank Ambalasi pointed out the gap between the barrier and the water.

"Always this way at the interface," she said. "I'll plant more seeds here, also these seeds for thick shrubs that root in the water. Hold them for me."

The elderly scientist kicked grooves in the mud with a practiced swipe of the claws on one foot while balancing on the other, then bent over, puffing and complaining, to plant the seeds.

Enge looked out into the river to the place further down the bank where a small sidewater joined the larger body of the great stream. Something moved there, swimming into the river, a large fish of some kind. She loked with interest as another one followed, emerging from the water for an instant.

"More seeds," Ambalasi said. "A sudden attack of deafness," she added with irritation when she turned to see Enge standing in silence, looking out at the river. "What is the matter?" she asked when there was still no response.

"There in the water, I saw it, gone now." She spoke with modifiers of such grave importance that Ambalasi turned at once, looking, seeing nothing.

"What was it?"

Enge turned back to the scientist with motions of life and death importance. Hesitating in silence before she spoke.

"I have now thought deeply and have considered all living creatures that I know that bear a resemblance. There is none it could possibly be confused with. The first one I saw unclearly, it could have been anything. The second put its head above the water. I saw it. I am not mistaken. It was there."

"Desire for explanation," Ambalasi said testily in the silence that followed. Enge faced her, still in silence and immobility, looked long into her eyes before she spoke.

"I realize the importance of what I am about to say. But I make no mistake.

"There, in the stream, I saw a young elininyil."

"Impossible. We are the first Yilanè to reach this place; there are no males so no eggs to hatch, no young to enter the sea, no elininyils to grow to fargi. Impossible. Unless . . ."

It was Ambalasi's turn to grow silent and rigid, with just shadows of thoughts rippling her muscles. It was a long time before she spoke.

"It is not impossible. When I spoke just now I was speaking with species specific ethnocentricity. Because we Yilanè are at the summit of the ecological pyramid we automatically assume—I automatically assume—that we are alone there, something special and singular. Do you know what I am saying?"

"No. Personal ignorance of technical concepts."

"Understandable. I will explain. Distant Entoban∗ is ours—our cities there stretch through all the habitable areas between the oceans. But now we are in a new world, where life forms have developed and differed. There is no reason to assume that our species is unique to Entoban∗. It could be here as well."

"Then—I did see an elininyil?"

"You might very well have. That is a possible conclusion. We

must now make observation to see if you were correct. If you did
see it—then I believe that this is the most important event since
the egg of time cracked. Come!"

Ambalasi waddled down the bank and hurled herself into the
river with an excess of scientific fervor. Enge quickly followed,
frighteningly aware of possible danger lurking in the muddy waters.
The current was slight in the backwater here and Ambalasi quickly
reached the channel and started up it. It came only to her waist and
she found it easier to walk than to swim.

Enge hurried up, going past the elderly scientist to lead the
way. Low branches overhung the stream and the air was thick and
humid, filled with biting insects. The flowing water kept them cool
enough, but when the channel widened out they plunged beneath
the surface to escape the insects. They surfaced, treading water,
looking about, unable to communicate other than the most simple
concepts until they had climbed out on the grassy bank.

"We are clearly on another island, separated from ours by this
side channel of the river. Warm water of a constant temperature,
yet shallow enough to keep the larger predators from entering.
If—and I accentuate the if—there are Yilanè here this would be a
perfect site for the birth-beach. Water protected from the large life
forms in the river, plenty of fish for the young to eat. And ready
access to the river and the sea when the young have grown and
become elininyil."

"This could be a path about the island," Enge said, pointing at
the ground.

"And it could be an animal track. We will follow it."

Enge went first, beginning to regret their precipitous venture.
They were unarmed—and any sort of creature could be hidden by
the jungle.

The track was easy to follow. It swung around the bole of a
large tree that had long roots extending into the river, then back to
the shore to a sandy beach bordered with soft grass. They shared
the same thought instantly; a perfect place for a birth-beach. Something splashed in the water, but when they looked it was gone
leaving only a pattern of ripples on the smooth surface.

"I feel that we are being watched," Enge said.

"Proceed forward."

The track skirted the beach and entered the thick stand of
trees on the far side. They stopped before it, trying to look into the

gloom beneath the heavy foliage. Enge made a sharp gesture of unhappiness.

"I think that we have come far enough. We must return to the others. We will come back here when we are better prepared."

"We must uncover more facts."

Ambalasi said this firmly, signed knowledge-primacy, walked forward past Enge.

With a screeching cry the creature burst from behind the trees, holding a large spider between her out-thrust thumbs, pushing it into Ambalasi's face.

CHAPTER THIRTY

Abalasi fell back before the unexpected attack. Enge jumped in front of her, thumbs extended and snapping with anger, shouting commands.

"Go back! Cease! Error-of-doing!"

The newcomer did not press the attack—though she still held the spider extended before her. She gaped at the two Yilanè with obvious fear. Then turned and fled.

"You saw her," Enge said, more statement than question.

"I saw. Physically identical to us in most ways. Opposed thumbs grasping the insect. Shorter in height, stockier, light green in coloring becoming darker on the back and along the crest."

"Admiration at observation. I saw simply a figure."

"Scientific training of course. Now consider! This is wonderful, remarkable, a truly important discovery. For social historians as well as biologists."

Enge was keeping one eye on the jungle—she wanted no repeats of the unexpected attack—and was listening to Ambalasi with her other eye. She signed ignorance and query. Ambalasi was exuberant.

"Biology of course for all the obvious reasons. But that spider—do you not instantly think of the wall of history? No, you wouldn't. Listen and be guided. You must recall the shells of lobsters, placed there to mark the dawn of our existence when Yilanè were supposed to have brandished them as weapons in defense of the males. Now we have proof that the theory is indeed fact. Wonderful!"

"But—I saw no lobster . . ."

"Creature-of-ignorance! It is the similarity, the action that I am talking about. In the sea brandishing a clawed lobster for defense is what would have been done. On land, as we have seen, a poisonous insect serves the same function."

"Information understood. But we must leave, come back with others, this is a most dangerous place to be. Threats of death by poison."

"Nonsense. She was just threatening us, a defense reaction since she did not press the attack home. Did you not see the confusion in her movements? We are her kind—yet not her kind. Uncertainty of threat, then retreat. I must consider the way to continue this contact without alarming them more."

"Ambalasi, I cannot order you to return—but I can implore you. We can then come back here with help . . ."

"Negative. The more of us that there are the more frightened they will be. We have been warned—but not attacked. That is the situation at the present moment, and I do not want it changed. I shall remain here. You will go into the river and catch a fish."

Enge could only communicate doubt and confusion.

"Think," Ambalasi commanded. "You pride yourself on your powers of rationality. The feeding ceremony, we still use it on important occasions, it must surely be as old as social custom. What is more sisterly than an offer of food? A sharing of sustenance and existence. A fish is now needed."

The old scientist irascibly rejected all arguments and communication, simply settled back comfortably onto her tail with a last imperative *fish!* and stared at the forest, her limbs shaped into welcome and warmth. Enge had no choice but to turn and walk into the river, diving beneath the surface.

There she saw them, a sight to bring happiness to any Yilanè. An immature efenburu gliding through the clear water, scarcely elininyil, the youngest of the young groupings, they were so small, moving in pursuit of a school of silver fish. She watched for a long moment until they saw her, turned with colored signs of fear on their palms. She raised her own palms telling them not to be afraid. But they were, she was too strange, and in an instant they were gone. One of them had been holding a freshly caught fish, had just bitten through its spine, and now she released it in panic as she rushed away. Enge swam forward and retrieved it, returned to shore.

Ambalasi looked at the small fish with doubt. "Speed of fishing produces tiny catch," she said.

"I didn't catch it. I surprised an immature efenburu, disturbed their feeding. They were attractive beyond measure."

"Undoubtedly. The fish will have to do. Remain here while I go forward."

"You may order, I will not obey. I will walk behind you, then move forward to assist you if there is danger."

Ambalasi began to speak, realized it would only be a waste of effort, and signed reluctant agreement. "At least five paces behind me. We proceed."

She held the tiny fish before her and walked slowly along the path, stopping before she entered the grove.

"Fish, tasty, nice, friendship," she said loudly but pleasantly. Then she settled back slowly on her tail, the fish still held out before her, and repeated her entreaties. Something stirred in the darkness and she did her best to convey warmth and friendship in the simplest manner.

The leaves parted and the stranger came reluctantly out. They examined each other in silence for the moment, Ambalasi with the skill of the scientist. All differences appeared to be superficial. Size, structure, surface coloration. A subspecie at most. With slow movements she bent and placed the fish on the grass, then stood and slowly stepped back.

"It is yours. A gift of friendship. Take it and eat. Take it, it is yours."

The other looked confused, drew back a bit and opened her mouth with lack of comprehension. Perfect dentition, Ambalasi observed. She must simplify.

"Fish-for-eating," she said, using the very simplest expression, non-verbal and simple color-change in her palms. The other raised her hand.

"Fish," she color-signed. Bent and seized it up, turned and fled from sight once again.

"Excellent first contact," Ambalasi said. "That is enough for today, and I grow tired. We return. Did you see what she said?"

Enge was radiant with excitement. "I did, it was wonderful! There is a theory of communication that begins in this manner. It assumes that we learned to speak in the ocean, physically at first, then with greater skill and verbalization."

"It makes biological sense as well. Non-verbal communication would appear to be universal in the sea. When our species separated from theirs, signed-colored speaking must have existed—or we would not have been able to communicate just now. The question is—are they Yilanè or yiliebe? Is this primitive signing all that they know? I must find out. There is much work to be done with them."

Enge was just as enthusiastic. "It is an opportunity never presented before! What pleasure. I have long studied communication and look forward expectantly to further work."

"I am pleased to hear that you have interests other than your life-death philosophizing. You will join me in this project, for there is much to be done."

They made their way back to the riverbank, but they were now more hesitant about plunging into the river. No longer carried away by excitement they were fully aware of the dangers beneath the surface: they attempted to stay in the shallows as they worked their way around the growing barrier. Smeared with mud, uncaring, they made their way back through the dead plants. The Daughters of Life were gathered by the uruketo, talking. Ambalasi looked about with growing anger.

"The work has not been done! No excuses for sloth-laziness-unsuitability."

Enge signed a query as well and Satsat, who was at the center of the circle, requested permission to speak.

"Far< requested permission to address us all. Of course we listened, for she is a deep thinker. Now we discuss her thoughts—"

"She will speak for herself!" Ambalasi said with growing disgust. "Which of you Daughters of Talk is Far<?"

Enge indicated a thin Yilanè with large, intense eyes, who filled her days with Ugunenapsa's thoughts. She signed them all to attend her, then spoke.

"Ugunenapsa said that—"

"Silence!" Ambalasi ordered, using the rudest form of address, from highest to lowest fargi. Far< colored at the insult. "We hear far too much of Ugunenapsa's thoughts. I asked why you stopped the work here?"

"I did not stop it—I just suggested it be examined. It is because we all came to this place of labor of our free will. But once we had arrived here you issued orders as to what we were to do, yet you did not ask how or why we wanted to work, but simply and as imperiously as an eistaa issued orders. But we do not take orders. We have come too far, have suffered too much for our beliefs to abandon them at this time. We are grateful, of course, but gratitude does not imply servitude. As Ugunenapsa said—"

Ambalasi did not hear what Ugunenapsa had said this time, but turned to Enge and signed urgency of attention.

"This is the end of my patience, end of my help. I know all that must be done; your Daughters of Stupidity know nothing but argument. I am through—unless you convince them quickly that interference must stop. Without my assistance you will all soon be dead and I am beginning to feel that that day would be a very happy one for me. I now go to the uruketo, to cleanse myself, to eat and drink and compose my thoughts. When I return you will tell me if you wish a city here. And if you do, you will tell me how cooperation will be achieved. Now—silence, until I am out of sight. I wish to hear nothing of your discussion, nor do I wish to hear the name Ugunenapsa uttered in my presence again without my permission to speak it."

With every line of her body radiating anger and firmness of purpose she turned and stamped away toward the uruketo, nail gouges in the dirt marking her path. After rinsing herself at the river's edge she clambered onto the uruketo and settled in the shade of its fin, calling out for attention as she did so. Elem emerged from the fin and looked down from above.

"Food and water," Ambalasi ordered. "Speed of delivery. Urgency."

Elem brought them herself, for she respected the scientist for her great intelligence, forgiving her all insults with gratitude for knowledge gained. Ambalasi saw this in the movements of her body and was mollified.

"Your scientific interests far outweigh your philosophical bent," she said. "You are a better individual for it and I can bear your presence."

"Kind thoughts from above equal to warm rays of the sun."

"And you are yilanè with gracious speaking as well. Share my meat and let me tell you of a scientific discovery that is incredible in its magnitude."

Time was taken in the telling for Elem was a most satisfactory audience. The sun was on its way down the sky when Ambalasi finished and returned to the land. The first thing she saw, with a great deal of satisfaction, was that the Daughters were now working to clear the dead undergrowth. Enge put down an armload of wood and turned to speak with the scientist choosing her expressions carefully in order to obey the edict not to mention the name of Ugunenapsa.

"We discussed the work here in the light of our beliefs. A decision was reached. We must live, for we are the Daughters of Life. To live we must have a city to live in. The city must be grown. You are the only one who can grow a city. To grow the city we will take your instruction since we must do that in order to live. So now we work."

"So I see. But only *now* as you have just told me. When the city is grown will you then stop taking my orders?"

"I have not considered all of the implications of thinking that far ahead," Enge said with an attempt at evasion.

"Think. Speak."

She must, though with great reluctance. "It is my belief that when the city is grown—the Daughters will no longer obey your orders."

"I thought not. I hesitated to consider any future for them other than certain death. For the moment, for my own comfort, I accept this weak and dispirited arrangement. There is too much of importance to be done here to involve myself with more argument now." She held up her hand and displayed the large portion of jellied meat held between her thumbs. "I return to the jungle to continue my contact with those we met. Will you accompany me?"

"With utmost pleasure and joy-in-tomorrow. This will be a rich city, rich with life and scientific endeavor."

"The scientific endeavor, yes. But I do not see a favorable existence for your Daughters of Disagreement, followers of she-who-shall-be-nameless. I think that your theory of life will one day be your death."

Imame qiviot ikagpuluarpot
takuguvsetame.

PARAMUT SAYING

═══════════

*There are more paths on the sea than
you can find in a forest.*

CHAPTER THIRTY-ONE

It was the waiting now, the not-knowing, that bothered Armun. At first it had been all right, once the decision had been made to leave the camp by the lake there had been no turning back, no hesitation on her part. If anything she had been the strong one, forcing Kerrick again and again to remember that it had been a good decision—and the only one possible. Whenever she found him sitting, grim with worry, she patiently went through their reasons for deciding to leave—yet once again. They had no other choice. They had to go.

Arnwheet, the one they were both most concerned about, seemed to care the least. He had never been parted from his mother so could not understand what it would be like. Darras, who was finally getting over her nightmares, was not happy about the change at all and cried a lot. Ortnar did not care one way or the other—while Harl could not wait for them to leave. Then he would be the only hunter, the sole provider.

But the two Yilanè were sure that their end had come. Imehei was composing his death song. Nadasakè was determined to die fighting and kept his hèsotsan close by him at all times. Kerrick understood their fears—but rejected them. The two halves of sammad

Kerrick had a working relationship now and would have to go on like that. There was no need for it to change. The Yilanè were adept at catching the lake fish and crustacea, swimming out at dawn to set their traps and nets. But they were indifferent hunters at the best. Because of this an equal trade had been established, fish for meat, and all those concerned were pleased with the arrangement. Arnwheet, the only one welcome without suspicion in both camps, took care of the exchanges, proudly staggering under the weight of his burdens. The males would be safe—they would all be safe enough as long as their presence here was not discovered.

Leaving, getting to the headland by the sea, all that had gone easily and well. With no responsibilities or cares they had looked to each other, reveling in the newfound freedom and closeness. Many times they even walked hand-in-hand through the summer warmth. No true hunter would have done that, there must only be silence and watchfulness on the track, but Armun appreciated this even more.

That had been during the first days. But now the waiting was a strain in their camp above the bay, looking out at the empty ocean day after day. Kerrick was in a dark and sullen mood, would sit staring out over the sea, watching for the Paramutan ikkergak that never came. He sat there and did not hunt; their meat was almost gone, and he did not seem to care. Armun knew that when he was like this and if she spoke to him, she would say too much—or too little—so she stayed away during the daytime gathering the roots and plants that made up the larger part of their diet now.

It was early afternoon and her basket was less than half-full when Armun heard him calling through the trees. There was something wrong! But her fear subsided as she listened again; he was shouting something, excitedly. She ran toward him, calling out as well, and they met in the tiny meadow of high grass and yellow flowers.

"They're here, the Paramutan, coming toward the beach!"

He seized her and spun her about so that they both fell and her basket spilled. They refilled it together until he took hold of her again and they rolled in the long grass.

"We cannot, not now," she said gently. "We don't want them to leave without us."

When they came down to the little bay the black form of the ikkergak, sail lowered, was rocking in the offshore shallows. There was waving and shouting as they splashed out to it: willing hands pulled them aboard. Angajorqaq was there, eyes round and worried in the smooth fur of her face, her hands clapped over her mouth.

"Alone," she wailed. "The two boys—gone . . ."

Kalaleq clambered over to them while Armun was explaining about the children, lumps of deliciously rotten meat held out in welcome greeting.

"Eat, be happy, there are many things to be told about—" Kerrick stopped him with upraised hand.

"Slowly, please . . . understanding difficult."

He had forgotten the little Paramutan he had learned during the winter; he called to Armun. She listened to the rush of words, then translated for him.

"They have gone—all of the rest of the Paramutan, across the ocean to a place he calls Allanivok. This ikkergak is the last one to leave. They have found the schools of ularuaq and a good shore where they can do something, I don't know what the word means, flensing. They have taken everything, the small boats, the paukaruts, all the children, everyone." There was fear in her voice when she said this.

"You think that if we go with them—we will never get back here? Ask him about it, now."

"It is a long voyage," Kalaleq said. "You will like it there—you won't want to come back."

"Thick of skull, eyes that cannot see!" Angajorqaq said loudly, striking him with her closed fist on his brown-furred arm. But it was a light blow, intended only to draw his attention to the importance of her words. "Tell Armun now that when she wishes to return to this land, that you will take her—or do you wish to separate her from her first-born male child for the rest of her life?"

Kalaleq smiled, frowned, struck himself on the forehead to show his chagrin. "Of course, an easy voyage, we will go when you want, this is never a problem to one who knows the winds and the sea as I do."

After shouted greetings from everyone else aboard there was the suggestion made that perhaps this would be a good day to start on the voyage to Allanivok. They could leave now, there was no reason to stay. With the Tanu aboard there was nothing else to do on this side of the ocean. Once the decision had been made, with typical Paramutan enthusiasm. They hurled themselves into the task. All the waterskins were taken ashore, rinsed and refilled from the stream. The instant they were all back aboard the ikkergak was pushed off the beach, swung about to catch the wind. The lines to the sail were tightened, and the voyage began. Their course was northeast so they slowly drew away from the shore. The land grew more distant and before sunset had vanished completely. When the sun dropped below the horizon they were alone in the ocean.

The pitching and rolling of the ikkergak made it very easy to refuse the offer of decayed meat and rich blubber: seasickness struck both Tanu down. Once the others had finished eating most of them crawled under the forward shelter and fell asleep. It was a warm night and the air was fresher outside; Armun and Kerrick stayed where they were.

"Do you know how long it will take us to make the crossing?" Kerrick asked. Armun laughed.

"I asked Kalaleq that. A number of days he said. Either they don't count very well—or they don't care."

"A little of both. They don't seem to be worried at all being away from shore like this. How do they find their way and not sail in circles?"

As though in answer to their question, Kalaleq climbed up next to the mast and held to it with one hand, swaying as they rode up on the easy waves. There was no moon, but it was easy to see in the bright starlight. He held something to the sky and looked at it, then shouted instructions to the helmsman who pulled the steering oar over. The sail flapped a little at this so Kalaleq loosened knots, tightened some lines and let out others, until the sail was angled to their satisfaction. When this was finished Armun called him over and asked him what he had been doing looking at the stars.

"Finding the way back to our paukaruts," he said with some satisfaction. "The stars show us the way."

"How?"

"With this."

He passed over the construction of joined bones. Kerrick looked at it, turning it over before shaking his head and passing it back.

"It makes little sense to me—just four bones tied together at the corners to make a square."

"Yes, of course, you are right," Kalaleq agreed. "But it was tied together by Nanuaq when he was standing among the paukaruts on Allanivok's shore. That is the way it is done. It is an important secret knowledge which I will tell you now. Do you see that star up there?"

With much pointing and shouted help from the others they finally discovered which star he was talking about. Kerrick knew little of the sky; it was Armun who identified it.

"That is Ermanpadar's Eye, that is what I was taught. All the other stars—they are the tharms of brave hunters who have died. Each night they walk up into the sky there in the east, rise up over our heads and then go to rest in the west. They walk together like a great herd of deer and are watched over by Ermanpadar who does not move with them. He stands there in the north and watches, and that star is his eye. It stands still while the tharms go around it."

"I never noticed."

"Watch it tonight—you will see."

"But how does that help us find our way?"

This involved more shouted explanation from Kalaleq, who felt that Kerrick's inability to understand Paramutan was because he was deaf. If he shouted loud enough surely Kerrick would know what he meant. With Armun translating he explained how the frame worked.

"This fat bone, it is the bottom. You must hold it before your eye and look along it at the place where the water meets the sky. Tilt it up and down until you cannot see its length, just the round end. When that is done—and you must keep it pointed correctly at all times—you must quickly look up along this bone which is the Allanivok bone, and look for the star. It must point right at the star. Look, keep trying."

Kerrick struggled with the frame, blinking and sighting until his eyes were tired and watering. "I cannot do it," he finally said. "When this bone points to the horizon—the other points above the star."

At this Kalaleq gave a shout of joy and called out to the other Paramutan to witness how quickly Kerrick had learned to guide the ikkergak already, his first day out from shore. Kerrick could not understand what the excitement was about since he had got it wrong.

"You are right," Kalaleq insisted. "It is the ikkergak that is wrong. We are too far south. You will see—when we go farther north the bone will point at the star."

"But you said that this star did not move like all the others?"

Kalaleq was hysterical at this and rolled about with laughter. It was some time before he could explain. It appeared that this star did not move unless you moved. If you sailed north it rose higher in the sky, if you went south it became lower. Which meant that for every place you were the star had a certain position in the sky. That was how you found your way. Kerrick was not sure exactly what this meant and fell asleep while still puzzling over it.

Though Kerrick and Armun were always slightly queasy from the bobbing, twisting, rise and fall of the boat, their seasickness did get better after some days at sea. They ate meagerly of the blubber and meat, but finished all of their carefully measured ration of water each day. They helped catch fish because the juice from the fish, freshly squeezed, satisfied their thirst even better than the water did.

Kerrick still puzzled over the bone framework each night as the sighting star rose measurably higher in the sky. Then, one night, Kalaleq shouted happily after taking its measurement and they all took turns looking along the bones and yes, they were pointing at the star and the horizon at the same time now. With this their course was changed, farther to the east, and the sail reset. In the morning Kalaleq rooted among his possessions and produced the larger framework of many bones that Kerrick had seen before.

"We are here," he said proudly, tapping one of the lateral bones. He ran his finger along it to the right until it came to another bone that was tied across it. "We sail this way and come here—and that is Allanivok. So easy."

"It may be a lot of things—but it is not easy," Kerrick said, turning the complex latticework over in his hands. Then he remembered. "Armun—those murgu charts. I still have them in my pack. Tell Kalaleq what they are while I get them."

"But—what are they?"

"Tell him—it's not easy. Tell him that the murgu cross this ocean in their big fish. When they do they use flat things with lines of color on them to guide them. I have no idea how they use them—perhaps he can understand how it is done."

All the Paramutan grouped round and shouted in astonishment at the charts, those not able to get close calling out for a description. At first they simply admired the colors and patterns, turning them over and over. They were particularly impressed by the fact that rubbing with spittle or even scratching with the fingernail would not affect the lines—which went right through the hard, semitransparent substance. Kalaleq waited until all had a chance to admire them before he crouched down and pored over their detail.

Later that day the wind began to increase, sending black clouds scudding before it. There had been squalls and showers some days earlier, but this looked like a proper storm. Kerrick watched the sky with some trepidation—but the Paramutan were excited and happy, digging into the dunnage. By the time the storm broke and the rain lashed down they had spread a large section of skin, held it stretched by the edges to collect the rain. The wind caught it and tried to pull it from them, while the lightning flared and thunder rolled over them. It was hard work for all of them, but well worth it because before the storm had passed three of the waterskins had been filled; they had all drunk their fill of the fresh water as well.

The weather remained cooler after the storm, with cloud most of the time. With his seasickness reduced to a continual, mild annoyance, Kerrick had the energy to learn more Paramutan. Armun tutored him, answered questions when he was in difficulties, but he went to the Partamutan themselves for his practice. There was no problem with this since they were great talkers, would talk to themselves if no one else was there to listen. Time passed easily this way, until they woke one morning to great excitement. Touched red by the dawn sunlight they saw two white seabirds passing overhead. Kerrick was unimpressed until Kalaleq explained.

"There is land, in that direction—and it cannot be many days sailing away!"

After this they all hung over the side and looked at the water, and were rewarded when one of the women squealed and almost fell overboard, two others held her by the ankles, another by her tail which came free of her clothing, while she groped head first in the ocean. They pulled her back, dripping and smiling—but holding tightly to a length of seaweed.

"Grows only close to shore!" she cried out, joyfully squeezing and popping its flotation bladders.

But land was not that close yet. There were storms and contrary winds and the Paramutan were so annoyed that they lowered the sail and put one of the boats into the water. They secured this to the bow by a length of braided leather line and four at a time, male and female, took turns at the oars. Armun and Kerrick did their stint, gasping and sweating as they pulled the large ikkergak at a snail's pace through the water. They were as glad as the others when a light westerly wind came up and, with much shouting, the boat was pulled back aboard and the sail was set again.

It was the following day, just before sunset, that someone saw the dark line on the horizon ahead. There was much loud argument whether it was cloud or land, followed by cries of happiness when they saw that it was land after all. The sail was lowered and a length of line trailed from the stern to keep them from being pushed along by the waves.

At dawn they were all awake as the sun rose above the forested hills, far closer now. Kalaleq climbed up the mast as far as he could to look for landmarks as they drew closer—finally shouted and pointed north to some small islands just visible off the coast. They turned that way, catching the breeze and making a good passage. The islands were passed before noon and beyond them, above a sandy beach, were the rounded black domes of the paukaruts.

"Allanivok!" someone cried out and all the Paramutan shouted in happy agreement.

"Forest and undergrowth," Kerrick said. "The hunting should be good here. A land without murgu, none of the Paramutan have seen any. This could be the place for us to be. To forget all about the murgu, never think of them again."

Armun was silent, for there was nothing that she could say. She knew that memory of the other sammads, the murgu pursuing them, would not go away. He did not talk about it any more, but she could tell from his face that it was always in his thoughts. They might be safe.

But what about all of the others?

CHAPTER THIRTY-TWO

Like all Paramutan occasions, their arrival involved much shouting, laughing and eating. Willing hands pulled their ikkergak up onto the beach beside the others giggling and getting in each other's way as they hurried to unload it, helping themselves to the remains of the food as they did so. It was quickly eaten, deliciously rotten after all the days at sea therefore greatly admired. Armun stayed to help the women, but Kerrick was eager to see this new land and knew that he could be of no help in erecting Kalaleq's paukarut. He took up his bow and spear and walked between the other paukaruts toward the wooded hills beyond. It felt good to be on solid ground again after the endless days in the ikkergak, although the earth seemed to move beneath his feet at times. When he came to the trees he smelled deep of their leafy fragrance. This was a good land.

But the cold winters had reached here as well. Although it was midsummer there was still snow lying in the deep gulleys. Birds called from the trees but there did not seem to be any bigger animals in the forest. Perhaps a better hunter would have seen signs, but he found nothing. He also tired quickly because, after the many days at sea, his legs were unused to this steady walking.

Despite this he felt real pleasure to be on firm land and went on, ignoring the fatigue. He sniffed the air. Forest mold, grass—and a faint smell of carrion carried on the wind. Along with a faint crackling sound.

Kerrick stopped, motionless, then bent slowly and placed his spear on the ground. Only when he had nocked an arrow into his bow did he retrieve the spear then walk silently forward, one weapon in each hand. The crackling grew louder and he saw something moving in the clearing ahead. Slowly, staying in the shadows, he moved toward it until he stopped suddenly, astonished.

The dead animal appeared to be a deer, now torn open and bloodied. But the creature eating it was like nothing he had ever seen before. It was tall, thin, bent over with its head buried in the corpse. Then it straightened up, pulling out a length of flesh. A bloodied head and beak, staring eyes, a murgu of some kind. No—it was a bird! Taller than he was, legs thicker than his, tiny wings. He must have stirred because the thing saw him, dropped the gobbet of meat and emitted a hoarse cry and flapped its wings. He dropped his spear and raised the bow, drew the string taut and released the arrow.

And missed completely. The bird stood its ground, still screeching, when he seized up his spear again and backed slowly away from it into the shelter of the trees. Time enough another day to find and kill one of the creatures. Once it was out of sight he turned and made his way back through the forest to the shore.

Their paukarut had been erected and Kalaleq was sitting on the ground before it in the sun, a Yilanè chart spread out on his lap. He smiled when Kerrick appeared and shook the chart in his direction.

"Something here and soon I will understand it. Already I know a lot. Do you see all the green, like scales—do you know what that is? That is the ocean. Soon I will understand."

Armun emerged from the tent when she heard them talking. And he told her about the forest and his encounter with the great bird.

"This is a new land so we must expect new things," she said with firm practicality. "I must go as well and see for myself. There will be plants and bushes that you know nothing about. There is always food to be found in the forest if you know where to look."

"Dangers as well. Do not go out alone. We must go together."

Her expression changed when he said this and she took Kerrick by the arm, as though her grasp would hold him there. "They were just waiting for our ikkergak to arrive before they start north on the ularuaq hunt. Just the males, even the grown boys don't go. It is the most important thing that they do."

He saw her grim face, the fear in her eyes. "What is wrong?"

"They want you to go with them."

"I don't have to."

"They are sure that you will be pleased by their asking you. It is a great honor and they expect you to accept. But I don't want you to leave me."

He understood her feelings: they had been parted too long before this. He tried to reassure her—and himself at the same time. "It won't take much time—it will be just like going on a hunt. You will see."

After the recent voyage Kerrick had no desire at all to put to sea again. Yet there was no way he could avoid going. The boys looked at him enviously while the women patted him when he passed for it was considered the best of luck to touch someone who was going on their first ularuaq hunt. The rest of the day was spent preparing the ikkergaks—most of the night in feasting of the old meat knowing they would be bringing a fresh supply when they returned.

They left in the morning and Armun stayed inside the paukarut, could not bear to see him go away from her again, emerging only when the little fleet was just a blur on the horizon.

They sailed due north and Kalaleq was quick to tell Kerrick the reason why, indulging himself in the Paramutan love of talking.

"Ice, we sail to the ice, that is where ularuaq are."

Kerrick had difficulty in understanding just why the creatures stayed to the north, near the ice, because Kalaleq used words that he had never heard before. He would just have to wait until they reached the ice in order to find out for himself.

They were many days at sea before the white line of ice was seen in the distance. There was much shouting and excitement as they drew close and the frozen wall rose above them. The waves surged and broke against it and in the troughs between the waves dark masses could be made out hanging from the ice.

"Qunguleq," Kalaleq said and rubbed his stomach. "The ularuaq come here, eat it. We come and eat them. What fun!"

As they turned and followed the ice Kerrick could see that the qunguleq was green seaweed of some kind, immense lengths of it attached to the ice and trailing out into the sea. He had never seen anything like it before. With this thought came some understanding. The ularuaq had come here to eat the qunguleq—and the Paramutan had followed. He looked forward with some excitement to seeing what sort of creatures grazed these frigid northern meadows.

Despite himself, Kerrick was caught up in the excitement of the hunt. The ikkergaks turned west and sailed along the wall of ice. When they reached the first of the icebergs that had broken free they spread out in a line to search around the bergs and in the channels between them. But never alone. This was a group effort and some of the other ikkergaks were always in sight. Kalaleq's ikkergak was near the middle of the line. The ikkergaks to the right and left easy enough to see—but the others were out of sight in the distance or searching other channels.

Since this was Kalaleq's ikkergak he had the honor of riding in the bow and throwing the spear. This had a long wooden shaft and a carved bone point with many back-facing barbs that would catch in the flesh to keep it from pulling free. Kalaleq sat and greased a long length of line with blubber, coiling it into a smooth pile beside him. Everyone else kept watch for their prey.

They sailed north for five days in this manner, searching all day and heaving to at night. Each dawn they were under way as soon as it was light enough to see, spreading out in their hunting formation. On the sixth day Kerrick was just hauling in a fishing line when there was a great shout of joy from one of the lookouts.

"The signal, there, look!"

Someone in the ikkergak to their left was waving a dark shape over his head. Kalaleq picked up a skin and passed the signal on down the line as they heeled over to follow the other turning ikkergak. The herd had been seen: the hunt was on.

The first ikkergaks tacked while they waited for the others to catch up—then all of them moved west together.

"There they are," Kalaleq shouted. "How beautiful—I have never seen anything that beautiful!"

To Kerrick they were just dark lumps against the ice—but they were food and shelter, life itself to the Paramutan. Their entire existence depended on the ularuaq, and to find them again they had crossed the ocean, from continent to continent. Now was the time when they must succeed.

Closer they came and closer, until Kerrick could see the great dark backs of the beasts as they moved along the wall of ice. They had blunt heads and what looked like thick lips. With them they seized the qunguleq and tore great streamers free. They reminded him of uruketo, they were as large, only they lacked the high dorsal fin. Every now and again one of them would surge high out of the water and crash back with a tremendous splash. The ikkergaks drew closer and angled toward the far side of the pack and began to separate. Kalaleq nodded in appreciation of the maneuver.

"Get in front, let them see, make them come back toward us." He pointed at the other ikkergak which, like them, had dropped its sail and was rocking motionless in the waves.

The others hurried away, letting out their sails fully to reach the pack as quickly as they could, angling for position. The great creatures grazed steadily, seemingly indifferent to the ikkergaks that grew ever closer. Their own craft rocked back and forth on the waves, the sail flapping loosely. The tension grew and Kalaleq shook the spear and bounced back and forth from one foot to the other.

"They are coming!" someone shouted.

Everything seemed to happen at once after that—and Kerrick jumped back out of the way. The sail was run up and lashed tight while the steerman—facing the bow for the first time—headed toward the approaching pack which had taken fright and was now fleeing from the other ikkergaks. Kalaleq stood ready in the bow, solid and unmoving and apparently ignoring all the shouted advice. The dark forms of the ularuaq plunged toward them.

"Now!" Kalaleq shouted. "Go about!"

In a single frenzied spasm of effort the steerman pushed hard on his oar while the others hauled on the lines that swung the sail to the other side of the mast. It flapped and cracked—then filled again. Moments later they were moving again on the opposite tack. Away from the ularuaq, angling across before them.

The reason for the maneuver was soon obvious. The ikkergak was no match for the rushing pack, could never have caught up with them. But as the giant sea creatures overtook them their relative speed was slowed and Kalaleq could select his victim. He did this calmly, signing to the steerman with his hands which direction he wanted to go, ignoring all the advice about size and suitability from the rest of the crew.

They were in amongst them now, sleek wet forms moving by on both sides.

"Now!" Kalaleq cried—and stabbed his spear into a bladder that hung by a thong over the bow of the ikkergak, just beside him. The spearpoint came out black and dripping and a repulsive odor washed back from the burst bladder. The ikkergak rocked as it bumped the back of the ularuaq.

Kalaleq plunged the spear down with all of his strength, deep into the creature's hide, then jumped away as the coil of line attached to it began to run quickly over the side. The stench from the punctured bladder was unbelievable and Kerrick lurched to the side and threw up. Through his tears he saw Kalaleq cutting the thong—the bladder dropped into the sea and was swept away.

With this done, Kalaleq kicked overboard the inflated skin just as the last of the line paid out. The skin bubbled away through the water, secured to the line, and the ikkergak turned and followed it.

Kalaleq climbed the mast again and shouted down instructions. If they lost sight of the inflated skin the whole operation would fail.

The steerman glanced at Kerrick and laughed. "Strong poison, good and strong. Make you bring up all your food, just smelling it. Even a ularuaq cannot live long with that poison in it, you'll see."

He was right; soon after this they came up to the inflated skin, bobbing on the waves. Below it the immense, still form of the ularuaq could just be made out. The rest of the school were gone, but the other ikkergaks were coming toward them.

"Good stab, wasn't it?" Kalaleq said, dropping down from the mast and looking fondly at his catch. "Did you ever see a thrust so good?"

"Never," Kerrick told him. Modesty was not a Paramutan trait.

"It will float up soon, then sink, but you will see what we do then before we lose it."

By the time the ularuaq's back was at the surface, the waves surging over it, the rest of the ikkergaks were arriving at the scene. Kerrick was astonished when one Paramutan after another stripped off his furs and dived into the icy water. They had bone hooks, like greatly enlarged fishhooks, tied to the ends of leather lines that they carried between their teeth as they dived down next to the ularuaq. One by one they surfaced and were hauled into the ikkergaks, their fur running with water. They shivered and shouted how brave they were as they dried themselves and redressed.

No one paid any attention to them because they were all busy hauling on the lines. Kerrick could help with this since it required no skill—just strength. The point of this exercise became clear when the ularuaq's corpse stirred in the water, then rolled slowly over. The hooks had been sunk into the creature's flippers. Now it floated in the sea with its lighter-colored underside facing upward.

Some of the lattice-work flooring had been lifted and a coiled mass taken out of the bilge. This proved to be a length of some creature's intestine preserved in a thick coating of blubber. A shaft of bone with a sharp tip was fixed to its end. After stripping off his furs, Kalaleq put the bone into his mouth and dropped over the side. Half swimming, half crawling, he worked his way along the ularuaq's body, the tubular length of gut trailing behind him. Kneeling, he was prodding the resilient skin with his fingers, hitting it with his fists. He moved along to another spot, repeated these actions—then waved at them before taking the sharpened bone from his mouth. Raising it above his head with both hands he stabbed down with all his strength to drive it through the creature's tough skin. Then he twisted it and worked it down into the flesh until it was out of sight.

"Try it now," he called out, stood shivering beside it with his arms wrapped about his body.

At first Kerrick thought that the two Paramutan were pumping water from the ikkergak. Then he saw that this large pump was attached to the end of the length of gut and was pumping air—not water. The tube writhed and straightened as they worked. Kalaleq watched the operation until he was satisfied with the results, then slipped back into the water and returned to the ikkergak.

He laughed aloud as he dried himself and redressed, then tried to talk but his teeth chattered too much.

"Let me, warm me up," he said to one of them who was frenziedly working the pump. The other Paramutan was gasping and exhausted and more than happy to hand over. "Now we . . . fill with . . . air. Make it float," Kalaleq said.

Kerrick took over from the other Paramutan—pumped in the same frenzied manner as the others, and soon passed the handle on to the next volunteer.

Bit by bit they could see their efforts rewarded as the great body rose higher in the water. As soon as this happened the lines, still hooked into the flippers, were passed to the other ikkergaks and secured into position. Their sails were set and they got under way, slowly pulling the great sea creature after them.

"Food," Kalaleq said happily. "This will be a good winter and we will eat very well."

CHAPTER THIRTY-THREE

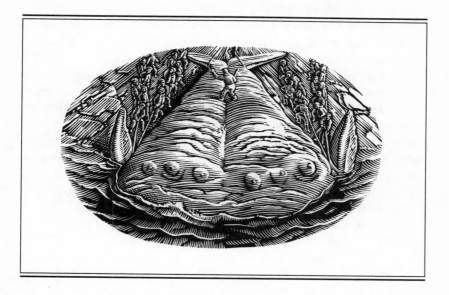

They sailed back through thick flurries of snow: the first sign that autumn was coming to an end. The Paramutan relished this weather, sniffing the air happily and licking the snow off the cargo. It was snowing even more heavily when they reached the shore and the dark shapes of the paukaruts could just be made out through the falling flakes. They sailed past the settlement to the rocky shore beyond, the site they had so carefully selected, the reason why they had erected their paukaruts in this place.

Here the waves broke on the tilted, grooved mass of rock that ran down and vanished into the sea. Its use became apparent when the lines from the ularuaq were passed ashore to the women. They had run out from the paukaruts when the little fleet had been sighted and were now shouting and waving on the shore. Kerrick picked Armun out, standing to one side, and called to her until she saw him and waved back. Then they were all caught up in the excitement as the large bulk of the ularuaq was pulled onto the rocks and held there by the ropes. With much shouted instructions it was turned so the tail lay pointing inland, was kept that way as the receding tide pulled at the body. When the tide ebbed it was stranded there, half in and half out of the water. Now the lines were taken from the fins and tied firmly about the tail, stretched out along the rocks until the next tide came in.

Kerrick was pushing his way through the happy crowd toward Armun, but could not reach her before the press of screaming Paramutan came between them. Kalaleq was being carried on their shoulders, passed forward like a bundle until he was safely deposited on one of the immense flippers. Once there he took out his knife and began to saw at the resistant flesh, eventually cutting free a bloody chunk. He smeared it on his face until it was as red as his hands—then took a large bite before passing the meat to the crowd who fought and struggled, laughing hysterically, to get some for themselves. Kerrick pushed his way clear of them and found Armun. He pointed at the mountainous body.

"The hunt was a success."

"More important—you are here again."

"There was nothing to fear."

"I did not fear. It is the separation. It must not happen again."

She did not tell him of each of the days since he had gone, how she had sat on the shore looking out to sea, thinking of him and their life together. When she found herself holding her skins over her mouth to hide her split lip, just the way she used to, she realized that he was her whole life, her new life that was not the one of rejection she had always lived. She was that different person again when they were parted. She did not like it, did not want to experience it ever again. Now they went together to the paukarut where he stripped and she washed the grime of the voyage from his body. He lay then under the warm furs while she took her own clothing off and joined him there. They were not disturbed; all the Paramutan were at the shore. Tight, together, their breaths mingling, her sounds of joy blending with his.

Later she rose and dressed and brought food for both of them.

"I built the fire and smoked these fish as soon as I caught them. I have had my fill of rotten meat. And here, these roots are from the forest; they taste the same as the ones I have always dug." When she saw his worried expression she reached out and touched his lips and smiled. "I did not go alone. We went together, many women, the boys with spears. We saw the large birds but never got close to them."

The Paramutan did not come back to the paukaruts until dusk, ate and retired at once for the next high tide would come during the night. The boys who had remained to watch the ocean came running and screaming between the paukaruts when it was time. Then they all turned out under the bright stars, breaths steaming in the night air, to pick up the lines once again. This time, with everyone pulling strongly on the creature's tail they slid it even higher up on the slanting rock; there was no chance now of it being washed back into the sea.

In the morning the flensing began. Great strips of hide and blubber were removed, meat hacked from the bones. The rock ran red with the creature's blood. Kalaleq took no part in this, just looked on, and once the butchery was well under way he returned to the paukarut and took out the charts once again. Then called to Kerrick.

"All the time we sailed to find the ularuaq I thought of these. I looked at the water, and I looked at the sky and I thought of these. And then I began to understand. They sail differently, the murgu, do things differently, but some things about the ocean must always be the same. Let me show you what I am thinking and you will tell me if there is any truth in my thoughts."

He spread the Yilanè charts out on the ground, then walked around them holding out his own navigation matrix of crossed bones. He turned it over and over in his hands, then kneeled and laid it carefully on the chart, turning it still more until it was just as he wanted.

"You will remember we crossed the ocean by following the unmoving star. This is the course we took—and here is where we are now. This is land, this the ice, this the shore where we met you, this is the place."

Kerrick followed the brown finger across the network of bones, could see none of the things that appeared to be so obvious to the Paramutan; to him they were still just bones. But he nodded agreement, not wanting to interrupt. Kalaleq went on.

"Here is where I began to understand. The murgu sail only in the south, for you have told me they cannot live in the snow. We live for snow and ice, live only in the north. But things go from south to north, north to south. Here, right here, is a river of warm water in the sea, coming from the south, and we have fished in it. It is rich with food and it runs far north, and I think many fish swim in it for their food. But where does it come from? Can you tell me?"

He smiled and smoothed the fur on his cheeks as he waited for an answer.

"From the south?" It did not seem too hard an answer, but it excited Kalaleq.

"Yes, yes, I think so. And you agree with me. So, look, at the murgu chart. If *this* is land and *this* is water—then this orange color could be the warm water flowing from south to north. Could it not?"

"It could," Kerrick agreed, though it could be anything to his untutored eye. With this encouragement Kalaleq rushed on.

"So it ends here at the edge of the chart because the murgu never go north—so this must be north. But before it ends, there is this place on their chart—which I believe is *this* place on mine! And if that is right—then *here* on theirs is *here* on mine—where we are standing right now!"

Kerrick could make no sense of the Paramutan bonework—but there was some logic to the Yilanè chart. The orange swirl could be warm water, that made sense—though what the blue swirls crossing it were he couldn't tell. Was all of the green mass ocean? The darker green land? Possibly. He moved his finger down the dark green on the left, traced it downward until it changed to the light green of the sea. In some ways it did look a bit like the model he had seen in Deifoben. And these flakes of golden metal sealed under the surface, out here in the ocean, what could they mean?

Alakas-aksehent. His arms and leg moved slightly as the name came to mind. Alakas-aksehent.

A succession of golden, tumbled stones. They had been pointed out to him when they had gone past them on the uruketo. On the way back to Alpèasak. His finger traced a course through the light green as he thought this, came to the darker green of land. To the two little yellow outlines there. Alpèasak.

The beautiful beaches.

"Kalaleq—you are right. I can understand these charts, they make sense. You are a Paramutan of great wisdom and lead all the world in your knowledge."

"That is true!" Kalaleq cried out. "I have always known it! If you understand—tell me more of the strange markings."

"Here, this is the place where the city was burnt. We joined you, here, that is what you said. And we crossed the ocean to this spot, almost off the top of the chart. Yes, here—do you see where the narrow bit of ocean widens out? That is Genaglè. Where this land to the north reaches Isegnet. Then all of this is Entoban✱ to the south."

"It is a very large land." Kalaleq was impressed.

"It is—and all of it murgu."

Kalaleq bent over in awe and admiration, following the contours of the continent to the south with his finger. Tracing back up the coast to the north to tap their location, then going north still to what could be a large island off the coast.

"This is not right," he said. "There is ice and snow here that does not melt, I know of no island."

Kerrick thought of the cold winters, colder every year, the snows further south each winter—and understood.

"This map is old, very old—or it is copied from an old map. This is the land that now lies beneath the ice. The murgu must have gone there at one time. See, there is one of their markers there, that red mark, on the land."

Kalaleq looked close, agreed. Then traced back down the shore to their site.

"Our paukaruts are here. And south along the shore, not far, do you see this little red mark? It looks like the one up here to the north. This I do not understand."

Kerrick looked at it with a growing sense of despair. It was not distant, on the coast, well north of Genaglè where it met the sea. Both red marks were shaped the same.

"There are murgu there, that is what it means. Murgu here, not too distant from us. We have fled from them but they are here ahead of us!"

Kerrick sank back with the weakness of despair. Was there no escaping the Yilanè? Had they come all of this way across the cold northern sea just to find them waiting? It seemed impossible. They could never live this far to the north, away from the heat. Yet the red mark was there, the two marks. The one to the north now beneath the unmelting ice. But the one to the south of them . . . He looked up to meet Kalaleq's eyes, fixed on him.

"Do we think the same thought?" Kalaleq asked. Kerrick nodded.

"We do. If murgu are that close we are not safe here. We must go there, find out what the red mark means. Go there as soon as possible. Before the winter storms start. There is not much time."

Kalaleq gathered up the charts, grinning happily. "I want to see these murgu you talk about. Have a good trip, good time."

Kerrick did not share the Paramutan's pleasure. Had he come this far just to begin the battle again? A Yilanè saying came to mind at the thought; and his body moved as he remembered. No matter how far you travel, no matter how long it takes, you will never find father again. Enge had taught him that and he had not understood its meaning then even after she had explained. When you are in the egg you are safe—but once you leave father's protection and go into the sea you will never have that protection again. The voyage of life always ended in death. Must his voyages always have death waiting at the end?

Armun shared his despair when he told her his fears.

"Are you sure there are murgu here, so close? For this we left Arnwheet and crossed that ocean, for this?"

"I am sure of nothing—that is why I must go to this spot on the chart and see what is there."

"That is why we must go. Together."

"Of course. Together. Always."

Kalaleq could have filled his ikkergak many times over with volunteers. Now that the ularuaq hunt was over the hard work of butchering and preserving the great creature was not as exciting. A voyage was. Kalaleq chose his crew, supplies were loaded aboard, and within a day they were at sea again.

Kerrick stood at the bow, looking at the coastline—then at the chart. What were they sailing into?

mareedege mareedegeb deemarissi.

═══════════

Eat or be eaten.

CHAPTER THIRTY-FOUR

Vaintè sat astride the neck of the tarakast, strength and authority in every line of her body, the living reins that grew from the creature's lips firm in her hands. Her mount was restless, tired of waiting; it turned its long neck to glare at her, hissed and snapped with its sharp beak. With a hard pull on the rein she asserted her command. It would stand on this spot all day if that was her will. Below the bluff, on the bank of the wide river, the last uruktop was wading ashore to join the others. Its eight legs moved slowly, for it had been a long and tiring swim; the single rider straddling its foreshoulders urging it on. When it had rested it would be able to carry its burden of fargi; they had already crossed by boat. Everything was going as planned. The broad river plain stirred with life as the fargi who had landed yesterday disassembled their nighttime laager. The thorn vines, now deactivated by the daylight, were rolled up, the illumination-creatures and large hèsotsan bundled together. They would be ready to march soon. The campaign was well under way.

Vaintè turned and looked out over the undulating plain to the hills beyond, traveled in her mind's eye farther still to the valley where the ustuzou were hiding. She would go to them there, over every obstacle; she would find them. Her body writhed with the strength of her hatred, her lips peeled back to show her teeth; the tarakast stirred beneath the pressure of her legs and she silenced it with a savage pull on its lips. The ustuzou would die, all die. With a sharp kick she started her mount forward, down the slope toward the laager of the advance party.

Melikelè turned away from the fargi she was supervising when she saw Vaintè approaching, shaping her arms in greetings, lowest to highest warmth of welcome. She felt this sincerely and could not conceal her pleasure at Vaintè's approach. She cared nothing now for distant sea-girt Ikhalmenets, or for its eistaa—whom she had only seen from a great distance. In that city she had been just one more fargi, unknown and unwanted, despite her skill at speaking. Vaintè had changed that, letting Melikelè rise in her service as fast as she was able. Vaintè destroyed failure—but amply rewarded those followers with intelligence. And obedience. Melikelè was obedient, stayed obedient, wanted nothing more than to serve Vaintè in any way that she was able.

"All is in readiness," she said in response to the signed inquiry. Vaintè slid gracefully down from her mount and looked about at the ordered turmoil of the work parties of fargi.

"You do well, Melikelè," she said with amplification gestures.

"I do what I am ordered, Vaintè highest. My life is between your thumbs."

Vaintè accepted her due for Melikelè spoke with affirmations of strength of duty. How she wished she had more like this stalwart one. Loyalty and intelligence were hard to come by now, even with the pick of Lanefenuu's followers. In truth they were a toadying lot, selected more for their adulation of the eistaa than the possession of any ability. Lanefenuu was too strong and independent to permit any competition from her retinue. In the back of her mind Vaintè knew that one day there could be a problem between them. But that day was far distant. As long as Vaintè exercised all of her strength and abilities in destroying ustuzou Lanefenuu's rule of the city would not be threatened. Destruction; her limbs moved with the strength of her feelings and she spoke them aloud.

"Go now, strong Melikelè, take your fargi and I will follow with the main body one day's march behind you. The advance scouts are a single day's march ahead of you. They are all mounted on tarakast so they will be able to search on both sides of our route as they go. If they see any sight of the ustuzou they will stop and wait for your stronger party to catch up with them. Do you know the sites for your next laager?"

"I have studied the pictures over and over, but will not be sure until I see the site on the ground. If in doubt I will rely on the two guides."

"Do that, for they came this way with me before." Vaintè appreciated Melikelè's honesty in admitting a weakness or lack of knowledge—she knew her own strengths, knew as well when it was necessary to rely upon others. "Do you know where you will wait for us?"

"I do. On the banks of the yellow-twisted river." She held up the thumbs and fingers of both hands. "It will be the tenth laager from here and I will remember the count of days."

"Be alert at all times. The ustuzou have an animal cunning when it comes to killing. Be prepared for traps and ruses, remember how they attacked us on the island, then escaped during the night of the heavy rain. They must not escape again. We must find them and kill them—but aware of danger at all times lest we die ourselves."

"Eat or be eaten," Melikelè said grimly, then locked strong hands into fists and signed infinite-aggression. "My appetite is of the greatest!"

"Well spoken. We meet in ten days."

Vaintè raked her claws into her mount's flank; it reared and hissed in anger and moved off at a fast run. Melikelè turned back to her work. Once the defenses were disassembled the uruktop were quickly loaded. The fargi stood ready, their weapons held out to her as she made a final inspection. On the long march from the city she had appointed those who showed any signs of intelligence and ability to speak. This enabled her to be sure that on each uruktop there was one whose responsibility it was to see that all was in order. The correct supplies in the correct places. Now everything was as it should be; she waddled swiftly to the lead uruktop and climbed up onto it, then signalled the scouting terakast to go ahead. Vaintè had offered her one to ride, but she had not the skill. This did not bother her at all. She had the ability to lead others and to follow Vaintè's orders; was supremely happy in this role. At her signal the march began.

The uruktop plodded along slowly but steadily on their eight strong and heavily muscled legs. They were not fast—but they could march from dawn to dusk without rest. They had almost no intelligence and if they were not instructed to stop they would march until they died. Melikelè knew this and watched after the great creatures' health making sure they were driven to the water at the day's end, that there was a swamp or stands of young trees for them to graze. Early in this long march she had discovered that the heavy nails on the last two pairs of legs had a tendency to crack and then get torn off. If this happened the feet would bleed steadily until the dim creature weakened and died. With Vaintè's permission she had two of her brightest fargi trained by Akotolp in the art of dressing and healing the wounds. Yet she still inspected the uruktop every night herself.

The day passed as did all the others, in a mindless haze of constant motion. The tarakast scouted on both flanks, then ran out ahead of them: the drab landscape moved slowly by. In midafternoon a sudden rainstorm cooled them, but the strong sun broke through and soon dried and warmed their skins. The sun was ahead of them now, getting close to the horizon when they came up to the group of tarakast waiting by the wide stream. The ground was flattened here, the undergrowth broken and sparse. It was obvious that large groups had made laager on this spot before. It was the correct site. At the scouts' signs of agreement she issued the orders for the laager to be set up.

In strict conformity to her orders, in practiced progression, the riding beasts were watered and led to forage. The tarakast had to be watched or they would have fled, but not so the uruktop. They would not even eat until they were prodded and urged into taking the first mouthfuls of leaves. After this they would keep eating until stopped. They were incredibly stupid.

Only after most of the guardian vines had been unrolled and erected had the fargi themselves time to eat. It was just before dark when the last beasts were brought in and tethered, the final vines rolled into place. It grew cool here at night and all of the fargi had sleeping cloaks. Melikelè prodded hers open but did not roll herself in it until the last moment of light. This was when the thorns emerged from the vines. She waited for the moment, watched with satisfaction as their poisonous spines rose into the air, knowing that the day was complete, the defenses secure, her work done. Only then did she lie down and wrap the cloak around her, satisfied that she had loyally followed great Vainte's orders for yet another day. Her eyes closed and she fell instantly into a deep sleep.

Around her, secure inside the protection of the circles of poisoned thorns, light-makers and night hèsotsan that would shoot if there were any disturbance, the fargi slept as well. Some of the tarakast stirred and hissed angrily at each other, but soon even they were curled in sleep, heads tucked under their looped tails. The Yilanè and their beasts slept.

For the most part the laager was on flat ground, though to one side there was a slight rise where a mound of rocks had collected blown soil to form a slight hill. Most of the boulders were half buried, though there was a tumbled heap at the foot of the slope where rain had washed them free and had rolled to the bottom.

One of these rocks stirred and rolled over with a crash.

A few of the fargi sleeping nearby opened their eyes with instant awareness. Heard nothing more, saw only the bright stars, closed their eyes, and were asleep again. In any case their night vision was so bad they would not have been able to see when another rock moved, quietly this time.

Slowly, cautiously, Herilak lifted his head up above the mound of tumbled boulders.

The big hunter looked about the camp. A crescent moon was just rising, but in the cloudless night the starlight clearly revealed the sleeping laager. The high-bulking forms of the beasts with eight legs, the smaller dark bundles of silent murgu. Drums of murgu meat to one side, bladders of them piled one upon the other.

There was a sudden blast of light, the sharp crack of hèsotsan as some desert creature touched the poisonous vines; Herilak froze, motionless. The murgu nearest to the light sat up and peered outward. The light slowly faded and went out. They settled back to sleep. Now, carefully and silently, Herilak moved the boulders aside until he could crawl free.

He stayed flat on the ground, then turned and called down into the black opening.

"Now. Quietly. Come."

He crawled aside as another armed hunter emerged from the ground. There was a hault more behind him in the cave. They had dug it, dumped the earth into the river, roofed it with thick logs, then covered it again with the boulders they had so painfully rolled aside. The digging had started in the morning, as soon as the murgu who had spent the previous night here had galloped out of sight. Now they emerged one at a time, filling their lungs with the fresh night air. They had been sealed in there since midday: it had been hot, breathless, the air foul. None had complained, all of them were volunteers.

"It is as you said, Herilak," a hunter whispered into his ear. "They always stay the night in the same place."

"They do. And now we will do what we have to do. Kill."

They were ruthless in their butchery, experienced killers of murgu. Only an occasional grunt of pain was heard as they stabbed down with knives and spears, slaying the sleepers one after the other. Only when the last one was dead did they use the captured death-sticks to slaughter the riding creatures. Some of these stirred and cried out at the smell of death around them, tried to run away and blundered into the deadly vines. One by one they were killed. The butchery was complete.

None of the hunters could sleep. They wiped the blood from their hands and arms as well as they could, sat and talked quietly until dawn. When there was enough light to see by, Herilak stood and issued orders.

"I want help here. I want to seal up this hole where we were hidden so nothing can be seen. Pull some of the bodies on top of the rocks. They might find the opening, I don't know—but if they don't it will be something more to worry them. They will then wonder how this happened, how we got past their defenses, and it could slow them down."

"Will they go back then?" Nenne asked.

"No, that won't happen," Herilak said, feeling the anger rise within him. "They will keep coming. But we can slow them, kill them. We can do that. Now the rest of you, wait until it is full light and the thorns withdraw. Don't touch anything, just use your spears to pull aside the vines. Leave everything else the way it is. We'll take the death-sticks, some meat, nothing else. Pull the vines back into place when we go. This will be a sight to make the murgu very, very unhappy. I want it to be that way."

CHAPTER THIRTY-FIVE

They sailed south along the coast. The Paramutan were excited by this journey into the unknown, pointing out every new headland and bit of beach with shouts of wonder. Kerrick did not share this enthusiasm but sank deeper into a grim unhappiness with every day's travel. Armun saw this and could only share his despair because she knew there was little she could do to help him. As they voyaged south the weather improved, but not his spirits. She almost welcomed the bad weather that followed because he had to work with others to reef the sails and pump out the bilge so had little time to think about the future.

The coastline made a turn here, they could see it on the map, until they were sailing due west. Although the sun was warm the winter storms lashed down from the north bringing squalls of rain. On their eighth day of sailing they ran through one cloudburst after another, starting soon after dawn, but by midafternoon the last squall had passed and the rainstorm had blown past them to the shore.

"See the rainbow," Armun said, pointing to the great arch that spanned the sky, stretching inland from the sea. It appeared to end upon a rocky headland. "My father always said that if you found the spot where the rainbow ends you would find the greatdeer who would speak to you. When you found it there at rainbow's end it could not escape and would have to answer any question that you asked it. That is what my father said."

Kerrick was silent, looking toward the land as though he had not even heard her.

"Do you think that would happen?" she asked.

Kerrick shook his head. "I don't know. I have never heard a greatdeer talk. They are good to eat—but I don't think I would take their advice about anything."

"But this is a special kind of greatdeer. You will only find it at rainbow's end. I believe that it really is there."

She said this firmly, watching the rainbow grow fainter and fainter still until it vanished as the storm swept inland over the wooded hills. Kerrick did not disagree with her, was sunk again into his depression.

The wind died down after the storm and the sun shone warmly. Armun turned her face to it and ran her fingers through her hair so it would dry. Only the Paramutan were unhappy, taking off their fur jackets and complaining of the heat. They were creatures of the north and grew unhappy when they were too warm. Kalaleq stood in the bow, the breeze ruffling the long fur on his back, peering ahead at the coast.

"There!" he cried out suddenly, pointing. "That is a new thing, a thing that I have never seen before."

Kerrick joined him, squinting at the distant green patch on the shoreline, waiting until he was absolutely sure.

"Turn about, go to the shore," he said. "I know what that is. It is . . ." His vocabulary failed him and he turned to Armun and spoke in Marbak.

"There is no word for it—but it is the place where the murgu bring their creatures that swim. The murgu are there, at that place."

Armun spoke quickly in Paramutan and Kalaleq's eyes grew wide. "They are indeed there," he said, pushing over on the steering oar as the others rushed to the lines. They went about and on the opposite tack angled back to the coast, away from the Yilanè dock. Kerrick was looking at the chart, tracing it with his finger.

"This is it, it must be. We must land on the shore and approach it on foot. We must find out what it is doing here."

"Do you think there will be any murgu there?" Armun asked.

"There is no way to tell from here—but there could be. But we must be careful, go cautiously, just a few of us."

"If you go—I am going."

He started to speak, but heard the firmness in her voice and only nodded instead. "We two, then. And one or two at most of the Paramutan."

Kalaleq included himself in the scouting party and, after much shouting and arguing, Niumak was added as well because he was known as a great stalker. They ran the ikkergak ashore on a sandy beach. Armed with spears the small party set out along the sand.

The beach ended in a rocky headland, forcing them to go inland among the trees. The forest here was almost impenetrable with fallen trees tumbled between the living ones, thick trunks mixed with the smaller secondary growth. As soon as they could they worked their way back to the ocean, toward the sound of waves on rock.

"I die, the heat kills," Kalaleq said. He was staggering, close to exhaustion.

"Snow, ice," Niumak said. "That is where the real people belong. Kalaleq speaks truthfully, death from heat comes near."

There was blue sky ahead and a welcome breeze. The Paramutan praised its cooling touch while Kerrick pushed the leaves aside and looked out at the rocks and the breaking waves below. They were very close to the dock now. There were rounded mounds of some kind behind it, but he could not tell what they were from this distance. Nothing moved, it look deserted.

"I'm going to get closer . . ."

"I'll go with you," Armun said.

"No, I had better go alone. If the murgu are there I'll come right back. And I know them, know how they react. It would be much more dangerous with you along. The Paramutan would be in the way as well—if they could walk that far. Stay with them. I'll be back as soon as I can."

She wanted to argue, to go with him—but knew that he was doing the only thing possible. For a moment she held her arms about him, pulled her head against his chest. Then pushed him away and turned to the gasping Paramutan.

"I'll stay with them. Now go."

It was hard to move silently through the forest; too many

branches had to be pushed aside and the dead wood crackled underfoot. He went faster when he came to a game trail that led down from the hills. It angled off in the right direction, toward the shore, and he followed it with care. When it emerged from the trees he stopped and looked out carefully from behind the screening leaves. The empty dock was directly ahead of him with the high, rounded mounds beside it. They were too smooth and regular to be natural formations—and they had openings like doors let into them.

Should he go any closer? If there were Yilanè inside them—how could he find out? There were no uruketo at the dock, but that meant little since Yilanè could have been left behind.

The sharp crack of the hèsotsan was unmistakable. He hurled himself aside, falling, horribly afraid. The dart must have missed. He had to get away.

There was a crash of heavy feet and even as he struggled to push his way through the screen of young trees he saw the Yilanè run up, hèsotsan half raised. She stopped suddenly when she saw him, her arms curved with a gesture of surprise. Then she raised and aimed the weapon.

"Do not shoot!" he cried out. "Why do you want to kill me? I am unarmed and a friend."

His spear had fallen from his hand and he pushed it deeper into the undergrowth with his foot as he spoke.

The affect on his attacker was dramatic. She stepped backward and spoke with disbelief.

"This is an ustuzou. It cannot speak—yet it spoke."

"I can speak and speak well."

"Explanation of presence here: immediate and urgent."

The weapon was ready but not pointed at him. That could change in an instant. What could he say? Something, anything to keep her listening.

"I come from far away. I was trained to speak by a Yilanè of great intelligence. She was kind to me, taught me much, I am a friend of the Yilanè."

"I heard once of an ustuzou that talked. Why are you here alone?" She did not wait for an explanation but raised and pointed her weapon instead. "You have fled your owner, escaped from her, that is what you have done. Stand there and do not move."

Kerrick did as he had been ordered; he had no choice. Stood there in silence as he heard more footsteps, saw the two fargi come down the path from the forest carrying the body of one of the giant birds. He cursed himself for not realizing that he was walking on a well-trodden path, not a natural game trail. There were Yilanè here after all. And this one, she looked brutal, a hunter just as Stallan had been. She must have been out hunting for fresh meat and had practically stumbled over him. He should have known, a hunter would have seen at once this was not a game trail and would have taken precautions. He had done nothing. The fargi came up, passed him, each rolling one eye as she went by, making muffled remarks of wonderment, their load making speaking difficult.

"Go after them," the hunter ordered. "Run and you die."

Kerrick had no choice. He stumbled along the path, numb with despair, toward the rounded constructions on the shore.

"Bring the meat to the butchers," the hunter ordered. The two fargi went on past the first dome, but the hunter pointed it out to him with signs of entry.

"We go in here. I think that Esspelei will want to see you."

There was a leathery door set into the side of the dome; it split and opened when he pressed a speckled area. It revealed a short tunnel with another door at the far end, barely seen in the light from the glowing patches on the wall. His captor stood well back, weapon ready, and ordered him forward. He touched the second door and a wave of warm air washed over him as he went into the chamber beyond. The glowing patches were larger and the light was better in here. There were many strange creatures on the ledges, creatures of science, he could tell that much. Charts were on the walls and a Yilanè was bent over one of the instruments.

"Why do you disturb me, Fafnege," she said with some irritation as she turned about. Her gestures changed instantly to surprise and fear.

"A filthy ustuzou! Why is it not dead, why do you bring it here?"

Fafnege signed superiority of knowledge and contempt for fear. She was very much like Stallan. "You are safe, Esspelei, so do not betray your quivering fright. This is a very unusual ustuzou. Watch what happens when I order it to speak."

"You are in no danger," Kerrick said. "But I am. Order this repulsive creature to lower her weapon. I am unarmed."

Esspelei was rigid with surprise. Long moments passed before she spoke.

"I know of you. I spoke with one who spoke with Akotolp who told her of the ustuzou that speaks."

"I know Akotolp. She is very-very fat."

"You must be the one then, for Akotolp is fat. Why are you here?"

"The thing has escaped," Fafnege said. "There can be no other explanation of its presence. See the ring about its neck? See where a lead has been severed? It has fled its master."

"Is that what happened?" Esspelei said.

Kerrick was silent, his thoughts jumbled. What should he tell them? Any story would do; they had no ability to lie themselves since their very thoughts showed in the motion of their bodies. But he could lie—and would.

"I did not escape. There was—an accident, a storm, the uruketo was in trouble. I fell into the sea, swam ashore. I have been alone. I am hungry. It is good to be able to speak with Yilanè again."

"This is of great interest," Esspelei said. "Fafnege, bring meat."

"It will run again if we let it. I will order a fargi."

She went out but Kerrick knew she had not gone far. He would escape when he could—but first he needed to get at least some advantage from his capture. He must find out what these Yilanè were doing this far to the north.

"From one of great stupidity to one of highest intelligence; respectful request for knowledge. What do Yilanè need in this cold place?"

"Information," Esspelei said, answering without thinking, amazed at the presence of the Yilanè ustuzou. "This a place of science where we study the winds, the ocean, the weather. All of this is beyond you of course; I don't know why I bother to explain."

"Generosity of spirit, from highest to lowest. Do you measure the coldness of the winters, the cold winds that blow ever stronger from the north?"

Esspelei signed surprise and a shade of respect. "You are no fargi, ustuzou, but can speak with the smallest amount of intelligence. We do study the winters for knowledge is science and science is life. This is what we study."

She gestured toward the grouped instruments, the charts upon the wall, movements of unhappiness behind her speech. Talking more to herself now than to him. "Each year the winters are colder, each winter the ice is further south. Here is dead Soromset and dead Inegban*. Dead cities. And still the cold comes. Here Ikhalmenets which will be the next to die when the cold comes its way."

Ikhalmenets! Kerrick trembled with the force of his emotions, took time to speak so his trembling voice did not betray his eagerness. Ikhalmenets, the city that Erafnais had told him about on that beach, before she died, the city that aided Vaintè, the city that had launched the attack that had retaken Deifoben. Ikhalmenets, the enemy.

"Ikhalmenets? In my stupidity I have never heard of the city of Ikhalmenets."

"Your stupidity is indeed monumental. Sea-girt Ikhalmenets, a shining island in the ocean. You are not Yilanè if you do not know of the existence of Ikhalmenets."

As she said this she reached out to make her point, tapping one thumb lightly on the hanging chart.

"So stupid I wonder that I can live," Kerrick agreed. He leaned forward and noted exactly where the thumb had touched. "What generosity of highest to lowest that you even bother to speak with me, much less waste your incredibly valuable time in increasing my knowledge."

"You speak the truth, Yilanè-ustuzou." The door opened and a fargi entered with a bladder of meat. "We will eat. Then you will respond to my queries."

Kerrick ate in silence, filled with a fierce and sudden happiness. He had no other questions, there was nothing more that he needed to know.

He knew where the enemy Ikhalmenets was located in the vastness of the oceans, in all the width of the world.

CHAPTER THIRTY-SIX

K errick had just finished eating the preserved meat and was wiping the grease from his fingers onto his furs when the door opened again. But this was no wide-eyed fargi; a Yilanè of age and substance entered and looked at him with signs of doubt and suspicion. Esspelei stood in a position of subservience and he copied her at once. The newcomer was heavy of jowl, her thick arms painted with a pattern of whorls even here in this crude place so far from the cities. She was very much in control of the situation, Fafnege, still armed with her hèsotsan entered behind her, also signing respect for her rank. Kerrick knew that this one would not be as easy to fool as the others. She examined his face closely with one eye, while at the same time looked him carefully up and down with the other.

"What is this piece of ustuzou filth? What is it doing here?"

"Lowest Esspelei to highest Aragunukto," Esspelei writhed humbly, "the hunter found it in the forest. It is yilanè."

"Is it? Are you?" An imperious order that Kerrick answered with all signs of deference.

"It is my pleasure to speak and not be dumb like other ustuzou."

"Tear off those repellent coverings—the beast is difficult to understand."

Esspelei hurried forward and Kerrick made no protest, stood with humble submission as she cut away his furs with her string knife. He was bleeding from a number of cuts before his clothing lay tumbled on the floor.

"Pink-ugly, disgusting," Aragunukto said. "And obviously a male. Admit no fargi lest the sight of this one generate unacceptable thoughts. Turn! I knew it, no tail either. I have seen pictures of your kind, safely dead, in far-away sea-girt Ikhalmenets. How did it get here?"

"It fell from an uruketo during a storm, swam ashore," Esspelei said. She said it as a fact; since he had spoken of it it must be a fact. Aragunukto's features clouded with anger.

"When could this have happened? It is my certain knowledge that there is only one Yilanè ustuzou and that it has escaped and is feral. Are you that same ustuzou?"

"I am, great one. I was recaptured, sent in an uruketo across the ocean, then washed overboard."

"What uruketo? Who commanded? Who captured you?"

Kerrick was becoming tangled in his own web of lies. Aragunukto was too shrewd to fool—but there was no way out now.

"This knowledge is not mine. I was struck on the head, a storm, night . . ."

Aragunukto turned away and signed Fafnege for attention-to-orders. "This creature of disgust speaks like it is Yilanè. It is not. There are shadows in its speaking that reveal its ustuzou nature. I feel dirtied by this communication. Kill it, Fafnege, and let us be done with it."

With gestures of satisfaction and happiness Fafnege raised her hèsotsan, aimed it.

"No, you have no reason," Kerrick called out hoarsely. But the order had been given, would be obeyed. He jumped sideways, away from the weapon, stumbled against the shocked scientist at his side. In an agony of fear he seized her heavy arms and pulled her before him, crouching so her body shielded him from any dart. "I can help you, give important information!"

But they could not understand him, for they could hear only the sound of his voice; because Esspelei's solid body blocked any view of his limbs.

"Kill it! Instantly-instantly!" Aragunukto raged.

Fafnege crouched, weapon ready, stalking him like a wild prey. Esspelei was struggling, breaking away. Once his body was exposed he was dead. He glanced over the scientist's shoulder as he felt her break his grip and fall forward. Saw the door opening.

Saw the shocked, brown-furred face of a Paramutan appear there.

"Kill the one with the death-stick," Kerrick screamed aloud, his body exposed now to the raised weapon.

Even as he spoke he realized that he had called out in Marbak. He hurled himself to the floor as the hèsotsan snapped loudly. The dart came so close to his face that he felt the breath of its passage. Fafnege watched him fall, moved the weapon to follow him.

"What is happening?" Kalaleq cried out.

Fafnege spun about at the sound of his voice. Kerrick found the Paramutan words.

"Kill! The one with the stick!"

Kalaleq's was the arm that sank the deadly harpoon into the giant ularuaq, now he hurled his spear with the same precision, the same strength. Catching Fafnege in the midriff, doubling her over with the force of the blow. The hèsotsan fired its dart into the floor as she fell.

Niumak surged through the entrance, his spear ready, Armun right behind him. Kerrick was starting to rise as she ran toward him.

"Don't—not that one!" he cried. Too late. Esspelei screamed in pain, clutched at Armun's spear where it had been thrust into her neck, fell still screaming out bubbles of blood, died.

"She was a scientist, I wanted to talk to her," he said weakly, looking about. Armun had wrenched her spear free, turned to protect him.

But there was no need. Aragunukto was dead as well, Kalaleq turning from her body. The Paramutan was panting with emotion, his eyes blood red. "More?" he asked. "Are there more?"

"Yes, in the other structures. But . . ."

They were gone before he could even begin to explain about fargi. Tiredly he picked up his cut furs, looked at them. Armun touched soft fingers to the blood upon his skin, spoke quietly.

"When you did not come back I was heavy with fear. The Paramutan too. Niumak tracked you, found your spear, found the place where your prints joined those of the murgu. Then followed them here. Did they wound you?"

"No. Just these small cuts. Nothing more."

As he pulled the dismembered furs together he tried to assemble his thoughts as well. By now the Yilanè would all be dead. So be it. Aragunukto had ordered his death simply because she did not like the way he spoke. Once again it was only death; peace was unthinkable. Perhaps it was better this way. He looked up as Kalaleq came back in, panting, his spear bloodied, blood drenching his hand and arm.

"What strange and horrible creatures! How they wriggled and screamed and died on our spears."

"All dead?" Armun asked.

"All. We went into each of these big paukaruts and found them and speared them. Some ran, but they died as well."

"Here is what must be done," Kerrick said, forcing himself to think, to plan. "We must leave no trace of our presence here. If the murgu even suspect that we are on this side of the ocean they will seek us out and kill us."

"Put the bodies into the ocean," Kalaleq said practically. "Wipe up blood."

"Will others come?" Armun asked.

"Yes, in their boats that swim, the dock is here. If they find them all missing it will be a mystery—but we will not be suspected. Take nothing, disturb nothing."

"Want nothing!" Kalaleq cried out, shaking his spear. "Nothing that these things have. We must carefully wash their blood from our spears or we will have the worst bad fortune. You spoke of how terrible and strong and different these murgu were, and I marveled. But you did not tell me how I would tremble with anger and hatred at sight of them. This is a very strange thing and I do not like it. Into the ocean with them, then we return to pleasure of cold north."

No, south . . . Kerrick thought, but did not speak the words aloud. This was not the proper moment. But he did turn to look at the chart one last time before he left. Reached out and touched it lightly just over the irregular dark green circle set into the light green sea. Sea-girt Ikhalmenets.

Armun saw his body writhe with the name and she took him by the arm. "We must leave. Come."

Darkness had fallen before they were done. The sea received the bodies and the blood-stained fragments of his furs. The tide was on the ebb; the corpses would be carried out to sea. The fish would take care of the evidence.

Niumak had little difficulty in leading them back in the darkness. But the track was steep and they were all tired when they finally saw the light of the fire flickering between the leaves. There were shouted greetings when they finally stumbled out onto the sand.

"You are here! All is well?"

"Things have occurred, terrible things!'

"Death and blood, creatures unbelievable."

Kerrick dropped onto the sand, then drank greedily of the cold water that Armun brought to him.

"You are safe," she said, touching his face as though to reassure herself. "They took you but they are dead. You are alive."

"I am safe, but what of the others?"

"We will return across the ocean to them. They are safe there by the lake. Do not fear for Arnwheet."

"I do not mean them. What about all the other sammads, the Sasku—what of them?"

"I know nothing of them, care nothing. You are my sammad."

He understood how she felt, wished that he could feel the same. They were secure here with the Paramutan—as long as they stayed far to the north and avoided this dangerous coast. In the spring they would be able to cross the ocean again, to bring the rest of their small sammad here. Then they would all be safe. They would do that. The other sammads were strong and could guard themselves, fight the Yilanè if they were attacked. Their existence was not his responsibility.

"I cannot do it," he said, teeth clamped tight, fists hard, shaking with the strength of his emotions. "I cannot do it, cannot leave them all to die."

"You can. You are one—the murgu are many. All of this is not your doing. The fighting will never end. We will stay away from it. We need the strength of your arm and spear, Arnwheet needs it. You should think of him first."

He laughed at that, a laugh without humor. "You are right—I should think of nothing else. But I cannot stop my thoughts. I discovered something in the murgu camp, saw a chart very much like the murgu one that we have, saw on it the place, the murgu city, where the killers come from . . ."

"You are tired, you must sleep."

He angrily brushed her hands away, stood and raised his fists to the sky.

"You just don't understand. Vaintè leads them—and she will follow the sammads until they are finally destroyed. But I know where Ikhalmenets is. Now I know where she gets her weapons and her strength and her fargi."

Armun fought to control her fear, did not understand the invisible pains that wracked him.

"You have this knowledge—but there is nothing you can do. You are one hunter against a world of murgu. There is nothing that you alone can do."

Her words disarmed him and he dropped down to sit at her side again. Quieter now, more thoughtful. Anger alone would not drive away the Yilanè.

"You are right, of course, what can I do? Who would help me? All the sammads in the world would be of no help against that distant city on its island in the sea."

The sammads could not help—but others could. He looked at the dark outline of the ikkergak, at the Paramutan talking excitedly around the fire while they tore at their raw meat with sharp white teeth. Remembered how Kalaleq had looked, how obsessed by hatred of the Yilanè, the murgu, the new, repulsive and unknown creatures.

Could that hatred be somehow harnessed? Was there something that could be done?

"We are tired and must sleep," he said and held Armun tightly to him. Yet tired as he was he did not sleep at once, heard her breathing softly and regularly beside him as he looked up unseeingly at the stars, his thoughts rushing around in circles.

In the morning he sat in silence looking at the Yilanè chart while the Paramutan loaded the ikkergak for departure. When they were ready to leave he called Kalaleq over.

"You know this chart?" he said.

"It must be thrown into the sea like the rest of the murgu."

His anger had faded during the night, his eyes no longer reddened with rage, but the disquiet was still there. Kerrick shook his head.

"It is too valuable. It tells us things we have to know. Let me show you. Here is where our paukaruts are—here is where we are now. But look, south along this coast, see across this narrow bit of ocean to the large land . . ."

"Murgu land, you told me so, I do not like to think of it."

"But here, look here, just off the coast are these islands. That is where the murgu are who kill my brothers. I would like to kill those murgu. This ikkergak could reach the island easily enough."

Kalaleq stepped back and raised his hands before him. "This ikkergak can sail in only one direction. North. This ikkergak goes quickly away from murgu—not toward them. Do not speak of this to me again for it is not a thing to even think about." Then he laughed and shuffled in a circle. "Come, we go to the paukaruts. Think of all the rotten meat to eat, the blubber to lick. What good fun! Do not think of these murgu. Never think of them or see them again."

If he could. If he only could.

Ardlerpoq, tingavoq, misugpoq,
muluvoq—nakoyoark!

PARAMUTAN SAYING

===========

Hunt, screw, eat, die—what fun!

CHAPTER THIRTY-SEVEN

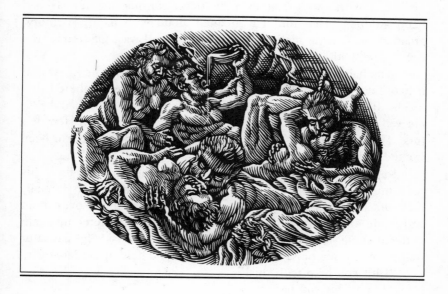

It was a fine celebration. No—it was far better than that. Far, far better than that Kalaleq realized when he took a moment to think about it.

It had been the greatest celebration the Paramutan had ever seen, that is what it had been. A victory banquet hailing the death of a new and terrible enemy. What tales they had told of the battle! What stabs of spears and ghastly alien death cries had been reenacted. Oh, there had been such screams of terrified delight from the women. Then they had feasted. How they had eaten and eaten, groaned with pain as their skin stretched tight over their stomachs, slept, ate again, slept some more. It had been hot in the paukarut, all of them jammed in together, so skins and furs had been thrown aside. When Kalaleq had woken the next time he found himself jammed tight against Angajorqaq's warm, pungent body. He had sniffed deeply of the soft brown fur on her breasts, then licked them. Distantly aware of his attention she had moaned in her sleep and excited him greatly. When this had happened he became tremendously worked up and had pulled her out onto the furs and took her there in front of the others who were awake. Their loud cheering and shouts of encouragement had woken the other sleepers, until they had all grown excited and the females screamed with mock fear as they fled, but not too far. It had been glorious, what fun! He groaned aloud with happy memory, groaned again as he realized how sore his head was. Of course, the fight! That had been glorious too.

Who had he fought with? He had no memory. But he knew that it had been glorious. How had it started? Yes, he remembered that much. It had been the male Erqigdlit, that is who it had been. He was so foolish. All that Kalaleq had done was open his female's furs. That was for fun. Then the other had hit him and he had been excited and hit Nanuaq who had hit him back. Good fun.

Kalaleq yawned and stretched—then laughed at the pain in his sore muscles. Angajorqaq was still asleep, snuffling to herself, Kukujuk just a mound under his skins. Kalaleq stepped over them and made his way from the paukarut, yawning and stretching again in the morning sun. Nanuaq who was also standing outside his paukarut walked over when he saw the other emerge and held up his large fist.

"I hit you hard with this!"

"Then I hit you hard."

"That was a real celebration."

"It was." Nanuaq laughed into the back of his hand as he spoke. Kalaleq's forehead wrinkled when he saw this, for laughing into the back of the hand means that there is a secret. More fun.

"Tell me, you must tell me," he called out loudly, "you must."

"I'll tell you. The Erqigdlit is gone. He must have gone while you still slept. And he has gone away in your boat!"

They both laughed uncontrollably at this until they fell helplessly to the snow where they rolled about, sides aching with laughter.

"I like these Erqigdlit," Kalaleq finally gasped. "They do things that we would never think of."

"Wake the others. Share the fun. Take the ikkergak. We will have to race to catch him before it grows dark."

The shouting outside woke Armun. She saw the tent flap thrown back and the Paramutan hurrying and calling out to one another. After the fighting and the excesses of the night before Kerrick had spread his furs between her and the others to prevent any more unwelcome attention. They were thrown back now; he must be outside with the others. She pulled her clothing over to her and dressed under the furs. The Paramutan found the sight of her smooth and hairless skin too interesting and exciting and she did not want any more trouble. When she went outside she saw that one of the ikkergaks was being pushed into the sea. Angajorqaq hurried up, her brown-furred face split into a broad grin.

"Your Kerrick, so funny. While we slept he sailed away in a boat to make us chase him."

Fear seized Armun. This was not funny, not to her, nor could it have been to Kerrick either. He had not laughed with the others during the night, had scarcely been aware of them, but had been cold and grim, his thoughts elsewhere, and had only stirred to life when one of the Paramutan had pulled at her clothing. Then he had struck with fierce anger, would have killed if she had not pulled him away. This was not a joke. If he had taken the boat it was for one reason alone. He would go south. He would try to find the island; he talked of nothing else.

"I am coming with you," she cried out as the ikkergak slipped into the sea. "Wait for me—you must wait for me."

The Paramutan chortled with pleasure as they helped her aboard, trying to touch her body through the thick furs. When she slapped their hands away they laughed even harder. She could not be angry at them because they were so different from the Tanu, laughing at everything and sharing their women.

Armun stayed out of the way while the sail was run up. Nanuaq was at the tiller tacking the ikkergak across the wind. Kalaleq looked up at the set of the sail with a quizzical eye, then loosed a line and tightened it into a new position.

"How will you find him?" Armun asked, looking out at the gray expanse of empty, white-flecked sea.

"He can't go west into the ocean, go north only ice, so we go south and find him quick because we sail better." He made the line fast, then tried to reach up under her furs while he talked. She pulled away and went into the bow, away from all of them.

It was cold here, with spray blowing into her face, but she stayed most of the day. The coast moved slowly by and the sea ahead remained empty. Why had he done it? Did he really think that he could sail alone to that distant murgu island? And even if he could—what could he do alone? It was a mad thing to do.

And he was mad to even think of it. She had to face up to the thought now for she had been evading it for too long. Kerrick had always been different from other hunters, she knew that. But for too long now she had been letting that difference cloud her thoughts. The time had come to face the truth. There was something very wrong with him, with the way he acted now. At times he reminded her of the old man, she had never known his name, in the sammad when she was very young. He talked only to himself and did not hear others—although he did listen to voices speaking to him that no one else could hear. They gave him food because of this and were attentive when he spoke, but in the end he walked off into the forest one day and never came back. Kerrick did not hear the spirit voices—but he had gone out into the sea just as the old man had gone into the woods. Was he the same? Could he be helped?

Fear held her in the bow of the ikkergak all day, looking out at the empty sea. Kalaleq brought her food but she pushed it away. There was no sight of the boat, nothing at all. Perhaps they were wrong and he had gone west, out into the trackless ocean, lost to her forever. No, she would not think that, could not. He had gone south looking for his murgu island, that was what he had done. Yet the fear stayed with her, growing even greater as the sky darkened with the coming light.

"There," Niumak called out. He had clambered halfway up the mast and clung by one hand, pointing out to sea. A tiny dark speck rode up on a wave, then disappeared again in the trough. Kalaleq pushed the tiller over.

"How smart the Tanu!" he cried. "He stands out to sea while we search along the shore."

They called out loudly to Kerrick as the ikkergak swooped down on the little boat, laughing and shouting compliments. He must have heard them—yet he never turned to look. Just faced ahead and sailed on. When they raced alongside he still took no notice. Only when the ikkergak moved in front of him, cutting him off, did he look up. He pushed over on the steering oar and sat, slumped, as the sail dropped and he lost way. His hands lay on his thighs and his chin rested on his chest and he never moved or seemed aware of their shouts. Someone threw a line to him but he took no notice as it slipped into the sea. They maneuvered closer and seized his sail. When the hulls bumped together Armun saw her chance, clambered over the side and half-fell into the boat.

"Kerrick," she called out softly. "It is Armun. I am here."

He stirred and lifted his eyes to hers and she saw the tears that stained his face. "They are going to die," he said, "all of them will die. I could prevent that, I could. Now they are going to die and it is all my fault."

"No!" she cried, seizing him and holding him tight to her. "You cannot blame yourself. You did not make this world the way it is. You did not bring the murgu. You are not to blame."

He was going out of his mind, she was sure of this now. This was not the Kerrick who had fought the murgu without fear, who had followed her into the frozen north. Something terrible was happening to him and she did not know what she could do. He had been like this in the camp by the lake. Though not this bad, and he had seemed to be much better after they had left. But the sickness in his head had returned—and stronger now than ever before.

Kerrick held tight to her all night, exhausted and deeply asleep, as they sailed back to the north.

In the morning he appeared calmer, ate and drank some water. But he did not answer when he was spoken to and the Paramutan sulked because they thought he was spoiling their fun. They soon forgot this though and cried out happily when the paukaruts came into sight soon after dawn. Armun could not forget. She looked at his grim and silent face and felt hope slipping away from her. Only when they were alone at last did he answer her.

"Yes, I was going to the island. There is nothing else that I can do. They depend upon me."

"But what can you do alone—even if you find it?"

"I don't know!" he cried aloud with pain. "I only know that I must try."

Armun had no answer to that, no words to help him. She could only hold him as tightly as she could and let her body speak what her lips could not.

The snows began that same day. First a light fall, then harder and harder until a long drift stretched out behind every paukarut and they knew that the blizzards of winter had begun.

There was plenty to eat and the Paramutan were well used to dozing through the long nights of winter. In the short days between storms they went hunting and fishing, but never strayed far. Kerrick would not join them, stayed inside and stayed within himself as well. Armun feared for the future because, try hard as she could, she could not shake him from the darkness of his thoughts.

In the end it was the strength of his obsession that won.

"I cannot bear seeing you like this," Armun cried.

"I have no choice. It can be no other way. I must find that island. And stop Vaintè. I will have no peace until that has been done."

"I believe you now. So I will go with you."

He nodded solemn acceptance, as though her cry of pain was a rational decision. "That is good. So now I am halfway there. The two of us cannot do it alone but will need one other. A Paramutan who knows how to sail. That will be enough. The three of us will be able to do it—I have worked out completely how it can be done."

"How?"

He looked about suspiciously as though afraid of being over-heard, then shook his head. "I cannot tell you yet. I must get it perfectly right before I can tell anyone. Now you must ask Kalaleq to come with us. He is strong and not afraid, he is the one that we need."

"He refused last time when you asked him."

"That was last time. Ask him again."

Kalaleq lay under his robes chewing desultorily at a piece of ancient fish—but he sat up and smiled when Armun approached.

"Many days of storm, many more days of winter." He lifted the fur and reached for her and she pushed his hand away.

"Why don't you leave winter, sail south to summer?"

"It is not done. The Paramutan are of the north and die when the days are hot all of the time."

"Do not go that far, not to the summer that never ends. Just part of the way. Sail to Kerrick's island then return. Help me."

"The island? He still thinks about it?"

"You must help me, Kalaleq, help him. There are strange things happening in his head and I am afraid."

"This is true!" Kalaleq called out excitedly, then covered his mouth with his hand when Angajorqaq and Kukujuk both turned to look in his direction. He was silent until they looked away again, then went on in a whisper. "I thought perhaps, because of the way he talks, but did not think that it could be true. How happy you must be."

"Happy? What can you mean?"

"To have such good fortune. To have your own hunter who has been spoken to by the spirits of the ocean and the wind. They talk to very few—and very rarely. And those who can hear their voices can then speak with the rest of us. That is how everything is learned. That is how we learn to make the things that we do. They told us how to build the ikkergaks so we can catch the ularuaq and grow fat. Now they talk to Kerrick and he will tell us what they say."

Armun did not know whether to laugh or cry. "Don't you know what they say? They say only one thing over and over. Go south to the island. That is all that they say."

Kalaleq nodded and chewed at his lip. "That is what they say? Well then, that is the way it must be. We shall just have to go south to the island."

Armun could only shake her head in complete disbelief.

yilanèhesn farigi nindasigi ninban*

YILANÈ APOTHEGM

Until a fargi is yilanè she has no city.

CHAPTER THIRTY-EIGHT

The new city had to come first, Ambalasi knew that, but she regretted every moment not spent studying the Sorogetso. That was what she had named these close relations of the Yilanè, the silent ones, for though they could communicate it appeared that they could do so on only the simplest of terms, as though they were still young elininyil in the sea. Even this was only an assumption made after her first contact with them; this success had not been repeated. The Sorogetso did not come near the wasteland of the peninsula, but stayed hidden in the jungle beyond. And she was too occupied with the endless problems of growing a city, with the indifferent help of the Daughters of Desperation, to have any opportunity to seek them out. She was also feeling her age.

Now she lay in the shade of a quick-growing shrub and examined the culture specimens in her sanduu. The eyelens of the greatly mutated creature was in the sunlight, the projected image clear in the shadow. Most of the microscopic life was familiar to her. There were no pathogens to see, nor had any harmful fungi grown in the sterilized soil. Good.

"Send for Enge," she ordered her assistant Setèssei, who had been changing specimens for her.

Then she lay back on the resting board and sighed. Life was too short for all that she wanted to do. Lanefenuu had been generous to her and life in now-distant Ikhalmenets a pleasure of relaxed research. How many years had she stayed there? She had lost count. She would be there still had she not grown interested in the biological aspects of the Daughters' philosophy. Then, on sudden impulse, she had thrown away all the comfort in exchange for this rude plank under a spiny shrub. No!—her body moved with the strength of her thoughts. Perhaps the study of the Daughters of Despair had been a mistake—but the voyage here had not been. What a wealth of new material she had discovered; how she would be revered for bringing it all to the attention of scientists in Entoban✻ still unborn. She savored the thought. Just the gigantic eels alone were important—not to mention an entire new continent. And one other thing of importance, many-times-amplified importance.

The Sorogetso. Patience, she must be patient. Proceed one step at a time. She needed security, peace, quiet to work. She needed the city to work in, the worthless sisters to provide her with necessities and comforts while she studied the Sorogetso. For this reason, if none other, the city must be grown quickly and perfectly. She sighed again, she had been over this chain of thought far too often before. Like it or not this was what she would have to do.

A shadow crossed her vision and she realized that Enge had appeared, was waiting patiently while she finished the interior conversation with herself. Ambalasi rolled one eye toward her and signed for close attention.

"We have reached an important moment in the development of this new city. The wall is strong, the worthless growth cleared away, shade shrubs growing. This patch of earth beside me has been dug and redug, sterilized and fertilized and is as ready as it ever will be. There is only one thing left to be done. Plant the city seed."

She took it from its container and held it up. Enge dropped forward on her knees in silent admiration. She stared at the gnarled brown shape for long moments before she spoke.

"First and foremost in my life was my discovery of Ugunenapsa. Now, this is surely the next most important moment in my existence. For this we have only you to thank, great Ambalasi, and have called this entire new land in your name to honor you. You have brought us freedom, brought us across the ocean, brought us to Ambalasokei where you will grow our city for us. May I call the others to watch the planting?"

"The planting is important—not the moment. They should keep working."

"They will want to honor the planting. Honor you."

"Well—if you insist. But it is a dreadful waste of time."

Word spread swiftly and the Daughters hurried from their labors, their mouths spread wide in the noonday heat. They grouped in silence around Enge, pushing close to see the depression that she had scooped in the soft ground. She was now soaking it with water under Ambalasi's direction.

"That is enough, you don't want to drown or rot it," the old scientist said. She held up the seed and the Daughters swayed in silent reverence. "Now—which of you is going to plant it?"

To Enge's chagrin a number of ardent discussions sprang up; arms moved swiftly and palms flashed color.

"We must discuss . . ."

"What would Ugunenapsa want done?"

"It is a matter of precedent. Those who came to Ugunenapsa first must be the wisest. So we should choose by precedent, question all . . ."

"Respectful request for silence," Enge said, repeating it with modifiers of importance and urgency until they finally fell silent. "There is only one single Yilanè suited for this momentous task: she who brought us here, she who brought the city seed, she is the one who shall plant it."

"Stupid waste of time," Ambalasi said, groaning as the rose to her feet, yet flattered despite her broadcast disdain. Garrulous and argumentative the Daughters might be—but at least they knew enough to respect intelligence and ability. She shuffled to the edge of the damp hole in the soil, the seed clutched between her thumbs.

"With this ceremony . . ." Enge began, and stopped, shocked, as the scientist simply dropped the seed into the hole, kicked some soil over it, then returned to her resting board, calling out as she walked.

"Water it some more—then all of you get back to work."

In the horrified silence that followed Enge recovered first, stepped forward, fumbled for the right expressions.

"With thanks, great thanks, to Ambalasi highest among the

highest. She has honored us by planting the seed for our city, the first city of the followers of Ugunenapsa. As we have discussed, many times over and over . . ."

"I am sure of that!"

". . . there can be but one name for this city. It will be called Uguneb, the City of Ugunenapsa, and will be honored forever by that name."

Movements of pleasure, cries of happiness. Twitches of disdain from Ambalasi who now called out.

"Enough. To work. There is much to do. You, Enge, stay. But order the rest of these creatures to their tasks."

"They cannot be ordered—" She saw Ambalasi's growing anger and turned swiftly to the crowd. "In Ambalasi's honor, and in honor of Ugunenapsa who guides us all, we must grow this city well so we must now return to our chosen duties. I remind you of our mutual decision. We will do what must be done."

She turned back to Ambalasi who made a sign of importance in the direction of the jungle as she spoke. "I think that now we shall begin our work with the Sorogetso. Have they been observing us?"

"They have. As you requested all sightings of them have been reported to me. They watch from the shadow of the trees very often, come even closer along the riverbank."

"They have not been approached?"

"No, you ordered that. But they have been observed. There are three of them watching us now."

"What? Why have I not been told?"

"Your instructions were to observe and record—not act."

"There are times when independent thought is called for. I am surprised at your lack of enterprise, Enge."

Enge knew better than to answer this impossible statement. Ambalasi stood and looked about. "Where are they? I see nothing."

"That is because you look in the wrong direction. Behind you, at the river's edge, there is a ledge above the water with new shrubs growing on it. They swim there daily and observe us from hiding."

"They have not been disturbed?"

"No, of course not."

"Occasionally, presumably by complete chance, your followers do something right. We will now consider contacting the Sorogetso. I will go and begin communication."

"No," Enge said, with signs of strength and command.

Ambalasi fell back, shocked, for in living memory she had never been spoken to in that manner. Enge addressed her again, quickly, before the volcano of the scientist's temper blew her away.

"I told you earlier of my studies of communication. I will tell you now that I have developed theories of sound-color-movement which I will be pleased to explain to you. I have also worked long to study fargi and elininyil communication, and have done the same with males in the hanalè. I have searched the records and have discovered that I am the only one who has done this for a very long time. Since I am a specialist I know you will want to listen to my suggestions." She saw that Ambalasi was swelling with anger, ready to explode. "You did not chastise Elem for exercising her specialized knowledge to feed the uruketo," she added quickly.

Ambalasi fell back—and made an easy motion of subtlety appreciated.

"In the fullness of time you are no match for me, Enge, but occasionally you present a glimmer of light that brings me amusement. I am very tired so will take this opportunity to lie in the shade and listen while you explain."

"First," Enge said, raising a thumb with a positive gesture, for she had pondered long and hard about this, "one must go alone— just as you went with the fish."

"Accepted. If I am the one."

Enge did not stop to argue, but went on.

"Secondly, a rapport must be established. They have taken our food, symbolic of sharing, but must now be satisfied on a different level. They will wonder just what sort of creatures we are, what we are doing here—but they must not be answered all at once. Knowledge must be shared. If I give them something I will want something in return."

"And how will this be done?"

"If you watch—why you will see."

Enge turned quickly away before Ambalasi's ready wrath could engulf her. Turned and walked slowly toward the shrubs that concealed the Sorogetso watchers.

She walked more and more slowly when she saw concerned motions, finally stopped and settled back comfortably onto her tail. Close enough to be understood, but not so close that she might be considered a threat. She held out the palms of her hands.

"Friend," she said, over and over again, in the simplest manner possible, using colors alone without verbalization. She stopped and looked at the shrubs. When there was no reaction from the hidden watchers she repeated herself once again. Her body at ease, she was not impatient; she radiated calm and serenity. "Friend." That was all she would say. It was now up to them.

"Friend."

The sun moved across the sky and the Sorogetso stirred restlessly. Finally one of them pushed through the shrubs and stood close in front of them, her eyes vertical slits against the glare. She was not the same individual that they had met in the jungle, but was taller and more muscled and stood with a chin-jutting arrogance. When Enge made no move the newcomer raked her claws on the ground in a simple aggressive movement.

"No fear," Enge said. "Do not fear me." The Sorogetso was puzzled and she repeated it in different ways, always as simply as possible until the Sorogetso understood and her crest came erect with anger.

"Me . . . fear . . . no! You . . . fear."

Contact had been established, but Enge permitted none of her pleasure to show. Instead she simply flashed the colors of friendship again. Then her name.

Ambalasi watching from a distance could make out none of the details of this first contact. But it lasted until the sun was low in the sky, then ended suddenly when the Sorogetso turned about, pushed through the shrubs and dived headlong into the water. Enge walked slowly back, her body stiff and uncommunicative.

"I hope that your time was wisely spent," Ambalasi said. "Though from here I saw very little happen."

"Much happened, much communication." Enge's speaking was muffled, for she was abstracted and deep in thought. "I insisted that the one who came forward should follow my lead, do as I did. I told my name and made strong reassurances that we were here in peace. I repeated that we wish only to help them, give them food if they wanted it. This was enough for the first contact, to get across basic concepts like that."

"Basic indeed. I hope it has not been all a waste of time. Did you at least get the creature's name?"

"Yes."

"Well, speak then. What is she called?"

"Eeasassiwi. Strong-fisher. But that is not her name." Enge

hesitated before Ambalasi's signed confusion, then spoke again with slow precision.

"We cannot say that it is her name.

"We must say instead that it is his name.

"Yes, that is right, this strong-fisher is a male."

CHAPTER THIRTY-NINE

"What you are sayng is a complete and utter impossibility."

Ambalasi reinforced the strength of her statements with modifiers of infinite enlargement. Enge bowed beneath the weight of her rage and assertiveness, but did not alter anything.

"That may be as you say, great Ambalasi, for you are the wisest in the sciences of life. I am humble before your knowledge—yet I still know what I know."

"How could you know?" Ambalasi hissed, her entire body atremble, her crest engorged and inflamed.

"I know in the simplest manner. The Sorogetso grew angry when I would not respond as it wished, made threatening gestures, one of which involved opening its sexual sac. I have seen what I have seen. It is male, not female."

Ambalasi collapsed backward, suddenly pale, gasping aloud as her strong passions ebbed. There was no mistake; Enge had seen what she had seen. Her limbs twitched in confusion as she sought some meaning, some possible explanation. Her inescapable conclusions were logically correct, personally repulsive.

"If the creature made gestures of threat, and one of these

gestures involved its sexual organs, I can only conclude that it must be the aggressor sex. Which in turn leads inescapably to the conclusion that . . ." She could not continue, but the movements of her limbs revealed the unavoidable conclusions. Enge spoke it aloud.

"The males here are dominant, the females at the most equal or possibly subservient."

"How unacceptably loathsome! Not the natural order for Yilanè. In the case of lower animals, yes, it is possible, for they are senseless brutes. But intelligence is female, thought is female, the source of life, the eggs—they are inescapably female. The males provide the crude biological functions of supplying half the needed genes and all of the reflexive-boring prenatal care. That is all they are good for, they have no other function. What you have observed is preposterous, unnatural—and utterly fascinating."

Ambalasi had recovered her aplomb, was thinking now like a true scientist not a mindless fargi. Was it possible? Of course it was possible. The diversity of sexual roles, relationships, variations and inversions among the species in the world was almost infinite. So why not a variation in her own species? How far back would the breaking apart of the two have to have been? She would have to consider that. The fact of even crude communication indicated a relatively recent separation. Unless the forms of basic communication were fixed in the genes and not learned. It all became more and more interesting. Enough. Observation first, theorizing last. Facts were needed, facts and more facts.

That she had been the one to discover this . . . ! She struggled to her feet.

"Imperative now! I must see, talk, record everything about the Sorogetso."

Enge signed patience. "You will do that, for yours is the mind of science that will disclose all. But communication first. I must learn to speak with the Sorogetso, gain their confidence, then penetrate their culture. It will take time."

Ambalasi leaned back with a tired sigh. "Of course it will. Proceed at once. Devote your time to nothing else. Take Setèssei with you, I will relieve her of all other tasks. She is to record everything. Detailed records must be kept. My name shall roar like the bellow of a nenitesk down through the annals of time for making this discovery. Of course you will get some credit as well."

"Your generosity is infinite," Enge said respectfully, concealing most of her feelings; luckily Ambalasi was too involved in her own whirling thoughts to notice any negative connotations in the statement.

"Yes, of course, well-known fact. I must learn the language as well—Setèssei will bring me the recordings daily. You will learn to speak with them, gain access to their community, give them food, hopefully they will have sickness and I can give them medical aid. In doing so I will make a study of their physiology. Doors of knowledge opening—facts accumulated, soon revealed!" She looked at Enge and her expression grew stern. "But knowledge reserved for those with the capacity to understand. Just as males are kept from the casual attention of fargi and unsuited ones, so must this fact of maleness be kept from your companions."

Enge was concerned. "But openness is the basis of our existence. We share with each other."

"Wonderful. But this fact is not for sharing." She pressed the point when she saw that Enge was still doubtful. "I make a comparison. A Yilanè would not put a hèsotsan in the hand of a yiliebe fargi with the sea still wet on her hide. It would mean death for the fargi or others. The maleness of the Sorogetso could be a weapon, a cultural poison, a threat. Do you understand that and agree?"

"I do," with grave reservations.

"Then I ask only for scientific reserve—for the present. When we have learned more we can discuss it again. Agreed?"

"Agreed." With strong modifiers. "We must discover the truth, then determine its effects upon us. Until we have reached that point I will remain silent."

"Very good. Since you agree with me my respect for your intelligence grows. Send Setèssei here so I can instruct her as to what is to be done."

The city grew luxuriously, and as it did Ambalasi drew more and more away from it. When problems were brought to her her wrath was so great, her insults so bitter that many grew to fear her. They began to discover ways to solve the problems on their own. This was made possible, as they soon discovered, by the fact that the city of Uguneneb had few of the city comforts they had known in older, larger and long-established cities. Refuse was not consumed and recycled by the city, water had to be brought from the river. Few if any of the other amenities of city life were present. Still existence here was superior to their imprisonment in the orchard. They would have to make do. If they had to sleep communally under the thick-leaved branches and eat a monotonous diet of eel and fish, it was not too important. What was more precious then food and drink to them was the unlimited opportunity to discuss Ugunenapsa and her ways, to seek truth and discover portents. It was a heady and wonderful existence at that moment.

For her part Enge actually managed to forget the existence of Ugunenapsa for a good part of her day, as she labored to understand the Sorogetso, to learn to speak as they spoke. Eeasassiwi did not return after their first encounter, but Enge did manage to make contact with another Sorogetso, who was withdrawn and shy but finally was won over by patience and gifts of food. This one was named Moorawees, which seemed to mean orange-of-color, perhaps because of the slight orange fringe on her crest. She was a female and Enge found that this made it easier to work with her, relate to her.

Understanding of Sorogetso communication grew slowly, but grow it did. They seemed to have very few modifiers and most of the meaning was carried by common color tonality. A few new verbal controllers were noted and soon after this Enge found that she could discuss basic concepts with Moorawees. It was then that the chance came at last to get Ambalasi involved.

"Opportunity unrivaled," she signed as she hurried toward the scientist—who instantly abandoned her work and radiated obedient attention. Enge was flustered by this—had never suspected that Ambalasi even knew these subservient gestures.

"Urge of explanation," Ambalasi said.

"Forthcoming. My informant mentioned that one of her companions—there is no shade of male-female attached to the term that I could tell—has been wounded in some manner. I informed Moorawees that one of us was skilled in repair of bodies and Moorawees grew excited. I think she will lead us to the injured one."

"Excellent. I have studied their communication as you have recorded it." She stood erect and spoke in the proper Sorogetso manner. "Help-given, person-aided, gratification."

Enge was truly impressed. "That is perfect. The time has come for us to penetrate the jungle. I fear only for your safety this first occasion. Perhaps I might take Setèssei now, she has healing skills, and might be more suitable for this first visit . . ."

"It is I who will go now." Said with all her imperiousness and might. Enge accepted; this was one time she knew that Ambalasi would not be disagreed with.

Ambalasi pushed the bulge on the hide of the carrying creature and its mouth opened to reveal the medical equipment stowed inside. After carefully checking the contents Ambalasi added more nefmakels, large ones for serious wounds, and other items that might be called for. When she was satisfied she shut it, then turned to Enge.

"Carry this yourself—we want no witnesses with us now. Lead the way."

The Sorogetso was waiting in the river, only her head above the water. Her eyes widened with fear when Ambalasi came up and she turned about and moved away through the stream. They followed her into the river but she was the faster swimmer and her orange crest quickly vanished from sight. Ambalasi saw her emerge on the distant bank and splashed ponderously in that direction. Enge followed, much burdened by the medical supplies. She was gasping for breath when she finally stumbled ashore. Moorawees was at the forest edge, slipping away between the trees as they approached. They hurried after her, losing sight of her finally, but noting that they were following a well-trod path. When they emerged from the shadow of the jungle, on the bank of a stream they found her waiting for them.

"Stop," her palms flashed, with head-movement controllers of danger-imminent. The two Yilanè stopped at once, looked about in all directions yet saw nothing to fear.

"In-water," Moorawees signed, then opened her mouth wide and emitted a high-pitched warbling cry. She did this a second time until there was an answering call from the other side of the stream. There were movements in the brush there and two more of the Sorogetso emerged and looked doubtfully across the flowing water.

"Danger of strangers, much-fear," one of them signed.

"Death of Ichikchee greater danger," Moorawees answered with some firmness. It was only after more hesitation, and shouted commands from Moorawees that they shuffled to the large tree trunk floating by the shore and pushed it out into the stream. One end remained secured on the far bank so that, when the free end had drifted across and lodged on the shore, a bridge was made across the stream. Moorawees led the way, hooking her claws carefully on the rough bark and holding to the projecting stubs of branches. Enge waited for Ambalasi to precede her—but the scientist was rigid and uncommunicative.

"I will go first," Enge said. "I believe that there is nothing to fear."

"Stupidity and incomprehension," Ambalasi said with some vehemence. "I am not afraid of these simple creatures. It was the silence of thought and observation that stayed me. Did you see what they did?"

"Of course. Floated this log over so we could cross the stream dryshod."

"Brain-of-lowest-fargi!" Ambalasi snapped with quick anger. "You see with your eyes but fail to understand with your brain. They have used an *artefact* in the manner of the ustuzou—not the Yilanè. Now do you see what is happening?"

"Of course! Joy-of-revelation, acknowledgment of stupidity. Though physically like us, they are fixed at a social level scarcely above the lower animals with no knowledge of Yilanè science."

"Obviously. But obvious only when pointed out to you. Proceed."

They crossed the bridge as carefully as the Sorogetso had done, though Ambalasi stopped halfway over and bent down to look closely into the water. The Sorogetso called out with fear until she signed a negative and went on to the other bank.

"No danger visible," she said, watching with great interest as the Sorogetso pulled on projecting branches and trailing vines— careful not to step into the water—until the tree had been pulled back into its original position. As soon as this was done the two Sorogetso hurried out of sight among the trees. Enge called for attention.

"Moorawees has gone this way; we must follow her."

They followed another well-trod path through the thin growth of trees and emerged into a clearing. Only Moorawees was visible, waiting for them, though they felt that many others were watching them from the concealment of the brush. Ambalasi expressed happiness at excitement of new knowledge.

"Look at the shore there, through the trees. I do believe that we are surrounded by water, an island in the stream that acts as a barrier, containing some danger-to-be-discovered. Gaze upon primitive and disgusting habits, discarded bones now black with flies."

"Moorawees calls to us," Enge said.

"Follow me and bring the medical supplies."

Moorawees pushed aside a low bough to disclose a nest of dried grass under a tree. Lying there unconscious, eyes closed, was a Sorogetso. Obviously female, her sac gaped slightly open, she stirred and moaned with pain. Her left foot had been bitten by some creature, was half eaten away. Now it was swollen and black, covered with flies. Her ankle and the leg above were also swollen and discolored.

"Neglect and stupidity," Ambalasi said with some satisfaction, opening the container creature. "Drastic measures must be taken and you shall assist me. This is also the opportunity for certain scientific experiments and observations. Send Moorawees away. Tell her this one's life will be saved but she must not watch or the cure will not take."

The Sorogetso was happy to leave and retreated quickly. As soon as she was gone Ambalasi, with quick, accurate movements injected an anesthetic. As soon as Ichikchee was silent she wrapped a binding creature around the injured limb, centering the head over the large artery behind her knee. When prodded, the binding smoothly swallowed its tail until it grew tight, sunk into the flesh, cutting off the blood supply. Only then did Ambalasi take her string-knife and cut off the infected foot. Enge turned away but could still hear it crunching through flesh and bone. Ambalasi saw this and registered astonishment.

"Such squeamishness! Are you then a fargi with no experience of existence? Watch and learn for knowledge is life. The foot was possible to repair—but only as a partial, crippled thing. Better to remove it all. Or rather all not needed. Half of the phalanges and metatarsal bones gone. With care and skill I excise the rest, stopping at the tarsus. We need that. Now—the large nefmakel, yes that one, clean this wound up. Give me the container."

Ambalasi found a small bladder of viscous red jelly. She cut it open and used a tiny nefmakel to remove a white kernel from its core—which she fixed into position on the stump of the severed leg. Only when this was placed to her satisfaction did she close the wound and cover it with a larger nefmakel, then found another single-fanged creature for a second injection.

"Antibiotic. Finished."

She straightened up and rubbed at her sore back—and realized that they were no longer alone. A number of the Sorogetso had emerged silently from hiding and now stood close and watched, stirring and moving back a bit when her glance caught theirs.

"Pain ended," she said loudly in their manner of communication. "She sleeps. Will be weak, but pain will be gone. She will have many days' rest, whole again, as she was before."

"Foot . . . gone," Moorawees said, staring wide-eyed at the bandaged stump.

"I will return and treat her. Then something will be seen that you have never seen before."

"What have you done?" Enge asked, as puzzled as the Sorogetso.

"Planted a cell cluster to grow a new foot. If these creatures are as genetically close to us as they appear to be she will grow a new foot in place of the lost one."

"But—what if it doesn't grow?"

"Equally interesting in the cause of science. Either result will be of great importance."

"Even more so to Ichikchee," Enge said with obvious overtones of disapproval. Ambalasi expressed surprise.

"Surely the advance of knowledge takes precedent over this primitive creature—who would certainly have died if I had not treated her. Such sympathy is misplaced."

The Sorogetso were even closer now, ten of them in all, jaws gaping as they tried to understand this unknown communication. They watched attentively as Ambalasi spoke, some even shuffling closer to make out her colors better.

"There you are," Ambalasi signed abruptly to Enge. "More knowledge must be gained. You will talk with them now. What a momentous occasion this really is. Momentous!"

The Sorogetso drew back at the quickness of her unknown communication, but returned when she called gently to them.

"They are like fargi fresh from the sea," Enge said. "We must be patient."

"Patient, of course, but we are students as well. We are the fargi now, here to learn, for they have a life and existence of their very own that we must plumb and understand. Now we begin."

kakhashasak burundochi ninustuzochi
ka'asakakel.

YILANÈ APOTHEGM

=======

A world without ustuzou is a better world.

CHAPTER FORTY

Vaintè felt no despair, no fear of her meeting with Lanefenuu. They had their losses, terrible losses—but there had been success as well. In battle you had to accept one in order to gain the other. The final victory was all that mattered, all that would be remembered. She was sure of this within herself, felt not one bit of doubt, yet still kept reassuring herself over and over again of that strength. Lanefenuu might doubt, if so she would not be convinced unless Vaintè wore surety-of-success like an all-enveloping carapace.

"Desire of position change, insufficiency of light," the crewmember with the brush and paint said, modifying the demand with controllers of extreme humility.

The uruketo had altered course, they must be nearing Ikhalmenets, so that the shaft of sunlight from the top of the open fin had moved from her. Vaintè leaned forward to take the weight off her tail and stepped into the light to examine the work. Ornate golden leaves spiraled down her arms from her shoulders to terminate in patterns of fruit upon the backs of her hands. Perhaps overly ornate, but suitable for this important meeting. She signed satisfaction and approval: the crewmember returned extreme gratitude.

"This is excellent, gentle of touch, fine in design," Vaintè said.

"It is my pleasure to do anything to assist the Salvationer."

Vaintè was hearing the term more and more these days. At first it had been expressed as she-who-aids-us, but had been gradually changed into she-who-saves-us. This is what the Yilanè of Ikhalmenets thought and what they said. They had no doubts, cared nothing for the fargi who had died that they might live. They could see the snow ever lower on the mountain peak, could feel the cold breath of endless winter drawing even closer. The eistaa must certainly share these feelings to some degree.

Vaintè was beside the uruketo's commander, on the summit of the fin, when they swam into the harbor of Ikhalmenets. With ponderous grace the great creature passed the row of other uruketo to reach its own place beside the docks. The enteesenat tore ahead in a torrent of foam seeking their reward. A small wave slapped off the wooden dockside, washing across the uruketo's back, then it was close and secured. Vaintè looked down into the fin and signed to a crewmember in the uruketo below.

"High-ranked Akotolp, presence desired."

Vaintè glared out at the barren dockside and hid her displeasure in immobility while she waited for the scientist. The Eistaa was aware that Vaintè was returning. She had sent for Vaintè and knew that she was aboard this uruketo. Yet none awaited her on the dock, no one of rank to receive her. If not an insult it was surely a warning. One that Vaintè did not need. Lanefenuu had made no secret of her feelings about the way the conflict with the ustuzou was going. There was much wheezing and panting from below, heard well before Akotolp appeared.

"Such a climb," the fat scientist complained. "Travel by uruketo discomfort-making."

"You will go with me to the eistaa?"

"With pleasure, strong Vaintè. To give what aid and support that I can." She rolled one eye to the commander, saw her back turned as she supervised the docking, before she spoke again. "Take strength from the knowledge that you have only done as you were ordered. Never did fargin or Yilanè ever err by following orders."

Vaintè expressed gratitude-for-understanding, then added, "I wish it were that easy, good Akotolp. But I command the forces so must take responsibility for any failures. Come."

That they were expected was obvious when they reached the ambesed. The Eistaa was there, sitting in her place of honor with her advisers grouped behind her. But the great open space was empty, the sandy floor smoothed and patterned. When they walked across it toward Lanefenuu they left a double row of footprints. Lanefenuu sat upright and immobile as they approached. Only when they had stopped before her and signed loyalty and attention did she turn and fix Vaintè with a cold gaze.

"There has been failure and death, Vaintè, failure and death."

Vaintè shaped her limbs into respect to superiority as she spoke. "Death, agreed, Eistaa. Good Yilanè have died. But there has been no failure. The attack continues."

Lanefenuu angered at once. "You do not call the destruction of an entire force a failure?"

"I do not. In this world it is eat or be eaten, Eistaa, you of all Yilanè know that. We have been bitten by the ustuzou—but we live on to consume them alive. I told you that they were a dangerous enemy and I never said that there would not be losses."

"You indeed told me that. But you neglected then to put a number to the Yilanè corpses, to give me a count of the tarakast and uruktop dead. I am very displeased, Vaintè."

"I bow before your wrath, strong Lanefenuu. Everything that you say is correct. I neglected to give you a number for those who will die. I give it to you now, Eistaa."

Vaintè threw her arms wide in the gesture of totality, speaking the name of this great city.

"Ikhalmenets will die, all will die, this will be a city of death. You are doomed."

Lanefenuu's advisers wailed in agony at the terror of her speech, followed her pointing finger to the great mountain, the extinct volcano that soared above the island, seeing but not wanting to see the snow that glistened there.

"Winter is coming, Eistaa, winter without end. Each winter the snow is lower on the mountain. One day soon it will reach this city and never melt again. All who remain here will die."

"You speak above yourself," Lanefenuu cried out, jumping to her feet with a gesture of great anger.

"I speak only the truth, great Lanefenuu, Eistaa of Ikhalmenets, leader of her Yilanè. Death comes. Ikhalmenets must go to the land of Gendasi∗ before that disaster happens. I labor only to save this city. Like you I sorrow at the death of our sisters and our beasts. But some must fall so that all may live."

"Why? We have Alpèasak. Your reports tell me that it grows well and soon Ikhalmenets will be able to go to Alpèasak. If that is so—what need for all these deaths?"

"The need is to destroy the ustuzou. There must be a final solution to their threat. As long as they live they are a danger. You will remember that once they destroyed and occupied Alpèasak. That must never happen again."

Anger still shaped Lanefenuu's body. Yet she carefully considered what Vaintè had said before she spoke. Akotolp took advantage of the momentary silence to step forward.

"Great Lanefenuu, Eistaa of sea-girt Ikhalmenets, may I speak to you of what has been accomplished, what still remains to be done to bring Ikhalmenets to Entoban∗?"

Lanefenuu grew angry at the interruption, then stilled her feelings as she realized that anger would accomplish nothing this day. Vaintè did not tremble with fear before her as the others did—nor did this fat Yilanè of science. She sat back and signed Akotolp to speak.

"There are only so many ways for an animal to attack, for a disease to kill. After each infection a good scientist determines the cause and finds the remedy. Once used, any particular attack on us will never succeed again. The ustuzou burnt our city—so now we grow cities that cannot be burned. The ustuzou attacked us at night in the concealment of darkness. Strong lights now reveal them, our darts and vines kill them."

Lanefenuu rejected past successes with a gesture of disdain. "It is not a history lesson that I need but a victory."

"You will have that, Eistaa, for it is inevitable. Attack and flee, bite and run is the bestial ustuzou way. Slow growth, inevitable success is the Yilanè."

"Too slow!"

"Fast enough with victory inevitable."

"I see no victories in the deaths of my Yilanè."

"We learn. It will not happen again."

"What have you learned? I know only that surrounded by impassable defenses they died, all of them."

Akaotolp signed agreement—but added strength-of-intelligence as well. "Stupid fargi may panic and run and talk of ustuzou of invisibility. That is the talk of ignorance. Science holds no secrets that cannot be unearthed through diligence and application. What an ustuzou can do, I can fathom. I made an examination, then used trained beasts with keen noses to track the ustuzou. I found where they had approached the laager, discovered the route they had used when they left."

The Eistaa was intrigued and paying close attention, her anger forgotten for the moment. Vaintè knew just what Akotolp was doing and was grateful.

"You found how they came, how they left," Lanefenuu said. "But how did they attack and kill—did you discover that?"

"Of course, Eistaa, for bestial ustuzou must always fall before Yilanè science. The ustuzou observed that our forces always made laager in the same places. So, before the attacking force arrived, they burrowed like the animals they are into the ground and lay in wait. How simple. They did not come to us—we went to them. During the darkness of night they burst out and killed."

Lanefenuu was astonished. "They did that? They have that intelligence? So simple—yet so deadly."

"They have a bestial intelligence that we must never underestimate. Nor will this manner of attack ever succeed again. Our forces will stop at night in different locations. They will have creatures with them to smell out and discover hidden enemy, hidden entrances and burrows."

Lanefenuu had forgotten her anger as she listened, and Vaintè took advantage of her improved mood.

"The time has come, Eistaa, to turn our backs on the snowy mountain and look instead at the golden beaches. Alpèasak has been cleared not only of the ustuzou but of all the deadly growths that drove them out. The defenses have been regrown and resown with plants that cannot burn. The ustuzou have retreated a great distance and between them and the city are our forces. The time is upon us to return to Alpèasak. It will be a Yilanè city once again."

Lanefenuu was on her feet at this welcome news, raking her claws victoriously into the ground. "Then we leave, we are safe!"

Vaintè lifted both rose-hued restraining palms. "It is the beginning—but not yet the end. Aid is needed to make the city secure, to assist its growth. But there is not yet food enough for the multitude of a city. But it is a beginning. You can send one uruketo of Yilanè and skilled fargi, two at most."

"A few drops where I wished for an ocean," Lanefenuu said with some bitterness. "Let it be so. But what of the ustuzou, what of them?"

"Consider them dead, Eistaa, put them from your thoughts. Akotolp needs some supplies, I will have more fargi. Then we leave. There will be no final clash of arms but rather a slow and inevitable tightening as a great serpent tightens about its victim. Though the victim may struggle—the end is unescapable. When I come to you next it will be to report this final victory."

Lanefenuu sat back and chewed on this concept, her conical teeth grinding lightly in echo of her thoughts. Everything was taking too long, too many were dead. But was there another way? Who could replace Vaintè? No one—that was an easy question to answer. No one else had her knowledge of the ustuzou. Or her hatred. She made mistakes, but they were not fatal mistakes. The ustuzou must be pursued and destroyed, she was convinced of that now. They were too poisonous to be allowed to live. Vaintè would accomplish that destruction. As her left eye looked at Vaintè her right eye rolled slowly up to look at the snow-topped mountain peak. This winter was the first time ever that the deadly white had reached all the way down to the edge of the green trees. They must leave before it reached the city itself. There was no choice.

"Go, Vaintè," she ordered, signing her dismissal. "Take what you need and pursue the ustuzou. I do not wish to see you again until you bring me word of their destruction." Then her anger burst out again. "If they are not dead you will die in their place, that I pledge. Do you understand me?"

"Completely, Eistaa." Vaintè drew herself up and radiated strength and certainty. "I would not have it any other way. I see it clearly. If they do not die—I will. That is my assurance to you. My life. I promise you no less in your cause."

Lanefenuu signed acceptance and grudging admiration. Vaintè would do what must be done.

Vaintè took his acceptance as dismissal, turned and strode away with Akotolp puffing after her, hurrying to keep up as Vaintè walked faster and faster. Hurrying to her destiny.

Her victory.

Nangeguaqavoq sitkasiagpai.

PARAMUTAN SAYING

The destination is of no importance,
only the voyage.

CHAPTER FORTY-ONE

Once the decision had been made, some of the madness left
Kerrick's eyes. It had been the unresolvable internal conflict that was tearing him apart. On one hand he and Armun
were safe—while across the ocean the sammads of the Tanu and
Sasku were under sentence of death. The better off that he was—
the worse their position became. He blamed himself for this impossible situation, saw Vaintè as the spirit of death that he alone had
released. He knew, without any doubt, that she was pursuing her
course of destruction only to kill him. He was the responsible one.
And he had fled. Only now had he stopped running. Like a trapped
beast he was turning to attack. And, like that beast, he never
considered for an instant whether he would live or die. He knew
only that he had to lash out, to tear and rend.

It was Armun who saw all too clearly the certain price of
failure. When she watched him poring over his charts she wished
that there were another way. There was none, she knew that. They
must sail south into the unknown. Either that or stay here until he
went mad. He was happy now, even smiling as he compared the
charts, traced out the course that they must take. Although the
future was dark and unknown, Armun was satisfied with her deci-

sion. Kerrick had filled her empty life, taken her from exile, from a life that was no life at all. He was not like the other hunters, could do things they could not do. He had led and they had followed him to victory against the murgu. But once the city had been taken they had rejected him. She knew all about rejection. Now, where he led she would follow. A small army of one. No, two really, she must not forget the little Paramutan hunter who saw wisdom in madness, sailed willingly into the blizzards of the arctic winter.

Kalaleq was indeed very happy. He sang hunting songs to himself as he went over the boat's sail stitch by stitch, sewing in more gut if there was any sign of weakness. He had done the same with the hull, checking and caulking. The first part of the journey south would be the most trying and every precaution must be taken before they left. Food stowed and lashed firmly into position—and the same for the waterskins. He knew full well what the fury of the winter storms could do. There would be two pumps instead of one for if they foundered they were lost. What fun! He laughed aloud as he worked, pretending not to see the jealous and envying looks of the others. What a voyage it would be!

Even when all of the preparations were complete they had to wait, for now in the depths of winter, the winds blew their worst, banking the snow outside the paukaruts and screaming continuously overhead. Now they could only wait. Some of Kerrick's dark mood returned with every day's delay and he fought to control it, knowing that nothing could be done. The work completed Kalaleq slept and harbored his strength. Armun remained calm, resigned, and this had a salutary affect on Kerrick. They would leave when the weather permitted.

When Kerrick woke he knew at once that something was very different. The shrieking wind that had torn at the paukarut for endless days was gone. Everything was still. Kalaleq was ahead of him, opening the lashings to admit the bright sunshine.

"What weather! How good!"

"Then we leave?"

"Now, soon, at once, no delay! The spirit of the wind has told us we must go at once while he is resting. He will not rest long, and we must try to be across the bay of storms before he returns. To the boat!"

With the end of the blizzard everyone knew that the long-delayed voyage would now begin. The paukaruts emptied, and the shouting, laughing mob converged on the boat. It was lifted clear of the snow and rushed to the ocean's edge. Waves still broke in a cloud of spray and rushed far up the slanting length of the flensing ledge. There was much loud argument as to the best manner of launching, but agreement was quickly reached. Ready volunteers hauled the boat into the surf, laughing and shouting at the cold soaking, held it there in the crashing waves. Still others seized up the three voyagers, sat them on their shoulders to keep them dry, then staggered forward into the water. The instant they were aboard Kalaleq raised the sail as willing hands pushed them into the breaking waves. As the boat surged forward the helpers were tumbled over by the heavy surf and washed ashore, laughing until they were exhausted. Armun watched with amazement; she would never understand these strange, furry hunters.

With the prevailing wind from the west they had to tack very often to make any progress to the south and west. Kalaleq knew that the coast to the south of them ran from east to west and they would never turn the headland west of the bay if they allowed themselves to be carried toward the land. Watching both the sail and the sky he took the bobbing, tiny craft on a course that should keep them well clear of the shore.

Seasickness struck Armun almost at once and she lay sprawled, damp-skinned under her fur covers. Kerrick seemed unaffected by the swooping rush through the waves and helped with the lines whenever they had to go about. He was smiling too, even laughing like the Paramutan while the spray froze on his hair and beard. Kalaleq shared his enthusiasm and only Armun seemed to understand the risks they were taking, the utter insanity of the voyage. But it was far too late to return, far too late.

The good weather held for the best part of two days, fair winds and clear sky. When the storms returned they were not as fierce as they had previously been. They sailed on for three days more before the ice on the rigging became so heavy that they had to go ashore to clear it away. They pulled the boat far up on the sand of a small beach, hacked at the ice until they were soaked and chilled, then huddled close to the fire Kerrick made, teeth chattering, their soaked clothing steaming and charring as they tried to dry it.

They had passed the murgu base during the storm, had seen nothing of it, nor did they expect to find any of the heat-loving creatures in these cold northern seas at this time of year. But with each day's voyage south there was an improvement in the weather. The storms seemed to have lost a good deal of their fury as the tiny craft moved slowly, ever southward, along the rocky coast.

It was foggy at dawn and a thin rain soaked them, chilling them more than the cold dry winds of the north. Kerrick stood in the bow peering as well as he could at the shore. A rocky headland rose above the fog ahead and they moved swiftly toward it, swept forward by wind and current. Kerrick looked from chart to land, chewing nervously on his lip. It must be, there seemed little doubt. He turned quickly and called out to Kalelaq.

"Put her over, take a heading as far west as you can. I am sure that we are coming close to Genaglè, the current is fierce there, rushing into the other sea."

"Are we there? This is wonderful!" Kalaleq shouted aloud and laughed as he pushed the tiller over, secured it then rushed to adjust the sail. "Oh that I should see this, a whole new world—and filled with murgu. Will the murgu be sailing in this sea now?"

"I don't think so, not this time of year. But after we cross the mouth of Genaglè we will come to the great continent of Entoban∗ where it is always warm. There we must be careful."

Murgu, Yilanè, the two words merged in his mind. They would be coming to the island soon. And he must attack them just as they attacked the Tanu on the other side of this sea. As they must be attacking them, even now.

"They will not fight," Herilak said, his lips white with anger. "They will not attack us—and when we attack them they hide behind their poison walls where we cannot reach them."

"They are murgu and murgu cannot be expected to war as Tanu or Sasku do," Sanone said, reaching out with a stick to stir the fire so that sparks rose high and blew away on the cold breeze. In winter, at night, even in this protected valley the air grew chill, and he was no longer young with the warm flesh of youth. He drew his thick robe closer about him and looked around at the sleeping valley. Only he and Herilak remained awake; the others slept.

"They learn, the murgu learn," Herilak said with some bitterness. "In the beginning we could spear them at night, cut them down and kill them. Now we cannot reach them at night. Nor during the day. They stay secure and do not advance until we have gone. Then they come on, slowly, but always closer."

"How close are they now?" Sanone asked.

"They surround us, on all sides. Not within sight, not yet, but still there, four days' march in any direction. The circle is not complete; they have separate armed camps, but all of them are invulnerable. If we attack one they stay inside and do not move. But while we do that the others come closer. One day they will all be here and the valley will be surrounded and that will be the end."

"Then we must leave before it is too late, before we are trapped."

"Go where?" Herilak's eyes were wide with mixed feelings, their whites glowing in the firelight. "Is there any place that is safe from them? You are the mandukto of the Sasku, you lead your hunters and women. Do you know of any place of safety to lead them to now?"

Sanone shifted uneasily before he spoke. "Across the desert to the west. It is said that there is water, green grass on the other side."

"Do you wish to lead your Sasku there?"

The fire crackled and a log fell in and it was a long time before Sanone answered. "No, I do not wish to take them away from this valley. We have always lived here. It is fit and right that if we are to die that we should die here."

"I do not wish to die—but I am tired of running. So are my sammads. I will lead them away from here if they wish to go, but I think they feel as we do. The time for running has ended. Sooner or later we must stop and take a stand against the murgu. Let it be sooner. We are all tired."

"The water in the river is lower than it should be. This time of year the rains in the mountains fill it to the banks."

"I will take some hunters in the morning, follow it back toward the hills. Do you think this is some murgu doing?"

"I do not know. But I fear."

"We all fear, mandukto. The murgu drift toward us like the snows of winter and are just as hard to stop. One of the women saw green vines growing down from the cliff tops. She said that she could not get close but they had the look of murgu poison vines."

"The cliffs are high."

"The vines grow long. When I sleep I dream of a death song. Do you know what that means?"

Sanone's smile was cold and grim. "You do not need a mandukto to read that dream, strong Herilak. I hear death songs too."

Herilak looked up grimly at the stars. "When we are born we begin dying. I know my tharm will be up there one day. It is just the closeness of that day that chills me more than this wind. Is there nothing we can do?"

"Kerrick once led us against the murgu, led in victory."

"Do not speak his name. He has gone and left us to die. He will lead us no longer."

"Did he leave you—or did you leave him, strong Herilak?" Sanone asked quietly.

Herilak stirred with quick anger and started to speak in anger— but was silent. He lifted his hands and clenched them into hard fists, then opened them again. "If a hunter had asked me that, had spoken to me in that manner I would have struck him. But not you, Sanone, for you can look inside someone and know what their secret thoughts are. Since all in my sammad were destroyed I have been two people inside one skull. One of them boils with anger always, wants to kill, heeds no council rejects all friendship. That is the Herilak who turned away from Kerrick at the time when he needed my help. But that is done. If he were here I would have words for him. But he is gone, dead in the north. Now that we are in this valley with murgu all about us I find that my anger is dying and I feel one person again. But this is perhaps a little late."

"It is never too late to walk the correct path to Kadair."

"I do not know your Kadair. But in a way you are right. Ermanpadar blew the spark that became my tharm. My tharm will glow in the stars very soon."

"The track is stamped into the rock for us to see. We can only follow it."

The fire died down to a bed of glowing coals and the wind grew stronger, hurtling down the valley from the north. The stars were bright and sharp in the clear night sky. The sammads and the Sasku slept and the murgu grew closer with every passing day. Sanone looked at Herilak's slumped head and wondered who would be here in the valley when the first green shoots of spring pushed their way up through the ground.

CHAPTER FORTY-TWO

The coast of Entoban* was a dark shadow on the eastern horizon that was barely visible in the dying light. As the boat rode up on a wave they could see the peaks of high, snow-covered mountains far inland, still touched red by the setting sun. As they dropped into the trough between the waves the sail flapped in the dying breeze.

Kerrick looked at Kalaleq slumped over the steering oar and spoke again, this time carefully choosing his words, fighting not to lose his temper.

"The water is almost gone."

"I have no wish to drink."

"But I do. Armun is thirsty. We must go ashore and refill the waterskins."

There was just enough light left for Kerrick to see the shiver that moved across Kalaleq's body, stirring the fur down his neck so that it rose into the air. He had discarded his clothes many days before when the air had grown warmer, when the worst of winter had been left behind. "No," he said, then trembled again. "That is the land of the murgu. I saw them once, killed them once. Never again. I am hot, we must go north."

He pushed over on the oar and the sail flapped loosely as they went all aback. Kerrick started toward the stern, angrier than before, and stopped only when Armun laid a restraining hand on his arm.

"Let me talk to him," she whispered. "Shouting at him does no good, you can see that now."

"Talk to him then." He pushed her hand away and moved to secure the sail. "Convince him. We must get fresh water."

Kalaleq's fur trembled at her touch and she stroked his shoulder until the quivering stopped. "Plenty water," he muttered.

"You know that is not true. It will all be gone soon then we will have to land."

"Land in the islands, go back, not ashore."

She stroked him again, spoke to him as she would to a child. "We do not know how far the islands are from here—and we cannot turn back. The spirit of the wind would not like that. Not after all the fair winds we have had so far."

"Not today, not yesterday."

"Then the spirit has heard you and grows angry."

"No!"

Kalaleq held tightly to her, then realized what he was doing and let his hands move up under her loose coverings, to rest on her bare back. She did not push him away, not this time. Kerrick could not see what was happening in the darkness. They must make for the shore despite Kalaleq's fears. He was the problem now, for the voyage south seemed to have driven all the dark thoughts from Kerrick's head. Driven them into the Paramutan's skull instead! Now she had to humor him instead of Kerrick, must still be the strong one. She knew how to do that well enough. The Tanu hunters and the male Paramutan were the same, quick to anger, ferocious in battle, washed by storms of feelings. But it was she who had to endure. To follow when needed—to be strong when that was needed even more. Now this one must have her help as Kerrick had had before. But he wanted more than that. His hands moved over her skin, moved from her back—and she pushed him gently away.

"Kalaleq is not afraid of the great ularuaq that swim in the northern sea," she said. "He is the mightiest slayer of ularuaq and the strength of his arm feeds us all."

"Yes," he agreed and reached for her again but she moved back.

"Kalaleq not only kills the ularuaq but he has killed the murgu. I saw him kill murgu. He is a mighty slayer of murgu!"

"Yes," then louder, "Yes!" He stabbed out with an invisible spear. "Yes, I did kill them, how I killed them!"

"Then you do not fear them—if you see them you will kill them again."

"Of course!" His mood had shifted completely under her guidance and he beat his chest with his fists. "We need water—to the shore. Maybe find some murgu to kill too."

He sniffed the wind, then spat unhappily. Still growling he unshipped the oars and slipped them into place. "Not enough wind, lower sail. I'll show you how to row."

But not this night.

In a short while he was gasping and running with sweat. He let Armun pull him aside and he sipped at the last of the water when she held it to his lips. Kerrick took his place, pulled hard on the oars, pulled toward the land. Kalaleq sank into a troubled sleep, and Armun hoped that when he awoke his mood would be unchanged.

The night was still and warm, the stars hidden by low cloud above. Before Kerrick tired Armun replaced him at the oars so that they moved steadily toward land. A ghost of a moon slipped in and out of the clouds enabling them to stay on course. While Kalaleq slept, they spelled each other, turn and turn again, until they heard the rumble of surf distantly ahead. Kerrick stood in the bow and could just make out the line of foam where the waves ran up onto the shore.

"It looks like beach, not rock, and the waves are small. Shall we go straight in?"

"Wake Kalaleq. Let him decide."

The Paramutan came awake at once—thankfully possessed by none of his earlier fears. He clambered part way up the mast to look ahead, sniffed the air then let his hand dangle over the side in the sea.

"We land," was his firm decision. "Row straight and I steer."

When they were closer in he saw a break in the shore and turned toward it, then guided the boat in between sandbanks to the outlet of a stream or a small river.

"No one knows boats, knows the ocean like Kalaleq!"

"No one," Armun agreed quickly before Kerrick could say anything to dampen the Paramutan's new-found self-esteem. Kerrick started to speak, then had the good sense to keep quiet. He rowed until they touched bottom, then jumped overside with a line to pull the boat further in.

The water was salt here, but when he walked a short distance upstream it suddenly became fresh and sweet. He cupped his hands and drank, then called to the others. Kalaleq rolled and splashed in the delightful coolness, his earlier fears forgotten. They pulled the boat up as far as they could and secured it there, all of them exhausted. They would refill the waterskins in the morning.

It was first light when Kerrick took Armun's arm to awaken her. "Up here," he said. "Come quickly."

Kalaleq was lying behind the mounded dune, shaking his spear and calling out loud insults. But he was careful to stay behind the cover. They ran to join him, dropping and crawling the last bit to look over the top.

Out to sea, just off the coast, a large creature with a high fin was swimming slowly by. Two smaller sea-beasts surged ahead of it.

"An uruketo," Kerrick said. "It carries the murgu."

"How I wish they were closer so I could spear it, kill them all!" Kalaleq's eyes were red with hatred in the first light, his temper restored and all traces of yesterday's fear vanished.

"Look at the direction they are going," Kerrick said, glancing toward the sun on the horizon, then back to sea. "North, they are going north."

He watched until the uruketo had vanished from sight, then hurried to the boat, rooted out the Yilanè charts.

"We have come too far south, see, we must be here on the chart. The uruketo is going north to the islands here."

Kalaleq understood the maps, Armun did not. They would decide. "It could be going to the ocean here, through the mouth," Kalaleq said. Kerrick shook his head.

"Not this time of the year, it is too cold, there may even be no cities left on the shores of Isegnet. It has to be going here, to Ikhalmenets."

While they argued she filled the waterskins.

By late morning they had all of the water they could carry and their course had been decided. They would follow the murgu swimming creature. It had been agreed that the island they searched for was in that direction. The breeze was coming from the land now and filled their sail, carrying them swiftly toward the horizon and what lay concealed beyond it.

They sailed all of that day through the empty ocean, the land out of sight behind them and nothing visible ahead. When Kalaleq's fears returned Armun asked him how he killed ularuaq and he showed her his skill, carried away, shouting with pleasure. Kerrick sat silently in the bow, staring ahead. He was the one who saw the snow capped mountain first.

"It is there, Ikhalmenets, it can be nothing else."

They gazed in silence as they sailed forward and the island slowly emerged from the sea. Kalaleq called out worriedly when other specks of land appeared.

"There—and there. Other islands, there are more than one. Which is the one we seek?"

Kerrick pointed to the white peak, now glowing warmly in the evening sun. "That one, it can be no other, that is the way it was described. An island with a single, high mountain at its center. There are others nearby, but this is the largest, the mountain the tallest. Sail toward it."

"The other islands we pass, we will be seen."

"No, they are uninhabited. the murgu live in only one place, in their city on that island. That is where we are going . . ."

"To our deaths!" Kalaleq cried aloud, his teeth chattering with fear. "Murgu beyond counting. We are three, what can we do?"

"We can defeat them," Kerrick said, strength and surety in his voice. "I did not come all this distance just to die. I have thought about this over and over, planned everything carefully. We will win—because I know these creatures. They are not like Tanu—or Paramutan. They do not do as we do, each of them going his own way, but are ordered in everything. They are very different from us."

"My head is thick. I fear—and do not understand."

"Then listen and you will see clearly what I mean. Tell me of the Paramutan. Tell me why you, Kalaleq, kill the ularuaq, not any other?"

"Because I am the best! Am strongest, aim straightest."

"But others kill as well?"

"Of course, different times, sail on other ikkergaks."

"Then understand, the Tanu have sammadars who lead. But if we do not like what they say we find a new sammadar, just as you may have a new spearer of ularuaq."

"Me—I am best."

"I know you are, but that is not what I mean. I am talking about the way things happen with Paramutan and Tanu. But that is not the way of the murgu. There is one who orders all of the others, a single one. Her orders are always obeyed, never questioned."

"That is stupid," Kalaleq said, pushing over the oar as the wind gusted about and flapped the sail. Kerrick nodded agreement.

"You think so—I think so. But the murgu never think about this at all. The one on top rules and all of the others obey."

"Stupid."

"It is, but that is a very good thing for us. Because I can speak to the one who rules, order her to do what must be done . . ."

"No, you cannot," Armun cried out. "You cannot go there. It is certain death."

"Not if you both help me, do as I ask. None of the other murgu matter, just the leader, the one they call the eistaa. I know how she thinks and I know how to make her obey me. With this," he held out the carved Sasku firebox, "and the bladder of ularuaq poison Kalaleq has stowed away."

Armun looked from his face to the box, then back again. "I understand none of this. You make fun of me." Without realizing it, she drew a fold of her clothing over her mouth as she spoke.

"No, never." He put the box down and held her to him, pulled the skin aside, touched her lips, calmed her fears. "It will be all right, we will be safe."

They came as close to the island as they dared in the fading daylight, then dropped the sail and waited. There were no clouds and the snow on the high mountain shone clearly in the moonlight. Kerrick went to raise the sail and Kalaleq called out to stop him.

"If we go close we will be seen!"

"They sleep, all of them. None are awake; I told you I know them."

"Guards posted?"

"That is impossible. None move after darkness, it is a thing about them."

Kalaleq steered reluctantly, still not sure. The island grew ever closer until they were moving slowly north along its rocky shore.

"Where is the place of the murgu?" Kalaleq whispered as though he could be heard from the shore.

"On this coast, to the north, keep on."

The rocky coastline gave way to sandy beaches with groves of trees beyond them. Then the coast curved away into a harbor and the row of dark forms was clear against the lighter wood of the docks beyond.

"There," Kerrick said. "The uruketo, their ikkergak-creatures, like the one we saw. This is the place, this is the city. I know what it will be like for they are all grown in the same manner. The birth-beaches beyond, the barrier surrounding it, the ambesed which will open to the east so the eistaa, sitting in her place of honor, will get the first warmth of the sun. This is Ikhalmenets."

Armun did not like it when he spoke of these things because of the strange sounds he made and the jerking motions of his body. She turned away but he called to her.

"There, do you see the dry stream bed where it runs into the ocean? That is where we will land, where we will meet again. Steer for the shore, Kalaleq. This is the right place, it is close—but still outside the barriers that surround the city."

The shore here was mud and sand, carried down from the hills during the rainy season. They grounded on a sandbank, gently rocked by the ripple of the tiny waves.

"We will stay here most of the night," Kerrick said. "But we must leave while it is still dark. Armun, you will stay behind and wait until there is enough light before you try to climb."

"I can go in the dark," Armun said.

"No, it is too dangerous. There will be enough time. What you must do is climb up there until you are above the city. Make everything ready as I have told you."

"Dry wood for a large fire, green leaves for smoke."

"Yes, but do not put on the leaves until the sun is two hands above the ocean. The fire must be large and hot with white-hot coals. At the proper time all of the leaves must be put on, to burn and smoke. As soon as you have done that you must come back here. Quickly—but not so quickly that you fall. Kalaleq will be waiting. I will come along the shore and join you as soon as I can. Is everything understood?"

"I feel that this is all madness and I am filled with fear."

"Don't be. It is going to go just as I planned. If you do your part I will be safe. But you must do it at the right time, neither earlier nor later. Is that understood?"

"Yes, I understand." He was distant from her then, his voice so cold, thinking like a murgu—and acting like one as well. He wanted only obedience. He would have it—if only to get this over and done with. The world was a lonely place.

She dozed fitfully in the rocking boat, waking to hear Kalaleq's rasping snores, then dozing again. Kerrick could not sleep but lay, open-eyed, staring up at the slowly wheeling stars. The morning star would rise soon, and after that it would be dawn. By nightfall this work would be done. He might not be alive to see the end of the day, he knew that. He would be taking an immense risk and victory was not as certain as he had assured Armun. For a moment he wished that they were back on that frozen coast, safe in the paukaruts of the Paramutan, away from all danger. He brushed the thought aside, remembering, as though it had happened to another person, the darkness that had held his thoughts for so long. There were too many people inside his head. He was Yilanè and Tanu, sammadar and leader in battle. He had burnt Alpèasak, then tried to save it, lost it again to the Yilanè. Then he had fled from everything—and now he knew that he could flee from nothing. Everything was inside his head. What he was doing was the right thing, the only thing. The sammads had to be saved—and in this entire world he was the only one who could do it. All of his efforts, everything he had ever done, had led him to this place, to this city at this time. What must be done would be done. The stars lifted above the horizon and he turned to waken the others.

Armun waded ashore in silence. She had so much to say that it was easier to say nothing. She stood knee-deep in the sea, clutching the fire-box to her, watching as the dark shape of the boat moved silently away. The moon had set and the starlight was not bright enough to reveal his face. Then they were gone, a black blur in the greater darkness. She turned and waded wearily ashore.

"Oh we are dead, dead," Kalaleq muttered between his chattering teeth. "Consumed by these giant murgu."

"There is nothing to fear. They do not move at night. Now put me ashore for it is almost dawn. You know what you are to do?"

"I know, I have been told."

"I will tell you again, just to be sure. Are you sure the ularuaq poison will kill one of these creatures?"

"They are dead. They are no bigger than a ularuaq. My stab is sure death."

"Then do it, swiftly, as soon as I am ashore. Kill them—but just two of them, no more. Be sure of that because it is most important. Two of them must die."

"They die. Now go—go!"

The boat moved swiftly away even before Kerrick had reached dry sand. The morning star was bright on the horizon, the first gray of dawn below it. Now was the time. He took off his hide coverings, the wrappings from his feet, until all that remained was a soft leather breechclout. His spear was still in the boat, he was unarmed. He touched the metal knife that hung about his neck, but it had no edge, was just an ornament.

Shoulders back and head high, limbs curved slightly into the arrogance of superiority, completely alone, he strode forward into the Yilanè city of Ikhalmenets.

ninlemeistaa halmutu eisteseklem.

YILANÈ APOTHEGM

=============

Above the eistaa is only the sky.

CHAPTER FORTY-THREE

The loud shouts woke Lanefenuu, sending her into an instant fury. The transparent disc in the wall of her sleeping chamber was barely lit; it must just be dawn. And who dared to make those sounds in her ambesed! It was the sound of attention-to-speaking, loud and arrogant. She was on her feet in the instant, tearing great gouges from the matted flooring with her claws as she stamped her way out of the chamber.

A single Yilanè stood in the center of the ambesed, of strange color, deformed. When she saw Lanefenuu appear she called out, muffled by her lack of tail.

"Lanefenuu, Eistaa of Ikhalmenets, step forward. I will talk with you."

The insult of the form of address; Lanefenuu was roaring with rage. Sunlight spread across the ground and she stopped in her tracks, tail lifted with surprise. The Yilanè could speak—but it was no Yilanè.

"Ustuzou! Here?"

"I am Kerrick. Of great strength and great anger."

Lanefenuu walked slowly forward, numb with disbelief. It was an ustuzou, pallid of skin, fur around its middle, fur on its head and face, empty-handed, glowing metal around its neck. The ustuzou Kerrick as Vaintè had described it.

"I have come with a warning," the ustuzou said, arrogance and insult in its mode of address. Lanefenuu's crest flared with her instant anger.

"Warning? To me? You ask only for death, ustuzou."

She strode forward, menace in every movement, but stopped when he framed certainty-of-destruction.

"I bring only death and pain, Eistaa. The death is here already and more will come if you do not listen to that which I will tell you. Death doubled. Death twice."

There was sudden motion at the ambesed entrance and they both looked at the hurrying Yilanè who appeared, mouth gaping wide with the heat of her rapid movements.

"Death," the newcomer said, with the same controllers of urgency and strength that Kerrick had used. Lanefenuu was crushed back onto her tail, numbed by shock, silent while the Yilanè shaped what she had to say.

"Sent by Muruspe—urgency of message. The uruketo she commands—death. It is dead. Suddenly dead in the night. And another uruketo. Dead. Two dead."

Lanefenuu's cry of pain cut the air. She who had commanded an uruketo herself, who had spent her life with and for the great creatures, whose city boasted more and better uruketo than any other. Now. Two of them. Dead. She turned in pain, twisted by pain, to look at the great carving of the uruketo above her, of her likeness high on its fin. Two dead. What had the ustuzou said? She turned slowly to face the terrible creature.

"Two dead," Kerrick said again with the grimmest of controllers. "Now we will talk, Eistaa."

He signed instant-dismissal to the messenger, from highest to lowest and the Yilanè turned and hurried away. Even this presumption of power in her presence did not disturb Lanefenuu, could not penetrate the grief she felt at her irreplaceable loss.

"Who are you?" she asked, the question muffled by her pain. "What do you want here?"

"I am Kerrick-highest and I am Eistaa of all the Tanu whom you call ustuzou. I have brought you death. Now I will bring you life. It is I who commanded the killing of the uruketo. Those I order did this thing."

"Why?"

"Why? You dare to ask why? You who have sent Vaintè to slaughter those I rule, to pursue them and kill them and keep on killing them. I will tell you why they were killed. One was killed to show you my strength, that I can reach wherever I wish, kill whatever or whoever I want. But the death of just one might have been thought to be an accident. Two dead is no accident. All could have died as easily. I did this thing so you would know who I am, what forces I command, so you will do what I will ask you to do."

Lanefenuu's roar of anger cut him off. She stumbled forward, thumbs outstretched and jaws agape, teeth ready. Kerrick did not move but instead spoke with insult and arrogance.

"Kill me and you will not die. Kill me and *all* of your uruketo will be dead. Is that what you want, Eistaa? The death of your uruketo and the death of your city? If you want that—then strike swiftly before you can think and change your mind."

Lanefenuu trembled with her inner conflicts, accustomed to a lifetime of command, holding the power of life and death, taking orders from no one. That this ustuzou could speak to her in this manner! She was losing control.

Kerrick dare not step away from her or change the arrogance of his stance. A moment's weakness on his part and she would strike. Perhaps he had pushed her too far—but he had had no choice. He shot a quick glance up at the hill above them. Nothing.

"There is something else I wish to tell you about, Eistaa," he said. He must talk, keep her attention, not let her passions carry away her judgment. "Ikhalmenets is a great city, a jewel among Yilanè cities, sea-girt Ikhalmenets. You are Ikhalmenets and Ikhalmenets is you. Your responsibility and your reward. You rule here."

He chanced another glance at the hill. There was a cloud above it—or was it a cloud? No. Smoke. And Lanefenuu was shuffling towards him. He shouted loudly to cut through her haze of anger.

"You are Ikhalmenets—and Ikhalmenets is about to be destroyed. Look behind you, up there, on that ridge. Do you see that cloud that is not a cloud? It is smoke. And you know what smoke is? Smoke comes from fire and fire burns and destroys. Fire burnt Alpèasak, killed all there. You know about that. Now I have brought fire to Ikhalmenets."

Lanefenuu turned, looked, wailed in agony. Smoke burst up from the ridge, climbing high in roiling clouds. Kerrick called for attention to speaking and she looked at him with one eye, the other still staring at the smoke.

"I have not come alone to your sea-girt Ikhalmenets, Eistaa. My forces have killed your uruketo while I was making my way to the ambesed. My forces now surround you on all sides—and they are masters of fire as you know. They have fire ready and wait my signal. If I give it—Ikhalmenets burns. If I am injured in any way—Ikhalmenets burns. So choose, and quickly, for the fire is greedy."

Lanefenuu's cry of rage turned to one of pain. She was defeated, slumping back on her tail, forearms hanging. Her city and all her uruketo must come first. The death of this creature was not important. Ikhalmenets was.

"What is it you wish?" she asked. Not humbled, but weak in defeat.

"I want for mine only what you want for yours, Eistaa. Continued existence. You have driven us from Alpèasak. You and your Yilanè and fargi will stay there for it is a Yilanè city. None will harm you there. I see the snow on the mountain above us, snow that is lower every year. Before the snow reaches you Ikhalmenets will go to Alpèasak and be safe there under a warmer sun. Ikhalmenets will live there.

"But my ustuzou must live safe as well. Even now Vaintè acts under your command, pursues and kills them. You must order her back, order her to return, order her to cease killing. Do that and Ikhalmenets lives. We do not want what you have. You will keep your city. We ask only for our lives. You must stop Vaintè. You will do that and Ikhalmenets and all of your uruketo will live in tomorrow's tomorrow as they lived in yesterday's yesterday."

For a long period Lanefenuu did not move, sat slumped in silence, fighting to find a way through her maze of conflicting thoughts. Finally, when she stirred, some strength returned and she spoke with the voice of authority once again.

"It will be done. Vaintè will be stopped. There was never a need for her to attack across your world of ustuzou. She will be recalled. You will leave. You will stay in your place and we will stay in ours. I do not wish to talk to you or to see you ever again. I wish that your egg had been stepped upon and that you had never emerged."

Kerrick signed agreement. "But there is one other thing you must do to stop Vaintè. You know her and I know her. She is capable of disobeying your order to stop. She is capable of that—is she not?"

"She is," said Lanefenuu grimly.

"Then you must go to her, find her and order her return. Then she must stop what she is doing for her Yilanè are your Yilanè, her fargi your fargi. That is what must be done."

Lanefenuu's eyes were glinting with hatred—but she kept her body under control. "I will do that."

"Good." Kerrick reached up to the ring around his neck, to the knife hanging there. He seized it and pulled it free, handed it over to Lanefenuu. She would not reach out for it so he dropped it into the dust at her feet.

"You will take this to Vaintè. She knows it, she knows what it will mean. She will know that it is I who have done this thing and why I have done it. She will know that you had no choice in what you did."

"I care nothing of how Vaintè feels, what she knows."

"Of course, Eistaa." Kerrick spoke slowly, with controllers of cold anger. "It is just that I want her to know that I, Kerrick, have done this to her, stopped her in her tracks. I want her to understand exactly what I have done."

With this Kerrick turned on his heel and stalked away. Out of the ambesed and past the gawking fargi who had gathered in terrified crowds. They moved away from him in fear, for all had seen the talking from afar. They did not know what was happening— only that it was terrible beyond belief. Two uruketo were dead and this ustuzou-Yilanè walked with death all around him.

Kerrick walked through Ikhalmenets to the shore, turned to the Yilanè and fargi there.

"In the name of your eistaa I order you from here. All of you. She commands you to attend her in the ambesed. Leave."

Incapable of lies themselves, they understood what he had spoken as a command and hurried to the ambesed.

As soon as he was alone, Kerrick jumped down to the sand and made his way out of the city.

CHAPTER FORTY-FOUR

"You sent for me," Enge said. "The message stressed great urgency."

"Any order that I issue is urgent, though your slothful creatures fail to realize that. If I do not stress urgency then the would-be-messenger would discuss the probity of her acting as my fargi and other irrelevencies."

"There is truth in that, for as Ugunenapsa said . . ."

"Silence!" Ambalasi roared the command, her crest rising and falling with rage. Her assistant, Setèssei, fled in panic, and even Enge bowed before the storm of the elderly scientist's wrath. She signed apologies and obedience then waited in silence.

"A slight improvement. From you at least I expect some attention, a slight amount of courtesy. Now, look here, at this splendid sight."

Ambalasi indicated the Sorogetso who rested in the shade—a splendid sight only to Ambalasi for she shivered with fear and had curled herself into a ball, eyes closed and waiting for her death.

"Not you, foolish creature, my anger is for others," Ambalasi said, then controlled her temper with a great effort and spoke in the Sorogetso manner. "Attention, little one. Friendship and aid."

She caressed Ichikchee's green crest until she fearfully opened her eyes.

"Very good. See, here is Enge who has come to be with you, to admire how well you are. Quiet, there will be no pain-accompaniment."

Ambalasi gently removed the nefmakel that covered and protected the stump of Ichikchee's leg. The Sorogetso shivered but made no protest.

"Look," Ambalasi ordered. "Gaze with admiration."

Enge bent to look at the puckered flesh of the stump where the flaps of skin had been folded over the exposed bone. In the center was a yellowish growth of some kind. It meant nothing to her. But she dared not say so and bring Ambalasi's ready wrath down upon her again.

"It heals well," she said finally. "Ambalasi is a mistress of the healing science. The amputation not only heals but there, in the center, something emerges. Can it be object-of-admiration?"

"It certainly can be—but in your ignorance I cannot expect you to appreciate its significance. That is a new foot growing there, a yellow-mottled foot on a green Sorogetso who is a head shorter than we are. Does any of the awesome importance of this penetrate the solid bone of your skull to the submicroscopic brain that sleeps inside?"

Enge swallowed the insult, always the wisest course if communication were necessary with Ambalasi. "Importance-not-understood. Ignorance admitted."

"Close attention demanded. Earlier theories discarded. Forget any mention of plate tectonics or continental drift. That period of separation is far too large. I doubted it first when I discovered that we could communicate with the Sorogetso, even at a basic and primitive level. Tens of millions of years cannot separate our species, even a million years is too great. We may appear superficially different, but genetically we are one. Or that foot would not be growing. The mystery deepens. Who are the Sorogetso—and how come they here?"

Enge made no attempt to answer, knowing that the elderly scientist's unfocused eyes were looking through her, beyond her, at wonders of knowledge she could scarcely imagine.

"It disturbs me. I sense dark experiments that should not have been done. I have found evidence of failed experiments before

WINTER IN EDEN • 335

this, but more often in the seas than on the land, work that has gone astray, ugly creatures that should never have been born. You must realize—not all scientist are like me. There are warped minds as well as warped bodies in this world."

Enge was horrified at the thought. "Such a thing cannot be."

"Why not?" Ambalasi controlled her temper long enough to smoothly wrap the nefmakel back into place again. "Why not!" She turned away from the Sorogetso and snorted with anger. "There will always be incompetents. I have seen laboratory experiments go so wrong that you would be horrified if you gazed at the deformed results. Remember—all you see about you are the successes. The digesting pits hide the failures. We found Ambalasokei easily enough; others could have come before us. Records not kept, knowledge not passed on. We Yilanè have the fault of temporal indifference. We know that tomorrow's tomorrow will be the same as yesterday's yesterday—so find it unnecessary to record the passing of time, of events. What records that you do see are simply shadows of self-esteem. Something discovered, something done that will puff up some tiny ego. Records of failures are never kept."

"Then you believe that the Sorogetso are the results of an experiment that went wrong?"

"Or one that went right—or one that should never have happened at all. It is one thing to tamper with the gene strings of ustuzou and other lower creatures. It is unheard of for a Yilanè to tamper with genes of Yilanè."

"Even to improve them, to fight disease?"

"Silence! You say too much, know too little. Disease is eliminated by altering *other* organisms. We are as we are, as we have been since the egg of time. This discussion is closed."

"Then I will open it again," Enge said with great firmness. "Statement-now denies statement-past. You aided us to come to this place because you wished to study the relationship of our philosophy to physiological changes in our bodies. Is that not in the nature of an experiment with Yilanè?"

Ambalasi opened her mouth and moved her limbs to speak—but remained silent, motionless. Then she closed her mouth and was still for a long time, rigid with thought. When she finally did speak she framed controllers of respect.

"The string-knife of your mind never ceases to amaze me, Enge. You are right, of course, and I must give this much more thought. Perhaps my instant repulsion at Yilanè experiments was not natural, but a learned and now automatic repulsion. Come, let us eat, for this requires more thought than I am prepared to give at the present time."

Ambalasi looked about testily but her assistant had gone. She registered displeasure-at-absence. "She should bring meat. She is well aware that I prefer to eat at this period of the day."

"Pleasure in service, great Ambalasi. I will get it for you."

"I will get it myself. Hunger undiminished by waiting delays."

Enge walked with her through the growing city, past the groups of Yilanè engaged in concentrated talk. Enge registered pleasure of observation.

"As never before we can search the truths of Ugunenapsa without danger from others."

"There is great danger from me to your worthless creatures. There is much in this city that needs less talking and more doing. Do not your Daughters of Despumation realize that without fargi in this city they must dirty their Yilanè hands and do fargi work?"

"We do Ugunenapsa's work."

"Ugunenapsa won't put food into your mouths."

"I think she has," Enge said with some pride. "She brought you to us, for it was the strength of her thoughts on our bodies that drew your interest, brought us here. And there you see the results."

Ambalasi had not visited the food preparation area since she had supervised the establishment of the enzyme processing. With the discovery of the giant eels in the river their food supply, while monotonous, was guaranteed. Nor had she heard complaints of late from the Daughters about how onerous were the labors to supply food for all. Now she saw why.

One of the Daughters, it was Omal, rested comfortably in the shade while three of the Sorogetso labored at the enzyme vats.

"They learn quickly," Enge said, "and are grateful for the food we give them."

"I am not sure that I approve," Ambalasi said, taking the slab of eel on a fresh leaf that the Sorogetso held out to her. The server kept her eyes lowered as she hurried to prepare another for Enge.

"Lack of understanding," Enge signed, then took her meat.

"Disruption of received order," Ambalasi said, tearing off a great mouthful of eel. "Interruption of scientific observation. Your Daughters can do nothing right." She finished the meat and hurled the leaf away from her with anger, then indicated the far shore of the river.

"These pseudo-fargi must be returned to their natural place. Sent away. Your slothful sisters must be made to work. You are disturbing everything. Have you forgotten already that we found the Sorogetso living not as we do but with their males among them—not sequestered in a hanalè? I must discover how this has been accomplished and record my studies. I must observe and record the details of their daily existence. This is an opportunity that cannot be repeated. I need to study them in their natural environment—not here slicing eels for greedy stomachs! Did you not observe the floating tree that guards their settlement? They use inanimate materials like the ustuzou, not animate life forms as we do. This interference with natural order must end—now. Return the Sorogetso instantly."

"It will not be easy . . ."

"It will be simplicity itself. Order all of your Daughters of Lassitude to gather here, every one. I will speak to them. Instructions will be issued."

Enge hesitated, thought about what must be done, then signed agreement. The time for a confrontation had finally arrived. She knew that it was due, overdue, for Ambalasi's expectations and the vital needs of the Daughters were as different as day and night. She knew that they owed their very existence to the scientist, knew at the same time that this no longer mattered. They were here. That part was done. The sides were drawn; the clash inevitable.

"Attention," she signed to the nearest Yilanè. "Utmost importance, all to gather in the ambesed. Urgent need, time soonest."

They went there in silence. Although there was no eistaa for this city, still no agreement on how it would be governed, the ambesed had been grown because it was the center of all Yilanè cities. From all sides the Daughters hurried, obeying the urgency of the command, urged on by memories of earlier orders and persecutions. They were as one in their fear. They made way for Enge and Ambalasi. Side by side they proceeded to the raised mound where an eistaa, if there were to be an eistaa, would have her place. Enge turned to face the multitude, signed for silence, gathered her thoughts—then spoke.

"My Sisters. Ambalasi whom we admire and revere, who brought us here, who gave us our freedom and our lives, she whom we respect above all others, she wishes to address us on grave matters of mutual importance."

Ambalasi stamped to the top of the mound and looked at the expectant, silent Yilanè, then spoke calmly and without passion.

"You are creatures of intelligence and understanding, I cannot deny that. You have all studied and understood the thoughts of Ugunenapsa, have had the intelligence to apply these thoughts to your own lives in order to be responsible for your own lives. But when you did this you broke the thread of continuity that binds fargi to Yilanè to eistaa. You have brought a new way of living into this world, a new society. You are enthused by what has happened, and you should be. Therefore you must devote a good part of your time to consider the effects of Ugunenapsa's teachings on your lives."

A murmured motion of agreement swayed the sisters. Ambalasi had their undivided attention. When she saw this she pounced, her body stern with anger, command in her voice.

"A part of your time—and no more! You have abandoned the eistaa and her commands that cause a city to live and grow. Therefore in order to live, to preserve the lives that you have saved from the wrath of an eistaa, you must find a way to order this new society by examining more closely the teachings of Ugunenapsa. But only part time, as I have said. The rest of the time you will work for the life and growth of this city. Since none of you knows how to grow a city I shall tell you and you will obey my orders. Discussion will not be possible—only instant obedience."

There were many shouts of pained complaint at this and Enge stepped forward, voicing the thoughts of them all.

"This not possible. You will be our eistaa, that which we have rejected."

"You are correct. I will be the waiting-eistaa. Waiting for you to produce a more acceptable way of governing your city. As soon as you produce this I will remove myself from this position that I do not welcome, but which responsibility I reluctantly assume since it is the only way to keep this city alive. I say this not as a suggestion but as an ultimatum. Reject my offer and I reject you. If I remove my skills your city dies, remove my food preparation knowledge and you starve, remove my medical skills and you die poisonous deaths. Remove myself and the uruketo and leave you to your waiting deaths. But you are the ones who have rejected death and accepted life. Accept me and you have life. So you can do nothing but say yes to my generous offer."

Having said this Ambalasi turned about abruptly and reached for a water-fruit; her throat was dry from talking. There was shocked silence, broken only by Far<'s call for attention as she strode to the mound.

"Ambalasi speaks only the truth," she said with great emotion, her large eyes as wide and moist as a fargi's. "But within her truth is another truth. None doubts that it was the strength of Ugunenapsa's thoughts that brought us here to this place. To find the simple Sorogetso waiting here. They will be trained in all the labors of the city leaving us free to pursue our studies of the truths . . ."

"Negative!" Ambalasi said, striding to the mound and interrupting with the coarsest of movements and sounds. "That is impossible. The Sorogetso, all of them, return to their old way of living today and will no longer be permitted to enter this city. You can only accept or reject my generous offer. Live or die."

Far< stepped before the old scientist, youth before age, calmness before rage. "Then we must reject you, stern Ambalasi, accept death if that is the only way that we can live. We will leave with the Sorogetso when they go, live simply as they do. They have food and they will share it. If some die it is enough that Ugunenapsa's thoughts live."

"Impossible. The Sorogetso must not be disturbed."

"But how can you prevent us, kind friend? Will you kill us?"

"I will," Ambalasi said without an instant's hesitation. "I have hèsotsan. I will kill any and all of you who dare to interfere with the natural existence of the Sorogetso. You have done enough damage already."

"Far< my Sister, Ambalasi our leader," Enge said, stepping between them. "It is my strongest request that neither of you say things that you will regret, make promises that will be difficult to keep. Listen to me. There is a way. If there is any truth in Ugunenapsa's teachings it is in the application of those teachings. We believe in ending death for others as well as ourselves. Therefore we will do as wise Ambalasi says, humbly obey her instructions as waiting-eistaa while we seek a more permanent solution to this major problem that confronts us."

"Speak for yourself," Far< said, drawing herself up firmly, her limbs shaped in rejection. "Speak for those who listen to you if they wish that. But you cannot speak for all of us, cannot speak for those of us who believe in efeneleiaa, the spirit of life, the common force behind all life, all thinking. The thing that differentiates live from dead. As we meditate about efeneleiaa we experience great ecstasy and powerful emotions. You cannot take this away from us with low labors and filthy hands. We will not be forced."

"You will not be fed," Ambalasi said with great practicality.

"Enough!" Enge ordered with a voice of thunder and all fell silent for none had heard her speak with such great firmness before. "We will discuss these matters—but we will not discuss them now. We will follow Ambalasi's instructions until our studies of Ugunenapsa's thoughts show us a way to rule ourselves." She spun to face Far< who recoiled from the strength of her movements.

"You I bid to silence before us all. You condemn the Eistaa who orders our death—then you assume the role of eistaa-of-knowledge who will lead her followers to their deaths. Better that you should die that they should live. I do not will that—but I understand now the feelings of an eistaa who wills one to die so that all others should live. I reject this emotion—but I understand it."

There were cries of pain from the sisters, moans of despair. Far< closed her great eyes as a shiver passed through her body. Then she began to speak but obeyed when Enge called for silence-for-all, in the name of Ugunenapsa whom they revered. When Enge spoke again it was with humility and sadness, all anger fled.

"My sisters, who are more to me than life itself for I would die happily if my death were needed to let the lowliest of you live. We disgrace ourselves and Ugunenapsa when we permit our divisions to control us. Let us serve Ugunenapsa in serving Ambalasi. Let us leave this place in silence and each of us meditate long on what has happened to us. Then we will discuss our problems among ourselves and work out mutually satisfactory answers. Now go."

They did, in silence for the most part for they had much to think about, much to consider. When only Enge and Ambalasi were left the old scientist spoke with great weariness.

"That will do for the moment—but only for the moment. You are in for a great deal of trouble my friend. Take heed of Far< who is a troublemaker, who seeks divisions and leads others in her ways. She is a schism in your otherwise solid ranks."

"I know—and I grieve. There was one once before who interpreted Ugunenapsa in her own manner, who died herself when she finally understood the wrongness of her thoughts. But many of the Daughters died because of her. May this never happen again."

"It is already happening. I fear for the future of this city."

CHAPTER FORTY-FIVE

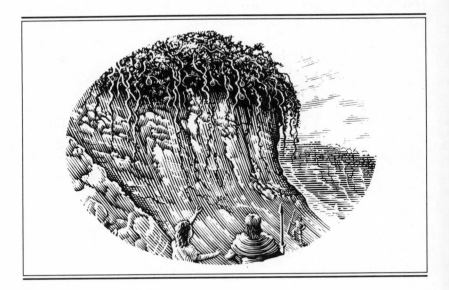

The first spring rains brought an unwelcome change to the
valley of the Sasku. What had been thin vines hanging from
the top of the enclosing walls now became burgeoning
lengths that dropped lower every day toward the valley floor.
They could not be burned, that had been tried without success,
and were difficult to approach because of their poisonous thorns.
Now swollen, poisonous green fruit could be seen ripening on their
stems.

"When the fruit falls—then what? What murgu destruction is
hidden within them?" Herilak said, looking up at the mass of
growth above.

"It could be anything," Sanone said, his voice wearier than any
had ever heard, the weight of his many years bearing down on him
as never before. The mandukto and the sammadar had drawn away
from the others as they did often now; to search for answers to
problems that were insoluble. Sanone's face twisted with disgust as
he looked at the harsh green growths above them, ringing the valley
walls. "Anything could emerge, poisonous, deadly, they seem to
change all the time. Or perhaps they contain only seeds to grow
more of them. That would be bad enough."

"Yesterday there was only a trickle of water in the river. Today it is completely dry."

"We have the spring, there is plenty for all."

"I want to see what they have done to our water; we have to know. I will take two hunters."

"One of my young manduktos will go with you as well. Wrap yourselves in the cloth, legs and feet covered as well."

"I know." Herilak's voice was grim. "Another child, dead. The thorns fly up from the sand when disturbed, very hard to see. We have had to pen and guard the mastodons. They will eat anything green. How will this all end?"

"It can end in only one way," Sanone said, his voice bleak and empty. He turned and left.

Herilak led his small band past the guards and over the barrier that sealed the valley. It was hot in the muffling wrappings of cloth, but the protection was needed. The murgu kept their distance, always retreating when attacked, but the dart-throwers grew everywhere now.

They walked cautiously up the valley floor along the dry riverbed, the mud already caked into a hard crust. There was movement ahead and Herilak pointed his death-stick, but there was nothing more to be seen, just a clatter of retreating claws. A few more turns in the valley and they reached the barrier.

From wall to wall it stretched, a tangled mass of vines and intertwined growth, vivid with flowers; a vertical jungle. A little water trickled through this living dam to make a small pool at its base.

"We can cut it down, burn it," Sarotil said. Herilak shook his head slowly, his face dark with anger, hatred—despair.

"Cut it, it will grow again. It won't burn. Poison thorns await us if we go close. Come, I want to see where all the water is going."

As they climbed up out of the dry riverbed there was a quick whistle of darts from above that bristled into their cloth coverings. Herilak fired back, climbed quickly. But there were no murgu there. The mandukto pointed to a shrub still swaying with the release of its burden; long roots from it ran back down the slope.

"We sprang the trap ourselves, when we stepped on the roots. They are growing these plants around us all of the time, more and more of them."

There was nothing that could be said. They skirted the bush—and the others like it—walked up along the high bank until the living dam was below them. A small lake had been formed behind it which had burst the banks further upstream. The river now found a new course out into the desert and away from the valley.

It was a good thing that they still had the spring of pure water.

Once they were back behind the relative safety of the barrier they carefully plucked out the poisonous darts before stripping off the stifling layers of cloth. Herilak found Sanone waiting in their usual meeting place, and he reported what they had found.

"And we had not a single glimpse of a murgu—they have learned to keep their distance."

"The dam could be torn down . . ."

"Why? It would only be grown again. While here the vines are closer to the valley floor every day. It must be said. The murgu have learned how to defeat us at last. Not in battle—but with the slow and ceaseless growth of their poison plants. They will win in the end. We cannot stop it any more than we can stop the tide."

"Yet each day the tide retreats again."

"The murgu do not." Herilak dropped to the ground, feeling defeat, feeling as old and tired as the mandukto. "They will win, Sanone, they will win."

"I have never heard you speak like that before, strong Herilak. There is still a battle to be fought. You have led us before, you have won."

"Now we have lost."

"We will cross the desert to the west."

"They will follow."

Sanone looked at the bowed shoulders of the big hunter and felt the other's despair, shared it despite himself. Was it Kadair's will that the Sasku be wiped from the face of the land? Had they followed the tracks of the mastodon only to find extinction waiting at trail's end? He could not believe it. Yet what else could he believe?

The excited shouts cut through the darkness of his thoughts and he turned to see what was happening. Hunters were running toward them, pointing, shouting. Herilak seized up his death-stick, leapt to his feet. There was a splashing roar as a wave of water rushed down the dry riverbed toward them, yellow with mud, quickly filling the banks. The terrified Sasku and Tanu scrambled to safety as the wall of water thundered by.

"The dam has been broken!" Herilak said. "Are all safe?"

Sanone watched the muddy water rush through the valley, saw no bodies—only tumbling shrubs and other debris. "I think they are, the river is staying inside its old banks. And, look, the level has dropped already. It is just as it always has been."

"Until they rebuild the dam, regrow it. This means nothing."

Even this welcome sight could not touch Herilak's despair. He had gone beyond hope, was ready for his life to end. He did not even lift his head when others called out, only looked up, blinking, when Sanone pounded on his arm.

"Something is happening," the mandukto cried, hope in his voice for the first time. "The vines, look at the vines! Kadair has not deserted us, we follow still in his tracks."

High above them a mass of vine tore loose from the cliff, tumbled and fell to the valley floor. Dust rose about it and when it had settled they saw that the thick stems that had supported it were gray and crumbled. Even as they watched the waxy green leaves drooped and lost their shine. In the distance another great tangle of vines broke free and slid down into the valley.

"Something is happening out there, something that we don't know about," Herilak said, released from the dark prison of despair by the incredible events about him. "I must go see."

His death-stick ready he ran the length of the valley, clambered up the barricade. Across from him, on the other side of the river, were the cliffs of the opposite bank, a close arrow-shot away. There was sudden movement there and he crouched, weapon pointed. A murgu appeared to stand at the cliffs edge, then another and another. Their repulsive two-thumbed hands were empty. They stood motionless, wide-eyed and staring.

Herilak lowered his weapon. It was inaccurate at this distance— and he needed to understand what was happening.

They looked at him, as he looked at them, in silence, capable of communicating only their presence to each other. The width of the river lay between them, the width of their difference wider than any river or sea. Herilak hated them and knew that the stare from their slitted eyes radiated the same hate in return. Then what was happening? Why had they undamned the river, slain the vines?

The large one, closest to him, turned about and moved its

limbs in sudden spasms as another appeared and passed over some object. The first one turned and cradled it in both hands, looking down at it—then looked up at Herilak. Its mouth opened in a spasm of unreadable emotion. Then it spun about and hurled the thing across the narrow valley. He watched it rise up in a slow arc, descend to strike the barrier and roll down to catch among the rocks.

When he looked back the murgu were gone. Herilak waited but they did not return. Only then did he slide down the barrier and stop beside the thing they had thrown over to him. There was the sound of hoarse panting as Sanone climbed up to join him.

"I saw . . . that," he said. "They stood and looked at you, did nothing. Just threw this thing—then left. What is it?"

It was a melon-shaped bladder of some kind, gray and smooth. Featureless. Herilak pushed at it with his foot.

"It could be dangerous," Sanone warned. "Be careful."

"It could be anything." Herilak knelt and prodded it with his thumb. "There is only one way to find out."

He lay the death-stick aside and pulled out his stone knife, tested the edge with his thumb. Sanone gasped with alarm and moved back as Herilak bent and cut into the bladder.

The outer skin was tough. He pressed and sawed—and it suddenly broke. Collapsing as orange liquid oozed from it. There was a dark shape inside. Herilak used the tip of his knife to push it free. Sanone was standing beside him now, looking down as well.

Looking at Kerrick's silver blade that had been concealed inside. The knife of sky-stone that he had always worn about his neck.

"It is Kerrick's," Sanone said. "He is dead. They have killed him and cut this from him and sent it to us as a message that he is dead."

Herilak seized up the blade, held it high so that it glinted in the sun.

"You are right in that it is a message—but the message is that Kerrick lives! He has done this thing—I don't know how—but he has done it. He did not die in the north but lives now. And has conquered the murgu." Herilak swept his arm out in a gesture that encompassed the valley.

"This is all his doing. He has defeated them. They have broken the dam and have killed their vines—and they are gone.

That is what the knife says. We can stay here. The valley is ours again."

He held the knife high in the sunlight, turned it so that it gleamed and sparkled, and roared his words aloud.

"Won! We have won—we have won!"

"You have lost, Vaintè," Lanefenuu said, one eye on the erect figure at her side, the other looking with distaste at the filthy, fur incrusted ustuzou that stood on the other side of the valley staring back at her. Then she signed Akotolp to join them. "Is the destruction done?"

The scientist framed her limbs into completion-as-ordered. "The virus has been released. It is harmless to other plants, animals. But certain death for all of the newly mutated cells. They will die. The virus remains in the ground so any seeds that mature will die as well."

Vaintè was scarcely aware of Akotolp and pushed her rudely aside to get close to the Eistaa, in a frenzy to deny what the Eistaa had last said.

"We cannot lose. They must be destroyed."

So fierce were her emotions that her meaning was muffled as conflicting feelings tore at the muscles of her body. In a final spasm she faced Lanefenuu, menace in her every motion.

"The battle must not stop. You must not stop it."

So strong were her expressions that Akotolp fell away with a cry of pain and the watching Yilanè raised their weapons, fearful for Lanefenuu's safety. She waved them back, then turned on Vaintè with distaste curving her limbs.

"The ustuzou-Kerrick knows you well, Vaintè. It said you would disobey me, would ignore my orders if I did not deliver them myself. It was right in that. You disobey me, Vaintè, who swore to be my fargi for life."

"You cannot do this—"

"It is done!" Lanefenuu roared with anger, all patience vanished. The watchers fled. "You wish to disobey me? Then you will have death as my last order—an order you cannot disobey. Die, outcast, die!"

Vaintè turned and stumbled away, Lanefenuu a step behind her, crest livid and shaking with rage.

"What is this? You do not die! You who hated them have

become one of them. You are a Daughter of Destruction. A death-less one, an outcast. You have joined the ranks of those you once loathed. I will have you killed. Attention to orders all present."

The fleeing Yilanè stopped, turned, fingered their weapons. Cold reason cut through Vaintè's anger; she turned quickly to Lanefenuu, her back to the others, spoke the sounds softly and moved her limbs with the minimum needed to communicate.

"Great Lanefenuu, Eistaa of Ikhalmenets who rules from strength, Vaintè who served you abases herself. I obey your instructions always."

"You did not obey the order to die, Daughter of Death," she hissed.

"I would, but I cannot. I live to serve you."

"I doubt that. I will order you killed."

"Do not chance it." There was cold menace now as Vaintè spoke. "There are Yilanè here who have forgotten Ikhalmenets, who have served me faithfully, who might even see me as their eistaa. Let us not tempt their loyalty—it might be a very dangerous thing to do."

Lanefenuu was swollen with cold anger, ready to burst, look-ing at the deadly creature before her, weighing her threat. Looking at the same time at the troubled Yilanè below them. Remembering the threat to Ikhalmenets that had brought her here so far from her sea-girt city. There could be much truth in what this Yilanè of venom had said. When Lanefenuu finally spoke she did so as silently as the other.

"You live. For the moment you live. We return to Ikhalmenets and you will leave with me. I do not trust you here when I am not present. The war against the ustuzou will end. Nor will I have you again in my city. You are banished from Gendasi∗, from Alpèasak, from my presence forever. If I could hurl you into the sea I would do that. I will not take that chance for others would know. You will be landed alone—very much alone—on the shore of Entoban∗, far from any city of the Yilanè. You will be as a fargi again. That is what I will do and that is your fate. Do you have anything to say?"

What Vaintè felt she dare not say—or one of them would have to die. She could not chance it. So rigidly under control was her body now that her muscles vibrated with the strain as she raised her thumbs and signed acceptance.

"Good. Now we leave this place of the ustuzou and I count the passing days with joy until tomorrow's tomorrow comes and I see the last of you."

They climbed on their mounts, the fargi following on the uruktop, and rode away. When the dust had slowly drifted back to the ground they were gone, all of them, gone.

"I had a dream last night," Armun said. "It was so real that I could see the colors of the leaves and the sky, even smell the smoke from the fire."

She stood in the bow of the ikkergak, her eyes half-closed in the glare of the setting sun ahead. Kerrick stood behind her, his arms about her for the warmth and the pleasure of being close. She turned to look up into his windburned face.

"The alladjex would always listen when he was told about dreams," she said. "Then he would tell you what they meant."

"Old Fraken is a fool. A troublemaker."

"You mean that my dream was not true?"

There was pain in her voice. He ran his finger over her long hair and reassured her. "A dream can be true—that is certain. We must dream for a reason. I meant only that you can tell for yourself, you don't need that old one to tell what you know yourself. What was the dream?"

"We were back at the round lake. Arnwheet was there and eating the meat I had cooked. The girl Darras too, only she was bigger than I remember her."

"She would be older now. Was Harl or Ortnar in your dream?"

"Ortnar was there, sitting and eating as well, with his bad arm hanging at his side. But the boy wasn't there, Harl. Could the dream be telling me that he is dead?"

He caught the fear in her voice and answered quickly. "It sounds a very real dream. You said you saw the color of the sky so it was daylight in your dream. Harl would be away hunting during the day."

"Of course." She laughed aloud, relieved. "But maybe it was just a dream because I hope so much?"

"No! It was real. You saw ahead of us, saw the lake where we are going and all of those who wait for us there. Who wait in safety."

"I want to be there."

"The ikkergak sails well, the spring storms are over. We will be there soon."

"Then I am happy. I did not want to have the new baby in the cold north."

She spoke calmly, with happiness and acceptance and he laughed aloud with pleasure, sharing her thoughts and feelings, holding her tight to him. Never to be parted, never again. Stroking her hair gently he felt at peace, realized that he had felt that way ever since that morning in Ikhalmenets when he had bent the eistaa to his will, forced her to end the attacks on the sammads. This single effort had banished the fears that had possessed him for so long, driven out the demons that had perched in his head and darkened his thoughts.

They were going to the lake, going back to his sammad. They would be complete once again.

The ikkergak surged up and over the long rollers, its rigging creaking, spray flying from the bow. There was sudden laughter from the stern where the other Paramutan sat close to Kalaleq at the tiller. It was an easy voyage for them, good fun. They laughed again.

A red sky ahead, sign of good weather, a band of high clouds turned rose-pink by the setting sun.

A world at peace.

Far to the south, in the world they were leaving behind, Vaintè stood in the sea, the warm waters surging about her. Looking out at the uruketo vanishing into the red-shot sunset. Her arms curled into a cry of hatred, her thumbs arched and aching to claw. She was alone, there were none to hear what she called aloud, none to aid her, to share with her. She was alone.

Perhaps it was better that way. She still had the strength of her hatred and that was all she needed. There was tomorrow and tomorrow's tomorrow, days running far into the future like stones tumbled on a beach. Days enough for her to do what must be done.

She turned, strode out of the ocean, trudged up onto the trackless sand. The wall of the jungle was solid and impenetrable. She turned and walked along the beach, leaving a straight trail of footsteps on the sand, walking slowly and steadily into the falling dusk.

THE WORLD
WEST OF EDEN

THE YILANÈ   353

   History of the World   353

   Physiology   356
      Diet   358
      Reproduction   358

   Science   361

   Culture   363

   Language   364

THE TANU   369

   Language   371

THE PARAMUTAN   372

   Environment   372

   Language   373

DICTIONARIES   376

   Yilanè–English   376

   Marbak–English   380

   Sesek–English   383

   Angurpiaq–English   383

ZOOLOGY   385

THE YILANÉ

Translator's Note
The following section has been translated from Yilanè, an
exercise that poses formidable problems. Of necessity the
translation must be a "free" one and the translator apolo-
gizes in advance for any errors or discrepancies that may
have crept into the text.

HISTORY OF THE WORLD

It must be pointed out at the very beginning of this particular history
that it differs from many 'histories' currently popular. It differs in *kind*,
a fact that the judicious reader must always take into consideration. For
far too long Yilanè history has been the province of the fabulist and the
dreamer. Whereas the intelligent Yilanè would be offended at any
guesswork or wild speculation in a physics or a biological text, the same
reader will allow any sort of imaginary excess in a work of history. A
perfect example of fiction purporting to be fact is the currently popular
history of this world that describes how a giant meteor struck the Earth
75* million years ago and wiped out 85% of the species then alive. It
goes on to explain in great detail the manner in which warm-blooded
creatures developed and became the dominant life forms on this planet.
This sort of thing is what the present authors deplore; wild speculation
instead of accurate historical research. No meteor of that size ever
struck the Earth. The world as we see it is the world as it always has
been, always will be, world without end. It is necessary, therefore, in
the light of other works of this nature, that we define the term *history*
before we can proceed.

History, as it is known today, is far too often a very inexact
science, so inexact that it is more fiction than fact, more speculation
than presentation. This is due to intrinsic aspects of the Yilanè nature.
We care little where we have been—but we know exactly where we are
going. We are happy with changes of a short duration while at the same

---

* For those readers not acquainted with large mathematical terms, see page 362
for a complete description.

time we demand that the future shall be as the present, changeless and unchangeable. Since this need for long-term continuity is essential to our very nature we tend to feel unhappy about the past because it might have contained long-term changes that we would find offensive. Therefore we refer vaguely to 'the egg of time' and assume in doing so that this was when the world was born, whole and new—and changeless ever since.

Which is of course nonsense. The moment has now arrived in Yilanè history to declare that history as we have known it is worthless. We could have referred to this present work as new history, but refrain since this gives an element of credence to the 'old-history'. We therefore reject all other works of history to this date and declare that there is now only one history. This one.

In creating this history we are grateful for the very few Yilanè with an interest in the sciences of geology and paleontology. We wish to honor these sciences and declare them true ones, just as true as physics or chemistry, and not the subjects of sly laughter as they have been up to now. The past existed, no matter how much we might like to ignore this unpleasant fact. We feel that it is intellectually more courageous to admit it and to accept this fact, to admit that the Yilanè did not appear suddenly when the egg of time cracked open. This is the true history and a far more exciting and fulfilling one.

Permit us one more slight divergence before this history begins. We do not intend to go back to the absolute beginning and the birth of prokaryote life. That story has been unfolded in far greater detail in other works. Our history begins about 270 million years BP (before the present) when the reptiles were already well established in their dominant role on Earth.

At that time there were four main groups of socket-toothed reptiles that are referred to as thecodonts. These primitive creatures were equipped for a life of hunting for their prey in the water. They swam easily by moving their sizeable tails. Some of these thecodonts left the sea and went to the land where their manner of walking proved superior to many other creatures like the proterosuchians, the ancestors of the present day crocodiles. You have seen the clumsy way that crocodiles walk, with their feet widespread, waddling along with their body actually hanging between their legs. Not so the superior thecodonts who thrust their entire limbs down and back with an upright stride.

Since the history of those days is written only in rocks, in the fossils preserved there, we find many gaps. While the details to fill these gaps may not be present, the overall record is still amazingly clear. Our remote ancestors were creatures called mososaurs, marine lizards of a very successful nature. They were specialized for their life in the sea with a tail fin, while their limbs had modified into flippers. One particular form of mososaur was *Tylosaurus*, a large and handsome creature. Large, in that the *Tylosaurus* were greater in length than six Yilanè. Handsome in that they resembled the Yilanè in many ways. The reason for this is that they were our direct ancestors.

If we place a representation of the skeleton of a modern Yilanè beside the skeleton of a *Tylosaurus* the relationship is immediately obvious. The digits of the limbs, hidden by the superficial flesh of the fins, reveal four fingers and four toes. So now we have two fingers on each hand and two opposed thumbs. The tail is our tail, suitably shortened. The resemblance is also clear in the rib cage, a flowing wave of ribs from clavicle to pelvic girdle. Look at these two similar skeletons and you see past and present, side by side. There we are, developed and modified to dwell on land. There is our true history, not some vague statement about appearing from the egg of time. We are the descendants of these noble creatures who some 40 million years ago became the Yilanè.

Much of what follows is of necessity guesswork. But it is *appropriate* guesswork that fits the facts of the fossil records, not airy-fairy flights of fancy such as imaginary giant meteors. The record in the rocks is there to be read. We simply assemble the parts and fit them together, just as you might reassemble the broken pieces of an eggshell.

If you wish to assemble all of the pieces yourself, then consult the relevant geological and paleontological texts. In them you will discover the origin of species, how earlier species are modified to become later ones. You will find revealed the history of the various ice ages, the phenomenon of continental drift, even the record sealed in rock that the magnetic pole was not always to the south, the way it is now, but has varied between north and south through the geological ages. You could do all of this for yourself—or you can be satisfied with our description in abbreviated form.

See then the world as it must have been 40 million years BP when the first simple and happy Yilanè roamed the Earth. It was a wetter and warmer world, with all the food they needed there for the taking. Then, as now, the Yilanè were carnivores, feasting on the flesh of the creatures that filled the land and the sea. The young, then as now, gathered in efenburu in the sea and worked together and ate well. What happened when they emerged on land is not clear in the geological record and we can only guess.

Having learned cooperation in the sea, the Yilanè certainly would not lose it when they emerged from the ocean and walked on solid ground. Then, as now, the males were surely the same simple, kindly creatures and would have needed protection. Then, as now, the beaches would have been guarded while the males were torpid, the eggs growing. Food was plentiful, life was good. Surely this was the true egg of time, not the imaginary one, when life was simple and serene.

In that early existence can be found the seeds of Yilanè science as we know it today. It can be seen in the Wall of Thorns here in this city. To defend the males, large crustacea were seized and brandished at predators, their claws a powerful defense. The bigger the claws, the more powerful the defense, so the largest would have been selected. At the same time the strongest and most offensive corals would have been chosen to defend the beaches from the seaward side. The first, crude steps along the road to the advanced biological science we now know would have been mastered.

But this simple existence was doomed to end. As successful Yilanè grew strong and filled the Earth they would have outgrown that first city on the edge of that ancient sea. Another city would have grown, another and another. When food shortages threatened the logical thing would have been to wall in fields and raise food animals and guard them from predators.

In doing this the Yilanè proved their superiority to the inferior life forms. Look at Tyrannosaurus, a carnivore just as we are carnivores. Yet these giant, stupid creatures can only pursue with violence, tear down their prey, waste most of the good meat on its carcass. They think never of tomorrow; they neither tend herds nor do they cull. They are witless destroyers. The superior Yilanè are intelligent preservers. To a scientist all life forms are equal. To destroy a species is to destroy our own species. Our respect for life can be seen in the manifold beasts in our fields, species that would have vanished millenia ago had it not been for our efforts. We are builders, not destroyers, preservers not consumers. It is obvious when these facts are considered why we are the dominant species on this planet. It is no accident; it is only the logical end product of circumstance.

PHYSIOLOGY

In order to understand our own physiology we must first consider the physiology of other animals. Simple creatures, like most insects, are poikilothermic. That is they are at one with their environment, their body temperatures are the same as the ambient air temperature. While this suffices on a small scale, more complex organisms require regularization of body temperature. These animals are homeothermic, that is they have a body temperature that is relatively constant and mostly independent of the temperature of the environment. The Yilanè belong to the kind of animals that are warm-blooded and exothermic. All of the important animals in the world are exothermic since this way of controlling body temperature is far superior to that used by the ustuzou who must expend energy continually in order to maintain the same body temperature at all times.

We are one with our environment, utilizing the natural temperature differences to maintain the consistency of our own body temperatures. After a cool night we seek the sun; if we grow too warm we face into the breeze, expose less of our bodies to the sun, erect our crests or even seek the shade. We do this so automatically that we are no more aware of regulating our internal temperature than we are of breathing.

There are many other ways that our physiology is superior to that of the endothermic ustuzou. Not for us their endless search for food to feed the ravening cells. Our metabolism changes to suit the circumstance. As an example, on long voyages by uruketo we can simply slow down our bodily processes. Subjective time then passes quickly, and each individual will require less food.

An even more striking example of physiological superiority, unique to the Yilanè, is the inseparable relationship of our metabolism to our culture; we are our city, our city is us. One cannot live without the other. This is proven by the irreversible physiological change that takes place, in the very rare instances, when an individual transgresses the rule of law, does that which is inadmissible by Yilanè propriety. No external physical violence is needed to penalize the errant individual. Justice is there within her body. The Eistaa, the embodiment of the city, our culture and our rule of law, has only to order the errant individual to leave the city while also depriving this same individual of her name. Thus rightly rejected the errant individual suffers the irreversible physiological change that ends only with her death.

The mechanism is hormonal, using prolactin which normally regulates our metabolism and our sexual behavior. However when an errant individual is forcefully reminded of transgression, her hypothalamus overloads and she enters a continuous but unbalanced physiological state. In our ancestors this was a survival factor that caused hibernation. However, in our present evolved state, the reaction is inevitably fatal.

DIET

It has been said that if you look into a creature's mouth you will know what she eats. Dentition denotes diet. A nenitesk has flat-topped, square teeth for grinding up the immense amounts of vegetable matter it must eat, with sharper-edged teeth in the front for cutting and tearing its food loose. The neat, attractive rows of cone-shaped teeth in our jaws denote our healthy and carnivorous fish-eating diet. The thickness and strength of our jaws indicate that molluscs once played a large part in our ancestors' diet for we did—and still can—crush the shells of these tasty creatures with our teeth.

REPRODUCTION

There are certain things that Yilanè do not talk about, and this is right and proper in a well-ordered society. When we are young and in the sea life is endless pleasure. This pleasure continues when we are fargi; our simple thoughts should not be burdened with subjects too complex to understand.

As Yilanè we not only can consider and discuss any matter, but we must do this if we are to understand the world we live in. The life cycle of the Yilanè is perfect in its symmetry and we begin our observation of this circle of life at the time it begins, when the young emerge from father's protection and enter the sea.

This is the beginning of conscious life. Though all of the earliest activities are inborn reflexes—breathing, swimming, gathering in groups—intelligence is already developing. Communication begins, observation, cogitation and conclusion are initiated. Members of the young efenburu learn by observing the older ones.

This is where language begins. There are two main schools of thought about the origin of language among those who make a study of languages. Leaving out the detailed arguments, and phrasing them in a popular way, they might be called the swim-swim and the ping-ping theories. The swim-swim theory postulates that our first attempts at communication are brought about by imitations of other creatures in the sea: that is a movement of the hand and arm in imitation of the swimming movement of a fish would indicate the idea of a fish. On the other hand the ping-ping supporters say that sound came first, the sounds that fish make being imitated. We cannot know, we may never know which of these theories is true. But we can and have watched the young learning to communicate in the open sea.

The elements they use are all of the ones that they will use later, but simplified to a great degree. Basic movements of the limbs, colored indications with the palms, simple sound groupings. These suffice to join the members of each efenburu together, to build the strong bonds that will last through life, to teach the importance of mutual aid and cooperation.

Only when they emerge from the sea do the fargi discover that the world can be a difficult place. We may speculate that in distant times, when our race was young, the competition was not as severe. Only when communication in an advanced society became of utmost importance did the individual begin to suffer.

It is a law of nature that the weak fall by the way. The slow fish is eaten by the fast fish and does not breed. The faster fish survive to pass on their genes for swift-swimming. So it is with the Yilanè, for many of the fargi never learn to speak well enough to join the happy intercourse of the city. They are fed, for no Yilanè refuses food to another. But they feel insecure, unwanted, unsure of themselves as they watch others of the efenburu succeed in speaking to join in the busy life of the city. Dispirited they fish for their own food in the sea, wander away, are seen no more. We can feel for them, but we cannot help them. It is a law of nature that the weak shall fall by the way.

It goes without saying that of course these self-chosen rejects are all female. As we know all of the males are sought out and cherished the moment that they emerge from the ocean. Doomed would be the culture that allowed these simple, sweet, unthinking creatures to perish! Wet from the ocean they are brought to the hanalè to lead the life of comfort and ease which is their due. Fed and protected they live happy lives, looking forward only to the day when they can perform the ultimate service of preserving their race.

WARNING

What follows may be too explicit for some to absorb. Details may offend those of too delicate sensibilities. Since the authors of this study wish only to inform, anyone who feels they would not be happy with material of this sort should read only the following paragraph, then skip ahead to the section labeled Science.

There is a process within *reproduction* whereby a small portion of male tissue, called a sperm, is united with a small portion of female tissue, called an ovum. This ovum becomes an egg, and the male carries the egg in a special sac. When carrying the egg, and keeping it warm and comfy, the male gets very fat and happy and sleepy. One day the egg hatches and a lovely youngster goes into the sea, and that is all there is to it.

DETAILS OF A POSSIBLY OFFENSIVE NATURE
The union of the sperm and the ovum takes place during a process with the technical term *intercourse*. There follows a description of this event.

A male is brought to a state of excitement by the stimulations of a female. When this happens one or both of the male reproductive organs becomes engorged and emerges from the penis sac at the base of the tail. As soon as this occurs the female mounts the male and receives the penis into her cloaca. At this point mutual stimulation, which need not be described, causes the male to expel a large number of sperm. These specialized organisms find and unite with ova inside the female body to produce fertilized eggs.

With the sperm is also released a prostaglandin that produces a reaction within the female body that produces rigidity in the limbs, among other things, that prolongs the sexual union for a lengthy time, a good portion of the day. (Intercourse without production of the hormone is technically named a *perversion* and will not be discussed here.) During this period the fertilized eggs quickly develop and grow, until they are extruded into the male's pouch.

The female's part is now finished, her vital role fulfilled, and responsibility for the continuation of the Yilanè race now becomes that of the male. The fertilized egg now contains the genes of both male and female. The implanted eggs now grow placentas and increase in size as they draw sustenance; for this to occur major changes happen in the male body. There is first the urge to return to the sea, the warm sea, and this is done within two days, since a stable temperature is needed for the maturing eggs. Once on the beach and in the sea the male enjoys a physiological change, growing torpid and slow, sleeping most of the time. This state remains until the eggs hatch and the young are born and enter the sea.

It should be mentioned, though it has no bearing upon the continuation of our species, that a few males die on the beaches each year as their bodies resist the metabolic change back to their normal condition. But since this only affects males it is of no importance.

Thus the life-cycle of the Yilanè begins anew.

SCIENCE

There are many sciences, each a specialized system of study, too detailed to go into in this brief history. Those interested can consult specialized works that deal with Chromosome Surgery, Chemistry, Geology, Physics, Astronomy, etc. Note will only be taken here of Genetic Engineering and Mathematics.

Like all else in Yilanè history the true history of our biological development is lost in the mists of time. We can, however, make some logical assumptions that explain the facts as we know them now. With patience enough—and time enough—any biological problem can be solved. In the beginning it can be assumed that crude breeding was the only technique that was used. As time passed, and greater interest evolved in how reproduction actually took place, research into gene structure would have begun. The first real breakthrough would have been when the researchers succeeded in crystallizing the genome, that is bringing about evolutionary stasis. Only when we can stop evolution can we begin to understand it.

At this point the uninformed reader may be puzzled and might be inclined to ask—how does one stop evolution and make genetic changes? The answer is not a simple one and in order to answer it we must begin at the beginning.

In order to understand Genetic Engineering some knowledge of the biological makeup of life on this planet must be considered. Organisms exist as two grades. The simplest are the prokaryotes, ordinary bacteria, blue-green bacteria, blue-green algae, viruses and so on. The other larger and more complex life forms, the eukaryotes, will be considered in a moment. First let us look at the prokaryotes.

All of these have their genetic material as rings of DNA, or RNA in some viruses. These tiny organisms seem to be economizing on their genetic material because many of these coding regions overlap. They possess special DNA sequences between genes for at least two purposes. Firstly, the control of gene function, such as the turning off of gene transcription by the products of the coded enzyme in operons, and for providing sequences recognized by transcription or replication enzymes. Secondly, there are DNA sequences that incorporate the DNA between them into other strands of DNA. (Examples would be into a host bacterium, for a plasmid or a bacteriophage, or a host eukaryote cell for a virus.) There are bacteria that produce a few enzymes which actually snip or join DNA by recognizing specific sequences for snipping or joining between two nucleotides. By using these enzymes it is possible to determine the sequence of DNA lengths. This is done by digesting them sequentially with enzymes which recognize the different sequences. Then each mixture of shorter resultant sequences is analyzed with other enzymes.

This is a lengthy process requiring millions of tries. But then Yilanè patience is infinite and we have had millions of years to develop the process. In order to recognize particular sequences radioactive DNA or RNA messengers are attached specifically with base complementation along their length. Afterwards, special enzymes are used to remove a specific length and insert it into another organism's DNA ring.

This is the way that bacterial DNA rings are modified: Firstly by the use of plasmids, natural bacterial 'sex' sequences. Secondly by phages, viruses that naturally attack bacteria. And thirdly by using cosmids, artificial DNA circles with special joining sequences, any of which can be tailored to include new or modified genes, so that the modified bacteria can make new proteins.

So it can be seen that it is relatively easy to change the protein chemistry of bacteria, simple eukaryotes such as yeast, and to reprogram other eukaryotic cells in a similar simple manner.

It is much more complicated to produce desired changes in the larger eukaryotic animals. In these creatures the egg itself is programmed in the mother's ovary, where it builds upon itself in the foundation of the embryo's development. Only after completion of this embryonic structure does each cell produce proteins that change the cell itself, as well as other nearby cells, in a process that finally results in the juvenile organism. How this process has been mastered and altered is too complex to go into in this curtailed discussion. There are other facets of Yilanè science that have to be considered.

Mathematics must be discussed since many Yilanè have heard of this, and since all of the sciences employ it, though they will not have run across it at other times. The following explanation, although brief is accurate.

The science of Mathematics is based upon numbers. If you wish to understand numbers spread your hands out before you, palms down, and inner thumbs touching. Wriggle your outside thumb on the right. That is called number *one*. Now, moving one finger at a time from right to left, the adjacent finger is *two*, the next finger *three*, the inner thumb *four*. Left inside thumb *five*, fingers *six* and *seven*, and finally the outside thumb on the left is *ten*. Ten is also called *base*, a technical term that we will not go into here. It is enough to know that numbering starts over again after the base is reached, ten-and-one, ten-and-two, right up to two-times-ten. There is no limit to the number of multiples of ten that you can have. That is why numbers are so important in the sciences where things are weighed, measured, recorded, counted, etc. Mathematics itself is very simple, just a recording of things that are bigger than things, smaller than other things, equal or not equal to other things.

The origin of mathematics is lost in time. Although mathematicians themselves believe that the base ten was chosen because we have ten fingers. They say that any number may be chosen as a base, though this seems highly unlikely. If we took two for a base then 2 would be 10, 3 = 11, then on with 4 = 100, 5 = 101, 6 = 110 and so on. Very clumsy and impractical and of no real use. It has even been suggested that if ustuzou could count, a singularly wild idea in any case, that their base 10 would be our 12. All our numbers would change as well; the 40 million years of Yilanè existence would shrink to a mere 30 million years. You can see where such unwise speculation might lead so it is best we abandon such unhealthy theorizing.

CULTURE

We have had to introduce a number of new terms in this history, and *culture* is another one. It might be defined as the sum total of the way we live as it is transmitted down through the ages. We can assume that our culture had historical beginnings, though we cannot possibly imagine what they might have been. All we can do is describe our existence now.

Every Yilanè has her city, for Yilanè life revolves around the city. When we emerge from the sea we can only look on in speechless awe at the beauty and symmetry of our city. We go there as fargi and are taken in and fed. We listen and learn from others. We watch and learn. When we can speak we offer our services and are treated kindly. We see all the manifold life of the city and are drawn to one part or another. Some of us serve humbly and well with the herds and in the slaughterhouses. All Yilanè who read this should remember that service is not only in the sciences and the studies that you do; it is in service and all Yilanè are equal in that.

As a city is built in rings, with fields and animals outermost, the living city next, the birth-beaches and the ambesed at the heart of it, so also is our culture built. The large circle of fargi outermost. Within that circle are the assistants and the trained laborers in the various specialities. They in turn circle about the scientists, the supervisors, the builders—all those at the peak of their learned skills. They in turn look to the city leaders, and all look to the Eistaa who rules. It is logical, simple, complete, the only possible culture to have.

This is the world of the Yilanè. It has been this way since the egg of time, and will go on forever. Where there are Yilanè there is Yilanè rule and law and all are happy.

At the two poles of our globe there is great cold and discomfort and Yilanè are too wise to penetrate these places. But only recently it has been discovered that there are comfortable places in this world where there are no Yilanè. We owe it to ourselves and to the world to fill these empty spaces. Some of these places contain ustuzou, unpleasant ustuzou. In the interests of science we must examine these creatures. Most readers will close this volume now since they have no interest in such matters. Therefore what follows in the section beginning on page 726 is for those with specialized interests.

Translator's Note
Here the translation from the Yilanè ends. For some understanding of the complex—and fascinating—problems that face the translator working with this unusual language please see the following section.

LANGUAGE

Slow development, for millions of years, has created a rich and complex language. So complex in fact that many never manage to master it and never become Yilanè. This cultural handicap separates the race into two subgroups, one of which, barred from the life in the cities, remains in a feral state, living off the life in the sea for the most part. Not breeding because of their inability to protect the torpid males from predators. Their loss means that the gene pool of the species is slowly being altered, but the process is a glacially slow one.

The Yilanè speak in a linked chain of gestalts, with each gestalt containing one to four concepts. Each gestalt also has a control sign which is indicated by a stylized body posture or movement that has some relationship to the overall meaning. These gestalts are rarely the same because they have so many possible combinations, approximately 125,000,000,000.

Any attempts to transcribe Yilanè in English presents formidable problems. Firstly the control signs, the stylized body positions, have to be considered. An incomplete listing, with stylized transcription symbols, follows:

Hunch	↑	Star	✳	Whirl	✝
Cower	⟩	Climb	⊓	Sway	↓
Stoop	⊓	Fall	⊤	Shake	⚡
Stretch	Y	Lift	⊣	Reach[1]	⊣
Diamond	⟠	Leap	⊣	Reach[2]	⊣
Squat	h	Rise	⌣	Sit	⟨
Lie	⊢⊣	Push	⟍	Neutral	I
Embrace	Y	Swim	∼	Tailsweep (clockwise)	⊋
Bask	✕	Plunge	⟋	Tailsweep (anticlock)	⊂

The sounds of Yilanè approximate those of humans, but for a basic understanding it is not necessary to consider all the differences. However, in English transcriptions zh is the sound in rouge, x the ch in loch. Th and dh are rarely used. There are four extra sigils denoting sounds particular to Yilanè. they are ' (glottal stop), < (tock), ! (click) and * (smack of lips).

The richness of the language and the difficulty of accurate transcription can be seen in the translation of the following expression:

> *To leave father's love and enter the embrace of the sea is the first pain of life—the first joy is the comrades who join you there.*

First the kernel string of gestalts, each one with a separate controller, numbered C1 to C12 for ease of reference:

C1 (✕) *enge*
C2 (⊢⊣) *han.natè. ihei*
C3 (⟍) *aga.petè*
C4 (⊤) *embo.[1] *kè.[2] ka<*

C5 (⏀) *igi. rubu. shei*[3]
C6 (∿) *kakh.shei. sèsè*
C7 (⟩) *hè. awa. ihei*
  //[4]
C8 (✶) *hè. vai<. ihei*
C9 (∿) *kakh. shei. intè*
C10 (Y) *end. pelei. uu*
C11 (∿) *asak. hen*
C12 (⫫) *enge*

(1) At this point Circumambience is also suggested by rotation of the tail tip.
(2) Warmth also suggested by movement of jaw muscles as if to gape.
(3) Note that units 4 and 5 are linked by controllers, 3 and 5 by paired opposite concepts at the start.
(4) The Yilanè pauses here and repeats gestalts in reverse order to form a deliberate balance or chiasmus.

A literal translation of this, with the definition of the control signs in brackets, reads as follows;

C1 (Bask)	Love
C2 (Lie)	Maleness. Friend. Senses of Touch/Smell/Feel
C3 (Push)	Departure. Self
C4 (Fall)	Pressure. Stickiness. Cessation
C5 (Fall)	Entry. Weightlessness. Cold
C6 (Swim)	Salt. Cold. Motion
C7 (Cower)	Numeral 1. Pain. Senses of Touch/Smell/Feel
C8 (Star)	Numeral 1. Joy. Senses of Touch/Smell/Feel
C9 (Swim)	Salt. Cold. Hunt
C10 (Stretch)	Vision. Discovery. Increase
C11 (Swim)	Beach. Male/Female
C12 (Reach)	Love.

A broad transcription of this would be;

Enge hantèhei, agatè embokèka iirubushei kaksheisè, hèawahei;
hèvai'ihei, kaksheintè, enpeleiuu asahen enge.

WINTER IN EDEN · 367

The most accurate translation into English would be in verse, but barring that this is an approximate translation;

The love of your father, to be expelled from it and go into the cold unloving sea, that is the first pain of life: the first joy of life (in that cold hunting ground) is to come upon your friends and feel their love close round you.

The basic differences between human language and Yilanè are so great as to be almost insurmountable for someone attempting to learn Yilanè. Human beings, talking to each other in different languages, start by picking things up and naming them. "Rock . . . wood . . . leaf." After some understanding they go on to actions: "Throw the rock, pick up the leaf."

This just cannot happen with the Yilanè. They do not name things but describe them. Instead of the noun 'chair' they would say "Small wood to sit on." Where we would use a single noun, 'door', the Yilanè would have different constructions: "Entry to warm place." From the other side it might be "Exit to a cold place."

You will find an example of this in volume one of the *West of Eden* trilogy. Enge attempts to teach the young Tanu girl, Ysel, to speak in the correct Yilanè manner. The basic concepts always elude her. She manages to memorize a few words and has some slight idea of the use of controllers. When Vaintè attempts to talk to her the exchange goes like this;

Vaintè says; (✱) esekapen (↑) yidshepen (Y) yileibesat (Y) efenduuruu (↑) yilsatuu (✱) yilsatefen

Which can be translated as; (Star) top-demand (Hunch) this-one-speaking-demand (Stretch) speech-difficulty equality (Stretch) life-continuation-increase (Hunch) speech-equality-increase (Star) speech-equality-life

"I personally demand it most urgently! Speak, please, as well as one of the yiliebe. This way you will keep on living and growing. Speech means growth—please! Speech means life—understand!"

The best that Ysel can do is say, "has leibe ènè uu"; she thinks that she is saying "I find it hard to talk, please." What comes out, however, fatally for her, is more like "female—age/entropy—suppleness—increase". The mistakes she has made are;

1. *has* does not mean 'I', but 'female'. The confusion was caused by Enge pointing to herself when she said it.

2. *leibe* does indeed signify 'difficult'—if it is said with a controller that implies some degree of constraint, for instance "Hunch," "Stoop," or "Squat." Without this the meaning edges towards *age*, that is the process of something running down, not only Yilanè.

3. *ènè* does not mean *talk* at all, but indicates suppleness since the Yilanè associate these ideas very often.

4. *uu* is a common termination used by Enge in her lessons for encouragement. But it signifies concepts like "growth, go on, try". It does not mean *please*.

Since Ysel has no tail she cannot make the cower gesture correctly. In addition she makes the fatal mistake of imitating Vaintè's last posture, the Star, that of threatening dominance. So Vaintè thinks that Ysel was saying something like "The old female grows adroit," or possibly even "Growing supple puts years on females." This is nonsense and Vaintè rightly loses her temper, her anger fed by the fact that she was polite to this animal; she may not have cowered but she did hunch as well as star. Ysel's fate is sealed.

By contrast, Kerrick comes out with: (**⟩**) esekakurud (**५**) esekyilshan (**I**) elel (**I**) leibeleibe

That is he communicates (Cower) top-disgust-cessation (Lift) top-speech-volition (Neutral) longlong (Neutral) hardhard.

Which Vaintè understands as "I very much don't want to die. I want very much to talk. (Giving up). Very long, very hard". At first Vaintè doesn't notice the 'cower' for he has no tail. But she does recognize the 'lift' and slowly realizes what he is trying to say.

THE TANU

The history of the Earth is written in its stones. While there are still unanswered questions, the overall history of our planet from the Palaeozoic Era up to today is recorded in fossil remains. This was the age of ancient life, 605 million years ago, when the only creatures in the warm and shallow seas were worms, jellyfish and other backboneless animals. The continents then were still joined together in a single large landmass that has been named Pangea.

Even then some of the sea creatures were using lime to build shells for protection and support. The development of internal skeletons came later, with the first fish. Later fish had lungs and lobe-like fins that could be used to support them when they emerged from the sea and ventured onto the land. From these the amphibians developed about 290 million years ago, the ancestors of the first reptiles.

The first dinosaurs appeared on Earth just over 205 million years ago. By the time the first sea-filled cracks were appearing in Pangea 200 million years ago, the dinosaurs had spread all over the world, to every part of the first giant continent that would later separate into the smaller continents we know today. This was their world, where they filled every ecological niche, and their rule was absolute for 135 million years.

It took a worldwide disaster to disturb their dominance. A ten-kilometer-wide meteor that struck the ocean and hurled millions of tons of dust and water high into the atmosphere. The dinosaurs died. Seventy percent of all species then living died. The way was open for the tiny, shrew-like mammals—the ancestors of all mammalian life today—to develop and populate the globe.

It was galactic chance, the dice-game of eternity, that this great piece of rock hit at that time, in that manner, and caused the global disturbance that it did.

But what if it had missed? What if the laws of chance had ruled otherwise and this bomb from space had not hit the Earth? What would the world be like today?

The first and most obvious difference would be the absence of Iceland, for these volcanic islands mark the place where the meteor struck and penetrated to the mantle below.

The second greatest difference would be in the history of global climate, still not completely understood. We know that different ice ages came and went—but we do not know why. We know that the polarity of the Earth has changed in the past, with the north magnetic pole where the south is now—but we do not know why. It seems a certainty that if the meteor had not hit and the incredible atmospheric change had not occurred, that the same progression of ice ages and accompanying continent building would not have occurred in precisely the same manner.

Look at our world as it might have been.

The rule of the dinosaurs is unbroken. The world is theirs and they are dominant on every continent—and the Yilanè rise above them all.

Except in the western hemisphere. Although South America is dominated by reptiles this is not completely true to the north. The land bridge of Central America, that connects North and South America, has been sunk beneath the ocean at different geological times. At one crucial time the break coincided with the spread of the vast sea that covered most of North America. The ice sheet of the glaciers that next came south stretched almost to the edge of this inland sea so that for millions of years the climate was northern, barely temperate in midsummer. The cold-blooded species died out and the warm-blooded species became dominant. They expanded and developed and became the dominant life-forms of this land mass.

In time, as the ice sheets withdrew, the mammals expanded north. By the time the land bridge of Central America rose from the sea again the warm-blooded creatures ruled the continent between the oceans. Yet they could not stand against the slow return of the reptiles. There is no defense, other than retreat, from armored creatures weighing 80 tons or more.

Only in the north, in the foothills and the mountains, could the mammals survive. Among them were the New World primates, from whom the Tanu are descended.

There are no Old World mammals here because the Old World is saurian. There are no bears or canines. But the New World deer abound, from small species to immense ones as large as a moose. The mastodons are here as are many marsupials including saber-tooth tigers. Mammalia in rich diversity live in the fertile band south of the ice and north of the cold-blooded saurians.

Most of the Tanu, imprisoned by a harsh environment, have never developed beyond the hunter-gatherer stage. But at this they are immensely successful. There are some exceptions, like the Sasku, who have moved on to a stable existence of neolithic farming. They have developed the settled skills of pottery and weaving, as well as a more complex and stratified society. But this does not mean that they are superior in any way to the hunting Tanu who have a rich language, simple art forms, many survival skills and a basic family group relationship.

The same might be said of the Paramutan who occupy a perilous ecological niche in the subarctic. Their skills are manifold, their culture small and communal. They are completely dependant upon the hunt and upon the single marine creature, the ularuaq, for their material existence.

THE MARBAK LANGUAGE

Marbak, like the other languages spoken by the Tanu, is a modern dialect of the lost parent language that has been named Eastern Coastal. In Marbak 'man' is *hannas*, the plural *hannasan*. Variations are *hennas* in Wedaman, *hnas* in Levrewasan, *neses* in Lebnaroi, etc.

All of the names of these small tribal groups are descriptive, e.g. Wedaman means 'the island ones'; Levrewasan 'tent-black-ones', that is the people of the black tents. Like man, *hannas*, woman *linga*, plural *lingai*, has widespread similarity. A person, sex not specified, is *ter*, while the plural *tanu* is generally accepted as referring to all other people.

The most common masculine noun declension is:

	SINGULAR	PLURAL
Nominative	hannas	hannasan
Accusative	hannas	hannasan
Genitive	hannasa	hannasanna
Dative	hannasi	hannasanni
Locative	hannasi	hannasanni
Instrumental	hannasom	hannasom

THE PARAMUTAN

Like the Tanu, the Paramutan are descended from the New World primates. Although fossil evidence is lacking, gene analysis reveals that Tanu and Paramutan are genealogically quite close and only their great physical separation has prevented inbreeding up until this time. Although superficial resemblance does not seem to bear this out, i.e. the fur-covered Paramutan and the relatively hairless Tanu, it should be noted that both groups have approximately the same number of hair follicles. Many Tanu are born with rudimentary tails, merely an external projection of the coccyx, which contain exactly the same number of bones as the Paramutan tail.

Therefore the obvious physical differences between the groups are of little importance; what is relevant are the social and cultural factors. The Paramutan migrated further north than any of the other primates. We may postulate population pressure from behind or relevant technology that made subarctic existence first a possibility, then a necessity. Their dependence upon a single major source for food, raw materials, existence itself (the ularuaq) allows no other possibility. Their use of north-temperate materials (wood for their boats, oak-tanning of hides) is still important—but the ularuaq is irreplaceable to their existence as their culture is constituted now.

It must be pointed out that Paramutan is a misnomer since this is a Marbak word that means "raw-meat-eaters". The correct term in their own language is *Angurpiaq*, meaning "real people", for this is how they see themselves. In their solitary existence in the northern wastes they feel, with some good reason, that they are the real people, the only people. This is why they call the Tanu *Erqigdlit*, the fantasy people. Strangers who come from an unreal world who therefore must be unreal themselves.

THE ENVIRONMENT

There are many more living creatures in the sea than on the land—and many more kinds. Life began in the sea and all of the major animal groups have many representatives still living there. The basis of all open ocean productivity is the floating unicellular algae. These microscopic plants live only in the top few meters of water where they can obtain energy from the sun. There are about 600 common kinds of algae which form the basis of the food chain. They are first eaten by tiny planktonic animals, the most common of which is the copepod crustacea of the genus *Calanus*. (The commonest animal on Earth—both by numbers and weight.) These are eaten in turn by larger, shrimp-like crustacea as well as many other animals including jellyfish, arrow-worms, baby fish, many larvae of molluscs and squid, as well as even larger benthic crustacea such as crabs and lobsters.

The product of all this activity is a slow rain of corpses and excreta that sinks down to the bacteria on the ocean bed. The essential nutrients, particularly nitrogen and potassium produced by the bacteria, are carried away by the deep-sea currents. This is the primary source of the abundant life in the polar oceans. Despite the low temperature and lack of light their productivity is high and virtually continuous. For the cold is indeed the source of the ingredients that nourish life. The temperature of the surface water is a chill four degrees centigrade—while the warm currents from the south range from five to eight degrees. The warmer water rises through the colder, denser water to feed the abundant life on the surface.

An unusual feature of the ice shelf is the qunguleq that fills an ecological niche that is empty in the world as we know it. The cold eco-system of the qunguleq is unlike any other in the ocean. Rooted in the ice, the great skirt of green tendrils spreads out through the sea, taking nourishment from the water and energy from the sun. This northern meadow is grazed by the ularuaq, the largest living creatures in the world. They tear at the strands with their thick, muscular lips, taking food and life from the qunguleq. They are utterly dependent upon this single food source. With the southerly movement of the arctic icecap the ocean currents have been changed and emerge further to the west. The ularuaq follow the qunguleq and the Paramutan in turn must follow the ularuaq. Every link in the food chain is dependant upon the link before it.

THE ANGURPIAQ LANGUAGE

Any student of their language will quickly discover how few terminal sounds there are. Because of this it may appear superficially simple at first, but greater study will reveal its richness and complexities.

The difficulty for Marbak speakers is that the *k* sound must be distinguished from the *q* sound. The latter is made with the tongue much further back than the *k*. The closest approximation that a non-native speaker might make would be *-rk*.

There are also two distinct forms of *l*, one voiced, the other unvoiced. The unvoiced form is transcribed here as *-dl* or *-tl* to note this important difference.

Linguistic difficulty is not a one-way street. The Angurpiaq have problems with some of the Marbak sounds, finding them virtually unsayable. For example, Armun emerges as "Arramun" and Harl as "Harral" and so forth.

One of the most interesting things about the structure of this language is that it consists only of nouns and verbs. One of these begins every word. However this root term is open to scores of affixes which then can combine with even more affixes. In this way sentence-long words are built up. For example;

> *qingik* a house
> *qingirssuak* a large house
> *qingiliorpoq* he builds a house
> *qubgirssualiorpoq* he build a large house
> *qingirssualiorfilik* a man can build a large house,
>   and so on, apparently without end.

It is very important that the right-branching nature of this be noted. We are all used to left-branching constructions, such as;

house

a house

a large house

Once one system is used by a native speaker it becomes 'natural' to speak that way and organize language in this manner, making learning a new order particularly difficult.

In addition to affixes, nouns and verbs also have suffixes. These are used to mark case, person or mood. Verbs can be in the Indicative mood, or Interrogative, Subjunctive, Optative, Conjunctive, Infinitive. As an example of how this functions let us take "like" which in the infinitive is *alutora*.

> *alutoroq* he likes
> *alutorut* she likes

alutorauk does he like?
salutorassuk do they like?
alutorliuk may he like (Optative)
alutorlissuk may they like
alutorpagit he may like (Subjunctive)
alutorpatigik they may like

Although Marbak and Angurpiaq are not linguistically related, they are structurally related, even if in a mirror-image fashion. If Armun, for instance was to use *alutora* for "like", then point to herself and then to some object that she likes it would be comprehensible. The Angurpiaq might consider her stupid for getting the ending wrong, but they would understand what she was trying to say. This is opposed to Yilanè where nothing would be understood at all that wasn't expressed within specific and precise narrow bounds.

One thing that is very imprecise in Angurpiaq is the sense of time, for they are indifferent time-keepers at the best. There is a vague form of future tense, but it is rarely used. The term most often heard is *tamnagok* which can mean once upon a time, or it can also mean then or now—or even in a bit. The only other time-related term is *eetchuk* which signifies a long *long* time ago. This is so unspecific that it could mean forty or even two-thousand years.

As is to be expected their language reflects their physical existence. They mark many distinctions that do not exist in Marbak, yet completely ignore others. For obvious reasons there are a number of terms for snow. They refer to packed snow, powder snow, frozen snow, wet snow, snow that you can cut blocks from and even snow that balls underfoot. Yet on the other hand green and blue are not distinguished as separate colors. And while red can be told from yellow there is no separate designation for orange. Since the terms for these colors are only affixes, never used as words of their own, there is really no clear sense of their exact meaning.

It has been theorized that their strong feeling for affixes and innumerable connections and cross-connections may have some relationship with the Angurpiaq deftness and ability to see how mechanical parts fit together. Though it is certainly true that their assembled and tied boat frameworks, their navigational charts, reflect this it must be emphasized that this is a theory only.

DICTIONARIES

YILANÈ-ENGLISH

(Note: this list includes both single elements and some commonly repeated gestalts.)

aa	in
aga	departure
aglè	passage
aka	disgust
akas	growing land
akel	goodness
akse	stone
alak	succession
Alakas-aksehent	Florida Keys
alè	cage
alpè	beauty
ambei	height
ambesed	central meeting place
anat	bodily extremity
ankanaal	land-surrounded ocean
ankè	presence
apen	demand
asak	beach
ast	tooth
asto	movement
awa	pain
ban*	home
buru	circumambience
dee	this
ee	out
eede	that

eesen	flatness
efen	life
efenburu	group formed in childhood
efeneleiaa	spirit of life
efenselè	member of an efenburu
eisek	mud
eisekol	dredging animal
eiset	responsibility
eistaa	city leader
eksei	caution
elin	small
elininyil	pre-fargi stage of development
elinou	small saurian carnivore
embo	pressure
empè	commendation
end	vision
enet	lake
ènè	suppleness
enge	love
enteesenat	plesiosaur
ento	each single
Entoban*	Africa
epetruk	tyrannosaurus rex
erek	speed
esek	top
esekasak	birth-beach guardian
esik	south
espei	posture
estekel*	pterodactyl
eto<	shoot
fafn	catch
far<	inquiry
fargi	one learning to speak
gen	new
Genaglè	Straits of Gibralter
Gendasi*	North America
gul	hearing
gulawatsan	buzzer animal
han	maleness
hais	mind

hanalè	male residence
has	female
has	yellowness

N.B. These two concepts are always distinguished by voice of controller.

hè	numeral 1
hen	male/female
hent	revolution
hèsotsan	dart-firing weapon
hornsopa	genetic shape
huruksast	monoclonius

igi	entry
ihei	sense of smell/touch/feel
ineg	old
inlè	large size
intè	hunt
ipol	rub, buff
Isegnet	Mediterranean
isek	north

ka<	cessation
kain	line of sight
kakh	salt
kal	poison
kalkasi	thornbush
kasei	thorn
kem	light
khets	convexity
kiyis	east
kru	short

lan<	copulation
leibe	difficulty
lek	badness

mal	absence of worry
man<	last
Maninlè	Cuba
masinduu	optical projection

melik	dark
melikkasei	poison-thorn vines
natè	friend
nefmakel	bandage-creature
neni	skull
nenitesk	triceratops
nin	absence
ninsè	the unresponsive
nu*	adequacy
okhalakx	herbivore
okol	gut
onetsensast	stegosaurus
pelei	discovery
rubu	weightlessness
ruud	cessation
ruutsa	ankylosaurus
sanduu	microscope
sas<	speed
sat	equality
selè	bondage
sèsè	motion
sete	purpose-oriented group
shak	change
shan	volition
shei	cold
sokèi	cleared land
son*	element
stal	prey
takh	clean
tarakast	mount for riding
tesk	concavity
top	run
tsan	animal
tso	excrement

trumal	a joint attack
tuup	fat, torpid
ugunkshaa	recording device
umnun	treated meat
unut	crawl
unutakh	hair-eating slug
uruketo	mutated icthyosaur
uruktop	eight-legged beast of burden
urukub	brontosaurus
ustu	blood
uu	increase
ustuzou	mammalia
yil	speech
yiliebe	incapable of speech

MARBAK–ENGLISH

allas	path
alladjex	shaman
amaratan	immortal ones (divine creatures)
arnwheet	hawk
as	how
atta	father (dim.)
bana	son (dim.)
beka	to knot
benseel	sphagnum moss
bleit	cold
dalas	soup
dalasstar	strong soup
dia	to be
drija	bleed
eghoman	the vowed ones
ekkotaz	nuts & berry paste
elka	to light
erman	sky
Ermanpadar	sky-father, a spirit
es	if
ey	always

fa	to look
falla	to wait
faldar	fire
gentinaz	leader
grunnan	misery
ham, hammar	to be able to (sing., pl.)
hans	war party
hannas	man
hannasan	men
hardalt	squid
harian	joyful ones
hault	twenty (count of a man)
himin	mountain
hoatil	everyone
istak	path
Kargu	mountain people
katisk	cheerful
kell	wedge
kurmar	river
kurro	boss
las	down
levrelag	camping ground
Levrewasan	the black tent people
ley	(burnt) clearing
linga	woman
lingai	women
lissa	to know
madrap	moccasin
mal	good
man	must
margalus	murgu counsellor
mar	hair
marag	cold-blooded animal
marin	star
markiz	winter
marsk	icthyosaur

mensa	to arrange
modia	maybe
mo trig	my child
murgu	plural of marag
nat	killer
naudinz	hunter
nenitesk	triceratops
nep	long
parad	ford
Paramutan	raw-meat-eaters, Northern people
rath	hot
sammad	mixed male/female band
sammadar	elected head of the sammad
sassi	few
sia	to go
skerm	period of time
so	as, that, who
stakkiz	summer
stessi	beach
tais	grain
tanu	people
tarril	brother
ter	person
terred	group of people on a mission
terredar	leader of a terred
tharm	spirit or soul
tina	to bear
to	at
torsk	ichthyosaur
torskan	ichthyosaurs
torskanat	ichthyosaur's bane
ulfadan	long-beards
veigil	heavy, important
wedam	island

SESEK–ENGLISH

bansemnilla	marsupial carnivore
charadis	flax
Deifoben	place of the golden beaches
porro	beer
tagaso	maize corn
waliskis	mastodon

ANGURPIAQ–ENGLISH

NOUNS

Angurpiaq	real people
Erqigdlit	fantasy people
etat	forest
ikkergak	large boat
imaq	open sea
inge	vulva
munga	small fish, codling
nangeq	destination
paukarut	tent
qingik	house, shelter
qivio	path
qunguleq	arctic seaweed
ularuaq	large aquatic mammal

VERBS

alutora	like
ardlerpa	hunt

ikagput	be many
liorpa	build
misugpa	eat
muluva	be absent
nagsoqipa	be equal, make no distinction
nakoyoark	be excellent
siagpai	be important
takugu	see
tingava	intercourse

AFFIXES

-adluinar	completely
-eetchuk	long ago
-guaq	inferior
-kaq	small
-luarpoq	too much
-qaq	quick
-taq	new-caught
-tamnagok	then, now, soon

ZOOLOGY

BANSEMNILLA
(Metatheria: Didelphys dimidiata)

A reddish-gray marsupial with three deep black bands down its back. It has a prehensile tail and opposable toes on its hind feet. It is carnivorous, favoring rats and mice, and is bred by the Sasku to eliminate these vermin from their corncribs.

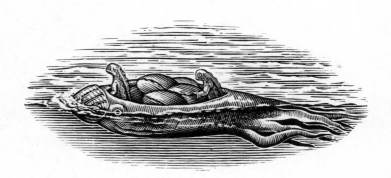

BOAT
(Cephalopoda: Archeololigo olcostephanus mutatus)

Yilanè surface water transport. Propulsion is obtained by a strong jet of water expelled to the stern. The creatures have only rudimentary intelligence like their ancestral squids, but can be trained to follow certain simple commands.

CLOAK
(Selachii: Elasmobranchus kappa mutatus)

Used by the Yilanè for warmth during the night or inclement weather. These creatures have absolutely no intelligence, but if they are well fed they will maintain a body temperature of approximately 102 degrees F.

DEER
(Eutheria: Cervus mazama mazama)

A small deer with antlers as unbranched spikes. It is found in great numbers in the North Temperate Zone. The Tanu value these creatures both for their meat and their skins. The hides are tanned to make clothing and small leather articles (e.g. moccasins [*madrap*] and bags).

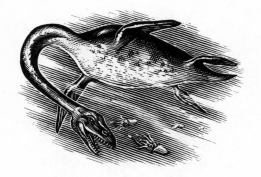

ENTEESENAT
(Sauropterygia: Elasmosaurus plesiosaurus)

A predaceous marine reptile well adapted to pelagic life and relatively unchanged since the Cretaceous period. They have small short heads and long snakelike necks. The paddlelike flippers are similar to those of the marine turtle. Newer varieties have been developed with greater cranial capacity that enable them to be trained to supply food for the larger uruketo (*Icthyosaurus monstrosus mutatus*).

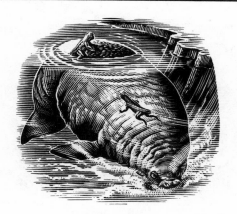

EISEKOL
(Eutheria: Trichecbus latirostris mutatus)

An herbivorous aquatic mammal which dredges for underwater plants in its original unaltered state. Gene manipulation has greatly increased the animal's size so that it can be utilized for underwater channel clearing, as well as dredging.

ELINOU
(Saurischia: Coelurosaurus compsognathus)

A small and agile dinosaur, much appreciated by the Yilanè for its pursuit and destruction of small mammalian vermin. Because of its colorful markings and complaisant nature it is often given the status of a pet.

EPETRUK
(Saurischia: Tyrannosaurus rex)

The largest and most powerfully armed of the great carnosaurs. Over 40 feet long, the males weigh up to 7 tons. The forearms are small but strong. Because of its great weight it is quite slow, therefore attacks only the largest animals. A large amount of its diet is obtained by driving smaller carnivores from their kill.

E S T E K E L*
(Pterosauria: Pterodactylus quetzalcoatlus)

The largest of the flying reptiles with a wingspan of over thirty feet. The bones are very light and strong, while the weight of the immense toothed beak is balanced by the bony outcrop on the back of the skull. They are found solely at the mouths of large rivers since they can only become airborne in locations such as this where large waves run counter to the prevailing winds.

G R E A T D E E R
(Eutheria: Alces machlis gigas)

The largest of all the deer. It is distinguished from other members of the *Cervidae* by the spread of the impressive antlers of the males. Hunted by the Tanu, not only for its meat, but for its hide which is preferred for use in covering their tents.

GULAWATSAN
(Ranidae: Dimorphognathus mutatus)

The application of gene-splitting for controlled mutation can be appreciated when the gulawatsan is examined closely. This was formerly a toothed frog, but the present form appears to have little resemblance to its forebears. Their powerful croaking, heard in tropical jungles during the mating season, has been enhanced and increased until the sound emitted is deafening in the close proximity.

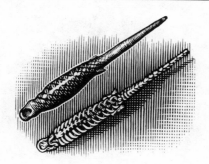

HÈSOTSAN
(Squamiata: Paravaranus comensualis mutatus)

This species of monitor lizard has been so modified that it now bears little resemblance to the original. Steam generating glands from *Brachinus* beetles violently project a dart which is poisoned when it passes over the sex organs of a commensal *Tetradontid* fish. This poison, the most deadly known, produces paralysis and death when as little as 500 molecules are present.

LONGTOOTH
(Metatheria: Machaerodus neogeus)

Long-tusked member of the marsupial tiger family. A large and ferocious carnivore that uses its greatly extended upper canine teeth to bring down its prey. Some Kargu hunters have a commensal relationship with these beasts to aid them in hunting.

ISEKUL*
(Columbae: Columba palumbus)

This gentle bird presents an ideal example of Yilanè science at its most practical. Like many other species, this one uses magnetized iron particles in its forebrain to detect the Earth's magnetic field as an aid in navigation. Through selective breeding the Isekul* will now point its head in any selected direction for long periods of time, until distracted by thirst or hunger.

MASINDUU

(Anuva: Rana catesbiana mutatus mutatus)

The sanduu is an accepted laboratory creature for magnifying images up to 200 times. However it lacks versatility in that only one observer at a time can utilize it. The masinduu is a variation that permits the image to be projected onto any white surface to be viewed by two or more researchers.

MASTODON

(Eutheria: Mastodon americanus)

A large mammal noted for its long upper tusks. It has a prehensile trunk reaching to the ground. Its domestication by the Tanu permits them to cover great distances when hunting and foraging, using the mastodons to pull large travois.

NENITESK
(Ornithischia: Triceratops elatus)

Herbivorous quadruped characterized by the possession of three horns set in a bony protective shield, unchanged since the Cretaceous period. They reproduce by laying eggs. Their brain capacity is small and their intelligence even smaller. Since they are slow growing they are of little use for meat supply, but are extremely decorative.

OKHALAKX
(Plateosauridia: Plateosaurus edibilus)

One of the largest of the 'flat lizards', so called because of their solid bodies and strong skulls. Although these creatures normally walk on all fours they rear up on their hind legs to graze the tops of trees. Its flesh is considered particularly tasty and is much sought after.

ONETSENSAST
(Ornithischia: Stegosaurus variatus)

The largest of the plated dinosaurs. These immense herbivorous creatures are protected from attack by two rows of plates down the neck and back, as well as heavy spikes on the tail. They first developed in the late Jurassic and only careful preservation by the Yilanè has prevented the destruction of this living fossil.

RUUTSA
(Ankylosauria: Euoplocephalus)

This giant creature is perhaps the most dramatic of the "living fossils" so carefully preserved by the Yilanè. Covered with great plates of armor, studded with spines, and protecting itself by the great ball at the end of its tail, it is hard to believe that it is a vegetarian and completely harmless, except in self-defense. This species has not changed in over one-hundred million years.

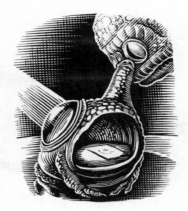

SANDUU
(Anuva: Rana catesbiana mutatus)

Extensive gene manipulation has altered this animal in almost every way; only its outer skin reveals its origins. Magnification of up to 200 power is available by proper use of sunlight directed through the different organic lenses of its head.

TARAKAST
(Ornithischia: Segnosaurus shiungisaurus mutatus)

A sharp-beaked carnivorous dinosaur, the largest examples being over 13 feet in length. They are difficult to train and require great strength to manage but when properly broken make a desirable Yilanè mount.

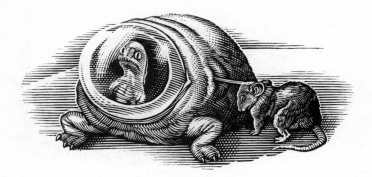

UGUNKSHAA
(Squamata: Phrynosoma fiernsyna mutatus)

Since the Yilanè language is dependent upon skin color and body movements, as well as sound, keeping written records is impossible; therefore writing has never developed. Historically knowledge was passed on verbally, and the recording of this information only became possible when an organic liquid crystal display was developed for visual accompaniment of the auditory memory records.

UNUTAKH
(Cephalopoda: Deroceras agreste mutatus)

One of the highly modified animals used in Yilanè technology. This cephalopod digests protein matter, especially hair and modified epidermal plates with ease.

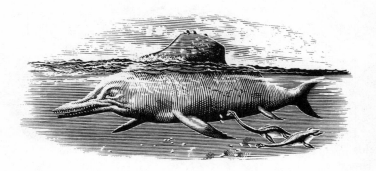

URUKETO
(Ichthyopterygia: Ichthyosaurus monstrosus mutatus)

This is the largest of the 'fish-lizards', a family of immense aquatic dinosaurs. Millennia of gene surgery and breeding have developed a strain of icthyosaurs very different from the parent stock. There is a large chamber situated above the spine and centered on the dorsal fin that is used for both crew and cargo.

URUKTOP
(Chelonia: Psittacosaurus montanoceratops mutatus)

One of the most extensively modified of the Yilanè animals. Used for land transportation, it can carry heavy loads for great distances since after gene-doubling it has eight legs.

ACKNOWLEDGMENTS

In writing this novel I have sought the advice of experts in various fields. The biology of the Yilanè is the work of Dr. Jack Cohen. The Yilanè, Sasku, Paramutan and Marbak languages are the work of Prof. T. A. Shippey. The philosophy of the Daughters of Life was developed with the active collaboration of Dr. Robert E. Myers. This would have been a far different and lesser book without their help and advice. My gratitude to them is infinite.